Thyme

Running

Out

The TARTAN of THYME
Part Two

Thyme
Running Out

by

Panama Oxridge

Thyme Running Out – The Tartan of Thyme – Part Two

Published in Great Britain by Inside Pocket Publishing Ltd.

A CIP catalogue record for this book is available from the British Library.

ISBN: 978-0-9567122-0-2

10 9 8 7 6 5 4 3 2 1

Illustrations by Adam Rex Pagoni
Cover graphics by Megan Rapidoxa

Printed and bound in Great Britain by
CPI Mackays, Chatham ME5 8TD

Visit
www.justinthyme.info

CAST of CHARACTERS

The Thymes

Justin Thyme – 13 year-old inventor and billionaire.
Robyn – his older sister.
Albion – their baby brother.
Sir Willoughby – their father, Laird of Thyme.
Lady Henny – their mother, a celebrity explorer.
Lyall Austin Thyme – their long-lost grandfather.

The Staff

Verity Kiss – the missing nanny.
Evelyn Garnet – the replacement nanny.
Professor Gilbert – Justin's private tutor.
Mrs Kof – the cook.
Angus Gilliechattan – the gardener.
Morag Gilliechattan – the housekeeper.
Peregrine Knightly – the butler.

Outsiders

Jock – a postman.
Horace – the Thymes' pilot.
Hank and Polly – Lady Henny's film crew.
Xavier Polydorus – retired conjuror, hypnotist & mind-reader.
Sergeant Awbrite and PC Knox – the local police.

Pets

Eliza – a computer-literate gorilla.
Burbage – Mr Gilliechattan's parrot.
Tybalt – Mrs Gilliechattan's cat.
Fergus – Jock's Scottie dog.
Haggis – a doddling.

But reckoning Time, whose millioned accidents
Creep in 'twixt vows, and change decrees of kings,
Tan sacred beauty, blunt the sharp'st intents,
Divert strong minds to the course of altering things.

William Shakespeare

Let us grasp the situation,
Solve the complicated plot —
Quiet, calm deliberation
Disentangles every knot.

W S Gilbert

CASTLE

North Tower

East Tower

A. The Library
B. Justin's Sitting Room
C. Justin's Bedroom
D. Justin's Lab
E. Archway & Castle Drive
F. Upper Corridor
G. Robyn's Room
H. Nanny's Room
I. The Nursery
J. Willoughby & Henny's Room
K. The Great Hall
L. Portrait Gallery
M. Professor Gilbert's Rooms
N. Schoolroom
O. Grandpa's Room
P. Guest Room
Q. Dining Room
R. Front Door
S. Eliza's Room
T. Mrs Kof's Room
U. Knightly's Room
V. The Kitchen
W. The Garage
X. Willoughby's Workshop
Y. The Kitchen Garden
Z. Gilliechattans' Cottage

*If you come across
any words you don't
recognise, the appendix
(a mini-dictionary at the
back of this book)
might help.*

CHAPTER ONE

Extinction

When Justin Thyme realised he'd been mistaken for a ghost, it came as something of a shock. The startling truth hit him as he stepped out of his time machine at dawn on the 1st of April 1662, and caught a fleeting sideways glimpse of his reflection in the chronopod's gleaming chrome bodywork.

He looked pale – much paler than usual – despite having spent the last three days on a remote sun-drenched island in the Indian Ocean. Naturally, a high factor sun-block had filtered out the harmful UV rays, but the real reason for his spectral pallor was time travel sickness.

Navigating the fourth dimension felt like a ride on the world's fastest, steepest rollercoaster; not something to attempt on a full stomach. This was his fifth and final excursion of the day – and so far, all he'd managed to force down was one dry oatcake and a few sips of iced water.

Justin stepped back from the egg-shaped pod and gazed at his distorted mirror image with pensive detachment. His dark hair stood up in untidy tufts – except for a single white forelock common to all male members of the clan, traditionally referred to as the "Thyme Streak". Illuminated by the ethereal afterglow of time travel, it stood out in the gloom of the cave like a small, silvery question mark hovering above

his forehead. Rimless designer shades completed the illusion, giving
his eyes a sunken look that transformed his youthful face into a gaunt
cadaverous skull.

His clothes – usually as monochrome as his hair – were all white in
an attempt to deflect the sun: A long white lab-coat, white knee-length
shorts and a plain white tee-shirt. It was hardly the reflection of your
average thirteen year old – but Justin Thyme was far from average.

An average teenage boy would probably live in a modern suburban
house, attend the local secondary school and spend his pocket money
on computer games and bags of barbecue-flavoured crisps. Justin on
the other hand, lived in a fourteenth century ancestral castle on the
banks of Loch Ness, had an IQ that surpassed most Oxford professors,
and had recently purchased a private Lear jet and a deserted tropical
island five kilometres east of Mauritius.

Everything about Justin Thyme was considerably above average.
Well, almost everything; he was a few centimetres short for his age –
but size isn't an issue when you're wearing the world's first *Hover-
Boots.*

He'd completed his preliminary design for the *Hover-Boots* several
weeks ago, despite the fact his *Jet-Blades* were still a phenomenal
world-wide craze earning more than half a billion in the last fifteen
months. But rogue companies in Taiwan and Korea were already
flooding the market with cheap pirated copies, so Justin knew the time
was ripe to launch a superior product and bankrupt the competition.

The *Hover-Boots* were *so* top-secret that no single manufacturer
could be trusted to produce the prototype. Individual parts, made by
various engineering companies had been hand-delivered to Thyme
Castle. The final component – a pair of pressure-sensitive computer
circuits – arrived just minutes before the Thymes had departed from
Scotland.

During the flight, Justin had left his family relaxing in the Lear jet's
luxurious cabin and retired to a small, custom-fitted lab at the rear of
the plane. He constructed the boots in complete secrecy, and then hid

them inside his time machine. Testing them on an uninhabited island a few hundred years in the past should prevent any corporate spies catching sight of them, he'd thought. However, that didn't mean he'd avoided detection entirely.

During a visit to 1601, a couple of shipwrecked sailors had spotted him gliding out of the forest, his white lab-coat fluttering in the breeze. They'd shouted '*Kaarspel, KAARSPEL!*' and ran off as fast as their sea-legs would carry them. At first, Justin had reprimanded himself for his negligence – but then he shrugged indifferently. Who'd believe them, anyway?

Justin hadn't inherited his mother's prodigious multilingual skills, but in less than a minute of surfing the net, he'd learnt that *kaarspel* was an old Dutch word for *phantom*. He'd been puzzled at the time – but now, as he stared at his haunting reflection, the remarkable synchronicity the situation gave him goose-bumps. It looked as if those terrified sailors *had* told a pretty convincing tale – so convincing, that many were *still* believing it centuries later.

Oddly enough, it was the local's fear of the Îlot du Mort that made the island so perfect for his latest project. Now, by a curious paradox of time, Justin realised *he* was personally responsible for its ghostly reputation.

Initially, the Mauritian government official Justin had contacted treated his e-mail enquiry as a practical joke, until the transfer of several million euros from a Swiss bank account opened the negotiations smoothly. Next, Justin had casually mentioned his mother, Lady Henrietta Thyme, and, as he'd anticipated, this secured Mr Papageno's undivided attention.

Lady Henny was an international celebrity – her TV wildlife show *"Thyme-Zone"* watched by billions worldwide. Whether she was rescuing condors in the Andean mountains, swimming with great white sharks in Hawaii, or wrestling crocodiles in the Australian outback, audiences loved the thrilling combination of her daredevil adventures and stunning wildlife photography.

Mr Papageno could hardly believe his luck; if some TV company wanted to pay a fortune for a few square metres of rat-infested real-estate, why should he object? He happily offered Justin a choice of eight or nine islands, describing them in glowing terms. But Justin had done his homework: Mouchoir Rouge was too small, Rocher Des Oiseaux was a barren guano-covered crag, Gunner's Quion was overrun with rabbits, and Pointe Bernache was swarming with tourists.

Justin had waited patiently until Mr Papageno ran out of steam, then explained that Lady Henny planned to establish a private wildlife sanctuary. He'd promised that in a few years, once their chosen endangered species was safely established, the island would be returned to the care of the Mauritian people; but meanwhile, Thyme Productions required *absolute privacy* for filming.

After a moment's hesitation, Mr Papageno had coughed diffidently and enquired whether the Thymes were superstitious. No, not in the least, Justin replied – and grinned, sensing that the Îlot du Mort was almost his. He was far too practical for superstition. There was always a simple scientific explanation for such apparitions he'd assured Mr Papageno – though admittedly, in this instance, the explanation had turned out to be anything but simple.

Strictly speaking, Justin hadn't been entirely truthful. True, Henny *was* establishing a sanctuary, but it wasn't for *endangered* wildlife; it was for wildlife already extinct. While she and her film crew had set up base camp and monitored the incubators, her son travelled back in time, collecting eggs from the 17th century.

Justin peered round the cave, inspecting his surroundings carefully before venturing further afield. It was, of course, the same cave he'd just left in the present – but there, his time machine – a converted motorbike and sidecar – had been surrounded by mounds of high-tech equipment.

With a wry smile, he reached back inside the chronopod and withdrew an old leather-bound diary. It was covered in an elaborate scrimshaw design of sailing ships and sea-serpents, and inscribed:

The Journal of Volkert Iversen

Until four days ago, (or 341 years in the future, depending on your perspective), it had been on display at the Oxford Natural History Museum between a macabre-looking dodo skeleton and a moth-eaten reconstruction. However, in return for a sizable donation and the promised loan of the Thymes' priceless Vermeer, the journal had returned, albeit temporarily, to the exact place it had been discovered.

Although the guarantee of privacy had attracted Justin to the Îlot du Mort, that wasn't his principal reason for choosing it. What fascinated him most was its unique place in history.

According to Volkert Iversen, this island was the last documented nesting-sight of the dodo – and, if the journal was to be trusted, its author and his companions would arrive in the next hour or so to seal that doomed bird's fate.

Justin walked to the mouth of the cave and gazed out in silence, scarcely able to believe that this peaceful island would soon be the scene of a brutal massacre.

In the first rays of the rising sun, the Îlot du Mort glistened like a precious jewel. Its dark emerald forest loomed beside a sparkling turquoise lagoon almost completely encircled by a crescent of soft, silvery-white sand. Where the forest bordered the beach, a fringe of dead twigs and crisp, brown leaf-litter mingled untidily with broken seashells.

And there, clustered beneath the ebony trees were the dodos – all asleep, except for an old alpha male on sentry duty.

Justin settled himself down on a warm, limpet-encrusted rock to wait. Carefully, he spread the fragile journal across his knees, opened it and started to read the final few entries:

5

The 12th day of February 1662

Storm Be Resentful! Laste nyght an angry storm overtook our valiant fleet as we sailed east beyonde Madagasikara. By morning, five of our shyps hath floundered, leaving only our owne vessel – the Arnhem – still afloat. She is damaged beyonde repaire, but her sloop remains seaworthy. Captain Willem Von Wybrant gives orders that all hands muste row towards the dystant coaste of Mauritius.

The 3rd day of March 1662

Aftare nineteen days and twenty nyghts, more than halfe our number hath perished. Those too sicke and injured to survyve arr caste overboard – others, madd from drynking seawater and weakened by constante rowing will followe them soon I feare.

The 10th day of March 1662

Our sytuation is desperate. Seconde Mate Pieter Hendrik proposes the plucking of straws to determyne whiche of our dwyndling numberr shalle be eaten firste. Mercifully, Captain Von Wybrant espies the Mauritian shore before we resort to such heathen cannibalism.

The 11th day of March 1662

Safe at laste! The Islande of Mauritius is goodly and pleasante, replenyshed with Palmyto-trees and Ebenwood as black as nyght. Refreshed with spryngwater and holesome palmfruite, we work to repaire our leaky olde sloop.

The 18th day of March 1662

Eight of our numberr electe to sail away againe in search of help. Our shyp's cooke – a Scotsman known to the crew as Arquebus Gunn – claims he preferrs to take his chance here on drye land. Five of us chewse to remain behinde with him: Sir Robbie and Lady Eugenia Bravesole, Padre Max O'Gain, Dr Stewart Nigelle Filby and myselfe.

The 31st day of March

Marooned for twenty days, we have eaten nothing butt palmfruite and fysh. How we yearn for fresh meat. We hath explored this fayre islande from shore to shore, yet we arr still unable to finde the legendary Dod-aarsen birde spoken of by shipwrecked sailors. The adult fowle are said to be tough and unpalatable, tho perhaps we may finde a tender yong doddling, or a new laide egg – creamie-whyte and large as a penny bun. Gunn has heard that the laste few specymens inhabit the Îlot du Mort (Islande of Death) – so called, because it is said to be haunted by the pallid ghoste of a yong childe floating amongste the nests.

We defy suche nonsense, and plan to visitt the islande tomorrow. Shortly aftare dawn, we estimate the tide will be lowe enough for us to paddle across the sandbar...

'*KraaARRRK!!*'

A sudden, guttural cry broke the island's tranquillity. It was a harsh, incongruous sound, like someone strangling bagpipes – but Justin, perfectly used to the discordant call of the dodo by now, merely glanced up from Iversen's journal and peered across the lagoon.

The old sentry dodo glared back at him mistrustfully and kraaked a second time, waking the last sleepy members of his colony. As they yawned and ruffled their feathers, Justin noticed there were far fewer than usual.

He withdrew a folding monocular from his lab-coat pocket and peered through it, taking a swift head count. There were eighteen adults, a couple of newly-hatched squabs and a week-old doddling – making twenty-one birds in total; less than a tenth of the dodos he'd observed on his previous trip in 1655.

Why had they died out so rapidly, Justin wondered. Surely they hadn't been hunted if they were as inedible as Iversen's journal suggested. Perhaps a new predator had been introduced. Or maybe some unknown virus had swept through the main colonies, leaving just a handful of survivors.

Once again, it struck Justin forcibly how different these birds looked to the few illustrations of dodos that had survived. These were no obese captive specimens, but were quick-witted, lithe and agile. At the start of the 17th century they had seemed docile – tame, almost – watching with apathetic disregard as Justin removed the occasional egg. But after years of being hunted indiscriminately by starving sailors they had grown wary in the extreme. Now, while the broody hen-birds squatted on their nests, the males – puffed up and ridiculous – stood guarding them.

As Justin watched, each drab grey female rose gingerly from its egg and defecated copiously. Crusty white peaks of steaming dodo dung encircled the squalid nests, reminding Justin horribly of lemon meringue pies.

Meanwhile, the males bobbed and bowed, making deep throaty burbling noises. Each climbed onto a nest and settled carefully on a single egg or squab. A few started to preen with their oversized beaks;

others basked in the morning sun, its light catching the iridescent sheen on their neck feathers.

The females stood for a moment on tiptoe stretching their stumpy wings, and then plodded off along the shore, foraging for crabs. The young doddling waddled after them, tripping over his huge yellow feet in an effort to keep up. His mother, a dull brownish bird, took her turn at sentry duty, whilst his father, the old male, closed his diamond-bright eyes and fell into a deep slumber.

Justin wondered how long it would take to establish a similar sized colony back in the 21st century. A while yet, he guessed. Anxious not to be the cause of the dodo's demise himself, he'd never taken more than a couple of eggs per decade – which meant the incubators contained just a dozen. And, of course, nobody knew how long they'd take to hatch, or at what age the dodos would be mature enough to reproduce.

In an effort to learn as much as possible, Justin's last few trips into the past had been pure fact-finding missions. He'd watched the same colony on each occasion, photographing their nest site with his digital camera and noting how their behavioural patterns changed with the seasons.

So far, he'd kept interaction down to an absolute minimum – and this, his final trip, was to be no exception. Justin assumed that Iversen and his companions would exterminate the remaining dodos with a ruthlessness to match their hunger, but that didn't give him the right to meddle with history.

'No interfering,' he reminded himself firmly. 'Remember what Dad said: you're here as an *observer* only.'

Sir Willoughby Thyme had extracted this solemn promise scarcely a couple of weeks ago, the morning *after* his son had completed the chronopod. When Justin casually mentioned that he'd tested the pod already, his father had embarked on a garbled lecture about disrupting the hypothetical space-time continuum. Justin had listened patiently, faintly amused by his father's grasp of the concept. But eventually, when the 24th Laird of Thyme had paused for breath, Justin promised to limit his forthcoming time travels to the confines of an uninhabited island. Sir Willoughby had sighed with obvious relief.

'Collecting the odd egg is probably quite safe,' he'd muttered, running his fingers though his hair until his Thyme streak stood on end. 'But that's all. Remember: interacting with the past can have irrevocable repercussions. The entire Mauritian economy depends upon the dodos' extinction.'

Sir Willoughby had worn an expression of such deadly earnest that Justin shivered as he remembered it. He was probably right. Most of the shops on Mauritius sold dodo souvenirs made out of everything from coconuts to seashells. Preventing the death of these last few specimens could destroy the tourist industry, or even create a parallel universe swarming with dodos.

Either way, it was hardly low impact.

Justin groaned silently. His father tended to be rather an old fusspot, imagining doom and despair round every corner; though when it came to time travel he had good reason to be wary. Years ago, (before Justin was born), he'd been tricked into building a prototype time machine for a bogus espionage company called *TOT Enterprises* – but it had a terrible, fatal flaw. It altered time *inside* the pod at the same rate as on the outside – which could have proved fatal for Willoughby if he'd been the first to test it. No wonder he'd been left with a warped view of time travel.

Fortunately, Justin had no such traumas to haunt him, and his grasp of time was second to none. He'd recently formulated his own theory on the subject – *Tartan Theory* – which proposed that individual timelines wove together like the threads in an everlasting multiversal tartan, forming the fabric of time itself. He was even writing a book about it.

As Justin thought about his next chapter: *The Standard Rules of Time Travel*, he leaned back against a sun-kissed rock at the mouth of the cave, and closed his eyes. He gave a wide yawn – and half-jokingly wondered if the first rule should be: *make sure you get enough sleep*. He listened dreamily to the gentle plish-plash of feet, and opened his eyes, expecting to see a dodo scavenging along the water's edge, but instead, he saw something that made him gasp.

10

Paddling through the shallows towards him was the bent figure of an old man. He wore a voluminous black robe which trailed in the water, and his face was obscured by a dark cowl.

Justin blinked. To his astonishment, he saw what looked like a rusty hourglass in the man's right hand, and a fearsome scythe carried over his left shoulder.

Old Father Time, Justin wondered – or was it the Grim Reaper? Surely he was dreaming. He rubbed his eyes, certain it was some sort of optical illusion caused by sunlight shimmering on the wet sand. But it wasn't.

The Grim Reaper lowered his scythe and pointed at him with a long skeletal finger. Justin's heart missed a beat. He wriggled his toes, desperate to activate the *Hover-Boots'* propulsion-thrusters and glide back into the cave, but in his panic he forgot how sensitive the new pressure circuits were. A sudden explosion of power sent him somersaulting backwards for several metres, slamming him against the chronopod.

The sidecar door swung open and, for a millisecond, Justin felt the urge to scramble inside and blast himself back to the present – but then he spied Iversen's diary outside, lying in the sand where he'd dropped it. After a deep breath, he allowed the logical left side of his brain to regain control. With his toes carefully clenched away from the *Hover-Boots'* pressure switches, he crawled on his hands and knees to the cave mouth and peeped out. The journal, its fragile pages fluttering in the breeze, lay just out of reach.

Justin glanced across the lagoon. Close behind the Grim Reaper, a group of men were now visible wading across a sandbar from a neighbouring island, towing a spoilt-looking girl on a rickety driftwood raft.

Instantly, Justin realised his mistake; Iversen and his companions had arrived early. As the man in long black robes reached the far side of the lagoon he pointed again – but this time it was obvious he was simply gesturing towards the dodos foraging along the shore midway between them.

Justin breathed a sigh of relief; it looked as if he hadn't been spotted after all. Hurriedly, he fumbled in his pocket for the monocular, and raised it to his right eye to examine the intruders in more detail.

The men looked unshaven and dishevelled, yet as Justin recalled their names from the journal he found it surprisingly easy to identify them.

From his sombre clerical robes, Justin guessed the Grim Reaper was Padre O'Gain. What he'd mistaken for a scythe, was simply a cutlass tied to the end of a long, sturdy branch; the hourglass turned out to be nothing more than a ship's compass. The old man pushed his cowl back and turned his face towards the gentle warmth of the sun. He had deeply hollowed cheeks and a cruel mouth half hidden by a scrubby white beard.

Of the others, the easiest to recognize was the ship's cook, Arquebus Gunn. He was a huge, red-haired man wearing a grubby singlet and kilt, and reminded Justin of the gardener at Thyme Castle. His arms were tattooed and muscular, and he brandished a hefty club in an enormous menacing fist.

Behind Gunn, a timid, scholarly-looking individual dithered, clutching a doctor's bag. His clothes were in a pitifully ragged state, and as Justin glanced back at the others he noticed they were all wearing bandages Dr Filby had torn from his own shirt.

Next in line came a lugubrious-looking sailor wielding a dagger. Squinting through his monocular, Justin spied a leather-bound journal sticking out of the man's pocket, and guessed this must be Volkert Iversen. He had greasy hair, a large sunburnt nose, and shifty-looking eyes that darted constantly at his fellow castaways. There was something about his veiled watchful expression that made Justin feel distinctly uncomfortable.

Finally, Justin peered at the Bravesoles. Perhaps because he'd assumed they would be an elderly couple, their appearance rather surprised him. Sir Robbie was a tall, gangly gentleman in his mid-thirties, with a stiff blonde moustache. His clothes, once of good quality, were now the threadbare shabby-chic of penniless gentry. Veins stood out on his forehead as he struggled to lift his young wife off the raft.

12

Lady Eugenia, who looked scarcely twenty years old, prodded her husband with a parasol, bombarding him with instructions in the petulant voice of someone used to getting her own way. As she spoke, she fidgeted constantly, playing with the frills and flounces edging her dress, or twirling her strawberry-blonde ringlets.

'Wobbie, tell these impertinent lickle men to kill those howwid, ugly birds wight away,' she whimpered, gesturing dismissively at Iversen and the others. 'I'm *fwightfully* hungwy.'

'Patience, my angel,' her husband replied in soft, cultured tones, as he lowered her gently onto the sand.

'Not *here*, you dwivelling dolt! It's *wet*. Over there ... on that big wock.'

Sir Robbie obeyed silently – only to be rewarded by a sharp kick in the shins. He smiled indulgently through gritted teeth – but through his monocular, Justin saw an icy flash of hatred in his flint-blue eyes.

'Och, fear not, ma wee lassie,' roared Arquebus Gunn. 'We'll kill every bird in sight if it'll make yer happy.'

Iversen and Padre O'Gain nodded in eager assent, while Sir Robbie withdrew a slender sword from inside his walking stick and swished it a few times, dangerously close to Lady Eugenia's ringlets.

'Either of you gentlemen fancy a wager?' he enquired, with a sly glance over his shoulder at the old hen dodo on sentry duty. Engrossed by the exploits of her bold young doddling, she seemed unaware of the impending danger.

'How about whoever bags most birds gets our final tot of rum?' suggested Iversen, slapping a hipflask in his jerkin pocket.

'And a kiss from her ladyship,' added the padre. He licked his cracked lips in anticipation and winked at a mortified-looking Dr Filby.

Lady Eugenia giggled coquettishly into her handkerchief, and Sir Robbie – who looked as if he'd rather kiss a dodo's bottom – shrugged with complete indifference. Then, mimicking the clarion of a huntsman's horn, he galloped along the shore with Iversen and Gunn lumbering after him. Meanwhile, Padre O'Gain grabbed his makeshift sickle and started swiping at the male birds guarding their nests. Dr

13

Filby followed him, half-heartedly plundering eggs and wringing the necks of defenceless squabs with clinical detachment.

Justin shuddered. So this was how the dodo had finally met its end, he thought: the hapless victim of a silly bet. This wasn't the theoretical extinction he'd read about in dusty academic books; it was extinction raw and savage, brought about by the most brutal creature on the planet.

He turned away, sickened by the senseless slaughter – but then he remembered Iversen's journal. He couldn't leave it. If the book had been for sale he could have bought it a thousand times over, but the museum had insisted it was on short-term loan only. Slowly, he inched his way out of the cave, dragging himself over the sand on his elbows. He kept his eyes lowered to avoid witnessing the carnage, but couldn't block out the distressed bird cries interspersed with callous squeals of delight from Lady Eugenia.

At length, Justin reached the journal. He slid it inside his lab-coat and edged slowly backwards. Then, pausing at the mouth of the cave, he took a reluctant glance across the lagoon – and immediately wished he hadn't.

The shore was littered with bleeding bodies. Justin watched as the terrified doddling scurried to each in turn, eventually huddling beneath the crumpled, blood-soaked carcass of its mother, uttering desolate cries of bewilderment and despair.

'Don't let the little blighter escape,' roared Sir Robbie, gesturing with his sword. 'It's the only bird worth eating.'

The men swiftly surrounded the doddling, advancing stealthily, arms at the ready. Even Lady Eugenia, unable to contain her excitement, kicked off her shoes, tucked up her petticoats and tiptoed after them, wielding her parasol. Moments later, they all stood shoulder to shoulder, encircling the world's last living dodo with their assorted weaponry held aloft.

Frozen to the spot, Justin boiled with rage at their cruel sport. He desperately wanted to help, but his father's warning kept ringing in his ears: *NO INTERFERING ... NO INTERFERING ...*

'All together,' Sir Robbie whispered, 'when I say *now!*'

14

'*NOOOooo!*' bellowed Justin, incapable of restraining himself any longer. But to his horror, the poised, bloodthirsty group awaiting his lordship's orders, mistook the cry and swung their weapons downwards.

Ever impatient, Lady Eugenia moved her parasol a fraction ahead of the others – and at that precise moment a freak gust of wind blew it open. In the ensuing collision of lace and steel the doddling squeezed between her legs and bolted along the shoreline, honking breathlessly.

'*Botheration!*' exclaimed Sir Robbie, struggling to disentangle the hilt of his sword from a rosebud-embroidered swag. With a sudden yank he tore it free, almost decapitating Arquebus Gunn in the process.

The Scotsman roared with fury and retaliated with his club – but Sir Robbie ducked, leaving Iversen to take the full force of the blow in his stomach. Within seconds, a vicious free-for-all broke out. Meanwhile, their first decent breakfast in nearly eight weeks ran towards the cliffs. Spying the sanctuary of a concealed cave, it scuttled inside bumping into something soft and white.

Assuming his mistimed cry had sounded the doddling's death knell, Justin had retreated into the cave choking back bitter tears of anger. When the blood-spattered little bird blundered into him he was both elated and petrified at the same time. Naturally, he was thrilled the dodo had survived – but he knew the trail of bloody footprints behind it would not go unnoticed for long. Sure enough, when he peered out, Sir Robbie, Iversen and the others were following them already.

Once again, the logical left side of Justin's brain advised him to leap into his time machine and leave the past behind – but something inside him baulked at the idea.

'This is *my* island after all,' he muttered, 'or at least it will be in a few hundred years. These people need to be taught a lesson.'

The problem was, there seemed very little a slightly shorter than average teenager *could* do, no matter how high his IQ. As the footsteps drew closer, Justin cast around the cave, desperate to find something ... anything ... to frighten off the intruders. But apart from some partially burnt driftwood and a couple of rusty chains, there was nothing.

Silently admitting defeat, he turned back to the chronopod, but as he stumbled towards it he found himself transfixed again by his ghostly reflection. With his long white lab-coat now smeared in dodo blood, he looked more ghoulish than ever.

Suddenly, in a dazzling burst of inspiration, Justin realised he had everything he needed to scare the trespassers senseless. He hurriedly scooped a short, charred branch off the floor, and using his forefinger smeared a dark ring of charcoal around each eye. Next, he grabbed the chains and draped them around his wrists. Finally, he wriggled his toes over the *Hover-Boots'* pressure switches, activating its antigravity units and acceleration-boosters simultaneously. With an almighty *whoooooosh*, he swept out of the cave and soared into the air several feet above the heads of the astonished dodo hunters.

'I AM THE GHOST OF THE ÎLOT DU MORT,' roared Justin, in what he hoped was a sinister-sounding voice. 'LEAVE MY ISLAND AT ONCE.'

For a moment the intruders looked as if they had turned to stone. Then Lady Eugenia leapt, whimpering, into her husband's arms, Iversen dropped his journal, and a large puddle appeared around Gunn's feet.

'LEAVE MY ISLAND OR DIE A HIDEOUS DEATH,' Justin bellowed. Then, with a blood-curdling scream he swooped down towards them, rattling his chains.

Sir Robbie Bravesole dropped his pretty young wife and sprinted off like an Olympic athlete. The rest swiftly followed his lead, and hurtled along the beach, tripping over each other in an attempt to splash across the sandbar first. Justin shrieked again, and did a couple more chain-clanking swoops for good measure, then glided back to the cave.

'Wow, I never dreamt being a ghost could be such fun,' he laughed, tossing the chains back where he'd found them.

Hurriedly, Justin searched the shadowy cave for the world's last living dodo – wondering what he was going to do when he found it. But as fate would have it, the decision was out of his hands. When he reached the chronopod, he discovered an exhausted little down-covered bundle curled up on the scarlet leather seat ... snoring cacophonously.

Justin lowered himself carefully into the pod, gently transferring the doddling onto his knees. Then, after double-checking the spatio-temporal coordinates for his return journey, he closed the pod door, automatically activating the subatomic wormhole-vortex accelerator.

The cool, efficient voice of the inbuilt computer commenced its countdown, but Justin wasn't listening. Oblivious to the spirals of multi-coloured plasma swirling round the pod, he chewed his lower lip pensively and wondered how many of the *Standard Rules of Time Travel* he'd just broken.

Standard Rules of Time Travel

Every means of transportation, by whatever vehicle, device or contraption, needs rules – and time travel is no exception. In fact, owing to its extraordinary manner of conveying passengers, the unique risks involved, and the need for complete secrecy, strict adherence to these rules is particularly important.

The safety of the traveller – or chrononaut – is vital, of course; but the welfare of those he or she might encounter must also be considered.

Apart from rules governing the basic navigation of the fourth dimension, each time-traveller should also observe a code of conduct when visiting another historical period.

The following section of my time travel guide will outline these rules. All potential chrononauts are advised to memorise them before embarking on their first journey through time.

CHAPTER TWO

Troubled Thymes

Justin opened the chronopod door and leaned out, peering anxiously at his surroundings. A shaft of late afternoon sunlight slanted through the mouth of the cave, transforming the uneven pebbled floor into a path of amber-coloured cobbles.

On his right, crates of supplies and bottled drinking-water were stacked against the cave wall; to his left, a portable generator droned beside a row of gleaming titanium incubators; and directly ahead, an untidy mound of high-tech surveillance equipment, cameras and recording apparatus lay half hidden beneath a spaghetti-like tangle of wires.

With a swift glance at his watch, he clicked its top right function-button, and instantly the second hand started ticking. Justin took a deep breathe and exhaled slowly; his left arm ached where he'd collided with the chronopod, but it felt good to be back in the 21st century. He stared at the warm, downy bundle on his lap. The little doddling snored soundly, unaware of its paradoxical situation. Nearly three and a half centuries had elapsed since it had collapsed, exhausted, into the chronopod, yet in real time it had been sleeping scarcely half a minute.

'Best not disturb you,' Justin whispered. 'You're even noisier when you're awake ... and I can't risk Hank or Polly hearing you.'

Hank and Polly were Henny's roving film crew. For the last nine years they'd travelled the globe with Lady Henrietta Thyme, shooting every episode of *Thyme-Zone*. Weary of their practical jokes, she'd fired them on no fewer than a dozen occasions – yet somehow they'd always managed to wheedle their jobs back in time for the next expedition. They were hardly the most reliable pair – but Henny maintained she'd trust them with her life.

Nevertheless, Willoughby absolutely insisted that the time machine be kept a secret, so Justin had concocted an elaborate cover story to explain their Mauritian assignment: dodo embryos, (genetically recreated by harvesting DNA strands from museum specimens), had been implanted into pelican eggs with a view to establishing a new dodo colony in their original habitat. Hank and Polly – thrilled by such an incredible career opportunity – appeared to accept this explanation quite readily. Just a month ago *Thyme-Zone* had faced the axe after a fall in ratings, but now they were both too busy mentally rehearsing their BAFTA acceptance speeches to ask any awkward questions.

Eggs were one thing, Justin thought, but the sudden appearance of a live doddling was certain to arouse their suspicions. He decided to consult his mother about the problem as soon as possible – meanwhile, the little bird had to be kept out of sight. Careful not to wake it, he carried the dodo over to an empty Perspex tank, settled it on a tartan blanket and switched on the inbuilt infrared heat lamp. Finally, he hid the tank by stacking several large boxes of equipment in front of it. As he stood back to check it wasn't visible, he heard the sound of footsteps approaching. An elongated shadow snaked across the pebbles towards him, as a tall, sunburnt man wearing a pair of baggy linen shorts stooped to enter the cave.

'You're back, then,' said Sir Willoughby. 'Thought I heard some—' His voice trailed off as he stared open-mouthed at Justin. 'What's happened?' he gasped, rushing forwards.

'It's nothing,' Justin assured him, hurriedly removing his blood-stained coat and rolling it into a bundle. 'I'm fine ... *really*.'

Sir Willoughby grabbed his son by the shoulders and examined him closely. 'Well, you don't appear to be injured,' he said, with a wry smile. 'But you look like you've seen a ghost.'

Justin laughed. Willoughby glanced at him sharply, unaware he'd said anything particularly amusing. He raised a quizzical eyebrow, folded his arms and waited for an explanation. But when his son remained silent, he sighed and started to rummage through a large food hamper labelled *Fortean & Mayhem*.

'If you can't trust your own father ...' he remarked sorrowfully, extracting a jar of whisky marmalade and a spoon, '*well* ...' Then leaving the half-finished phrase hanging awkwardly in mid-air, he shrugged and ambled back outside, whistling tunelessly.

In the dimly lit cave Justin blushed a fiery red. Sir Willoughby never whistled when he was happy – quite the reverse; he whistled when he was in a foul mood and wanted to disguise his true feelings. Something was bothering him.

'Of course I trust you, Dad,' Justin called after him 'It's just that ...'

He stopped short, knowing that if he said *you're always so paranoid*, he'd make matters even worse. 'I er ... I didn't want to worry you,' he concluded lamely, as he hurried out into the dazzling sunshine. He paused for a moment or two with his eyes screwed up, squinting along the shoreline.

It was astonishing how little the Îlot du Mort had altered with the passing of time. Tropical storms had toppled several of the oldest ebony trees, but a dozen healthy young saplings had sprouted up in their place. Now, where the ancient dodo had once stood on sentry duty, Henny worked, covering a hide with camouflage netting. She stepped back to admire her handiwork, resting her thumbs in the belt loops of her khaki shorts. Then, with the uncanny intuition of a wild creature, she sensed her son's gaze and swung round to face him, laughing as a huge wave crashed on the shore, spattering her bronzed cheeks and blonde elfin-short hair with sea spray.

With his own pallid reflection still fresh in his memory, Justin waved to her, thinking for at least the hundredth time how little he took after her.

Further along the lagoon, Hank and Polly bickered good-naturedly as they rigged a remote surveillance unit to the top of a tall palm tree.

They were an odd-looking couple: Hank, the cameraman, coal-black and built like a sumo wrestler – and Polly, who usually did sound and Henny's makeup, as pale and slender as a stick of celery.

Balanced precariously on Hank's enormous muscular shoulders, Polly rummaged through his trouser pockets complaining loudly.

'Have you seen my five-eighths star-headed screwie?' he grumbled, tucking a loose strand of flaxen hair back into his ponytail. 'I think I've dropped it ... *again*!'

Hank groped inside his shirt collar and fished out two rubber bands and a stick of chewing gum.

'Just as well you're not using a sledge hammer,' he sighed, finally withdrawing a tiny screwdriver and tossing it into the air.

Polly caught it. 'Thanks, Hank. Promise I won't drop anything else.' But behind his small, round spectacles, his denim blue eyes sparkled mischievously as he withdrew a fake rubber tarantula from his shirt pocket.

Henny exchanged an exasperated glance with her son, then returned to adjusting the hide. Seconds later, when Hank left Polly dangling from the treetop as he hurtled along the beach wailing like a banshee, nobody raised so much as an eyebrow.

Sir Willoughby seemed oblivious. He scowled at the horizon and licked the back of a marmalade-covered spoon with absentminded detachment. Justin crept up behind him, reached over his shoulder and whisked the sticky jar off his stomach.

'That stuff'll *ruin* your teeth!' he whispered.

Normally, this would have prompted a roar of mock fury from his father, swiftly followed by an amicable chase along the shore, but Willoughby didn't flinch. Justin lowered himself into a vacant deck-chair and tried again.

'What's up, Dad?'

As he waited for a reply, Justin kicked his shoes off, squeezed warm sand between his toes, and peered at the crumpled newspaper on his father's lap. It was yesterday's copy of the Drumnadrochit Gazette. Justin had arranged for it to be couriered over from Scotland as a surprise for his dad, but now he wondered if it was responsible for his

22

sudden mood swing. He craned his neck and squinted sideways, trying to catch a glimpse of the front page without appearing to do so; unfortunately, Sir Willoughby noticed and snorted like a constipated rhinoceros.

'Utter *bunkum*!' he roared, thrusting the paper into his son's hands. 'We'll have tourists swarming all over the estate. *Dash it all!* There's even a photo of the damn castle.'

For a moment, Justin failed to see the problem. Apart from a nondescript little man with a Scottie dog in the foreground, it was the standard scenic view of Thyme Bay found on almost every postcard sold between Inverness and Fort Augustus, usually with a grotesque cartoon plesiosaur looming out of the water. Then, with a sickening jolt, Justin remembered the one subject guaranteed to rile his father: he utterly despised all talk of the Loch Ness Monster. The first time Justin saw Nessie, Willoughby had been scathing and dismissive; he'd kept his second sighting a secret.

The headline confirmed his worst suspicions:

ɒdrochit Gazet

May 31st 200

POSTIE SEES NESSIE

Local Loch Ness postman, Jock McRosie, had a monster shock yesterday morning whilst emptying Dores postbox. Fergus, his constant canine companion, started barking. Hearing a sudden loud splash, Mr McRosie turned swiftly and saw what looked like a long scaly tail disappearing beneath the surface of the loch. Later, during an interview with our reporter, Mr McRosie seemed lost for words - although, according to his neighbours this isn't particularly unusual. When asked if he thought it was Nessie, he merely replied, "Aye," and nodded, returning to

23

'Never a man of many words,' Justin laughed. 'Still ... I bet he's thrilled; he's been delivering mail round the loch for almost twenty years, and he's never seen a sign of Nessie.'

'Hardly surprising, considering the monster doesn't exist,' sneered Willoughby. 'Anyway, how do *you* know what he has or hasn't seen?'

He's told me at least three or four times a week for as long as I can remember,' explained Justin, smothering a grin. 'Jock isn't much of a conversationalist. His *I've-never-seen-Nessie* lament is precisely one fifth of his entire verbal repertoire!'

Willoughby shrugged indifferently; he couldn't remember the last time he'd so much as glanced at a postal worker, let alone chatted to one. 'People see what they want to see ... especially naive people with overactive imaginations.'

Now it was Justin's turn to scowl. He had an uncomfortable feeling this was a well-aimed dig at his beloved Nanny.

Nanny Verity Kiss saw "*the Beastie*" as she called it, with monotonous regularity. Justin had always suspected she'd seen nothing but driftwood, but now he wasn't so sure.

'Leave Nanny out of this,' he hissed, fiercely loyal to her despite the trouble she'd caused lately.

Willoughby feigned a look of surprise, as if the thought had never occurred to him, but the glacial glint in his eyes showed that the memory of her miraculous disappearance still needled him. The local police force had been equally frustrated; it wasn't every day a prime suspect vanished out of a locked room leaving nothing behind except a pair of regulation handcuffs and an air of mystery. The following night, Justin had received an e-mail from Nanny Verity, implying that someone at Thyme Castle had helped her escape, but, so far, he'd kept this startling information to himself.

'Admittedly, Nan's a lot sharper than she's always let on,' continued Justin, remembering her artfully contrived mistrust of computers. Then, provoked by his father's innocent expression, he added: 'But she's not the only one, is she, Dad?'

As soon as the words flew out of his mouth, he regretted them. Willoughby's cheeks flushed beneath his tan – though whether this

24

was due to anger or embarrassment, Justin couldn't tell. He held his father's gaze for a few seconds, then turned away, the shock of learning his father's secret still fresh in his memory.

For the last thirteen years, Sir Willoughby had pretended to be the victim of an electrical mind-wipe procedure, playing the part of a stereotypical absentminded inventor convincingly enough to fool everyone. True, he'd had his reasons: he'd explained that a deadly spy known as Agent X probably kept him under constant surveillance, and the deception had been necessary to ensure the safety of his family. But discovering the skeleton in the Thyme family closet had shaken Justin's faith in his father. No matter how well-intentioned his lies had been ... they were lies nonetheless.

The worst part of it was the guilt, Justin thought, frowning at the sand as he traced random patterns across it with his fingertips. Every time he doubted his father's word he suffered a pang of conscience from deep within, as if *he* were in the wrong for feeling so suspicious. Even now, he half-wondered if his father was keeping something else from him – and the constant reproachful look on Willoughby's face only compounded his mixture of anger and shame.

As always, on these occasions, Justin reminded himself that his father's life had not been entirely without tragedy: his mother had drowned when he was barely three-and-a-half years old, and thirteen years later his younger brother, Deighton, got thrown from a horse and broke his neck. By a bizarre coincidence, exactly thirteen years after this second fatality there appeared to be a third: Willoughby's father, Sir Lyall Austin Thyme, was swept away in an avalanche on Ben Nevis, and until quite recently had been presumed dead. Now, another thirteen years on, Willoughby had become obsessed by what he called "*The Thyme Curse*", gloomily prophesying that a grisly and inevitable death awaited one of the Thyme family.

Utterly devoid of logic, thought Justin, but upsetting him won't solve anything. Perhaps I should tell him what's just happened in the past and ask for his help with the doddling; it might take his mind off things.

'Dad, I need your advice,' he said, looking gravely serious.

It worked. Willoughby brightened at once and raised his eyebrows.

'You were right,' Justin continued. 'Something happened during my last time-warp. I dozed off by the mouth of the cave; when I woke up I saw this old man wearing long black robes, carrying what looked like a scythe and an hourglass.'

'The Grim Reaper!' exclaimed Sir Willoughby.

Justin grimaced and gave a phoney gothic laugh – but after a swift glance at his father, he realised he was laughing alone. Willoughby's face had turned a maggoty shade of grey and his eyes had a hollow haunted look.

'The Harbinger of Death,' he groaned. 'It's ... it's a sign. You must be next. *Aaaarghh*, this is terrible ...'

'Not the dreaded curse,' sighed Justin, rolling his eyes in exaggerated despair. 'I thought ...'

'WE *CAN'T* GO HOME,' shouted Willoughby, pounding his knee with a clenched fist. 'Absolutely NOT. It's as simple as that. As long as we stay right here, you'll be safe; I can't possibly see the ... er ... erm ... I ... I can't possibly see the harm in that.' He glanced along the shoreline to where his wife, disturbed by the sudden outburst, peered at him enquiringly, and yelled 'WE'RE STAYING HERE.'

'For the rest of the week?' Henny called back.

'REST OF THE YEAR IF NECESSARY!'

Henny laughed, assuming it was a joke – one she didn't get. Despite living in Scotland for most of her adult life, she still found the British sense of humour somewhat perplexing. With a shake of her head she returned to her work.

'Listen, Dad,' said Justin, taking the authoritative tone frequently required when his father went off at the deep end. 'I thought you'd abandoned all this curse nonsense. Now Grandpa's back safe and sound, that means there hasn't been a death in the clan for twenty-six years.'

Justin spoke with considerably more confidence than he felt. The old man, who'd turned up scarcely a month ago, certainly *seemed* the genuine Sir Lyall – but Nanny Verity, the only person apart from Sir Willoughby with clear memories of the previous Laird, had told Justin in strictest confidence that he was undoubtedly a fraud. At the time, he'd taken Nanny's tale with a pinch of salt, assuming his dad was perfectly capable of recognising his own father. But now, insidious doubts crept stealthily into the back of his mind.

'You *are* certain it's him, aren't you?' he asked, watching his father's face closely for blinks, twitches and other signs of dishonesty.

'Absolutely,' replied Willoughby.

If that's a lie, it's a convincing one, Justin thought – then a voice from deep within him calmly pointed out that, when it came to lying, his father had had thirteen years of practice. Justin pushed the thought away, but not before a blaze of guilt once again flashed through him like a forest fire.

'Stop worrying, Dad,' he said, forcing a grin. 'Anyway, I've seen stuff like that before without dropping dead. I never told you, but the morning Grandpa turned up I almost mistook him for Old Father Time. I was looking out of my lab window when I noticed someone standing at that fork in the road just outside the castle gates. He had a bundle over one shoulder, and was tossing a coin to ...'

'... To decide which fork to take,' concluded Willoughby, barely audible. His face had turned from grey to the waxen white of a corpse. With a terrible groan, he buried his head in his hands.

'What's wrong?' begged Justin, baffled.

Sir Willoughby remained frozen. 'Shhh ... let me think.'

Feeling guiltier than ever, Justin stared at his father, wondering why his words had caused such alarm. One thing was certain: his father wasn't acting now; that sudden deathly pallor couldn't possibly be faked.

After a minute of total silence, Willoughby rose from his deckchair and started pacing up and down the shore. The knot in Justin's stomach tightened and twisted as he mentally willed his father to stop festering and tell him the truth. Finally, Willoughby halted in front of his son and held out his right hand.

'Give me the motorbike keys,' he said. 'There'll be no more *you-know-what* travelling for you. I should never have agreed to it the first place. You've no idea what danger you're in.'

27

Justin disagreed, but the look on his father's face told him this wasn't the time to quibble.

'The more trips you take, the greater the risk of paradox,' Willoughby continued. 'You might think you can handle it, but the cerebral strain is mind-blowing. Panic attacks, identity crisis, nervous twitches, tinnitus – you could end up having a complete mental breakdown. Hand them over. NOW!'

Reluctantly, Justin reached into his pocket and gave his father the keys to the old Norton bike and its chronopod sidecar. There'd be plenty of time to negotiate with him later, he reasoned ... once he calmed down.

'That's the last time you'll be going anywhere – past, present or future! As soon as we get back home I'm ...'

'I thought you were staying here,' said a gently mocking voice. It was Henny. Attracted by the commotion, she'd crept up behind Willoughby, signalling to her son to keep quiet. Justin was more than willing to leave things to his mother; she was an expert at diffusing the Thyme-bomb, as she sometimes called him.

'Far too ... erm ... HOT,' snapped Sir Willoughby. 'We're leaving first thing tomorrow.'

Justin's eyebrows rose almost imperceptibly as he exchanged a furtive glance with his mother. Even by Willoughby's standards, this was a spectacular about-turn.

'Of course, Honey,' Henny cooed. 'All this *beastly* sunshine and palm trees. You're missing the mists and pining for pines. I understand perfectly. This is no place for a Scottish Laird. Where's that invigorating north wind gusting across the heather? The horizontal rain? That sky the colour of lead? It was selfish of me to drag you away.'

Willoughby deflated visibly, and Justin marvelled for the umpteenth time at his mother's skill and father's credulity.

'But ... but ...' Sir Willoughby faltered.

'No more butting you stubborn old Billy goat,' laughed Henny. 'I'll contact the pilot tonight and tell him to have the jet ready for tomorrow morning. Unfortunately, I'll be busy here until next weekend, so I

28

can't come with you.'

'But ...'

'Time to call it a day, I think,' Henny concluded, checking her watch. 'Let's get back to the villa. Hank and Polly haven't finished the security set-up yet, so they're camping in the cave tonight, to keep an eye on our equipment.'

'That reminds me,' said Justin, remembering the dodo. 'There's a *slight* problem. I was trying to tell Dad when ...'

'Not something else?' groaned Willoughby.

'Oh, *do* stop fussing, Willo,' said Henny. 'Life's full of little hiccups – that's half the fun!' She took a firm hold of her husband's arm, and the two of them followed Justin into the cave.

It was less than a month since Lady Henny had been kidnapped, kept tied up, and then almost drowned; yet not only had she'd taken the experience comfortably in her stride – she'd come remarkably close to enjoying it! Life's constant challenges had taught her that worrying about trivia was futile. If a crisis cropped up, she dealt with it in the blink of an eye and moved on.

When Henny caught sight of the baby dodo, she barely flinched. While Sir Willoughby paced round wringing his hands, she grinned cheerfully and lifted the little creature out of its tank.

'You can't let Hank and Polly see it,' twittered Willoughby, 'or they'll guess about the ... er ... *you-know-what.*'

'*Obviously*!' said Henny. 'You'll have to take it home with you until the rest hatch out.'

'But ...'

'If anyone asks just say it's an orphaned er ... condor, or something.'

'What about Professor Gilbert?' asked Justin. 'He's an ornithologist.'

'*Ornithologist my foot*!' scoffed Henny. 'That's nothing but a load of old *bullfinches*! Remember that kiwi I looked after last summer? He never even asked to see it. I'll bet he wouldn't recognise a baby condor if it pecked him on the butt.'

Justin said nothing. He suspected the professor had simply been too overawed by Lady Henny to speak.

'But ... but ...' said Willoughby. Henny quelled him with a steady stare, forcing him to silently mouth the words 'Agent X.'

'So what?' laughed Henny. '*He* knows about the time machine already.' Willoughby winced like someone with severe toothache, but before he could remind his wife not to say the forbidden words, she continued: 'The dodo might even help you flush him out. You can watch how people react to it; this X guy is the only person likely to guess the truth.'

Willoughby shook his head in silent defeat. As always, Henny's solution was the last he would normally consider – yet, try as he might, her perverse logic defied all argument.

'I'll start the boat,' he mumbled, and trudged back outside.

The Thymes had rented a secluded villa on the eastern coast of Mauritius. Obscured by a dense wall of foliage, it was all but invisible from the nearest road – and only a dilapidated wooden jetty and a narrow flight of stone steps were observable from the sea. The average passer-by would assume they led to nothing grander than a fisherman's hut, but this misleading impression was a security ploy. In the unlikely event of strangers coming ashore, they wouldn't reach the high-tech burglar-alarmed gate without being tracked by a dozen CCTV cameras.

Justin ran ahead and keyed in the access code; his mum and dad strolled behind him, Henny carrying the little dodo wrapped in a blanket, Willoughby muttering disconsolately about Nessie, Agent X, the Grim Reaper and the Thyme Curse.

'Relax, Willo,' drawled Henny, unruffled as always by her husband's perpetual anxiety. 'What you need is an ice-cold mango daiquiri and a spell in the hot tub.'

Willoughby nodded grudgingly. Henny had never taken his curse theory seriously; the practical, prosaic American in her rejected anything so unscientific. Once indoors, he brushed past her and marched straight to the kitchen. He hauled a large frosted jug out of the icebox; only the sound of his wife's approaching footsteps prevented him from putting his lips to the spout and gulping down the whole lot.

After settling the dodo in a quiet corner, Henny rummaged through the kitchen cupboards looking for something it could eat. Justin, still feeling rather queasy, opened a bottle of highland spring water and sipped it slowly as he headed towards the muffled sound of a television.

The rooms of the villa were deceptively rustic in style. Beams of sun-bleached driftwood arched across whitewashed walls, and rattan paddle fans rotated restfully in cool tented ceilings. Beside the windows, buttery swags of muslin undulated in the breeze, their reflection in the polished granite floors creating the illusion of rippling water underfoot. Here and there, a few priceless artefacts stood amongst lavish yet understated furniture. It was not the sort of place you'd expect to find a gorilla ... unless you were a Thyme.

Sprawled over an ivory linen sofa, a banana in one hand, a TV remote in the other, sat 267 lbs of bulging muscle covered in dense black hair. The plasma television skipped from station to station, and judging from the pile of banana skins littering the floor, the ape had been channel-hopping for quite some time. Amongst the peel sat a baby wearing an angelic smile and a nappy. He waved a chubby hand at his big brother, and gurgled happily as he pointed to the screen. Justin patted Albion on the head then turned to the gorilla.

'Anything on, Eliza?' he asked, flopping into an armchair that appeared to almost swallow him whole.

The gorilla grunted softly and opened a laptop computer fastened to a harness around her waist. Her huge black fingers flickered over the keyboard, and a synthesised voice replied: 'No cartoons for baby.'

Eliza acted like a member of the family, but she was no pampered pet; Lady Henny had rescued her from the Congo as a baby and had taken her back to Scotland, hoping to teach her to communicate by using sign language. However, as Eliza had grown, she'd displayed an aptitude for computers, so Justin built her a special reinforced laptop loaded with a complex vocabulary of pictogram symbols. The prototype had limited function and a poor quality sound unit, but the latest version was state-of-the-art. It could record brief vocal samples, then replicate a voice so accurately it was indistinguishable from the original. Entire phrases could be stored in its memory, all instantly accessible via her keyboard.

'Where's Robyn?' Justin enquired.

There was a brief pause as Eliza opened her laptop's vocal menu and jabbed QUEEN with a huge leathery finger. 'Bad girl outside,' she replied in her favourite regal-sounding voice. 'Robyn very bad human. Make Henny angry.'

'So that's why you've gone all royal, is it?' asked Justin, wondering what his sister had done *this* time. 'You think Mum's going to blame *you.*'

'Poor Eliza always get blame.'

Justin couldn't deny it. After Nanny Verity disappeared, Henny had put Eliza in charge of Albion. She was used to helping out occasionally, but the sudden responsibility of being a full time nursemaid troubled her greatly – and it's never wise to trouble a gorilla. She'd grumbled, but eventually complied. However, during the last couple of weeks she'd grown ever more surly and irritable, frequently complaining that Albion was a '*bad baby.*' Justin had reminded his mother that Eliza shouldn't be treated as an unpaid servant – but Henny had swept his concerns to one side, insisting it was all good practice for when Eliza had a baby of her own.

Once they'd landed in Mauritius things swiftly deteriorated. Left to her own devices, Robyn soon got bored and sought retail therapy. Within days she'd frittered away ridiculous amounts of money and flirted with every local male between the ages of fifteen and fifty. Finally, after Robyn had picked the lock on the drinks cabinet and tried to invent a new cocktail, Henny blamed Eliza for not keeping a strict enough eye on her. In Justin's opinion, this was the last straw that broke the gorilla's back!

'I'd better talk to Mum,' he sighed, hauling himself out of the armchair. 'Don't worry Eliza, whatever Robyn's done, it's not your fault.'

Justin glanced uncertainly at the enormous ape. Eliza pursed her lips broodingly for a moment, then wrinkled her nose. 'Gorilla still get blame,' she said, and scooped Albion up onto her broad muscular back, making him squeal with excitement. Then, as Justin turned and headed towards the kitchen, she prowled slowly and majestically behind him.

Lady Henny had opened several tins before discovering that sardines in tomato sauce were the doddling's favourite. Unfortunately, it was a messy eater. Accustomed to living food, it shook each mouthful vigorously before swallowing, splattering the walls with droplets of ketchup. Henny smiled, unconcerned that the once pristine kitchen was starting to resemble an abattoir.

Justin hovered in the doorway, trying to choose his words with care. He didn't want to get his sister into any unnecessary trouble; after all, he didn't even know what she'd done yet. But before he could speak, Albion slid off Eliza's back and landed on the floor with a squishy thud. Spying his father, he squeezed between Justin's legs and sped across the kitchen on his hands and knees.

'Fourteen months old tomorrow and *still* crawling,' grumbled Henny. 'You and Robyn were walking by eleven months – and talking properly too.'

Justin felt tempted to reply that if Albion spent more time with his mother instead of a gorilla, his behaviour might be a little less apelike, but he didn't want to hurt Eliza's feelings. 'He's just a late developer,' he murmured. 'His Thyme Streak hasn't come through yet either.'

'Baby walk – baby talk,' announced a royal voice behind him. Eliza marched into the kitchen. She frowned darkly as her huge fingers rattled over the laptop's keyboard. 'Baby walk and talk already.'

By now, Albion had reached Sir Willoughby and was using his father's legs to drag himself upright. 'Dad!' he chortled, then, as if trying to prove the truth of Eliza's words, took a few faltering steps before flumping down in an explosion of wind and giggles.

'Steady on, little chum,' said Willoughby, his face suddenly relaxing into a grin for the first time that day. He tickled Albion's nose affectionately. 'Your first proper word! My goodness – what would Nanny say if she could hear you?'

'Nodna!'

'He's trying to say Nana now,' laughed Justin. 'Alby, say Jus–'

'Not first word,' Eliza interrupted, her face like a thundercloud. 'Bad baby talk before.'

'Eliza!' gasped Henny. 'I'm surprised at you. You're jealous because he's starting to talk for himself and you have to use a computer. Or is this about you wanting a baby gorilla?'

The furrow on Eliza's rubbery black brow deepened. She swayed to and fro making breathy grunting noises, and then swiped with her fist at a kitchen stool, sending it spinning across the tiled floor. Albion chortled happily. For a moment, the merest flicker of irritation clouded Henny's normally placid features, then she took a deep breath and smiled serenely; it took more than primate displacement behaviour to faze *her*.

'Say Mommy,' she called, with her arms outstretched. 'Mom-mom-mommy.'

Albion stared at his mother, his lips puckered in an expression of bewilderment. Then, with a bemused scratch of his head he turned back to the gorilla. He glanced from one to the other looking increasingly confused, until finally, he pointed to Eliza.

'Mum!' he said decisively, and chuckled.

Justin found it impossible to decide who looked most offended – the human or the simian. Henny looked uncharacteristically put out, but was trying to hide it beneath a breezy, carefree laugh. Eliza made no such pretence; she roared with anger and beat her chest with her fists. Albion beamed, clenched his own tiny fists and aped her behaviour to perfection. Willoughby sniggered, but catching his wife's eye hurriedly turned it into a cough. Justin managed to subdue his own amusement by pinching the bridge of his nose and screwing his eyes tight shut. Startled by the pandemonium, the little doddling cowered on Henny's lap, dribbling ketchup down her shorts.

'Come to Mommy, my sweetie-pie,' Henny cooed, beckoning to Albion desperately. 'Come and see the funny birdie.'

'No!' said Albion, in the wobbly kind of voice that threatened tears

34

before bedtime. He thrust his lower lip out, then, after some deliberation, hooked a slimy green bogie from his nose and flicked it in his mother's direction.

The nonchalant smile Henny had worn so resolutely slipped a little; then, as her baby son crawled stubbornly towards Eliza, it slithered off completely, leaving an expression of simmering resentment in its place. Determined to maintain her composure, Henny closed her eyes and took a few more deep, calming breaths. Meanwhile, she pondered how to change the subject as naturally as possible, unaware the worst was yet to come.

'I wonder where Robyn's got to?' she droned, asking no-one in particular.

Eliza glowered angrily and clattered at her laptop again: 'Robyn outside,' she said. 'Bad girl get skin-picture.'

'SKIN-PICTURE?' shouted Henny, her hazel eyes flashing with undiluted fury.

Lady Henrietta Thyme practically *never* lost her temper – but on the rare occasions when she *did*, there were no half measures. Like molten lava, Henny's anger boiled and bubbled deep within her, and when the eruption came it made your average volcano look like a damp squib.

'DOES THAT MEAN WHAT I *THINK* IT MEANS? HAS THAT DARN GIRL GONE AND GOTTEN HERSELF A BLITHERING TATTOO?'

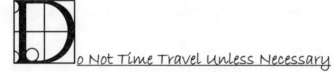# Do Not Time Travel Unless Necessary

Unlike the time travel of fiction, real time travel isn't just a convenient way to take vacations in the past. The danger of using a time machine is considerable and should never be underestimated.

Apart from the obvious risks of materialising suddenly in the past, there may be long-term physical effects from travelling faster than light, not to mention the mental strain of encountering paradox.

Before any trip through time, a chrononaut must consider whether their journey is really necessary. What do they hope to gain? Will the traveller's historical discoveries make a significant contribution to the present-day sum of human knowledge?

In short: do the potential advantages outweigh the hazards? Only after careful risk assessment should the chrononaut proceed.

CHAPTER THREE

Card Tricks

Lady Henny rose to her feet, seething with suppressed rage. When she spoke, her words came out in a slow, soft snarl, more terrifying than a tiger with toothache.

'*Whhhhere ... issssss ... shhhheee?*'

Justin took an involuntary step backwards. Willoughby edged behind the fridge door, Albion clutched Eliza, and the little doddling cowered beneath the table in a puddle of ketchup.

Eliza stood firm – and Justin, half wondering whether he was seeing things, watched the ghost of a smile drift across her thick, dark lips. Calmly, she rattled her fingers over the computer's keyboard:

'Robyn outside. Bad girl sleep on water.'

'WELL, SHE'S IN FOR A RUDE AWAKENING,' roared Henny. She stormed through the villa and out onto the rear terrace.

'I'll er ... keep an eye on Alby, shall I?' Sir Willoughby called after her, clearly guessing it was safest to remain in the kitchen and blend with the wallpaper.

Justin followed at a cautious distance – curious to see his sister, but not wanting to get caught in the inevitable crossfire. He peered through the living room curtains as Henny marched down the steps and across the lawn. Meanwhile, Robyn lounged nonchalantly on a lilo in the centre of the swimming pool, head back, fingers trailing in the cool, clear water. She seemed oblivious, but Justin suspected her strategic position was all part of a carefully laid battle plan.

She wore a purple bikini and a pair of glitzy designer sunglasses, neither of them covering more than a few square centimetres of skin. Yet from his vantage point, Justin couldn't see the tattoo anywhere. It must be on her back, he thought, trying to imagine the design: a life-size vampire bat, perhaps ... or a basilisk ...

'You've gone too far *this* time, my girl,' growled Henny.

Robyn stretched luxuriously, yawned, and then eased herself side-ways onto one elbow. Her long black hair tumbled around her neck and shoulders.

'Oh, hi Mum. What's up?'

'WHAT'S UP?' Henny spat the words like a venomous cobra. 'Don't toy with me you ... you ... WHERE IS IT?'

'Where's what?'

'You know darn well. The TATTOO!'

Henny prowled around the edge of the pool, desperate to examine her daughter from every angle – but with a casual flick of one hand, Robyn continually thwarted her by spinning the lilo gently.

Mmmm ... definitely on her back, Justin decided. But she can't stay in the water for ever – and antagonising Mum isn't the smartest move.

'Get *out* of that pool THIS INSTANT,' Henny thundered, her patience now completely evaporated.

Robyn sighed. 'If you insist.' She rolled off the lilo and swam underwater towards the shallow end, then hauled herself up the steps, her long hair plastered to her face and neck. As Henny strode forwards with a towel, Robyn lifted her arms and did a slow 360° pirouette.

Justin gasped. He couldn't see so much as a freckle.

'Satisfied?' Robyn asked, taking the towel from her mother and wrapping it around her waist. But before Henny could reply, she turned and strolled casually towards the villa.

Puzzled, Lady Henny watched her for a moment through narrowed eyes, then grabbing another towel she called, 'Aren't you going to dry your hair?'

'Er … no,' said Robyn, walking a little *less* nonchalantly. 'It'll soon dry in this heat.' After a lightning glance over one shoulder, she broke into an uneasy trot up the villa steps – which Justin considered a definite tactical error.

With a triumphant gleam in her eyes, Henny moved like a hungry cheetah with her sights set on the dumbest-looking gazelle on the Serengeti. She raced up the steps and grabbed hold of Robyn's wrist, jerking her round so they faced each other almost nose to nose; using her free hand, she withdrew a comb from her pocket.

'Here – you mustn't let it dry in a tangle.'

Frowning now, Robyn tried to pull and twist away, but Henny simply tightened her grip, and waited for her daughter to stop struggling.

'So ... it *is* on your neck, then?'

Robyn remained silent, but her mutinous pout was answer enough. After an exasperated sigh, Henny combed the damp hair off Robyn's neck, then shook her head slowly.

'How old did you say you were?'

'Nineteen.'

'And they bought that?'

'I'm not a *child*, you know?' snapped Robyn, her eyes suddenly flashing with resentment. 'Perhaps if you were home more, you'd have noticed! Nanny always ...'

'That's *ENOUGH*!'

Mother and daughter glowered at each other until the air between them seemed to crackle with electricity. Then, leaning forward and wagging her forefinger right in Robyn's face, Henny snarled: 'Well, listen up, young lady: whether I'm home or not, you're GROUNDED for the rest of the YEAR!'

Justin could tell supper was going to be an uncomfortable meal. Lady Henny had been slamming things around in the kitchen for the last hour; Sir Willoughby kept frowning distractedly out of the window, muttering under his breath; and Eliza, who'd just finished putting Albion to bed, was slouched over her laptop, frowning darkly. Only the little doddling looked happy, snoring contentedly on a tartan blanket.

'*Really*, Eliza,' remarked Henny, juggling with a steaming pan and a colander. 'I *told* you to keep an eye on Robyn.'

Justin watched the gorilla hitting the floor with her knuckles – and wondered why his mother, an expert in primate behavioural psychology, couldn't read the usual danger signs. With an irritable grunt, Eliza tapped at her keyboard, replying, 'Gorilla not human nanny,' for the fourth time in five minutes.

'That's no excuse,' Henny continued. 'You should've stopped her.'

Loosing all patience, Eliza slammed her laptop shut and stormed off outside, roaring with frustration. Moments later, a potted plant flew past the kitchen window. Henny flinched as it smashed into a palm tree, then, with a martyred sigh, she spooned congealed lumps of overcooked pasta onto several plates and banged them down on the table.

'Supper's ready,' she said, seeing Justin hovering in the doorway. 'Go fetch your sister.'

Robyn – quite wisely, in Justin's opinion – had shut herself in her bedroom. He knocked softly on her door. After what seemed like ages, it opened, and a defiant-looking face peered out, glittery purple mascara not entirely disguising her puffy red eyes.

As they returned to the kitchen, Justin glanced surreptitiously at his sister's neck, trying not to look too curious. Robyn saw him and grinned.

'Well, what do you think, then?' she asked, bending her head to one side and flicking her hair back. 'It's my own design.'

The tattoo wasn't as large or elaborate as he'd expected – just a small bird with outstretched wings, carrying a sprig of leaves in its beak.

'Hmmm ... surprisingly tasteful ... for you,' laughed Justin, dodging a friendly punch on the arm. 'I'm guessing it's a robin.'

'Obviously!'

'And the leaves?'

'Thyme, of course!'

'Coooool.' Then before his sister could look too pleased with herself, he added: 'And really handy if we ever forget what you're called!'

Back in the kitchen, both their parents were already seated at the table. Sir Willoughby was staring at the contents of his plate with ill-concealed dismay, but after a sideways peek at his wife, took a deep breath and shovelled a forkful of the unappetizing mess into his mouth.

'What's *that* supposed to be?' asked Robyn.

Henny, about to risk her first mouthful, ignored her.

'One of Mum's famous pasta-mutations, I think,' Justin whispered, settling in his chair.

'No, not that ... *THAT*,' said Robyn, pointing to a heap of rubbery-pink flesh in the corner of the room.

'Oh, er ... it's a baby dodo,' explained Justin. '*Raphus Cucullatus*; hitched a ride back on my last trip.'

'It looks like a badly-made haggis.'

The little doddling woke up, stretched its wing-stumps, and shot a stream of fishy poo over the floor.

Robyn covered her nose. 'Yuck ... disgusting freak!'

'There's *nothing* disgusting about it,' snapped Henny. 'Perfectly natural. If you want to talk about freaks, how about people who disfigure their own skin, tattooing it with indelible ink?'

'I've told you – it's body-art.'

'GRAFFITI,' Henny shouted. '*Permanent* graffiti. And mark my words: one of these days you'll regret it.' Lady Henrietta turned to her husband 'Back me up, Willo – she's your daughter too.'

Sir Willoughby looked up from his plate, wearing a puzzled, distant expression. He glanced across the table at Robyn, clearly wondering what the problem was, then, noticing her food still untouched, said: 'Eat up, Bobs ... it's not as bad as it looks!'

Henny groaned. '*Arrghhh* ... you haven't been listening to a single word I've said, have you?' She slammed her fork down and appealed to her eldest son for support. 'Surely *you* don't ...'

'Please, Mum – let it drop,' Justin murmured. 'It's only a tattoo. What's done is done ... and can't be undone!'

'*Fffuhhh*! Find me a lemon-zester or some sandpaper and I might be tempted to disprove that theory!'

41

Once supper was over, Sir Willoughby drained his glass, and after murmuring a few words in his wife's ear, hurried outside. From the kitchen window, Justin watched him trot down the narrow stone steps to the jetty and start up the boat.

'Where's Dad off to?'

'Oh ... things to arrange for tomorrow,' replied Henny vaguely. 'Which reminds me: I'd better phone that pilot.' She leaned over and rummaged through a battered-looking leather handbag beside her chair; after grabbing her cell phone she stepped out onto the terrace, scrolling through her contacts menu.

Justin opened the dishwasher and began stacking the dirty plates. Robyn watched him, frowning pensively – then, to his enormous surprise, offered to help. She jumped up and grabbed her own plate, knocking a fork spinning onto the floor.

'Oh, crud-crumpets!' she muttered, scrabbling on her hands and knees beneath the table. By the time she emerged, Justin had almost finished. Robyn held out the fork to him, grinning apologetically – but when he tried to take it from her she kept a firm grasp of it until she had his undivided attention.

'Hey, Dustbin,' she said. 'Thanks for sticking up for me.'

Later that night, his bags ready packed for their morning departure, Justin lay in bed trying to wind down. It had been a long day – several hours longer than anyone else's if he counted his time in the past – yet, as tired as he was, he couldn't sleep. His left arm hurt where he'd been thrown against the chronopod, and when he removed his wristwatch he was shocked by the number of bruises.

The watch had taken quite a knock too, but to Justin's relief it was still ticking away steadfastly, although the bracelet catch seemed looser than usual. The thought of his wristwatch getting damaged horrified Justin; it was by far his most treasured possession, even though he still had no idea who'd actually given it too him. But that wasn't his worry tonight. As he mentally replayed the last few hours, something – or someone – left him feeling decidedly unsettled.

Robyn's prickly defiance was nothing new, of course. And it wasn't his mother, he decided. True, he'd never seen her get so angry before, but discovering Robyn's rebellion minutes after Alby's rejection made it pretty understandable.

Was it, perhaps, his father's behaviour that had unsettled him? On reflection, that seemed a distinct possibility ... yet the more Justin thought about it, the more confused he felt.

Bizarrely, Sir Willoughby's preoccupied manner at supper would have looked perfectly normal a few weeks ago. For as long as Justin could remember, his father had been the vague and distracted type, never quite in touch with the real world – but he now knew this had always been an act.

'And Mum's known for years,' he reminded himself, wondering whether the pretence was being kept up for Robyn's benefit alone ... or was just a useful habit Sir Willoughby slipped into to avoid getting embroiled in family arguments.

At first, the thought annoyed him ... then a momentary twinge of guilt made him question his judgement. Carefully, he analysed the day's events again, and realised that his father's anxiety had started hours before supper.

'The Grim Reaper apparition,' he whispered. 'I should've guessed telling Dad about it would trigger his curse fears. But why did it make him want to stay *here*?'

Try as he might, Justin couldn't see how remaining in Mauritius would protect anyone from the Thyme Curse ... even if it *was* real.

'And what changed Dad's mind so abruptly?' he muttered into his pillow. 'When I told him how I almost mistook Grandpa Lyall for Old Father Time, he was suddenly *desperate* to get back home.'

Two strangely similar visions; two radically different reactions. Justin knew there had to be a logical explanation ... some connection ... but hours later, as he heard his father creep back into the villa, he was still no closer to finding one.

Exhausted, Justin closed his eyes, casting his mind back to the momentous day he turned thirteen; the day he'd cracked the enigma of time travel. Slowly, he felt himself drifting into that surreal hypnogogic phase between wakefulness and sleep, crossing the hazy boundary between truth and dreams. He felt like two people in two different places; part of him knew he was asleep in a Mauritian villa, yet, simultaneously, he was standing in his laboratory at Thyme Castle. He could feel the warm sunshine through the leaded windowpane; run his fingers over each crack and crevice in the ancient stone sill; even smell the stale chemical fumes of a recently abandoned experiment. Everything seemed in pin-sharp focus and glowed with a dazzling radiance that transcended reality.

He knew, without a particle of doubt, that it was the 1st of May, a few seconds before ten o'clock. Curious to witness the strange apparition a second time, he reached for his telescope and turned it towards the castle gates, zooming in on an old man with white hair and a long, snowy beard – the man he now called Grandpa. As the tower clock started to strike, a shaft of sunlight pierced through a cloud, creating a strange semi-transparent hologram that shimmered around the old man so there appeared to be two figures: an ethereal linen-robed stranger carrying a scythe and hourglass superimposed over a ragged-looking vagrant tossing a coin.

It was exactly as he remembered. Hoping, this time, to spot some previously-overlooked detail that might make sense of it all, Justin tried to freeze the image in his mind – but it was like trying to grasp hold of smoke, distorting the memory into something sinister and new. With each reverberating chime, the hologram seemed to pulsate and darken – gradually, almost imperceptibly, transforming Old Father Time into the skeletal black-clad figure of the Grim Reaper. As the final note rang out, the hologram shattered into ten glittering fragments each containing a different image: a blood-stained scythe lying just beyond the castle gates, cold cerulean eyes burning with hatred, a table set for thirteen, the last grains of sand trickling through an hourglass, a smoking gun, crimson rose petals, a monogrammed handkerchief, three broken bottles, a hangman's noose and, finally, a single playing card ... the joker.

One by one the fragments flickered and vanished, until only the joker remained, toppling forward until its face leered through the castle window, its spindly fingers tapping on the glass ...

Tap ... tap, tap ... tap ...

Justin woke with a jolt, his heart pounding. For a moment, the pale sunshine streaming through the muslin curtains dazzled him so much he could scarcely see. He picked up his wristwatch and squinted down at its face through half-closed eyes; in a couple of minutes it would be a quarter past six. Justin flopped back on his pillow ... then froze as he heard the sound again ...

Tap ... tap, tap ...

Holding his breath, he turned slowly towards the window where, to his horror, he saw the shadow of a slender hand beyond the curtains.

'Who ... who's there?' he gasped.

There was a pause, then a relieved voice whispered, 'Oh, hi Justin ... it's me, Polly. Did I wake you?'

'Er ... not exactly.'

'Phew, glad I got the right window; didn't want to disturb your mum and dad this early.'

Justin slid off the bed and padded across the room. After drawing the curtains aside, he unlatched the window and leaned out, yawning widely. 'What do you want?'

Polly shuffled his feet. 'A favour, actually,' he said, pulling a crumpled envelope from the back pocket of his jeans. 'Sir Willoughby sailed over to collect your motorbike last night. He said you were flying back to Scotland this morning ... so I wondered if you could deliver this for me.'

'Why didn't you just give it Dad?'

'Oh ... I er … hadn't written it then. I only got the idea after Sir Willoughby left. It's to *my* father, you see; since Daddikins retired he's been terribly lonely. He's missing the hustle and bustle of the circus dreadfully – especially now he's alone in that draughty old house with no one to talk to. I thought a letter might cheer him up.'

'Yeah ... okay,' said Justin, taking the envelope.

'I could've mailed it, I suppose,' Polly continued. 'I just thought if

45

you delivered it in person he'd have someone to talk to. And I know it's a lot to ask, but ...' He hesitated, looking a trifle embarrassed. 'I ... I wondered if you might take Robyn ... and stay for half an hour ... have afternoon tea or something.'

There was an awkward pause.

'Well ... er ...' Justin mumbled, uncertain what to say. Scarcely a couple of weeks ago he'd suspected Polly's dad was Agent X, Sir Willoughby's old enemy. Xavier Polydorus had even visited Thyme Castle the very morning Nanny Verity had inexplicably disappeared out of a locked room. 'Hmmm ... the thing is ...'

Blushing now, Polly interrupted him, back-pedalling furiously. 'No, no ... it's okay,' he spluttered. 'I *really* shouldn't have asked. *So* sorry. Forget it; forget the letter too,' he added, snatching it back. 'Must dash; Hank rowed me over – he's waiting by the jetty ...'

The more Polly apologised the worse Justin felt. It seemed so mean. After all, there'd been absolutely no *real* evidence against Mr Polydorus – just a few circumstantial coincidences and his name starting with an X. 'Don't be silly,' Justin insisted hurriedly. 'Of *course* we'll visit your dad ... if he invites us.'

Within nanoseconds, Justin was regretting his hasty offer. If he'd been wide awake he'd have come up with a polite plausible excuse ... but still half-asleep, he'd been caught completely off-guard.

'Oh, he will, he will!' gushed Polly, his blue eyes suddenly sparkling. 'I promise it won't be *too* awful. Dear old Daddikins! He's a harmless sweetie-pie, really – probably bore you both senseless with his cards tricks. And I should warn you ... he tells the most *ghastly* jokes.

The atmosphere at breakfast was a degree or two less frosty than supper, but nowhere near a complete thaw. There was an uneasy truce between the females of the family, although the icy glares Robyn gave her mother conveyed more defiance than mere words could ever express.

Eliza kept her laptop closed, and all attempts at starting a conversation with her were greeted with noisily blown raspberries and a dismissive flick of one hand.

Sir Willoughby, who looked as if he hadn't slept a wink, was hunched silently over his coffee mug. And Albion, grinning wickedly, appeared to have decided that food was for throwing, and that mothers were for target-practice!

Despite all this, Lady Henny looked unaccountably pleased about something – and Justin couldn't help wondering if she was secretly glad to be seeing the back of them all in a couple of hours.

'Any pancakes, Mum?' he asked, knowing that, despite her dodgy cooking, these were reasonably fail-safe.

'Wow! Someone's still speaking to me,' laughed Henny. She opened a fresh packet of *Aunty Meridian's All American Microwaveable Pancakes*, stacked them in the microwave and punched the ten second button three times.

'Thanks, Mum,' said Justin, helping himself to couple and pouring warm maple syrup over them. As he dug into his first pancake, he noticed Albion watching him, his eyes as round as marbles. With both arms outstretched towards Justin's plate, he wriggled his little fingers and made cute gurgling noises.

'He's back to his usual incomprehensible baby-talk again,' Henny sighed. 'Can't understand more than one word out of five; I swear he's doing it just to annoy me!'

Instantly, Albion stopped gurgling. He turned to his mother and regarded her for a long moment with his head on one side; then, as if coming to a decision, screwed up his face and strained until his cheeks turned red and an unpleasant smell wafted across the breakfast table.

'Pude!' he said, slapping the front of his nappy ... and looked at his mum with an expression that seemed to say: *Any problems under-standing that?*

'I guess he needs his diaper changing, Eliza,' said Henny, her tone of voice clearly implying this was an instruction. She leaned back in her chair and took a casual sip of coffee, as if to emphasise she had no intention of performing the task herself.

Eliza had other ideas; she hoisted the baby up by the back of his romper-suit, dumped him unceremoniously on Henny's lap and strolled out of the kitchen. Once again, Justin could sense the gorilla's growing resentment. He'd never felt afraid of her, not for an instant – but for the first time in his life he wondered what might happen if, one of these days, his mother pushed Eliza just a bit too far.

By ten o'clock the Thymes' luggage had been packed into the big red people-mover hired to take them to the airport. After kissing his wife goodbye, Sir Willoughby clambered into the front seat, while Justin, Robyn, Eliza and Albion settled themselves in the back.

Eliza had grudgingly agreed to take care of Albion until they got home – but only because Henny had promised that she would be relieved of her duties once they were back at Thyme Castle.

The doddling was snoring peacefully inside a small pet crate. Henny had given it a mild sedative (concealed in a kipper), hoping this would make its journey as stress-free as possible. She placed the crate on the seat beside Robyn, who scowled and edged away.

'Eurgh ... it smells like a mouldy fishcake,' she grumbled.

'You'll just have to get used to it,' said Henny, keeping her voice calm and measured. 'From now on, it's your job to look after him.'

'You've *GOT* to be JOKING!'

'It's high time you learned to shoulder some responsibilities,' Henny continued. 'In future, whether I'm home or not, I'll be setting you regular assignments; if you complete them satisfactorily, you'll get a weekly allowance, if not, well ...'

Robyn stared at her mother, her mouth hanging wide open.

'Weekly allowance? I ... I don't need a ...'

'Oh, I think you will do,' said Henny, opening her left hand to reveal several shards of brightly coloured plastic. 'I snuck into your bedroom last night and cut up your credit card.'

'YOU DID *WWHHHHHAAAATT?*' screamed Robyn. 'You CAN'T *DO* THAT ... YOU ... YOU ...'

Henny glanced down at her watch. 'You'd better get going, Willo – it's nearly five past; the pilot won't want to miss his timeslot for takeoff.'

Sir Willoughby nodded, his face serious. 'Take care, Hen – don't get yourself kidnapped again.'

'*Fffuhhh*! It's you I'm worried about; looks like you're in for a turbulent trip.'

With a swift eye-rolling glance at Robyn through the rear-view mirror, Willoughby switched on his iPod, and wedged its earbuds firmly inside his ears. He grimaced at Henny and turned the ignition key. As the people-mover pulled away Justin tried to shout goodbye, but, unable to make himself heard over Robyn's rage, he waved to his mum instead.

Henny waved back – smiling the serene smile of a mother in full control.

Robyn's screams of indignation continued unabated as the people-mover purred along the narrow road – but the instant Sir Willoughby steered round a sharp bend, the ear-splitting shrieks stopped as abruptly as if someone had pressed a mute button.

'Round one to Mum,' Justin remarked, guessing his sister wasn't going to take this lying down.

'HAH! As if.' Robyn reached down and removed her left sandal. After checking their father's attention was fixed on the traffic, she tipped the inside of it towards Justin. 'Yep ... it's mine,' she whispered, noticing her brother's eyes widen as he saw a credit card wedged along the insole.

'But ... but ... I mean ... how?'

'I guessed something like this would happen, so I took precautions. Mum's been threatening to destroy my plastic ever since I got my navel stud ... yet last night at supper, no mention! Suspicious, huh? I guessed her idle threat was about to become a reality. When she stepped outside to make that phone call, I dropped my fork under the kitchen table so I could raid her handbag. Once I'd "borrowed" one of her credit cards, I simply swap—'

'*Borrowed*?'

49

'She's got it back now, hasn't she? It's not my fault she cut it up.'

'But ...'

'Serves her right for sneaking about in the dark. She assumed I was asleep, but I was faking; I watched her take her own card out of my purse and hack it up. Epic fail! How I kept from laughing I'll never know! Round one to me, I think!'

'Hmm ... what about having to care for the dodo?' asked Justin.

Robyn shrugged. 'Granted, I didn't see that coming – but how hard can it be? Just sling a few scraps of food at it three times a day.' She peered through the mesh front of the pet carrier, holding her nose. 'I still say it looks like a badly-stuffed haggis!'

Lady Henrietta Thyme strolled back inside the villa, planning a peaceful cup of coffee before heading over to Îlot du Mort. Passing a tidy bin, she tossed the fragments of credit card into it – but one small, shiny triangle of plastic remained stuck to her palm. Scarcely paying attention, she flicked the piece off with a fingernail – but her brain, busy planning the day ahead, subconsciously registered the few random letters embossed across one end – and as she walked away Henny felt an indefinable sense of something being wrong.

Very wrong.

So wrong, in fact, that half way to the kitchen Henny turned around, sprinted back and retrieved the piece of plastic out of the bin. She glared at it, her eyes blazing with a cold fury.

'So you want to play hardball, do yer?' Henny whispered to herself. 'Well, watch out ... cos no fourteen year-old girl's gonna get the better of me.'

esearch Your Destination Period

Ideally, while visiting the past, the time traveller should stick to unpopulated locations. However, when human contact cannot be avoided, it is vital he or she blends in perfectly with the populace of the period.

Research the era thoroughly, familiarising yourself with the customs, language and currency, as well as ensuring your hairstyle and clothes are appropriate. Never wear sneakers in Victorian London, or use a digital camera in the Iron Age – it will attract unwelcome attention and lead to complications.

When visiting the recent past, careful planning is still essential ... perhaps even more so if there's a chance of meeting people you know, (including yourself). With careful research, the chrononaut should try to deduce the whereabouts of others, and so avoid problematic encounters.

– CHAPTER FOUR –

Thymes Fly

The Lear jet was ready and waiting – its sleek white fuselage gleaming in the Mauritian sunshine. It was parked beside one of the small private hangars the airport usually reserved for visiting Heads of State.

Sir Willoughby drove past the main entrance and stopped outside a pair of sliding security gates. He tooted his horn, and a uniformed guard with a clipboard hurried out of a kiosk and marched towards them. After a cursory nod at the people-carrier's tinted windows, he opened the gates and waved the Thymes through.

Sir Willoughby breathed a sigh of relief. Henny had given him her Zoological Specimen Import License and a sheaf of paperwork claiming the dodo was a legally captured parrot ... but this made things undeniably simpler.

'Bit lax on security,' he remarked, glancing quizzically at his son.

Justin laughed. 'It'll be the Krataslavian Crest on the tail-fin, I bet. He probably thinks we're royalty.'

Justin had bought the Lear jet less than a week ago, after hearing on the grapevine that the Crowned Prince of Krataslavia needed to liquidate a few surplus luxuries to cover his gambling debts. Within twenty-four hours he'd wired the money through, hired a pilot, and dispatched him to collect the plane – but there hadn't been time to get the tail-fin repainted.

Sir Willoughby parked beside the hangar and checked his watch.

'Okay, get your bags, everyone,' he said, leaving the ignition key behind the sun visor.

Robyn scowled as she lugged the pet-carrier off the back seat, heartily wishing some airport official would materialise and confiscate it; Eliza settled Albion on her shoulders then tucked a suitcase under each arm; and Justin, hoping his time machine was already stowed on board, grabbed his travel bag and *Hover-Boots*.

As the Thymes crossed the tarmac, their pilot, waiting beneath the plane with his arms folded, glowered at them with such simmering intensity, that Justin felt the hairs on the back of his neck prickle. He shot his father a swift sideways look. The Laird of Thyme wore a grim, fixed expression – like someone steeling themselves to visit the dentist.

In Sir Willoughby's opinion, the new pilot didn't look like a pilot at all; he half suspected the agency had misheard his son's instructions and sent a pirate instead. Proper pilots, he'd insisted, were little chaps with crisp, navy blue uniforms and handlebar moustaches; whereas this man was at least six and half feet tall, wore flowing black robes and a turban. He *did* have a moustache – and a beard too, of sorts: just a narrow angular line along his jaw that looked as if it had been drawn onto his coffee-coloured skin with a black marker-pen.

Even Justin had to admit he didn't behave much like a pilot either. He didn't salute smartly while his passengers embarked, or make bracing comments about the weather.

And those eyes! They were so impenetrably dark it was impossible to distinguish between the iris and the pupil; they were the eyes of a shark, Justin thought – only less friendly.

'If looks could kill ...' muttered Sir Willoughby. Then, giving the pilot an ingratiating smile, he called out: 'G'morning, Horace. All ready for takeoff?'

The pilot said nothing; he merely nodded – or to be precise, his head twitched a fraction of a millimetre which was as near to nodding as he ever seemed to get. Silently, he lowered the Lear's steps, and stood back. One by one, the Thymes filed past him: Sir Willoughby first, looking awkward and attempting a nonchalant whistle. Justin came next, and found himself giving the pilot a nervous grin and immediately wishing he hadn't. Eliza followed; to Albion's delight, she paused to reacquaint herself with the pilot's spicy aroma. With complete lack of embarrassment, she snuffled noisily in his face, then tapping at her laptop announced in the voice of the castle cook: 'Flying man smell like ginger cake.'

Robyn came last of all and, after Eliza's performance, was struggling to subdue a fit of the giggles. 'Looks like you've got yourself an admirer,' she remarked to the pilot, tipping him a slow wink.

The pilot stared right through her, his face as stony and impassive as the sphinx. Once his passengers were settled in their seats, and their luggage safely stacked in the hold, he secured the cabin door. Without a word, he swept past them into the cockpit, moving with the sinuous grace of a black panther; then, utterly *unlike* a panther, he withdrew a razor-sharp scimitar from within his robes and stowed it beneath his seat. Seconds later, the jet's powerful engines started to thrum and the plane taxied slowly along the runway.

'Has anyone heard him say *anything* yet?' hissed Robyn, once she was certain the pilot was safely out of earshot.

'Just his name,' Willoughby groaned. 'And I wasn't sure I heard *that* properly. I mean, Horace Aerobus doesn't sound very likely, does it? But I hadn't the nerve to say pardon. The look on his face could've stopped Big Ben!'

'What's his background?' asked Robyn.

'Pilot and personal bodyguard to the Sultan of Borborygmus,' Justin replied. 'Until we offered to double his wages.'

'Well, the least he could do is say hello,' said Robyn, annoyed at having wasted one of her most alluring winks on him without the merest flicker of a response.

Eliza finished fastening Albion's seatbelt and then reached for her laptop. 'Flying man not need words,' she said.

Justin laughed, struck by the gorilla's innate ability to read people. She was absolutely correct. The pilot didn't need to speak; his impassive silence manoeuvred them all into handling him with kid gloves.

'Didn't your mother talk to him?' asked Sir Willoughby. 'I seem to remember her visiting the cockpit when we flew out.'

'That's *right*,' said Justin. 'I almost forgot. *Greek father; Egyptian mother; probably born in Nepal*, she thought. You know Mum ...'

Robyn nodded. Henny had a rudimentary grasp of every language from Arabic to Zulu. The moment someone spoke, from their accent and dialect she could usually deduce where they were from and attempt a few words of greeting in their native tongue.

Justin turned to his sister. 'I'm surprised *you* can't get him chatting.'

Although Robyn had inherited her mother's linguistic skills, she seldom bothered to use them. However, she found the pilot rather intriguing in a dark and dangerous kind of way, and was eager to rise to the challenge.'

'Hmmm ... I'm absolute *pants* at Egyptian,' she mumbled trying to look suitably disinterested. 'But my Greek's not bad.'

As the plane took off, Robyn closed her eyes and imagined the pilot confiding his life story to her, his stern face gradually relaxing into an enigmatic smile ...

Once the Lear jet reached a stable cruising altitude, Sir Willoughby undid his seatbelt and helped himself to a drink from the galley. Catching his son's eye, he motioned with his head towards a steel door at the rear of the plane. Curious, Justin jumped up and followed him.

The custom-built lab had been hurriedly fitted out to Justin's specifications; basic yet practical, and equipped with the best portable field apparatus available. It was, however, a small area designed for just one person working alone; with two inside it felt decidedly cramped, especially with Justin's Norton motorbike and sidecar already taking up half the floor space.

Justin gazed at the chronopod, wondering if it was too soon to negotiate for the return of its keys.

'I brought her over from the island last night,' explained Sir Willoughby, running his fingers over the registration plate on the bike's front wheel.

'So I see,' Justin remarked, guessing his father had something far more pressing to say, and was searching for the right way to begin. He decided to help out: 'Is there anything bothering you, Dad?'

An expression of something like relief seemed to flood across Willoughby's face – but a split-second later it turned into a look of frazzled anxiety.

'It was something you said yesterday,' he whispered. 'It made me wonder if ... no, *no* ...' He paused, shaking his head. 'You see, I think there's a chance that ...' Then, slamming one fist down on the motorbike's leather saddle, he groaned: '*Aarghh*, dash it all ... it doesn't add up!'

'What doesn't?'

Again Sir Willoughby hesitated. 'I ... I'd rather not say ... in case I'm wrong.'

'But ...'

'I need to know something,' he said, and took a deep breath before carrying on. 'Tell me again *exactly* what you saw the morning Grandpa arrived. I ... er ... well, it's important.'

Justin leaned back against the door and rubbed his forehead. 'Like I said before. I saw him standing at that fork in the road outside the castle gates. It looked like he was trying to decide which way to go – so he tossed a coin in the air and ...'

He stopped, uncertain whether to go on. Although Sir Willoughby was doing his best to hide it, Justin sensed that every word he uttered was causing his father acute discomfort. 'What's wrong, Dad?'

'Nothing ... go on.'

Justin shrugged. 'Okay. Well, I saw this weird vision, right? Not a hallucination or anything – more like some trick of the light; for a moment or two there was Old Father Time carrying his scythe and hourglass ... and in an explosive flash of inspiration I suddenly understood everything I'd ever struggled to grasp about time.'

Sir Willoughby closed his eyes and hunched over, withdrawing into himself.

'As you know,' Justin continued, 'there isn't a solitary stream of time. It forks ... and forks again, *ad infinitum*! Yet, bizarrely, our passage through time is often a matter of chance, like the tossing of a coin at each fork in the road.'

'And once you realised that, you instantly saw how time travel was possible,' whispered Willoughby, straightening up again.

'Exactly!'

Sir Willoughby leaned forward, placing his right hand on Justin's left shoulder, and stared intently into his eyes as if trying to read the thoughts hidden behind them.

'I'm going to ask you a *very* important question; will you promise to answer me truthfully?'

'Of course!'

'Have you *ever* described this incident to anyone else ... anyone at all?'

'Well, er ...' Justin felt his cheeks flush as he spoke. 'I ... I might have mentioned it to Professor Gilbert. Not the Old Father Time bit ... just about somebody tossing a coin at a fork in the road, and how that made me think of plotting conceptual timelines in binary code. But the prof's trustworthy ... I'm certain.'

Willoughby shook his head gloomily.

'Look, you mustn't talk to *anyone* about this, no matter how much you think you can trust them. You've got to remember that Agent X is still out there ... still every bit as dangerous ... still desperate to get his hands on *this*,' he said, patting the chronopod. 'Have you forgotten all the trouble we went to making it look like *I* was the one building it?'

'Hardly!' replied Justin, his voice a shade too defensive. 'It was *my* idea. But it's built now. Why keep misdirecting him? Or have you been acting for so long you can't stop?'

Sir Willoughby shrank back as if he'd been slapped across the face. The hurt in his eyes made Justin squirm uncomfortably – yet looking deeper into them, he saw a flicker of something else there too ... resentment, perhaps ... or guilt. For a while, father and son faced each other in stony silence, then Willoughby turned away and spoke in a tone that sounded cold and detached.

'Of course I can't stop; I *daren't* stop. I sacrificed my career to

57

protect my family ... and if acting is the best way to keep you all safe, then I'll do what needs to be done.'

'I didn't mean ...'

'If you think I'm trying to take credit for your work, I assure you I'm not,' Sir Willoughby continued. 'Your safety is more important to me than anything ... *anything!* A brain as exceptional as yours is far too valuable to risk. You alone have been the focus of my every thought and action for the last thirteen years; ensuring you had the best education, a fully-equipped lab, the freedom to experiment and develop at your own pace in an environment designed to foster genius. I've guided you, inspired you, answered your questions ... all the while assuming the role of a burnt out old has-been. And why? To keep you safe until you reached the point I was once at myself, before ... before I lost everything. Don't repay all that by putting yourself in danger.'

Justin felt sick. 'Please, Dad ... don't be angry ... I only ...'

Holding up one hand to silence his son, Willoughby pressed on, a note of agitation creeping into his voice. 'I'm not angry with *you*; I'm angry with *myself*. Damned fool. I should've seen this coming. I always knew you'd be brilliant, of course ... but ...'

He stopped abruptly and gave a long shuddering sigh. Justin stared at his father, uncertain what to say. Clearly, the emotional strain of the last few years had almost become too much for him; he looked as if he was about to crack.

After several deeps breaths, Sir Willoughby seemed to regain control. He turned back to Justin, looking him squarely in the eyes.

'Understand this: Agent X is ruthless and deadly – but he's smart, too. I doubt he'll try kidnapping again. My bet is he'll target the inventor next time – apply a little motivational pressure; an incentive, if you get my drift ... probably something lingering and painful. Which is why we can't let him discover the truth. If he ever finds out *you're* the one who built this dratted contraption, you could be in terrible danger.

'Fortunately,' Sir Willoughby concluded. 'I *now* have a pretty good idea who he is; as soon as we're back at Thyme Castle I intend to settle the matter, once and for all.'

Robyn leaned round the cockpit doorway, wondering what to say next. In her best Greek she'd already tried: *"Hello"* – *"Nice view up here"* – *"How long have you been a pilot?"* – *"Which is your favourite Greek island?"* ... and after noticing an eye design on the back of his right hand, *"Would you like to see my tattoo?"* None of which got even the slightest reaction.

Seeing as the only Egyptian phrase she could remember was *"Does your camel bite?"* – Robyn finally resorted to English, but after several polite questions were studiously ignored, her patience snapped.

'Can't you say *ANYTHING*?' she groaned.

The pilot turned towards her slowly, his lips drawn back in a contemptuous sneer.

'How's this?' he whispered. 'May your right ear wither and drop into your left pocket!'

Back in the main cabin, Sir Willoughby poured himself a large drink and downed it in a single gulp. After eyeing the bottle thoughtfully he replaced the cork, fetched a tartan blanket from one of the overhead lockers, and settled himself in a chair well away from the others.

Across the cabin, Eliza was sharing a bunch of grapes with Albion – although Alby, who usually loved grapes, kept wrinkling his nose and spitting them out. He squashed one in his fist and extracted a couple of small, slippery pips with thumb and forefinger.

'Ips!' he grimaced, waving them at Eliza. He placed them on the arm of his chair beside several others, then, frowning with concentration, flicked them one at a time onto the floor.

Meanwhile, Justin opened the fridge door and grabbed a bottle of highland spring water. He wasn't particularly thirsty, but it gave him something to do with his hands while his brain struggled to process all that his father had just said. Flumping down in an empty chair, he half glanced at his sister without focussing. Robyn, looking moody and irritable, was tossing chocolate raisins into her mouth and chomping them viciously.

'Want one, Dustbin?' she asked.

For a moment or two Justin stared at her, unaware she'd even spoken – then noticing her eyes rolling in despair, muttered, '*Oh* ... erm, pardon?'

'*Urrgh*,' Robyn groaned. 'What's the matter with everyone today?'

'Jetlag?'

'Yeah ... we've only been flying one hour. Have you and Dad had a row?'

'No.'

'As *if*. I think one of us is fibbing ... and, oooh, it's not me!'

Justin frowned, trying to think of a safe ambiguous reply, but soon realised his inventive genius was better suited to hi-tech mechanical gadgets.

Robyn gave a short, hard laugh. 'When you and Dad came back in he looked like someone had ripped his guts out and sold them on eBay! And *you* ... well, you looked ten times worse!'

Silently, Justin had to admit that Robyn wasn't far wrong; the conversation with his father had left him feeling pretty shaken. It had been a wake-up call, he decided – and probably one that he'd needed. He hadn't forgotten Agent X, of course, or the threat he still posed to the Thymes. A few weeks ago it had all been frighteningly real – but, safe with his family, these last few days in the warm Mauritian sunshine had given him a false sense of security. Far from Thyme Castle and any potential impostors, he'd let his guard down – while his father, after years of relentless vigilance, had kept the ongoing danger sharply in focus.

And clearly, Sir Willoughby's thirteen-year act had been no simple charade; more like walking a tightrope, where one false step could have ended in catastrophe. It explained a lot, Justin thought. Particularly his mercurial behaviour, moods switching unpredictably in the blink of an eye; perfectly justifiable given the strain such a continual pretence must have been. Yet, for all that, Justin knew there was something his father was hiding.

It rankled.

'Why won't he tell me what's bothering him if he thinks I've got such an exceptional brain?' Justin muttered to himself. 'Maybe I could help.'

'Help who?' asked Robyn, raising one eyebrow and peering sideways at him.

Justin took a quick look at his father, now snoring beneath his blanket. 'Dad,' he whispered. 'Something's bugging him – but he won't explain.'

'Typical.'

He shot another wary glance across the cabin and lowered his voice further still. 'Okay, I get that he's pretty scared of X, but ...'

'X?'

'Agent X – that's the codename Dad's old enemy uses.'

Robyn's eyes widen for a moment, and her cheeks flushed – but when she said nothing, Justin continued.

'Something I said made Dad think he suddenly knows who X is.'

'Who?'

'He wouldn't tell me! The Professor, I *think* ... or maybe Gra—'

'*Ffuhhh*! Professor Gobbledygook? Don't make me laugh.'

'Shhhhh ... you'll wake Dad.'

'Not after a triple whisky,' chuckled Robyn. 'Hey, we *are* still looking for him, aren't we? This X guy ... when we get back?'

Justin hid his surprise. When their mum had been kidnapped, it was Robyn who'd suggested they should try to solve the crime – but once Henny was safely back home, her ambition of being a private investigator seemed to evaporate.

'I think Dad wants us to keep out of danger,' Justin told her.

'That's parents for you,' snickered Robyn. 'Got to feel they're in charge ... caring for the little chickies in the nest. Gives them a sense of purpose in their declining years, I suppose.'

Justin gave a noncommittal shrug, guessing this was more about her conflict with Henny ... but a small part of him wondered if she was right ... sort of.

'Maybe Dad just needs to feel in control,' Justin murmured, half to himself. 'Proving he can still protect his family without the help of us kids.'

'Anyway,' said Robyn, 'I'm still going to catch this Agent X ... even if *you're* too scared.'

'Of course I'm not; I rescued Mum, didn't I?'

Robyn grinned. 'Yeah, a bit of action, for once ... but that's my department, remember? You're the brains, Dustbin – *I'm* the action!'

'The Thyme-team!' laughed Justin.

Not for the first time, Justin thought how much he appreciated Robyn's forthright attitude. He knew his dad wouldn't approve of their plans – but, despite their many similarities, he didn't want to become too like his father. Justin realised that tackling problems head on would never be his natural inclination, and that it would be all too easy for him to slip into Sir Willoughby's strategy of avoiding trouble by camouflage and evasion. That was where his sister helped out.

'Okay, let's talk suspects,' said Robyn, rubbing her hands together.

'Based on Dad's description, we're after a man in his late fifties,' Justin reminded her. 'We know he's a talented actor, and a whiz at disguising himself ... so he could look older or younger.'

'Yeah ... and if he's infiltrated Thyme Castle that means we've only three possible suspects' said Robyn. 'Mr Gilliechattan, Knightly, and your precious professor.'

'Four,' insisted Justin. 'You've forgotten old Sir Lyall.'

Robyn made huffing noise and shook her head. 'I'm *sure* Grandpa's for real.'

'Well, Nanny Verity didn't think so. And speaking of Nanny ...'

Justin stopped abruptly, remembering his sister didn't know the *full* truth about Verity Kiss. After Nanny disappeared, Henny had persuaded Sir Willoughby to tell everyone she was on vacation recovering from her "accident" – although Robyn, guessing this was a smokescreen, assumed she'd gone into hiding until her assailant was caught.

At first, Justin had wanted to tell his sister the truth – but out of loyalty to Nanny Verity, he'd finally decided to keep the facts to himself. After all, if Nanny wished to tell Robyn about her unhappy marriage to Agent X, surely that was her prerogative.

But keeping Nanny's secret had been like navigating a minefield. The day she'd vanished, she'd taken Robyn's old laptop with her. Justin had managed to explain its sudden disappearance by saying he was giving it a virus-check – but that was the easy part. He'd also needed to hack into Robyn's hotmail account to delete Nanny's e-mail. If Robyn had spotted it in her sent items folder, it would've prompted an avalanche of awkward questions.

'Go on,' said Robyn, nudging him. 'What *about* Nanny?'

'Oh ... it's nothing.'

Robyn's face puckered into a sad frown. 'I worry about her, you know. Don't you think it's weird she left without saying goodbye ... or leaving us a message?'

'I suppose.' Justin took a slantwise peek at his sister, wondering if she was close to guessing the truth. 'What do *you* think happened?'

'Well ... you know how everyone came to welcome her home from hospital that day? Maybe her attacker was right there in our kitchen. What if Nanny *didn't* leave of her own free will? What if this X guy abducted her ... and ... and ...'

'Silenced her permanently?' Justin whispered.

Robyn nodded, her eyes brimming with tears.

Justin wasn't about to admit it, but, at first, the same terrible thought had occurred to him, too. There'd been something undeniably odd about the way her e-mail was worded.

'I'm pretty sure Nan'll be safely hidden somewhere,' he said quietly. 'We checked her room, remember? She wouldn't have packed any clothes if she'd been abducted.'

Robyn nodded, looking reassured.

'Yeah, you're right,' she sniffed. 'And maybe X isn't at the castle. You always said he'd have a spy there, doing his dirty work. Perhaps he lives nearby, keeping a close eye on things ...'

'Like Mr Polydorus!' exclaimed Justin, almost forgetting to whisper in his excitement. 'He's renting the old house across Thyme Bay ...'

'And Polly could let him know whenever he overhears anything.'

Justin gave a sudden gasp and thrust one hand into his trouser pocket. 'Polly asked me to give this letter to his dad; *hey* ... d'you

63

suppose he saw the doddling and wrote to tell him?'

'Well, there's an easy way to find out,' sniggered Robyn, snatching the envelope out of his hand.

'*No* ... give it here,' Justin hissed. He glanced nervously across at his father, but Sir Willoughby didn't stir. 'We can't just read someone else's private correspondence.'

'Maybe *you* can't,' said Robyn, tearing the envelope open. 'But *I* can. Honestly, Dustbin, you'll have to toughen up if you want to catch this guy; think what he did to Mum.'

She unfolded a sheet of lilac notepaper and read it aloud:

> *Dearest Daddikins,*
>
> *How's tricks? I hope you're well, and not feeling too lonely. The weather here is so hot and sunny I have to use a Factor 10 sun-block to avoid getting burnt!*
>
> *When I get home, remind me to check if there's any Starglow in my spare makeup box. Henny hates her new foundation.*
>
> *Hanky-panky sends his best wishes. Don't let the past get you down. I'm sure, in time, everything will work out for the best!*
>
> *Do, do try to keep positive!*
>
> *Lots of Love,*
>
> *Polly-Wolly-Woo.*

By the time she'd finished reading, the disappointment in Robyn's voice was plain. 'Perhaps it's in code,' she murmured; then sounding a little more hopeful, added, 'Yeah, look – it's got the words *past* and *time* in it.' She read the letter again, slower this time, tapping each word with a glittery pink fingernail.

Justin wasn't listening; a faint musical sound drifting across the cabin had distracted him. It was the theme tune of Eliza's favourite computer game: *Ape-Invaders*. The big gorilla was hunched over her laptop, with Albion beside her, chuckling happily.

Before he could turn back to Robyn, something about Eliza's body-language struck Justin as unusual; she seemed alert and focussed – although *not* on the computer screen – and her forehead was creased by a frown of deep displeasure.

She's listening to us, he thought. But no sooner had the idea flashed into Justin's mind, than he instantly dismissed it.

The music stopped, and a robotic voice announced '*Game Over – You have won zero bananas!*' Eliza blinked slowly, and then tapped the keyboard with a huge black finger.

'Baby try now,' she said, using a deep hypnotic-sounding voice, then pushed the laptop towards Albion.

After a few bleeps the music started again – but louder this time, making Sir Willoughby twitch in his sleep. With a long, shuddering snore, he tossed his head sideways, and one hand shot from beneath the blanket as if to shield his face.

'No, no ... can't see it ... mustn't look,' he murmured. Then, with a muffled sob, he turned over and went back to sleep.

Justin and Robyn exchanged glances.

'What was *that* all about?' Robyn asked.

'Nightmare, I guess,' whispered Justin, remembering his own peculiar dream from the night before. All at once, he felt an overwhelming weariness sweep over him; an hour ago he'd felt glad to be heading back home – but now that all too familiar knot of anxiety was tightening in his stomach. A return to Thyme Castle would mean a return to living on a knife-edge; constantly looking over one shoulder and being unable to trust even one's oldest friends. Justin marvelled how his dad had coped for so many years, and felt a sudden rush of pity for him.

With a deep sigh he glanced warily at Eliza, wondering if he'd imagined her strange expression. She seemed her usual placid self now, trying to soothe Albion, who had started to whimper.

Hmm ... now I'm getting as paranoid as Dad, Justin thought, shaking his head. He turned to his sister, realising she'd been speaking and he hadn't heard a word.

'... and the morning Nanny disappeared, Mr Polydorus was doing conjuring tricks in the kitchen,' concluded Robyn. 'He even pretended to read my mind; I wish I could remember exactly what he said ...'

Justin took Polly's letter from her and returned it to his pocket.

'Actually,' he said, feigning a yawn, 'I think I'll take a nap myself.'

'Shouldn't we be reviewing our clues?' asked Robyn, looking disappointed. 'Getting ready to reopen the investigation?'

'I've got all our clues stored on my computer; let's wait until we get back home.'

His excuse, though perfectly truthful, was only part of the reason. From now on, Justin decided, he wasn't going to discuss the case within earshot of anyone ... even a gorilla!

'Wake me in a few hours,' he muttered, checking his watch. Then, after reclining his chair as far back as it would go, Justin took a deep breath and closed his eyes.

It was raining in Scotland. As they approached the runway, Justin stared forlornly out of the window, watching endless lines of wind-blasted droplets dance horizontally across the glass, glistening against the steel-grey sky.

Now they had their own plane they could land at Inverness Airport, instead of being restricted to scheduled flights in and out of Prestwick. The Lear jet touched down with a gentle bump and taxied slowly into their private hangar. Once the engines had stopped, the pilot swept into the main cabin and opened the door. He stood at the top of the steps as they disembarked, glaring at them silently, with his arms folded across his chest, looking like an angry headmaster waiting for a line of naughty pupils to vacate his study. Sir Willoughby muttered something incoherent about an excellent flight, which earned him a look of scornful disdain; the rest had the good sense to keep quiet.

Peregrine Knightly, the Thymes' butler, was waiting for them; he'd brought the Bentley, and as they filed down the Lear's steps he strode forward to take their hand luggage. He had a face like the reflection in the back of a spoon – and wearing his black tailcoat and pinstriped trousers, Justin thought he'd have made a good undertaker if his shoes hadn't squeaked.

Meanwhile, the pilot lowered the tailgate; after hauling out their cases, he wheeled Justin's motorbike and sidecar down the ramp. He stepped back, gazing at it, his coal-black eyes almost hungry with admiration – and for a moment Justin thought he was actually going to speak. But as Sir Willoughby reached to take the bike's handlebars, the pilot turned briskly away, his black robes swirling as he slammed the tailgate shut.

'I'll drive old Bessy home,' Sir Willoughby told Justin, pulling on an old-fashioned leather helmet and a pair of goggles. 'You lot go ahead in the car – I'll follow.'

The Bentley was roomy, but its back seat couldn't quite stretch to two teenagers, a baby, a doddling and a 267 pound mountain gorilla. Justin and Robyn raced to the front passenger door; Robyn grabbed the handle first and grinned infuriatingly – so Justin found himself wedged in the back between Eliza and an extremely smelly pet crate.

As Knightly steered the Bentley out of the hangar, Robyn wound her window down and shouted to the pilot: 'Bye, Horace – thanks for the lovely chat!'

'He actually spoke to you?' asked Justin, astonished.

'Of course,' Robyn laughed. 'Once he got going I couldn't get a word in edgeways. Honestly, that guy could talk the skin off a wooden leg!'

Cold rain blew across Loch Ness, lashing against the Bentley's windows. The sky was getting dark now, and Justin thought he could hear a distant rumble of thunder. On the plus side, being a stormy Monday evening, Glen Thyme Road was fairly quiet – the majority of tourists in one pub or another, clustered around blazing log fires sipping hot toddies.

At least we're warm and dry in the car, Justin thought; Dad'll be soaked to the skin. He twisted round, peering through the car's back window. Sir Willoughby was about fifteen metres behind them, gripping the handlebars but with his head turned away from the loch, as if half-blinded by the driving rain. He swerved to and fro, his speed never slackening.

'Keep your eyes on the road, Dad,' Justin muttered under his breath. 'Or pull over and catch up with us later.'

Gradually, imperceptibly, Sir Willoughby drifted to his right, getting dangerously close to the oncoming traffic. Justin waved frantically, trying to attract his father's attention, but with his face turned away from the lashing rain, Willoughby couldn't see, and his drift continued towards the centre of the road.

'HORN,' Justin yelled. 'Knightly, sound the horn ... *NOW!*'

The sudden loud blaring noise grabbed Sir Willoughby's attention not a second too soon. Lifting his head, he swerved back onto the left side of the road, narrowly avoiding an oncoming truck. He slowed slightly, still unsteady, then as the road headed inland a little, seemed to regain control of the bike. Five minutes later the Bentley turned in through a pair of towering wrought iron gates and headed up the drive to Thyme Castle. Sir Willoughby followed, and Justin breathed a huge sigh of relief.

The castle, which normally looked so homely to Justin, seemed strangely ominous and forbidding; a gothic silhouette against a storm-ravaged sky.

Knightly drove into the courtyard, pulling to a smooth halt outside the castle door. Moments later, Sir Willoughby chugged through the archway, then steered his bike round the east tower to his workshop, spraying gravel chippings left and right.

As Justin climbed out of the Bentley, he heard the workshop door slam shut, the rattle of a lock, and then feet crunching over the wet gravel. His father strode to the front of the garage, beckoning him over, and for a fraction of a second Justin thought he was going to be given the motorbike keys.

'Are you okay, Dad?' he called, running over. 'Did your goggles mist up?'

'Never mind about that now,' said Sir Willoughby brusquely, dragging Justin inside. He marched past the cars – Henny's Porsche, the family VW, and Grandpa's vintage Rolls Royce – until he reached the internal door connecting the garage to his workshop. He locked this door too, and then ran his hand along the lintel above it.

Justin's heart sank; he'd hoped his dad would forget about the spare key.

Sir Willoughby bunched the workshop and motorbike keys together in one hand, and thrust them deep into his trouser pocket. Then he turned to Justin and spoke breathlessly, his voice low, his eyes wide and staring.

'I know this isn't what you want to hear, son ... but your time-travelling days are over. Permanently. You won't be using that damned machine ever again!'

nly Use Each Set of Coordinates ONCE!

Time travellers must learn to think four-dimensionally. When driving a standard road vehicle in the present, the same three-dimensional location can be visited over and over again without risk; this is because the time of the visit is ALWAYS different.

Likewise, when travelling into the past, a specific location can be revisited at a different time – or, alternatively, the chrononaut can materialise at the same time but in a different location.

However, because it is impossible for two different solid objects to occupy the same spatial position simultaneously, the combined time and place CANNOT be visited more than once. Identical spatiotemporal coordinates must NEVER be used a second time otherwise the time machine will collide with itself.

CHAPTER FIVE

Kof Drops

The first thing Justin noticed as he stepped through the front door of Thyme Castle was a delicious smell wafting from the east tower.

'Supper will be ready in five minutes, sir,' Knightly droned, helping the Laird of Thyme out of his dripping mackintosh. He shook the coat vigorously, making the dewdrop on the end of his nose wobble. 'Cook thought you might prefer a simple meal in the kitchen after your long, tiring journey,' he added, with a sniff of disapproval.

'Excellent – just enough time for me to change out of these wet clothes,' Sir Willoughby replied, his voice clipped and formal. 'Robyn, take *that* up to your room,' he said, pointing to the pet-crate. 'Eliza, you'd better get Alby ready for bed, then bring him down for some hot milk or whatever he usually has.'

Knightly eyed the huge mound of luggage at the foot of the stairs with an air of gloomy resignation. 'I'll see to everyone's bags whilst you're dining,' he muttered.

Sir Willoughby marched off briskly, his footsteps echoing on the stone floor; Eliza, cradling a sleepy-looking Albion, strolled after him; and Robyn followed lugging the pet-carrier, grumbling to herself.

Justin remained behind. Despite the burgeoning knot in his stomach and the confiscation of his time machine, he felt surprisingly hungry.

After four days of his mother's cooking he could hardly wait to see what Mrs Kof had prepared for them, and had no intention of hiking all the way to the south tower first. He hid his *Hover-Boots* in the downstairs cloakroom, hurriedly washed his hands, and then dashed along to the kitchen.

As he pushed the kitchen door open, Justin's eyes widened and his stomach rumbled appreciatively. The enormous pine table was piled high with enough food to feed Nessie herself: a huge honey-roast ham, mounds of grilled venison sausages, stuffed mushrooms, garlic bread, dishes of butter-glazed vegetables and a mountain of curly French-fries.

On the kitchen worktops Justin could see a selection of mouth-watering desserts: a sticky-looking chocolate torte stood between a toffee-apple crumble and a gigantic raspberry mousse. There were jugs of whipped cream and steaming custard ... not to mention mounds of scones and shortbread.

At the far end of the kitchen, taking a towering cheese soufflé out of the oven was the castle cook herself. Mrs Kof was the largest woman Justin had ever met; she looked like a troll on steroids, and had muscles that would shame a champion bodybuilder. She was barefoot, as usual, and wearing a starched white apron over her favourite mud-brown smock. Her cheeks glowed like two ripe red apples, and her bald head gleamed beneath the halogen spotlights. Catching sight of Justin she grinned broadly, showing the gap in her teeth. After placing the soufflé on the table, she tanked over and gave him a bear-hug that almost cracked his ribs.

'Ahoy! You wants big punch in the mug?' she asked, beaming down at him happily.

'Pardon?'

'Punch ... hotty and fruitful,' she explained, pointing to an enormous crystal punchbowl with several large silver mugs hanging round its rim. 'Full of spies.'

'SPIES?' gasped Justin.

'Ya, ya ... synonyms and clothes,' Mrs Kof explained in her deep guttural voice. She unhooked a mug, dipped it into the bowl, and handed it to Justin. He took a cautious sip; it tasted of tangerines, cherries and ginger, and had cloves and cinnamon sticks floating on the top. Within seconds Justin felt its delicious spicy warmth flood through him to the tips of his fingers and toes.

The rest of the family appeared a couple of minutes later, and Mrs Kof insisted on hugging each of them in turn – although when she advanced on Sir Willoughby with her arms outstretched, he edged backwards so swiftly he tripped over the edge of his long silk dressing-gown.

'No, no ... really, I'm fine,' he muttered, grabbing a dinner plate and holding it up like a shield.

'Then I gives you punch instead,' said Mrs Kof decisively.

Justin exploded with laughter at the alarmed expression on his father's face. 'Don't worry, Dad – she's not going to hit you.'

The meal was a huge success, and by the time they'd finished dessert everyone looked happy and relaxed. Justin and Robyn had eaten a little of almost everything; Eliza had devoured a record-breaking number of banana fritters; and Albion got the hiccups. Even Sir Willoughby gave a contented smile as he swallowed his final mouthful of apple crumble.

By then Knightly had returned, and while Mrs Kof cleared the dishes away, he served the coffee. As he handed Sir Willoughby a cup, the kitchen door creaked open and Grandpa Lyall tottered in, his footsteps slow and unsteady. He looked vacant-eyed – his hair tousled, and his snowy-white beard uncombed. Justin had always thought he looked rather like Old Father Time, but in his long cotton nightshirt the resemblance was extraordinary.

Sir Lyall stared at the Thymes, his mouth hanging wide open in bewilderment.

'Who are all these people?' he asked, turning to Mrs Kof. Then gesturing towards Eliza, added: 'And what's *that* thing?'

Eliza grunted huffily. She chose the prim voice of Nanny Verity from her vocal menu, and after announcing it was *'past baby's bedtime,'* tucked Albion under one arm and prowled off upstairs.

'Hi Grandpa,' said Robyn, jumping up. She ran across the kitchen and gave him a peck on the cheek. 'It's us ... your family. Remember?'

The old man peered at her, his face puckered into a puzzled frown. With long, pale fingers he touched the place Robyn had kissed him, and shook his head slowly.

Justin glanced at his father. Normally, Sir Willoughby would've greeted the old man with an affectionate handshake, but tonight he stared at him coolly, his lips drawn together in a hard line.

'Oh, er, did I miss supper?' Sir Lyall yawned.

'No, no ... you beans for supper early and went offal to bed,' Mrs Kof explained, her gruff voice surprisingly tender. She dried her hands on a tea towel and took his arm gently, helping him towards a chair. 'You wants I make you special cocoa again?'

Grandpa nodded.

Physically, Justin thought, the old man was looking much healthier now. When he'd first turned up at the castle gates he'd been a homeless wanderer desperately in need of a square meal. But in the last month his skin had lost its translucent pallor and, thanks to Mrs Kof's cooking, he was clearly better nourished. His mental condition was less easy to quantify. There had been times when Justin seriously wondered whether his memory problems were all part of a sophisticated con-trick. Tonight, however, his eyes had the glazed faraway look of a person not quite in touch with reality.

Mrs Kof tipped a handful of chocolate truffles into a pan of hot milk, stirring them slowly. Leaving it to simmer, she took a tiny key from her apron pocket and unlocked a wooden cabinet beside the pantry. She took a small glass bottle, and carefully shook three drops of dark liquid into the cocoa.

'Dreamy-drops,' she explained, seeing Justin's questioning glance. 'Make Grandpa Liar go sleepy.' She poured the steaming cocoa into a mug and placed it on the table beside the old gentleman.

Knightly bent down and whispered discreetly in Willoughby's ear. 'I'm afraid Sir Lyall's been sleepwalking, sir,' he murmured. 'A couple of nights ago we spotted him wandering along the battlements to the west tower – stark naked! It took us half an hour to stop him climbing the flagpole. Since then, Cook has been giving him one of her herbal concoctions to make sure he sleeps right through.'

'Oh, er ... right ho!' said Sir Willoughby, uncertain what else to say.

Knightly turned to Robyn next. 'If you've finished your coffee, Miss, I should perhaps mention that while I was in the west tower I heard a curious honking noise coming from your room. Maybe it's something you'd like to attend to.'

'*Uurghh*, I clean forgot about Haggis,' Robyn groaned, gathering a few scraps of fish and hastily mixing them with some mushy peas and a spoonful of raspberry mousse.

'That's what you're calling it then?' asked Justin. 'Haggis?'

But Robyn was already half way through the kitchen door. 'Yep,' she called back as she hurtled across the entrance hall, 'unless you can think of a better name.'

Knightly coughed diffidently. 'Hhrrm ... that reminds me, sir. Her Ladyship phoned this morning and instructed me to engage a replacement nanny.'

'Really?' remarked Sir Willoughby, looking rather taken-aback. 'How odd! She never mentioned anything about it to me.'

'Arhh, I believe she got the idea shortly after you left, sir – and knowing the time difference, thought she'd catch me before breakfast so I could attend to the matter today.'

'But we *have* a nanny,' said Justin. 'She's just ... just ...'

'Her Ladyship fears it may be some time before Mrs Kiss returns,' Knightly continued. 'The agency sent three candidates this afternoon; following her Ladyship's orders, I interviewed them and arranged for the most qualified applicant to start work tomorrow.'

'Tomorrow!' Justin exclaimed. 'Wow, that's fast work – Eliza will be pleased.'

'Hmm ... although her Ladyship considered young Master Albion's requirements, she was most emphatic that the new nanny should also be a fully qualified governess with experience of controlling er ... spirited young ladies. My impression was that there had been a minor altercation with Miss Robyn and ...'

'Thank you, Knightly,' Willoughby interrupted. 'That will be all, for now.'

'Very good, sir.'

Justin glanced at his father. 'Who's going to tell Robyn?' he asked quietly.

Willoughby ignored his question. 'I'd better phone Hen,' he muttered. 'I wish she'd told me first; I'd have preferred to handle this myself.'

Grandpa Lyall drained the last of his cocoa, pushed his chair back and struggled to his feet. 'Goodness, I'm sleepy,' he yawned. 'I'd better get off to bed. Goodnight gentlemen.' He nodded to Justin and Willoughby as if they were strangers. 'Kind of you to visit. Thanks again for the cocoa, Mrs Wight.'

Sir Lyall Austin Thyme shuffled slowly out of the kitchen, seemingly unaware of the commotion behind him. Willoughby took a sudden sharp breath and sat bolt upright, whilst Mrs Kof dropped an entire plateful of jam tarts.

Sir Willoughby grasped Justin's arm and half opened his mouth to speak – then, glancing mistrustfully at Knightly and Mrs Kof, changed his mind. A dozen different emotions seemed to flicker across his face: excitement, hope, bewilderment, doubt, fear, and others too ephemeral for Justin to identify. Willoughby gave his son a pointed look, and motioned to the kitchen door with a twitch of his eyebrows. They edged past the cook and butler busy picking jam tarts off the floor, and hurried out into the entrance hall.

Grandpa Lyall was just starting up the north tower staircase. Sir Willoughby dashed over to him; he removed his dressing gown and placed it solicitously round the old gentleman's shoulders. After wishing him an affectionate 'Goodnight, Pops,' he loped back to Justin.

'Great Scott!' he hissed. 'Did you hear him? He called her Mrs Wight.'

Justin frowned pensively, rubbing his lower lip. The name *did* seem vaguely familiar. 'Who's Mrs ...?'

Sir Willoughby glanced towards the kitchen then put one finger to his lips. 'Shhh, not here,' he whispered, 'follow me.' He led Justin

76

through the dining room and into the portrait gallery, pausing to shut the door behind them.

The gallery ran between the north and west towers. It was a long, narrow room with arched stained-glass windows overlooking the courtyard on one side, and wood-panelled walls hung with handsomely framed portraits on the other. The chandeliers were unlit tonight. Raindrops spattered against the windows, and cold slivers of moonlight sent their shadows trickling like tears down the faces of Justin's ancestors.

Father and son walked along side by side, speaking in hushed voices.

'Mrs Wight was the castle cook when I was a boy,' Sir Willoughby explained. 'You must've heard Nanny talk about her. When I was four she caught me hiding gingersnaps inside my old teddy and walloped me with a wooden spoon. But she was a good sort really; she adored Deighton – and always used to pack us off to school with heaps of tuck. Anyway,' he said, pausing to catch his breath. 'If Grandpa remembers her, then surely he's genuine. And for the last twenty-four hours you've had me convinced he's Agent X.'

'*I've* had you convinced? How come?'

Justin peered sideways at his father waiting for him to answer, but Sir Willoughby seemed oddly flustered and uncomfortable.

'Well, all that whatnot about seeing him outside the castle gates, tossing a coin,' he muttered irritably. 'You've got to admit ... you made it sound dashed suspicious.'

Justin kept his face bland, his voice calm – determined not to rise to the bait.

'Look Dad, I hate to burst your balloon, but I'm not convinced this proves anything. Actually, her name *does* ring a bell ... but if *I've* heard Nanny mention it, so could Grandpa ... if that's who he really is.'

For a moment, Sir Willoughby looked so dejected that Justin felt sorry for him.

'You're right, of course,' he sighed. 'I just *so* want him to be Pops.'

'I understand. But remember what you said to me on the plane. We can't trust anybody.'

Sir Willoughby gave a solemn nod. 'Yes ... yes, absolutely. What was I thinking?'

'Don't worry, Dad ... you've just got a lot on your mind,' Justin reassured him. 'We'll track Agent X down sooner or later, you'll see.'

'Thanks, son, I know I can rely on you.'

They walked along the gallery in companionable silence, passing several generations of ancestors. By the time they reached the bottom of the west tower staircase, Willoughby had brightened a little.

'I've got some of Pops' old journals and papers in my desk; I think I'll sort through them tomorrow; see if there's anything that'll help prove whether the old chap's genuine or not. And if that doesn't work out ... well ...' Willoughby's voice trailed off into an incoherent mumble; Justin got the impression he didn't want to think that far ahead.

'So, if Grandpa's not Agent X, who is?' he asked. 'Knightly?'

Sir Willoughby laughed, his voice echoing up the stone tower. 'No chance! Dashed impertinent of him interviewing staff without so much as a by-your-leave from me ... but I'm sure he's got nothing to do with all *this* nonsense.'

'Hmmm ... Nanny Verity thought that too.'

'Really?' said Willoughby, looking a little surprised. 'Well, it figures, I suppose. He didn't start work at the castle until *after* your mum was kidnapped.'

Justin felt his line of reasoning wasn't entirely logical, but refrained from pointing it out.

'My money's still on our so-called gardener,' Willoughby continued. 'Chap's admitted he's an actor ... and I'm convinced Agent X had theatrical connections. I've told you how his acting fooled me in the past, and his makeup skills were astonishing.'

Justin nodded. A few weeks ago Robyn had discovered that Angus Gilliechattan was, in fact, a retired thespian and budding playwright; he and his wife had taken jobs at the castle merely to practice their starring roles in his forthcoming play.

'Why he doesn't drop that dreadful bogus accent now we all know the truth, I can't imagine,' Sir Willoughby sighed, leaning in the doorway of his bedroom. 'And Mrs G's just as bad. I play along, of course, pretending I believe them ... but ...'   He shrugged and grimaced as if lost for words. 'Ah well, time for bed, eh?'

'Yeah ... g'night Dad; sleep well.'

'Goodnight.' Then, as Justin turned towards the south tower, Sir Willoughby called: 'I say ... you wouldn't mind just popping upstairs to tell Robyn about the new nanny, would you? Thanks.'

And before Justin could reply, his father's bedroom door closed with a firm click.

Typical Dad, thought Justin. Absolutely classic. He'd just been thinking that his father was starting to look a little less stressed out, and had been wondering whether it was the hot fruit punch, the fabulous meal ... or just being back at Thyme Castle. But now he realised the truth: Willoughby was simply opting out as usual. Justin trudged up the west tower stairs, wondering why the difficult jobs always seemed to get dumped on him. It wasn't enough that he shouldered the family's finances – everyone came to him with their problems as well. He didn't complain, but occasionally, there were times when it all felt like too much pressure for one thirteen-year-old boy.

On the next landing he bumped into Eliza, dragging a pile of blankets out of the nursery.

'Shhhh, baby sleep now,' she said, her computer set to whisper.

Justin peered into the darkened room. Albion was in his cot, snuggled under a quilt, clutching his favourite teddy. His eyes were closed and his lips made the shape of a perfect little 'o'.

Outside the nursery door, Eliza started to pull and wind the blankets around herself, just like a wild gorilla making a nest of foliage in the Congo rainforest.

'You should be back in your own room by tomorrow night, Eliza,' Justin told her. 'Mum's arranged for a new nanny to take care of Alby.'

Eliza reached for her laptop. 'Good, good,' she said, her computerised voice still whispering. 'Bad baby make Eliza feel sad.' Then, hearing a loud honking noise from the top of the tower, she added: 'Stop noise please – make bad bird stop noise now.'

In Justin's opinion, his sister's bedroom was a psychedelic migraine-inducing nightmare; a chaotic fusion of glitter-balls and multi-coloured lava lamps – part futuristic fashion boutique, part seventies-style disco.

Justin poked his head round the door, and found his sister looking harassed and flustered. She was busy pushing bits of food into the doddling's open beak. After gulping each mouthful it threw its head back, making a noise that sounded like a cross between an old-fashioned car horn and someone vomiting. Robyn kept backing away, hoping the little dodo had eaten its fill – but it followed her tenaciously round the room constantly demanding more. The doddling paused, and Robyn sighed with relief ... until it squirted a stream of poo across her favourite bubblegum-pink shag-pile rug.

'Having fun?' Justin enquired.

Robyn glared at him. 'You've got to help me, Dustbin. I'll never manage this day after day; it's insane. Can't you rig up some kind of machine – a robotic bird that'll feed it at regular intervals?

Justin laughed. 'A dodobot? It'd probably take me a couple of days to do it properly. Maybe I can come up with something temporary in the meantime.'

'Well, get thinking ... *please* ... or I won't get a wink of sleep.'

'Hmmm ...' said Justin, frowning thoughtfully. Then he turned and dashed out of the room, shouting: 'I'll be back in a two ticks.'

Ten minutes later, Justin returned with a mound of household oddments, and carried them into Robyn's bathroom.

'I'm setting everything up in the bath,' he called to his sister, 'so you can swill any dodo poop away with the shower.'

First, he took a blanket, some cushions and one of Mrs Gilliechattan's old feather dusters, and formed them into the approximate shape of an adult dodo for the doddling to snuggle under. He placed this at one end of the bath on top of a couple of hot water bottles; at the other end he put Robyn's bathroom scales. Next he took a piping-bag Mrs Kof used to decorate cakes, and filled it with mushed-up food. He knotted the piping-bag and inserted it into a pair of inflatable water-wings (that Alby wore in his paddling pool) and hung these above the scales. Finally, he wired the scales to an air-pump and ran a length of plastic tubing from the pump to the water-wings. With some fine tuning he fixed it so that when the dodo stepped on the scales its weight activated the air pump, which gradually inflated the water-wings, squeezing out a slow, steady stream of food; once the fully fed doddling moved off the scales, the current to the air pump stopped, and the flow of food dribbled to a halt.

'It's a bit crude,' Justin apologised, demonstrating the contraption to his sister. 'But it'll do for a day or two until I can build something more sophisticated.'

They placed the doddling in the bathtub, and watched it squirm beneath the cushion-dodo. Before long it was snoring peacefully. Robyn turned to her brother and gave him a gentle punch on the arm.

'Hey,' she said, 'has anyone ever told you, you're a genius?'

The tower clock struck eleven, making everything in Justin's bedroom vibrate slightly. A few years ago he'd been given the entire south tower to himself – mainly because no one else could stand the noise. By now, Justin was so used to the steady ponderous ticking that permeated the tower walls, he scarcely heard it; sometimes he didn't even notice the chiming, unless he was working in his lab directly beneath the enormous bronze bell.

Justin climbed into bed and lay quietly, making a mental list of everything he needed to do that week.

For a start, he'd have to get up an hour earlier tomorrow and finish his homework. Professor Gilbert had slipped a note beneath the door to the south tower, telling him that lessons would start, as usual, at ten o'clock sharp, and reminding him not to forget his essay on quantum entanglement. Of course, the professor thought the Thymes had been on a family vacation, and didn't realise his pupil had been working up to twenty hours in a single day. Still, Justin had managed to get most of it written on the flight home, and knew it wouldn't take him long to finish it in the morning.

What else? Well, sometime between breakfast and lessons, he thought he'd like to have a quick search round Nanny Verity's room. The new nanny would doubtless insist on sleeping next-door to the nursery, so Mrs Gilliechattan, the castle housekeeper, would need to get it ready as soon as possible. Before she started clearing out all Nanny V's belongings, Justin wanted to take one last look to see if he'd missed anything.

He thought again of the e-mail she'd sent him after her disappearance; it had said *not* to search for her, and that she hadn't left any clues ... but, oddly enough, that only made Justin wonder if she had ... otherwise why mention it?

And he had to agree with Robyn; it was hard to imagine Verity Kiss going away without leaving *some* kind of message.

Which reminded him: he'd forgotten to tell Robyn about the new nanny – so he'd have to deal with that too, worse luck.

Justin sighed. There'd probably be a pile of business mail to catch up on – but hopefully, the professor would let him take the afternoon off to get up-to-date. Now the *Hover-Boots* had been tested, Justin knew he needed to calculate the cost of mass production and formulate a specific long-term business plan – and that would mean lengthy negotiations with his usual manufacturers and suppliers. Which reminded him of something else: he needed to fetch his *Hover-Boots* from the downstairs cloakroom and lock them in his safe.

And he mustn't forget to sketch out a plan for some kind of robotic dodo-feeding device for Haggis.

Of course, Justin knew that every minute of every day he'd be pondering over the possible identity of Agent X, keeping an eye on the various suspects and a sharp lookout for any clues.

Maybe ... just maybe ... he thought to himself, if I can catch him, then Dad might let me have the time machine back. He hoped so; in just ten days' time it was his parents' wedding anniversary, and he had something special planned for his mum ... but he'd need the time machine to make it possible.

'That means I've got little more than a week to unmask X,' Justin groaned.

A tall order indeed, but if he could pull it off, surely it would be the best anniversary present his dad could possibly wish for.

Anything else? Justin racked his brains, certain there was something he'd forgotten. Ah, Polly's letter, of course! It would need delivering to Mr Polydorus – which might provide a useful opening for some investigation.

Justin sighed, it looked like it was going to be a hectic few days. He leaned over and set his alarm clock for 7:15, then removed his watch, placing it carefully on the bedside table. The tiny scythe-shaped catch had worked looser still; yet another job to include on his things-to-do list.

Justin closed his eyes, trying to clear his mind; he knew he'd need a really good night's sleep with so much pencilled in for tomorrow.

'Ah well,' he yawned, 'at least I'm not going to be woken at dawn by someone tapping on the window!'

Justin's eyes flew open; something had disturbed him – and it wasn't his alarm clock. He held his breath, listening carefully and peering over the top of his bedclothes. A soft pearl-grey light filled the room; he could hear the distant sound of water lapping gently against the cliffs, and a blackbird singing in the rose garden.

'Must've been dreaming,' he mumbled to himself. He yawned, thumped his pillow and turned over. And then he saw it outside the window ...

A hand.

Tap ... tap, tap ... tap ...

For a moment or two, Justin knew what it was to feel petrified. His limbs – as lifeless as if they'd been fossilised – stubbornly refused to function. Only his eyes moved, watching the hand as it scuttled around the edge of the window, its fingers scrabbling over the ivy-covered stones.

A blade appeared ... then a face ... flaming red hair, craggy eyebrows and a bushy ginger beard.

'Mr Gilliechattan!' Justin gasped. 'What on earth ...?'

He threw back the bedclothes, leapt out of bed and ran across to the window.

Seeing Justin suddenly appear behind the glass, the gardener gave a roar of surprise and almost fell off his ladder. In an explosion of white feathers, Burbage, his pet cockatoo, rocketed into the air with an ear-splitting screech. He flapped in a wide arc over the loch, flying back to his master's shoulder as Justin opened the window.

'I say, what the dickens are you trying to do? Frighten me to death?' boomed Mr Gilliechattan, his ruddy face pale, and his green eyes flashing. 'Bother! Slipped right out of character; shock probably.' He cleared his throat and spoke again: 'Hhrrrm ... have a care, laddie! A thought ye werra wee bogle, sendin' me doon to ma grave.'

The gardener's exaggerated highland accent had always sounded peculiar to Justin – but today it seemed hilarious. And the thought of him up a forty foot ladder wearing a kilt, made it even harder to keep a straight face.

'Sorry, Mr G,' he said. 'You scared me too. What are you *doing* up here?'

'Ah'm a trimmin' the ivy. A did'na ken you werra back home yet, Jimmy.'

Justin swallowed a chuckle. In full Scottish mode Mr Gilliechattan tended to call everyone Jimmy.

'Oh, we got back last night – a week early,' Justin explained. He wondered if the gardener really *had* been pruning the ivy, or whether he'd been trying to break in. After all, the ancient windows were probably the tower's one security flaw. Justin's three rooms had special fingerprint-sensitive locks that opened only to his touch, and Mrs Gilliechattan had been banned from cleaning the south tower since she'd accidentally teleported her cat whilst prying in his laboratory.

Burbage raised his sulphur-yellow crest. '*O call back yesterday, bid time return,*' he cackled, sidling along the gardener's shoulder and nuzzling his whiskers.

For the umpteenth time, Justin found himself wondering if Angus Gilliechattan's shaggy red beard was real, and what he might look like without it. Then, as he stared at the gardener, he had a sudden idea.

84

'By-the-way, has Mrs G finished your scrapbook yet?' he asked. 'I'd love to take a look at it sometime.'

Mr Gilliechattan – or Oliver Marsh to give him his real name – seemed to swell with pleasure. He beamed at Justin, and replied in ringing theatrical tones:

'I say, how jolly nice of you. There's a splendid photo of me as King Lear, and one of us both in "Twelfth Night" ... hhrrrmm, I mean ... Aye, Jimmy, ah'll tell Mrs G to fetch 'em over forr ye.'

'Thanks,' said Justin, shutting the window.

He walked slowly towards the bathroom, grinning to himself.

'Now we'll finally get to see what the real Oliver Marsh looks like,' he whispered to his reflection in the mirror. 'There's bound to be *some* old photos of him without a beard. I'll get Dad to take a look at them – and if our stage-struck gardener really *is* Agent X there's an excellent chance Dad'll recognise him.'

rite ALL Coordinates in a Log-book

Because reusing a set of spatiotemporal coordinates will inevitably result in disaster, it is imperative that a careful and comprehensive record of all trips be kept.

A modern time machine designed to use computer technology should automatically store ALL previously used coordinates in its memory. However, a wise chrononaut will also keep a personal hand-written log-book on their person at all times in case of computer malfunction.

Not only should all destination and return coordinates be recorded, but also the precise duration a time machine is standing in any given spatial location past or present. If a chronopod is mobile, a note should be kept of ANY place it is moved to. Again, a modern time machine would store such data automatically.

– CHAPTER SIX –

Poetry and Pistols

The good thing about being woken at dawn by a mad Shakespearean gardener, Justin decided, was that it gave him a head start on his things-to-do list. By half past eight he'd finished his quantum entanglement homework, cleared his backlog of business e-mails, and sketched out a few rough plans for a dodobot ... and there was still another thirty minutes before breakfast. Just enough time to stop by Nanny Verity's room on the way down to the dining room.

Before he was half way along the upper corridor, Justin heard a loud crying noise coming from the west tower. As he crept past the nursery bathroom he peeped through the half-open door. Eliza was trying to wash baby Albion. Although she'd managed to remove his pyjamas, he clearly had no intention of surrendering his favourite teddy bear; he clutched it to his chest, screaming angrily whenever Eliza's huge black fingers inched towards it.

Justin chuckled to himself. He pushed Nanny's bedroom door open, and stood for a moment on the threshold, taking everything in. It was a small, fussily decorated room smelling of dried flowers, talcum powder and peppermint. He stepped inside and shut the door behind him, intending to work his way round methodically, looking for anything, no matter how insignificant, that seemed odd or out of place.

If Nanny *had* left any clues they wouldn't be obvious in case Agent X or another of his spies came checking. However, the curtains were closed, and a fine layer of dust everywhere reassured Justin that nothing had been disturbed since the day Nanny disappeared.

He started by checking under the bed, then ran his hands beneath the pillows and patchwork quilt; no clues there. To the right of the bed was an old wooden rocking chair piled with crocheted cushions. To its left stood an oak bedside cabinet; it had a frilly lamp on top, and a small leather-bound book with Nanny's door key resting on its cover.

Opposite the bed was a narrow wardrobe; inside it Justin found several starched grey and white uniforms, a couple of old-fashioned flowery dresses, a handbag full of knitting needles, and a squashed straw hat. Next to the wardrobe was a whatnot shelf of pottery robins, each one resting on its own lace doily. Beside the window stood an old fashioned writing bureau; it was locked. A pincushion and Nanny's sewing box lived right on the top where Albion couldn't reach. Near the door through to the nursery was a little trolley on which Nanny kept a primus stove for warming milk, a tin of custard creams, and a stack of satin-bound baby albums.

Justin sank onto the bed, feeling dejected – and it wasn't just because everything looked exactly the same as always; it hit him forcefully how paltry and few Nanny's belongings were. Suddenly Justin realised that he'd rarely seen her out of her uniform, and that she had no jewellery except for that old Victorian cameo she always wore fastened to a broad band of petersham ribbon around her throat. He immediately resolved to treat her to something really special the instant she was safely back at Thyme Castle.

With a sigh, he drew back the curtains and reached for one of Nanny's baby albums, wondering if she'd hidden a letter between the pages. But there was nothing – just countless photos of her grand-children, all with hand-written captions like: *Tristan and Leopold are building a sandcastle, Poor little Milo wants his din-dins,* or *Here's Beowulf dressed as a baa-lamb!*

'Babies, babies and yet more babies,' Justin groaned, helping himself to a stale custard cream. He ploughed doggedly through the rest of the albums, thinking how confusingly similar they seemed; the oldest were clearly identical twins, and one of the others looked just like Albion. There were no photographs of Nanny's three daughters though, or, unfortunately, of her villainous ex-husband either – not that Justin expected to find any. For as long as he could remember, Nanny had told everyone she was a widow, and it was only recently he'd uncovered the truth.

Justin stood up, tossing the last album onto the trolley. He took a final desperate glance round the room – but it all looked so utterly normal; as if Nanny Verity had just stepped into the nursery, and at any second would come bustling back twittering about the weather or the ridiculous price of corn-plasters.

'A place for everything ... and everything in its place,' Justin muttered gloomily. He'd been hoping Nanny had left something slightly *out* of place ... something that would look perfectly ordinary to anyone else.

Then, as he turned to leave, a sparkle of light caught his eye; the key resting upon the old leather-bound book on Nanny's bedside cabinet gleamed in a dazzling shaft of sunlight.

I suppose *that's* out of place, Justin thought; it's usually in her bedroom door. With a sudden prickle of excitement he wondered if Nanny Verity was trying to hint that something inside this book would unlock the secret of her whereabouts.

Curious now, Justin slid the key to one side, and recognised the book immediately. It was one of Nanny's favourites: "*The Romantic Verse of Lord Byron.*" As he picked it up, it fell open at a page with its corner folded down – a poem entitled "*When We Two Parted.*" A shiver ran down Justin's spine like a trickle of icy water. It *couldn't* be a coincidence, he thought; it *had* to be a clue. He started to read the first verse under his breath, but, hearing footsteps outside the door, hurriedly snapped the book shut and stuffed it into his trouser pocket.

The door swung open, and Mrs Gilliechattan marched in tugging a vacuum cleaner hung about with an assortment of mops, brushes and feather dusters. She was a small wiry woman with a sallow complexion, copper-coloured hair, and eyes that looked as if they could burn holes through reinforced steel. Her face, at rest, looked sour and disapproving – but when circumstances required it, (as they did now), she could manage a sickly, simpering smile.

'Och, good morrrning, young sair,' she said in her overly-refined highland accent. 'Mr Knaightly said to clear this rrooom for the new nairny.'

She glanced at the mirror, adjusting her cairngorm beads. Meanwhile, a pair of jade-green eyes peered from behind her long tartan kilt, then a strange eight-legged cat scuttled across the floor like a giant black spider. Justin took an automatic step backwards, even though he knew Tybalt was quite harmless. It was all those legs that did it, he thought – and the guilt.

Justin shuddered at the memory. His doomed teleportation project had come to an abrupt halt after Tybalt and a spider were accidentally fused into an arachno-feline monstrosity, and Sir Willoughby had smashed both teleport-pods. To this day, Justin was adamant that he'd closed the pod door properly, and that Mrs G must have been prying. But whenever he clapped eyes on the octo-puss, he suffered a pang of guilt, wondering if it really *had* been his fault after all.

'Hi Tybs,' he mumbled, rubbing the cat's head. He felt Mrs Gilliechattan's eyes boring into him, and could tell she sensed his discomfort and relished it.

'Angus said ye wanted to see oour wee scrapbook,' she said, running one finger along a dusty shelf. 'I've poot it on the corfee table in the great hall for ye.'

'Oh, thanks, Mrs G,' said Justin, edging towards the door. Then, hearing the tower clock strike nine, he smothered a relieved sigh and added: 'Better go ... I'm late for breakfast.'

As he ran along the portrait gallery, Justin grinned. He guessed Mrs Gilliechattan would spend a happy hour or two rifling through Nanny Verity's belongings; thank goodness he'd found Nan's hidden clue first.

By the time Justin reached the dining room, the rest of the family had already started breakfast without him. Sir Willoughby was spreading whisky marmalade on his toast, Robyn was sipping orange juice, Eliza was feeding Albion his porridge, and Grandpa Lyall was nodding over a bowl of rice crinklies.

Justin fetched a plate from the sideboard and helped himself to a chocolate-filled brioche – but before he could sit down, he heard the distant ringing of the telephone. Sir Willoughby groaned irritably, and threw his napkin down onto the table.

'Stay there, Dad,' said Justin. 'I'll get it.' He took a quick bite of his brioche, hurried out into the entrance hall and scooped the phone up. 'Hello – Thyme 802701.'

'Ah, good morning,' said a brisk familiar voice. 'Sergeant Awbrite, Inverness constabulary. I wonder if I could speak to Sir Willoughby.'

'Oh, hello, Sergeant – it's Justin here. Dad's having breakfast at the moment; can I take a message?'

'I'd like to call round about two o'clock this afternoon, if possible,' said Awbrite. 'Give Sir Willoughby an update on the situation with Mrs Kiss.'

'You've found her?' gasped Justin.

'Erm ... no,' replied the sergeant, sounding a little discouraged. 'Quite the reverse, unfortunately; we've come to a dead end. I was hoping your father might be able to help.'

'Oh, okay – I'll tell Dad to expect you later. Bye sergeant.'

As Justin walked back to the dining room, he wondered whether he ought to tell Sergeant Awbrite about the book from Nanny's room. After all, locating Verity Kiss was probably their best chance of unmasking Agent X. But something told him the policeman wouldn't take such an unorthodox clue seriously.

'Who was it?' asked Willoughby through a mouthful of toast.

'Sergeant Awbrite; he's coming to see you after lunch.'

'Oh ... I wonder if ...' He stopped mid-sentence – the unmistakable sound of squeaky shoes warning him their butler was approaching.

Knightly breezed in bearing tea and coffee pots on a silver tray. He glided round the table filling cups; when he reached Sir Lyall, he paused uncertainly and cleared his throat.

91

'Hhrrrm.'

Sir Willoughby glanced across the table, rolled his eyes and exhaled with a loud huff. Grandpa was fast asleep – his head resting in his cereal bowl; each time he snored half a dozen rice crinklies flew into the air and wafted across the tablecloth.

'A large black coffee for Sir Lyall,' Willoughby suggested. 'And perhaps a little less of Mrs Kof's sleeping potion in future.'

'Very good, sir – I'll tell Cook. However, I should mention that the old gentleman was sleepwalking again last night. I found him at three o'clock this morning wandering around in the great hall. Mrs Kof had to make him another special cocoa ... which is probably why he's doubly relaxed this morning.'

Willoughby exchanged an alarmed glance with his son, though whether it was the thought of Grandpa roaming the castle in the wee small hours, or the butler, Justin couldn't tell. Once Knightly headed back to the kitchen, Sir Willoughby returned to the subject of Sergeant Awbrite: 'I wonder if the police have found ...'

'He didn't say,' Justin interrupted hurriedly. He gave his dad a warning look to remind him that others were listening, none of whom knew the truth about Nanny Verity's disappearance.

Willoughby frowned. There was an awkward silence for a few minutes ... until Grandpa Lyall awoke, jerking suddenly upright.

'Stop it, Roxanda,' he said sternly. 'Leave your poor sister alone!' He glared round the table, rice crinklies stuck to his left eyebrow and milk trickling down his beard. Then, as swiftly as he'd woken up, he nodded off again.

'I miss Nanny V,' said Robyn, with wistful glance at her empty chair.

'Well, one thing's certain,' Willoughby remarked. 'If Nanny had been keeping an eye on you, you'd never have got that tattoo. You're not even fifteen until September.'

'Mrs Kof got *her* first tattoo when *she* was fourteen.'

'Well, Mrs Kof's spent most of her life in the circus,' snapped Sir Willoughby. 'Assuming what she says is true.'

'She's been more honest with us than the Gilliechattans,' muttered

Robyn.

'Oh, that reminds me,' said Justin. 'I asked Mr G if we could borrow his scrapbook.'

Robyn's eyes widened. 'Cooool! Did you know Mrs G was married to Templar Tercel when she was a teenager? She mentioned it during my last acting lesson. It was years before he became a megastar, of course. He ditched her as soon as he got his big break in Hollywood.'

'Fascinating, I'm sure,' drawled Willoughby. 'But why would *I* be interested?'

'I thought you might be curious to see what our gardener looked like without his beard,' Justin explained.

Sir Willoughby's eyes opened wide. 'Brilliant! I can check whether he's ...'

He stopped short as the dining room door flew open again; this time the castle cook marched in brandishing a large rotary whisk.

'Who wanting X this mornings?' she bellowed in her deep voice.

Sir Willoughby almost fell off his chair. 'X?' he spluttered. 'What ... what do you know about ...?'

'Ya, ya ... I know all about X,' said Mrs Kof, nodding. 'Scrambled X, poached X, boiled X, fried X sunny-side up. Who wanting any?'

Sir Willoughby made a quiet noise that sounded like the air being let out of a bicycle tire. 'Scrambled, please,' he replied, his startled expression fading a little.

While the rest of the family ordered their eggs, Eliza hoisted Albion on to her back. He giggled happily, full of porridge and warm milk.

'Eliza take baby walk outside,' she said, prodding her laptop carefully. 'When new Nanny arrive?'

'*New* nanny?' gasped Robyn. '*What* new nanny?'

'Oh, I thought Justin'd told you,' sighed Willoughby, with a reproachful glance at his eldest son. 'Your mum organised it with Knightly yesterday.' Then turning to Eliza he added: 'Miss Garnet will be here at four o'clock.'

'Good, good,' said Eliza. 'Gorilla happy now.' She closed her laptop and prowled off with Albion clinging tightly to her neck.'

'But what about Nanny Verity?' Robyn demanded, turning to her father. 'She's coming back, isn't she?'

'Probably.'

From the alarmed glint in Robyn's eyes, Justin knew his dad's dismissive comment had reawakened her fears for Nanny's safety.

'What do you mean, *probably*? She can't stay away *forever*.'

'Well, your mum isn't prepared to have you running wild in the meantime. I phoned her this morning, and she's absolutely furious. You've only got yourself to blame, you know. Which reminds me ...' Sir Willoughby pushed his chair back and stood up. 'I won't be two ticks,' he said, and loped out of the room.

'I can't believe you knew about this and didn't tell me,' said Robyn, glaring at her brother.

'Sorry, Bobs,' said Justin. 'Slipped my mind. I had every available brain cell concentrating on your dodo problem at the time.'

Robyn gave him a scornful look. 'You know where Dad's gone, of course?'

'No.'

'Obvious. He's legging it up to my room. Mum'll have told him to get my credit card. *Fffuhhh*! Like I wouldn't see that coming.'

'Ohhhhh ... don't tell me Dad's about to destroy one of his own cards.'

'Tempting, but no,' Robyn snickered. 'Never play the same trick twice if you want to stay one jump ahead! I've left a note in my purse, saying that if he asks me *very* nicely I'll give it to him.'

Justin groaned. 'Then what?'

'He can have it. I don't fight battles I don't need to win. Most stuff I buy is online, so I memorised the number ages ago: 1425–0215–1813–0109 ... *ha*! You pay my credit card bill, so nothing's changed.'

'Apart from caring for Haggis.'

'Okay, so I have to feed that dratted dodo, and ...'

'Shhh,' whispered Justin, pointing to Grandpa Lyall with a sideways flick of his thumb.

Robyn rolled her eyes. 'And Alby gets a temp nanny. Big whoop! Though why Dad thinks that's anything to do with me I can't imagine.'

Justin shrugged, hoping his sister would interpret this as tacit agreement – but Knightly's words flashed into his mind: *a fully qualified governess with experience of controlling spirited young ladies!*

'Nanny Verity's bound to come home sooner or later,' he said, hoping it was true. 'Everything'll get back to normal then.'

'I just wish she'd told us where she'd gone,' sighed Robyn plaintively. 'A message or something ... but I suppose after that bang on the head she couldn't risk it.'

'Yeah,' said Justin, trying to avoid eye contact with his sister. He hated keeping the truth from her, but he was determined to stay loyal to Nanny Verity. Still, there was no harm in telling her about the book he'd found. After checking Grandpa Lyall was still snoring soundly, he whispered: 'Actually, I think she *might've* left us a clue. Something only *we'd* spot.' Carefully, he slipped the old book out of his pocket and held it beneath the table where Robyn could see it. 'This was by Nanny's bed; take a look at the poem on the only page with its corner folded down – it's called: "*When We Two Parted.*"

Robyn stared at him wearing a doubtful expression. 'Nanny's had that book for donkey's years. What makes you think it's some special secret message?'

'She left a key on it,' Justin explained. 'Like she's telling us this book is the key to finding her. And don't you think the folded page corner's odd? Nanny always used to give us *such* a telling off if *we* did that. I bet it's because she knew it'd look unusual to us ... but perfectly ordinary to anyone else.'

'Barmy!' Robyn laughed. 'Stark staring bonkers. I heard there was a fine line between genius and insanity – I think you just crossed it!'

Justin blushed. His theory had seemed so believable up in Nanny Verity's room – but since he'd said it out loud, he had to admit it *did* sound pretty crazy. 'Yeah, you're probably right,' he muttered, stuffing the book back in his pocket.

'Listen Dustbin, we need to do something practical,' said Robyn. 'If we catch this X guy, then Nanny'll feel safe enough to come home.'

'SHhhhhh!' hissed Justin, pinching her arm. 'We shouldn't discuss this where we can be overheard.'

Robyn sniggered. 'What, him?' she said, glancing at Grandpa Lyall.

'Forget it! He doesn't know whether it's new year or New York! Look, how about delivering that letter to Polly's dad? We could get him talking ... find out where he was the day Mum was kidnapped.'

'Okay, tomorrow then,' said Justin, ready to agree to almost anything as long as she stopped talking. 'Shhh, I think that's Dad coming,' he added, hearing footsteps along the stone floor of the portrait gallery.

'Let's see if he's done what Mummy told him ... at least we'll know who wears the pants in the Thyme family.'

'Listen, Bobs – don't be too hard on him; he's got a lot on his plate right now.'

'*Fffuhhh!* Dad *never* has a lot on his plate – he dumps it all on yours, in case you haven't noticed. You earn all the money, pay all the bills – but he still treats you like a little kid ... *and* you *let* him. I'm surprised he didn't persuade you to nick my credit card ... get someone else to do his dirty work.'

'I'd never do that,' said Justin quietly.

The dining room door crashed open, and Sir Willoughby strode in, white with anger. 'I suppose you think that's funny,' he growled. 'Hand it over ... NOW!'

Robyn took the credit card out of her jeans pocket, slapped it onto the table and sent it skimming across to her father. 'Here – treat yourself to a *World's Best Dad* T-shirt.'

Sir Willoughby simmered silently as the butler appeared with a tray of scrambled eggs and bacon. The instant Knightly left the dining room, Willoughby turned to Robyn.

'If you ever speak to me like that again, young lady, you'll lose more than your credit card.'

Justin stared at his plate, hoping his father wouldn't draw him into the argument. He knew that if given half a chance Sir Willoughby would try to enlist his support – especially now Nanny Verity wasn't around to back him up. His appetite spoiled, Justin nudged his food around with his fork, mulling over what Robyn had said.

It's true, he thought. Dad *does* treat me like a child – though he never objects to me shouldering the responsibilities of an adult. It's *my* income everyone relies on; Mum's wages wouldn't cover the upkeep of a castle, and we'd be penniless if it was left to Dad. He was happy for me to build the time machine – *and* rescue Mum – so why should he stop me using it?

He turned to Robyn – slumped down in her chair, scowling at her breakfast– and gave her a sympathetic smile ... but somehow it was misinterpreted.

'It's *not* funny,' she yelled. Then choking back a sob, she jumped up and ran out of the dining room, slamming the door behind her.

The old grandfather clock in the entrance hall struck half nine, its chime echoed by a distant sonorous clang from the south tower. After taking a small stick of Edinburgh rock out of the hall table draw, Justin unlocked the castle door and stepped outside.

His timing was perfect. A bright red mail van came trundling through the archway and pulled to a halt a few metres from the castle doorstep. Its front door swung open, and a Scottish terrier leapt out; it bounded over to Justin, barking ferociously and bristling with excitement.

'His bark's worse than his bite,' said the postman, easing himself out of the van.

Justin laughed. Jock had said the very same thing at least five times a week for as long as he could remember.

'Poor ol' Fergus – I know he's a big softy, really,' Justin replied, tossing him the Edinburgh rock. 'That wagging tail gives him away.'

The Scottie sprang up, catching the rock in midair, and then jumped back into the van, crunching it like a bone. Justin marvelled how the little black dog and his master were so utterly different – one noisy and lively, the other taciturn and dull.

Jock reminded him of how people looked on television if you dialled down the colour. Grey hair, grey eyes, grey spectacles, grey personality – the sort of person who liked train-spotting or collecting stamps.

'Aye,' said Jock, nodding blandly. 'Grand weather.'

It was at this point the conversation usually stalled; having used two

97

of his five stock phrases, the postman would shuffle uncomfortably and return to his van.

In all the years Jock had delivered their mail, Justin had only heard him say something different on one occasion: the morning Albion was born. Collecting the mail, Justin had proudly announced the birth of his new little brother, and to his astonishment Jock had hesitantly asked if he could see the baby. Clearly embarrassed by his own audacity, Jock had followed him up to the nursery, still clutching his heavy mailbag – but by the time Justin had fetched Nanny, the poor chap was so overcome with shyness he muttered his excuses and left.

'I saw your photo in the newspaper,' said Justin, wondering if he could spur him to new conversational heights.

'Aye,' Jock replied.

'So, you finally got to see Nessie, then?'

'Aye.'

He nodded silently as he handed Justin a wad of envelopes. Fergus licked the last few crumbs of rock out of his whiskers, and put his paws on the dashboard. Jock climbed in beside him, and seconds later the little red van disappeared through the archway.

After checking through the morning mail, Justin collected his homework and set off for his lessons a minute or two early for once. As he stepped out of the upper corridor into the north tower he heard the faint sound of singing from the schoolroom; clearly the professor was in a good mood. Justin pushed the door open slowly.

Professor Gilbert was busy writing equations on a whiteboard; he had his back to the door, and continued to sing, unaware he was no longer alone.

I've wisdom from the East and from the West,

That's subject to no academic rule;

You may find it in the jeering of a jest,

Or distil it from the folly of a fool.

9

I can teach you with a quip, if I've a mind;

I can trick you into learning with a laugh;

Oh, winnow all my folly, folly, folly, and you'll find

A grain or two of truth among the chaff!

Justin coughed to announce his arrival. The professor turned quickly and gave his pupil a warm, welcoming smile. He had short, dark hair, a perfectly trimmed beard, and dark eyes that sparkled with intelligence. His hands moved nervously, forever straightening his bowtie or brushing invisible specks off his herringbone jacket. Everything about him radiated orderliness and precision, tempered with a gentle sense of humour. But no matter how genuine his smile, there was always a deep underlying sadness in his eyes. Justin suspected there was a tragedy in his past; the loss, perhaps, of someone very close. The professor never spoke about his personal life. In fact, owing to a pronounced stammer, almost every word was a struggle.

'I know it's my first day back,' said Justin, handing Professor Gilbert his homework. 'But I wondered if I might have the afternoon off; I've got rather a lot to catch up on business-wise.'

The professor pretended to look shocked, but Justin knew he was teasing. 'I g-guess that can be arranged,' he said quietly. 'To be honest, it's a struggle to f-f-find anything to challenge you these days; I sometimes think *you* should be the one teaching *me*.' He glanced down at the first page, humming contentedly to himself as he read it through. 'Hmm ... quantum en-entanglement,' he murmured. 'Have you had any ideas about p-p-practical application?'

Justin shrugged. Actually, he'd given the matter considerable thought, but since his father had warned him not to trust anybody, he felt decidedly wary about saying too much. He felt bad not trusting his tutor, but Professor Gilbert had always shown an avid interest in his time-fork theories, often asking some very awkward questions.

'W-will Robyn be joining us this morning?' enquired the professor, trying look as if the prospect pleased him.

'I don't think so.'

The expression of relief on Professor Gilbert's face was unmistakeable.

With Sir Willoughby's concerns uppermost in mind, Justin decided to test the professor out. 'Actually, Robyn's busy caring for a rare bird.'

'Hmmm,' replied the professor, still scanning through Justin's homework.

'It's one of Mum's specimens,' Justin continued. 'I thought you'd be interested ... you being an ornithologist.'

'Oh, er ... yes ... of course,' muttered Gilbert, sounding bored stiff.

Justin persisted. 'What's your speciality? Finches? Waders? Magpies, perhaps?'

The professor fixed Justin with an uncharacteristically hard stare, and hesitated a moment before replying. 'Birds of prey,' he said, his voice a tad snappish. 'Especially the nocturnal species; Lately, I've been observing a pair of *Strix aluco* – which, as I'm sure you know, is the Latin name for the tawny owl. Now, if you've f-f-finished testing my ornithological knowledge, perhaps you'd k-k-k-kindly turn your attention to the equations on the whiteboard.'

At two o'clock sharp Sergeant Awbrite rapped on the castle door. He marched briskly into the entrance hall where Willoughby and Justin were waiting to receive him.

'Good afternoon, sir,' he said, removing his cap, and tucking it under one arm. He nodded solemnly at Justin, then took a handkerchief from his pocket and mopped the perspiration off his shiny bald head.

'Well, Sergeant,' Sir Willoughby enquired. 'What's the news?'

'Bad news, I'm afraid, sir' sighed Awbrite, looking so dejected his luxuriant moustache seemed to droop. 'We've lost track of Mrs Kiss.'

'You mean to tell me that a middle-aged children's nanny has managed to outwit the entire Inverness Constabulary?'

'She's led us quite a merry dance, sir, I can tell you,' Awbrite replied. He opened his note book and took a deep breath: 'On Thursday the 15th of May at 10:15 a.m, a taxi collected Verity Kiss from the gates of Thyme Castle and drove her to Inverness Station. Here Mrs Kiss used her credit card to buy a train ticket to London. However, we've since discovered she left the station on foot, catching a bus to Fort Augustus instead ... where she purchased a second train ticket with cash. This train took her directly to Prestwick Airport; she then booked and paid for nine different international flights ... but according to our investigations she didn't catch *any* of them.'

'And by the time you'd checked the passenger lists and interviewed all the flight attendants, her real trail had gone stone cold,' said Justin, smothering a laugh so as not to hurt the sergeant's feelings. 'Go Nanny!'

Awbrite continued: 'After she'd booked the flights, CCTV cameras showed her wandering round the gift shops for a while – with her bandaged head and nanny's uniform she was easy to spot in the crowd. She was last seen entering a public toilet on the main concourse, then we lost track of her.'

'She must've changed clothes and removed her bandages inside one of the cubicles,' said Justin. 'Did the cameras show anyone coming out who didn't appear to go in?'

'We can't be sure,' said the sergeant, shaking his head. 'The airport was incredibly busy that day ... and people often exit the restrooms after taking off their coat, or putting on a pair of glasses. We're hoping the airport was another of her false trails, and she's hiding somewhere in Scotland. That's why I wanted to talk to you, Sir Willoughby. To ask if you have *any* idea where she might be?'

'What about her family?' Willoughby suggested.

'Brighton Constabulary checked with them, but they haven't heard from her.'

Hardly surprising, thought Justin – with her ex-husband on the watch, that'd be the last place she'd want to hide.

'I won't detain you any longer, sir – just let us know if she gets in contact, or if you come up with any useful leads.' He tore a page out of his notebook, scribbled down a number and handed it to Justin. 'This is my direct line. Call me any time ... night or day!'

To Justin's relief, he cleared through his backlog of business mail surprisingly quickly. After answering the final letter, he leaned back in his chair, watching a thumb-sized brass beetle as it scaled down the laboratory wall and dropped onto his desk.

Six months ago a corporate spy posing as a telecom engineer had bugged the castle. Since then, Justin had upgraded his security, determined to protect his inventions. This particular microbot – Bug-Seeker Number 3, or Bugsy for short – patrolled the south tower, constantly searching for hidden microphones or transmitters. It scuttled over to the computer and plugged its snout into a USB port; the word RECHARGING glowed dimly across its exoskeleton, and its eyes turned from red to flashing green.

As Justin stood up and stretched, he glanced across at the huge mosaic face of the old tower clock. From inside, the shadow of its hands across the opal white glass read a quarter past eight, which meant it was actually fifteen minutes to four. Justin walked to the small narrow window overlooking the driveway, wondering if the new nanny had arrived. A solitary figure was heading towards the castle, marching up the drive like a regimental sergeant major.

Curious, Justin reached for his telescope – but catching sight of his wristwatch, he changed his mind. Sir Willoughby had told the family to be in the great hall by five minutes to four, ready to welcome the new nanny for afternoon tea. Justin strolled over to a large circular hole in the floorboards; taking a deep breath, he grabbed a shiny fireman's pole and slid down to the first floor. The descent was as hair-raising as ever – but it was certainly more fun than the stairs.

Despite its grand name, the great hall was really the Thymes' sitting room. It was a cosy traditionally-decorated room, with a tartan sofa and several comfy chairs grouped around a large coffee table. An antique Chippendale desk stood between the two arched French windows overlooking the rose garden, and there was a faded tapestry of the Thyme family tree hanging above the old stone fireplace.

As he ran along to the great hall, Justin wondered if his father had checked out the Gilliechattans' scrapbook yet. For a moment, he imagined Sir Willoughby sitting in his favourite armchair, flipping through the pages – suddenly roaring with excitement when he discovered photo after photo of his old enemy. Then, in a flash, Justin realised the idea was ludicrous; if Mr G *was* Agent X he'd be far too smart to hand over incriminating photographs of himself.

Feeling disheartened, he pushed the door open, expecting to find his father poised to make a good impression on the new nanny – but to his astonishment, Sir Willoughby was leaning over his desk, tossing papers left and right as he burrowed frantically through a mound of old journals. Every drawer had been wrenched open, envelopes and crumpled news clippings littered the floor, and dozens of notebooks lay strewn across the rug.

'Lost something, Dad?' asked Justin.

Sir Willoughby turned towards him, his face haggard, a look of panic in his eyes.

'D'you remember me saying I was going to sort through some of Pops' old things? Well, I keep them in here,' he muttered, dropping to his knees in front of a bottom drawer and yanking it out even further. 'Apart from his highland journals, some old letters and a few legal documents, there was a pair of antique pistols that belonged to your great-grandfather. And *now* ... one of them is missing!'

103

The Return Coordinates CANNOT be Identical to Those you are Leaving.

The precise coordinates a time machine leaves must always be recorded – and, to avoid self-collision, it is vital that these NEVER match the coordinates of your return trip.

Either the temporal or spatial coordinates must be changed slightly. Both have their problems.

If you return to the SAME PLACE, then it must be to a TIME AFTER you left. An ideal setting would be about 5-10 seconds later, but preferably no longer than one minute, or this would constitute a trip to the future (which has its own set of problems).

Should you return to the SAME TIME, then it must be to a DIFFERENT place, although this might be inconvenient if the traveller's laboratory is cramped.

CHAPTER SEVEN

Hard Lines

'A gun?' gasped Justin. 'Do you think it's been stolen?'

'Must've been,' groaned Sir Willoughby, running his fingers through his hair in desperation. 'But there's no sign of a break-in.'

'Perhaps it's slipped down the back of a drawer.'

'I've checked; had every drawer right out. And anyway, both pistols have always been kept in this.'

The Laird of Thyme slid a carved wooden box towards his son. Justin opened it carefully; the inside was lined with blood-red velvet, recessed to hold two weapons and ammunition. In the top indentation lay a silver-coloured gun; it had a rosewood grip inlaid with mother-of-pearl, and had *Chekhov-XXX* engraved along its barrel. The bottom much smaller recess was empty.

'They were given to your great grandfather, Sir Mark Thyme, when he married Lady Margo Paxidean,' explained Willoughby.

Justin wrinkled his nose. 'Weird wedding gift.'

'Times were different then,' Sir Willoughby continued. 'Gentlemen carried firearms for protection – ladies too, sometimes. These were a custom-made matching pair, his and hers – one standard size gun, and a miniature pistol just the right size for a lady to conceal in her handbag ... or the garter of her stocking. They were very fashionable at the time.'

'Would they still work after all these years?'

'I'm afraid so. A few months ago, your mum took them into Paige and Romax, that place that services her tranquiliser guns. She only wanted them valued, but old Mr Paige went ahead and restored them as a special favour.'

'And the missing one – is it dangerous?' asked Justin, tracing its indentation in the velvet with one finger. 'It must be tiny.'

'Don't be deceived; it's no toy,' replied Willoughby. 'Over a distance it wouldn't have the power or accuracy of a larger weapon, but at close range it'd be deadly.'

Justin shuddered. 'A burglar would've taken both,' he said, frowning thoughtfully as he spoke. 'Which means it must be someone here in the castle.'

'It's that damned blighter masquerading as your grandpa,' growled Willoughby. 'Probably came rummaging in here last night. Sleep-walking ... PAH!'

'But when he mentioned Mrs Wight, you were convinced he was genuine.'

'No wonder. What an actor! That vague manner ... nothing over-played; the casual way he slipped her name into the conversation. Must've found it written in one of Pops' old journals, of course. And all that tosh about someone called Roxanda – just a clever smoke-screen to convince us he really *has* got amnesia.'

'But how did he know the guns were there?' Justin asked.

'Because, like a complete fool, I showed him,' replied Willoughby, shaking his head in dismay. 'It was a few weeks ago, after supper. I hoped they might trigger some memories. Old fraud! You should've seen the act he put on. Broke down sobbing, and kept repeating that something was all his fault; it took me and Robyn half an hour to calm him down. At the time it only convinced me more.'

'Why?'

'Well, apparently, your great-grandfather was meant to have shot somebody; killed them. I don't know the details. Pops never liked talking about it. However, he once let it slip that old Sir Mark was completely innocent; he'd confessed to protect someone else. I never learned who ... but Pops would've been about twenty-one when it hap—'

Sir Willoughby broke off as the door to the great hall creaked open; Knightly glided in carrying an enormous tray, which he placed on a low table.

'Afternoon tea, sir,' he droned. 'Cucumber sandwiches, scones and Dundee cake. Would you like me to serve now ... or shall I fetch the new nanny along first? Miss Garnet's just arrived.'

Willoughby sighed. '*Urrghhh* ... wheel the old girl in.'

'Very good, sir,' said Knightly. He eyed the ransacked desk with a stern sniff, then marched off, his shoes squeaking as usual.

'Better clear up this mess, I suppose,' said Willoughby. Then, turning to his son he added: 'Just nip upstairs and fetch Robyn, would you? Better remind Eliza to bring Alby down, too.

'Okay, Dad. Just one last question ...'

'Well?'

'Exactly how long is it since you showed Grandpa the guns?'

'Hmmm ... let me think. Well ... it was before Nanny Verity vanished, because I remember her taking Albion up to bed; she gave me one of her disapproving looks as she left. Then Knightly came in to close the curtains ... ah yes, *now* I remember... it was the day Knightly arrived.'

'So the little pistol could have been stolen any time in the last three weeks,' said Justin, counting back. 'Unless you've seen it since.'

'No.'

'Okay, let's think this through logically. If Knightly noticed the guns, he might have told Mrs Kof about them. The Gilliechattans probably knew already; there's not a drawer or cupboard in the castle Mrs G hasn't rummaged through. Professor Gilbert was away at the time, but someone could've mentioned the guns when he got back. I guess Nanny V could've taken the little pistol when she escaped, though I doubt she'd have got it through airport security. And with Grandpa, that makes seven possible suspects.'

Sir Willoughby nodded gloomily. 'What shall I do with *this* one?' he

107

asked, gesturing to the full-sized weapon.

'Throw it in the loch,' replied Justin solemnly. 'A gun only has one purpose – nothing good can come from keeping it.'

'Oh, I couldn't do that – it's a family heirloom,' said Willoughby. He made a hurrying motion with his hands. 'Robyn ... Alby ... *now*!'

Justin, paused by the door, turning back. 'Then put it somewhere safe, Dad,' he said. '*Very* safe ... or you might just live to regret it.'

Justin strode up the west tower staircase, considering each suspect in turn. It was hard to imagine any of them stealing a loaded pistol, he thought – except, perhaps, Mrs Kof. She was, after all, a convicted murderer. When she'd arrived, the cook had spoken openly about her past, although Justin had never heard her story firsthand.

Despite her outlandish background, Justin found it almost impossible to believe Mrs Kof was a danger ... but given the latest turn of events, he knew he'd have to talk to her as soon as possible, if only to reassure himself.

At the top of the west tower, Justin hammered on his sister's bedroom door.

'Bobs? Miss Garnet's arrived. Dad wants us down in the great hall ... *now*.'

He held his breath, not really expecting an answer; the atmosphere at lunchtime had been subzero. But after a loud honking noise from Haggis, Robyn shouted back, sounding her usual defiant self.

'Okay, Dustbin ... nearly ready.'

Justin hurried down to the next floor, with an uncomfortable feeling that trouble was brewing. He peered into the nursery, where Eliza was busy changing Albion's nappy.

'Tea downstairs in a couple of minutes,' he called. 'The new nanny's here.'

Eliza reached for her laptop. 'Good, good – Eliza happy new human nanny come. Bad baby make Eliza sad.'

As Justin stepped back into the great hall Sir Willoughby glanced up nervously.

'Ah, good, it's only you,' he said, cramming a final tartan-covered journal into a drawer and forcing it shut with some difficulty. He strode over to the mirror and straightened his tie – then tried, rather unsuccessfully, to smooth down his hair. 'Before everyone gets here, there's ... er ... something I want to ask you.'

Justin thought he could guess what was coming. He closed his eyes and took a deep breath, determined not to let it irritate him. But before his father could continue, there was a smart knock on the door, and Knightly entered, standing back to announce the new nanny.

'Miss Evelyn Garnet,' he said in a hollow voice.

The new nanny marched in briskly. She had a sharp nose, eyebrows that met in the middle, and wire hair scraped back into a severe bun. Her stiff iron-grey uniform gave her an amour-plated look, and the knife-edged pleats down the front of her starched white apron looked positively lethal. She seemed all angles and edges, and cold rice pudding and sensible shoes.

Stepping forward, she grasped Sir Willoughby's hand and gave it a single swift downward tug like someone tightening a knot.

'Garnet,' she barked.

'Er ... welcome to Thyme Castle,' said Willoughby, flexing his fingers to see if they still worked. 'This is my eldest son, Justin; he has his own private tutor, so you probably won't need to ... er ...'

'I'll still be keeping a close eye on him,' she said, glaring at Justin as if he was a worm she'd found after biting into an apple. 'Where's the rest of your family?'

'They'll be down shortly,' Willoughby assured her. 'Perhaps you'd like some tea while we wait?'

'Splendid ... I'll pour,' said Miss Garnet, pushing Knightly aside.

Seeing the butler's wounded look, Sir Willoughby caught his eye. 'Thank you, Knightly. That'll be all, for now.'

'Very good, sir.'

As the butler hurried out, Eliza prowled in with Albion clinging to her back. Evelyn Garnet gasped, but stood her ground. She turned swiftly to the Laird of Thyme.

'Why isn't that filthy animal in its cage?' she demanded. 'It'll get fleas all over the baby.'

'She's spotlessly clean,' said Justin, seeing the hurt look on Eliza's face.

'Quiet!' snapped Miss Garnet. 'Little boys shouldn't correct their elders.'

Meanwhile, Eliza deposited Albion at the new nanny's feet, then edged back, grunting unhappily.

'Ah ... so this is Baby Thyme,' said Miss Garnet, in the tone of voice someone might say *ah ... so this is an ingrown toenail*.

'His name's Albion – Alby for short,' Sir Willoughby explained. 'Alby, say hello to Nanny Evelyn.'

'Eva ... hi,' said Albion, smiling sweetly and waving one chubby hand.

'Clever boy,' said Justin. 'He's just starting to talk,' he told Miss Garnet proudly.

Nanny frowned. 'Mm ... he's just starting to be impertinent.' She picked Albion up and held him in the crook of one arm. 'It's *Nanny Evelyn* to you,' she said, prodding him with a bony finger.

Justin looked at his father, hoping he would say something. Sir Willoughby, feeling his gaze, grimaced back, yet remained disappointingly silent. Then, as Justin gave him a firm nudge, the door flew open with a resounding crash, and Robyn swaggered in.

For a moment Justin almost exploded with laughter. In an attempt to make the worst possible impression on the new nanny, Robyn had given herself a sort of gothic-punk makeover. She wore a black leather miniskirt, a black halter-neck top slashed to ribbons, thigh-length boots wrapped in chains, and a pair of fingerless lace gloves. One half of her hair was gelled into spikes, while the rest had been plaited into about two dozen braids with keys dangling from them. Her eyes were ringed with deep purple eye-shadow and thick mascara, and her lips and fingernails were the disturbing blue-grey of a corpse. She looked like a cross between a pirate, a zombie and a mentally deranged locksmith.

Biting the insides of his cheeks to keep his face straight, Justin glanced at his dad, hoping to detect a faint glimmer of amusement beneath his outraged expression.

'So, you're the difficult young lady I'm here to discipline,' said Nanny Evelyn, not looking the least bit fazed.

'Yep, that's me,' grinned Robyn. 'Think you're up to it?'

'She's going to be a tough nut to crack, Sir Willoughby,' Miss Garnet remarked. 'But crack her I will, make no mistake.'

'Well, you have my permission to do whatever it takes to keep her in line, Nanny.'

'I'm authorised to punish the children as I see fit?'

Sir Willoughby hesitated, running his forefinger around the inside of his shirt collar before replying. 'Erm ... yes ... those are my wife's instructions.'

Justin frowned, realising this was entirely the wrong way to handle Robyn, and that sooner or later things would spiral out of control. Nanny Verity never had this trouble, he thought. She'd always been three steps ahead of Robyn – and could get the best out of her no matter what her mood. If Robyn had tried a trick like this, Nanny V would've smiled brightly and said, 'that looks nice, dear – let's take a walk into the village,' knowing Robyn would rather die than humiliate herself in public.

'Come on, Dad,' he said quietly. 'This isn't what Mum had in mind.'

Miss Garnet turned on him like a pit-bull. 'You insolent boy – it's not your place to dictate to your elders. Write me five hundred lines: *I must not tell my father what to do*.'

Justin said nothing – but looked directly into his father's eyes and held his gaze steadily.

Sir Willoughby glanced round the room uncomfortably. 'Hhrrmm, well, I er ... must er ... things to do and all that.' He helped himself to a cup of tea and a scone, whisked a newspaper off a nearby armchair, and muttered, 'I'll leave you all to make friends,' as he scuttled out of the door.

After the Laird of Thyme had left, there was a strained silence – eventually broken by baby Albion yawning.

'Won kot,' he said, rubbing his eyes.

Nanny Evelyn frowned at him.

Eliza opened her laptop and prodded its keyboard. 'Baby sleepy – baby want sleep in cot now,' she said, using the voice of an old-fashioned radio announcer.

'Animals *don't* talk!' snapped Nanny Evelyn.

'Well, this one does,' said Robyn, with a chuckle.

'Hm ... not while I'm here, it won't. It's bad enough getting backchat from children – I won't tolerate it from some dirty beast.'

Frowning unhappily, the gorilla typed again: 'Eliza good clean gorilla – Eliza not dirty.'

'Tell it to give me that computer, at once ... then lock it in its cage.'

Justin felt anger bubbling inside him. Eliza had always been treated like one of the family ... in fact, she *was* one of the family. He wasn't about to stand by and see her robbed of the ability to communicate by some hatchet-faced old bully.

'You can't do this ...' he began. But Eliza bounded over to him, and gently placed one huge dark finger on his lips. Her eyes locked onto Justin's, speaking without words; the pain and sadness he saw in them brought a lump to his throat ... but more than anything else he saw wisdom. Justin marvelled at her depth of insight; somehow, she instinctively knew that arguing would only make things worse.

Slowly, she moved back, unfastening her laptop from its harness. After leaving it on the coffee table beside the Gilliechattans' scrapbook, she took two bananas from a large fruit bowl and solemnly handed one each to Justin and Robyn, patting their arms and grunting softly.

Finally, turning to face Nanny Evelyn, she rose majestically to her full height and gave a deafening roar, beating her chest with clenched fists. Then she blasted through the door and stormed along the portrait gallery, sending a marble bust of Sir Jolyon, 13th Laird of Thyme, crashing to the floor.

Albion goggled in stunned silence. Justin glanced at his sister, and noticed a single tear trickling through her mascara. But her face wasn't sad; it was seething with barely-suppressed fury. Justin could tell she didn't even trust herself to speak – and he knew exactly how she felt.

Evelyn Garnet surveyed her two eldest charges with a satisfied nod. 'Hm ... now, follow me upstairs ... quick march.'

Nanny Verity's old room looked cold and impersonal without her homely chintzy clutter. No photo albums, no lace-edged doilies, no sachets of lavender. All that remained was the faint floral scent of potpourri.

Miss Garnet sniffed disapprovingly then strode over to the windows and pushed them wide-open. She carried Albion through to the nursery, and after dumping him in his cot, walked round the room appraising it with a critical eye.

It was a bright cheery room, its stone walls were whitewashed, and a pair of pale blue curtains fluttered in the warm breeze wafting through the barred windows. Justin and Robyn hovered in the doorway, and watched Albion dragging his teddy from beneath a pillow. Nanny Evelyn, who had been examining shelf upon shelf of fabulous toys, looked at it with distaste.

'What a nasty, unhygienic-looking thing,' she muttered, reaching for the bear with her thumb and forefinger as if it was a dirty old sock.

Albion clutched it to his chest, and screamed. But *what* a scream! Never in his entire life had Justin heard such a racket. It was like a banshee with toothache being flattened by an express train as it whistled through a tunnel. Miss Garnet jumped back as if she'd been burnt. Meanwhile, Albion clung to the teddy as if his life depended on it, his face gradually turning from red to a dangerous purple.

'Sammy Bear's his favourite,' Justin explained, once Albion had quietened down. 'He used to be mine – and, before that, Dad's. I know he's a bit grubby and loose at the seams, but Alby can't get off to sleep without him.'

Nanny Evelyn looked sorely tempted to test that theory ... but even *she* couldn't endure such a dreadful noise a second time. 'Hmm ... I'll get it once he's dozed off,' she muttered, ushering Justin and Robyn through to her room. 'He can have a nice clean plastic building-block instead.' She walked over to a bell-pull and gave it a brisk tug, then turned to face her two charges with a cold, thin smile. 'Now, while Baby Thyme has his afternoon nap, I'm going to unpack my things. Supper is at seven-thirty, I believe?'

'Yes,' muttered Justin and Robyn together.

Miss Garnet glared at them, her eyes glinting like two chips of ice. 'Pardon?'

'Yes, Nanny Evelyn.'

'That's better. You can both report back here at six o'clock sharp. *You* had better be dressed in something decent,' she told Robyn. 'And you, boy – bring a pen and paper to do your lines.'

'I can do them in my room right now.'

'Hm ... I wasn't born yesterday,' replied Miss Garnet. 'I've heard you like inventing little gadgets; my guess is you're planning to make something that'll write the lines for you ... so you'll be doing them where I can keep my eye on you.'

'You can't force him,' said Robyn angrily. 'Me neither.'

'No, but I can punish you, young lady.'

Robyn laughed. 'So, what've you got in mind? Whipping us? Starving us? *Hello* – this is the 21st century not a Victorian orphanage.'

'You seem fond of that revolting ape; if either of you misbehave, I'll simply phone Edinburgh Zoo and have it taken away.'

'Mum wouldn't allow you,' said Robyn. 'Eliza's part of her TV show.'

Miss Garnet gave a short barking laugh. 'Lady Henrietta contacted me this morning; she's already worried the beast's behaviour is getting unpredictable. I'll tell her it tried to attack the baby ... that it became so wild and dangerous it had to be got rid of for the safety of the family.'

'She'd never believe you,' Justin said quietly.

'She wouldn't have any choice. Famous TV celebrities can't afford bad publicity. One phone call from me and every national newspaper will proclaim she puts an animal's happiness above the welfare of her own baby. The authorities would insist on the creature being put down – and your mother's reputation would be in tatters.'

'You wouldn't dare!' cried Robyn.

'Do you really want to take that risk?' Nanny asked, propelling them both out of the door. 'Think it over. If you're smart, you'll choose to cooperate. Now, be back here at six o'clock sharp.'

'Can't you give her the sack?' hissed Robyn. 'I bet you anything you're the one paying her wages.'

The two of them were huddled together on the west tower landing, whispering furtively.

'You're probably right,' Justin agreed. 'But maybe it's best if we cooperate for the time being, or Mum'll dig her heels in all the more. I'll phone her first thing in the morning and explain; I'm sure she hasn't a clue what this woman's like. It's Dad that disappoints me most,' he conlcuded, shaking his head. He was tempted to add that if Robyn hadn't gone out of her way to make things worse, their father might've been more supportive.

'D'you think she's bluffing about Eliza?' asked Robyn.

Justin frowned as he considered the question. 'I don't know ... but for Eliza's sake I'd rather not take any chances.'

'If only we could find Nanny Verity,' Robyn sighed. 'I wonder if ...'

Justin put one finger to his lips. 'Shhhh.'

Hearing the sound of squeaky shoes climbing the west staircase, he and Robyn crept up a few steps until they were out of sight. They held their breath, listening as the butler rapped on Miss Garnet's bedroom door.

'Ah, Mr Knightly,' said Nanny Evelyn. 'Can you get me a couple of large trunks, preferably with padlocks?'

'I think there are some in storage, Miss Garnet. Shall I fetch them now?'

'Yes ... and I could do with about a dozen black plastic bin-bags as well.'

Justin exchanged a baffled glance with his sister.

'Very good – I'll attend to it directly,' droned Knightly. 'Will that be all?'

'Hm ... I need to talk to Sir Willoughby. Do you know where I can find him?'

'I believe he's in the library.'

'Splendid,' said Nanny Evelyn. Justin and Robyn heard her step onto the landing and close her door. 'Leave the trunks in my room if I'm not back. Quietly, though – Baby Thyme's just gone off to sleep.'

Robyn scowled darkly. 'What's she up to now?'

'I'll follow her,' whispered Justin. 'You'd better go and feed Haggis. Make sure he keeps quiet – and don't forget to lock the bathroom door afterwards!'

Justin peered along the upper corridor leading to the south tower, making sure Nanny Evelyn was safely through the far door before creeping after her. As she made her way down to the library, he hurried into his private sitting room, tiptoed over to the fireman's pole and knelt beside it, peeping through the hole in the floor.

The library fire was unlit, but Sir Willoughby was sitting beside it in his favourite leather armchair. Justin could just see his feet resting on the hearthrug; he noticed them twitch as Nanny Evelyn rapped on the library door and marched in.

'Everything okay, Nanny?' Willoughby asked, sounding a trifle nervous.

'Excellent,' barked Miss Garnet. 'Soon have them toeing the line.'

'What can I do for you?'

'When I spoke to Lady Henrietta earlier, she mentioned keeping a tranquiliser gun in the castle. I'm concerned the children may come across it and accidentally hurt themselves.'

'Oh, I don't think that's likely,' Sir Willoughby assured her.

There was a long silence, broken only by the rustling of Sir Willoughby's newspaper. Justin watched his father's feet shuffling uneasily, and imagined Nanny Evelyn glaring at him. When she spoke again, her tone of voice made it clear she meant business.

'Her ladyship also told me the gorilla has been rather bad-tempered with Baby Thyme recently. I got the distinct impression she wanted me to keep her tranquiliser gun loaded and close at hand in case of any problems. She knows I'm a fully-trained markswoman.'

116

Justin fumed silently, certain his mother had never suggested anything of the kind. Clearly, Miss Garnet wanted the gun to intimidate Eliza, and was lying through her teeth to get it. He made a mental note to ask his mum when he phoned her tomorrow.

'That doesn't sound like Henny,' Willoughby replied uncertainly.

'Check with her first, of course,' said Nanny Evelyn. 'But if Baby Thyme is injured in the meantime, I assume you'll accept full responsibility.'

Sir Willoughby jumped to his feet. 'Great Scott! I'll go and fetch it right now,' he said, a note of panic in his voice

Justin heard his father hurry out of the library. Keeping perfectly still, he listened carefully, wondering what Nanny Evelyn would do while she waited. He heard brisk footsteps, then another much fainter sound he couldn't identify, and wondered if he dared risk poking his head through the hole – but he knew that if Miss Garnet glanced up and guessed he'd been eavesdropping, she'd be utterly furious.

After a minute or so, Justin heard more footsteps followed by the creak of the library door. He listened as Nanny Evelyn marched upstairs and across the south tower landing, and barely had time to dive behind the sofa before she opened his sitting room door and peered inside. Justin lay as still as stone, hardly breathing, until Miss Garnet turned on her heels and hurried further up the south tower staircase, jangling what sounded like a large bunch of keys.

Justin wondered whether she was looking for him, or just prying. It didn't matter; both his bedroom and laboratory doors were locked – and nothing except the touch of his right thumb would open them. Before long, he heard Nanny trotting back downstairs huffing irritably; she let herself into the library, and had just a few seconds to compose herself before Sir Willoughby reappeared.

'Here you are, Nanny,' he said, slightly out of breath. 'We're lucky to have someone so dedicated to caring for Alby.'

'Thank you, Sir Willoughby, replied Miss Garnet. 'You can be assured I'll keep it loaded and on me at all times.'

The instant Miss Garnet left the room, Justin slid down into the library, landing with a gentle thump. Sir Willoughby, who was standing in front of the mantelpiece frowning at the old Thyme Clock, jumped.

'I say ... what ...?'

Justin cut him off, struggling to keep the frustration out of his voice. 'Really, Dad ... I can't believe you've just handed over Mum's tranquiliser gun to a complete stranger. What *were* you thinking?'

'I gave it to a responsible safety-conscious adult who ...'

'Yes, I noticed it was the word *responsibility* that sent you rocketing out of your armchair!'

'That's enough!' roared Willoughby. 'No wonder Miss Garnet gave you those lines; it's clear your sister's having a bad influence on you.'

'Thanks to Robyn my eyes are wide open,' Justin snapped back at him, unable to hide his feelings any longer. 'An hour ago, you said you wanted to ask me something. I'd bet half my bank balance I can guess what it is. You want to know what you should do about Grandpa, don't you?'

He paused, waiting for his father to say something, but Sir Willoughby, unsettled by his sudden outburst, looked too shocked to speak. Justin continued, his voice growing steadily louder. 'Grandpa's now top of your suspect list, but you daren't boot him out just in case you're wrong. So what do you do? You want *me* to decide for you. As usual, you dump the responsibility in *my* lap.'

'Well, I ... I do value your opinion,' Sir Willoughby mumbled.

'Of course you do – because if things turn out fine you can pretend it's what you'd have done anyway, and if not, you've got someone to blame. I bet there are millions of kids who'd love to be in my shoes, having their dad come asking for advice – but I've had it up to here,' said Justin, holding one hand level with his nose. He paced across to the library desk and took a pen and paper out of the top drawer. 'Well, I'm off to do my lines now' he said. 'Do you remember what they are?'

Sir Willoughby shrugged awkwardly. 'Look, son ... I er ...'

'I'll remind you,' Justin continued. 'I've got to write: *"I must not tell my father what to do,"* five hundred times. So, hard lines, Dad! From now on, you can make your own decisions!'

At six o'clock Justin and Robyn knocked on Nanny Evelyn's bedroom door. Robyn was now dressed quite sensibly – for her – although Justin suspected her metallic pink hot-pants and denim jacket wouldn't entirely meet with Nanny's approval.

'Ghastly!' barked Miss Garnet, the instant she opened the door. She pointed to a pile of black plastic bin-bags on the bed. 'Take those upstairs,' she instructed Robyn. 'I'll be along in a minute to go through your clothes; any that are unsuitable will be bagged up and locked in these trunks. One week of good behaviour and I'll return a single item; if you misbehave ten garments will be burnt. Understand?'

Robyn nodded gloomily, then shot Justin a look that said he'd better sort things out rapidly or there'd be big trouble.

Justin suspected there'd have been a major battle already if he hadn't warned her about the tranquiliser gun. It was now obvious to them both that Evelyn Garnet held all the cards, and that Eliza would suffer if they didn't cooperate. He'd promised his sister that, somehow, he'd make things right ... but he knew Robyn's patience wouldn't last indefinitely. The gun was now tucked into a broad leather belt cinched around Nanny's waist – clearly her way of showing she was a force to be reckoned with.

'You, boy,' she snapped. 'Over there, where you can keep an eye on Baby Thyme while I'm upstairs.' She pointed to one of the trunks Knightly must have brought. Justin placed his pen and paper on top of it and drew up a chair. He glanced through the doorway into the nursery; Albion was sitting in his playpen, pushing a shiny red racing car in and out of the bars.

'Das ... reh-sek!' he gurgled happily, waving the car at his older brother.

Justin grinned and gave him a double thumbs-up.

'Concentrate, boy,' said Nanny Evelyn. She leaned over and riffled through the sheets of paper as if she suspected something was hidden between them. As she straightened up, Justin was surprised to notice she was wearing an old-fashioned hearing aid. 'Well, get busy,' she snarled, drumming her fingers on the gun's handgrip. 'And remember: no jiggery-pokery ... I'm leaving my door open so I can check on you!'

Justin had never written lines before. On the few occasions he'd forgotten to do his homework, the professor had simply accepted his apology, knowing the tedious repetition of some written phrase would merely waste his pupil's time.

The boredom Justin could cope with ... and the cramp in his hand – but what bothered him most was how each line reminded him of the wounded expression on his father's face. Part of him wanted to patch things up as soon as possible – but another part kept stubbornly insisting he had no reason to feel guilty. Usually, kids asked their fathers for advice – not the other way round.

Of course, the real fly in the ointment was Evelyn Garnet, he decided. But the question was: had she driven a wedge between father and son ... or exposed one that already existed? The same thing was happening with Henny and Robyn, Justin thought anxiously. If he could only find Nanny Verity, he was sure everything would return to normal; in truth, she'd been the glue that held the Thyme family together.

'Only two hundred and thirty lines to go,' Justin sighed, flexing his stiff fingers.

He wondered how Robyn was coping. For the last half hour her infuriated shrieks had been echoing down the west tower – but now these were accompanied by the skirling cry of a hungry doddling. Justin listened with bated breath, hoping his sister had remembered to lock Haggis in the bathroom. Moments later he heard heavy footsteps tramping across her bedroom floor, followed by Robyn shouting: 'No, stop ... you can't go in there ... please, no ...'

With a sigh of resignation Justin put down his pen. But before he could head upstairs there was a startled roar from Nanny Evelyn, and Haggis came tumbling down the west tower staircase, honking breathlessly.

The doddling glanced back – but, seeing Miss Garnet marching after him, scurried across the landing into the nursery. He ran past Albion's playpen and dashed through the connecting door into Nanny's room, skidding to a halt in front of Justin.

Half crouched, with his hands held out, Justin advanced slowly on the little bird – but as he dived forwards, Haggis squeezed under the bed.

Peering beneath the patchwork quilt, Justin watched the dodo wriggle between Nanny Evelyn's slippers and a torch, which went clattering across the floor as he scrambled out the other side. A split second later, as Nanny sprinted through the nursery, Haggis shot out of the bedroom door and down the next flight of stairs.

'Flux!' yelled Justin, jumping to his feet. He vaulted over the bed and ran onto the landing, overtaking his sister who was already racing downstairs after Haggis.

At the foot of the west tower, he swerved past Mrs Gilliechattan and hurtled into the portrait gallery with Robyn a few paces behind. Tybalt, his eyes gleaming like polished emeralds, scuttled rapidly after them licking his lips.

One after the other, they dodged round Grandpa Lyall as he gazed dreamily at the painting of Lady Isabel.

As they dashed through the dining room, Justin almost caught up with Robyn – but the octo-puss, his eight legs a blur, outstripped them both. He catapulted himself onto the dining table – and would've pounced on poor Haggis if he hadn't collided with Knightly setting the table for supper. Justin slammed the door behind him, trapping Tybs in the dining room.

Haggis rushed across the entrance hall, zipping between Professor Gilbert's legs as he stepped in through the front door, then ran into the kitchen.

'G-g-g-good gracious!' gasped the professor. 'W-w-what was that?'

But Justin and Robyn were already out of earshot. They raced through the steam-filled kitchen, almost tripping over Mrs Kof's huge bare feet as they dived out through the open back door.

Tiring now, Haggis crossed the lawn, wheezing and honking like a bagpipe with hiccups. After trampling an entire row of radishes, he galumphed past Mr Gilliechattan kneeling by his vegetable basket, and blundered into a net stretched over some strawberries. Quickly, Justin emptied the basket, popped it over the doddling, then collapsed beside it, gasping for breath.

'You forgot... huh ... to lock ... huh ... the bathroom door... huh ... didn't you?' he panted to his sister.

'No way!' said Robyn, giving him a dark conspiratorial look. 'Nanny Evelyn's got her own set of skeleton keys!'

ome Coordinates Should be set Before Departure

As a safety precaution, it is best to set the return coordinates whilst still in the present. The traveller cannot know what awaits them in the past, and might have to abort their exploration instantly to avoid danger or detection. Preset coordinates allow them to simply hit the launch button and disappear.

My own chronopod is programmed to automatically set the return coordinates to exactly five seconds after whatever time I depart; I can manually override this if necessary.

When a proposed trip looks likely to be hazardous, a chrononaut might alter BOTH the temporal AND spatial home coordinates, (choosing somewhere close by, a few seconds BEFORE leaving). This would allow them to witness their safe return shortly ahead of departure.

CHAPTER EIGHT

A Midnight Message

Supper was a ghastly meal. Robyn refused to speak to her father – and even Justin found it a struggle, although he was determined to act normally in front of Grandpa and Knightly. Old Sir Lyall seemed quite clear-headed for a change, remembering their names and asking about their trip to Mauritius. He tickled Albion's feet, and then winked at Nanny Evelyn.

Eliza's place was empty; she'd taken her banana bucket out onto the east tower roof and was venting her feelings by hurling it along the battlements.

Even the food that night was dreadful. As soon as Nanny Evelyn saw the delicious-looking cheese and ham pies set before Justin and Robyn, she instructed Knightly to take them straight back to the kitchen.

'Tell Cook the boy and girl will have a lightly boiled egg each, with a slice of brown bread,' she snapped. Then, glancing at the raspberry trifle and fabulous chocolate-cherry gateau on the sideboard, added, 'And a prune apiece for dessert.'

Two minutes later, Mrs Kof stormed into the dining room, her huge muscular arms folded squarely across her chest.

'What wrongful with my cookings?' she bellowed at Miss Garnet.

The site of Mrs Kof flexing her biceps would have turned most

Nannies' knees to jelly – but Evelyn Garnet didn't flinch.

'Rich fatty foods aren't good for the children,' she said. 'And desserts loaded with sugar – it's no wonder they're so hyperactive and insolent. Trust me,' she continued, turning to Sir Willoughby. 'I used to be a prison officer. A sugar-free diet cut inmate riots by twenty percent; I find it reduces nursery insubordination likewise.'

Sir Willoughby muttered something inaudible and shuffled uncomfortably, avoiding eye contact with his son and daughter. He gulped his meal as swiftly as possible, then disappeared without a word, much to Nanny's disapproval.

Justin glanced across the table at his sister. Apart from her robin tattoo and the defiant gleam in her eyes, she was almost unrecognisable. Nanny Evelyn had scrubbed off her makeup and nail polish, plaited her dark hair into two long, schoolgirly pigtails, and forced her into a drab grey skirt and blouse. Robyn kept grumbling she looked like a housemaid in a TV costume drama, but Nanny Evelyn adamantly refused to let her wear anything else, and insisted it looked very appropriate.

Knightly returned with their boiled eggs on a large silver platter, and despite his outwardly bland expression, Justin got the impression he found their meagre rations somewhat amusing.

Justin stared at his lonely egg, and would've felt thoroughly gloomy if Mrs Kof hadn't drawn a smiley face on it. Better still, after swallowing the last mouthful he found a message scrawled on the bottom of his eggshell:

Don't pan-nick
Pig-nick later!

Once supper was over, Robyn hurried upstairs to check on Haggis. After his mad dash through the castle, the little doddling had been carried back to her room where he'd collapsed in an exhausted heap at the foot of her bed.

Nanny Evelyn, who disapproved of pets, had objected strongly at first, but once she discovered that caring for the bird was a punishment, she seemed pretty okay with it.

Justin volunteered to help Knightly clear away the dishes, hoping he'd get a chance to talk to Mrs Kof alone – but to his dismay Nanny Evelyn suspected he was after more food, and trailed after him.

The kitchen was a hive of activity. Apart from Mrs Kof and Knightly doing their usual after-supper chores, Grandpa Lyall had turned up, waiting for his special cocoa; and Professor Gilbert – who always dined alone in his room – had trickled down to collect his supper tray and a glass of beer.

Nanny Evelyn marched past everyone, shoving them aside. After plonking Albion in his highchair she snapped her fingers at Mrs Kof.

'You ... I'd like some warm milk for Baby's bedtime bottle ... now!'

'Ya, ya' replied the big cook, nodding placidly. 'I just finish Grandpa Liar's cocoa first.'

Evelyn Garnet hovered impatiently, watching Mrs Kof pour the hot chocolate into a mug and add three dreamy-drops.

'What's that?' she barked, snatching the little glass phial. 'Something illegal?' She gave it a cautious sniff, her nose quivering like a bloodhound's.

'No, no ... not ill eagle,' said Mrs Kof, looking puzzled. 'This my own herbivorous sleepy potion.'

'Most unsuitable!' grumbled Miss Garnet. 'Probably *highly* dangerous. If I catch you using it again, I shall speak to Sir Willoughby.'

She turned away from the cook and, for a moment or two, her eyes became narrow, calculating slits. Then, with a crocodilian smile, she spoke again, this time her voice as smooth as oil.

'My, how delicious that cocoa smells. I'm sure Robyn and Justin would love some; I know I would. Perhaps you could make some for all of us, Mrs Kof.'

Without waiting for a reply, Nanny swept across the kitchen and opened the crockery cupboard, still clutching the little glass phial of dreamy drops.

Meanwhile, Mrs Kof refilled the milk pan and tipped in another generous handful of chocolate truffles. After checking Miss Garnet had her back to them both, she tossed the last one to Justin, who crammed it in his mouth before the new nanny turned round.

'I thought we weren't allowed sugary stuff,' he said, as Nanny Evelyn returned carrying three mugs on a small round tray.

After placing it on the table next to Albion's highchair, she took the pan of cocoa from Mrs Kof and filled the mugs, stirring each one in turn.

'No harm in a little treat occasionally,' she told Justin, still smiling like a hungry crocodile. 'There now! My mug's the one with the spoon in it.'

Meanwhile, Mrs Kof filled Albion's bottle with warm milk and handed it to him – but after just one sip he squealed and threw it on to the floor.

'Am tig-ni!' he shouted crossly, while everyone scrabbled beneath the kitchen table.

Nanny Evelyn emerged first looking flushed and angry. 'What's that supposed to mean?' she snarled, slamming his bottle on the tray. 'Doesn't he *ever* speak properly?'

'He manages *some* words,' Justin laughed, ruffling his little brother's hair. 'But he likes to make up his own silly baby-talk, too. Don't you, Alby?'

'Yas,' grizzled Albion, nodding. 'Speeka zil-ee!'

'Perhaps his milk's too hot,' suggested Grandpa Lyall, feeling the bottle with the backs of his knobbly fingers. 'The twins used to scream the place down if their drinks weren't cool enough.'

Justin glanced curiously at the old man, making a mental note to check if there were any twins on the Thyme family tree.

'I think I know what's best for Baby,' remarked Nanny Evelyn, glaring at Sir Lyall as she lifted Albion out of his chair.' She turned to Justin. 'Bring the tray and follow me back to the nursery ... quick march.'

As Justin reached for the cocoa, Mrs Kof grabbed his arm, whispering furtively in his ear. 'You want I scream?'

'Pardon?'

The cook pointed to two large wicker baskets by the pantry door. 'I scream, I scream!' she hissed. 'You want I bring you sums in pig-nick basket laters?'

'Oh ... I see,' Justin gasped. 'No ... no ice-cream, thanks. And please be careful; Nanny'll be furious if she catches you.'

'No worrits! Nanny Evil not catch Missiz Kof.' She winked and gave him a wide gappy grin as he hurried out into the hall.

Professor Gilbert trotted after Justin, glancing warily at the new nanny as if she might bite him.

'Th-th-that bird you were chasing – is it the one your sis-sis-sister's looking after?' he stuttered, trying just a little too hard to sound interested. 'W-w-w-what is it?'

'Oh, yes ... it's a doh ... er, a Dominican dabchick,' Justin invented wildly.

'Ahh, y-y-yes ... from the Do-Do-Dominican Republic,' replied the professor, nodding sagely. 'I th-thought so.' He wished his pupil good-night and headed up the north tower, leaving Justin to follow Nanny Evelyn along the portrait gallery.

Once Evelyn Garnet had settled Albion in his cot for the night, she placed a mug of cocoa on her bedside table, and then handed one of the others to Justin.

'Now, make sure you drink it while it's hot,' she told him, her voice still oddly unctuous. 'Then off to bed, nice and early. Your mother's told me what a night-owl you are.'

'I find it's a good time to get things done,' Justin explained, hoping she wouldn't get cross.

But instead Nanny Evelyn gave an icy-cold snigger. 'Me too,' she replied, and then marched off upstairs with the third mug of cocoa for Robyn.

Justin didn't feel the least bit sleepy; in fact, his brain was buzzing like a beehive.

It was less than twenty-four hours since he'd got home, and his things-to-do list had been growing at an alarming rate. His homework and business mail were now up-to-date – and he'd decided that making a dodobot for Haggis would have to wait. But that still left several problems in need of urgent attention.

The mysterious theft of the little pistol was perhaps the most worrying. It appeared to prove that either X or his spy had infiltrated Thyme Castle – but Justin knew that discovering their identities wouldn't be easy.

I'd better remind Dad to look through the Gilliechattans' scrapbook, he thought – and first thing tomorrow I must phone Mum about Nanny Evelyn.

Then there was the letter he'd promised to deliver to Polly's father; somehow, he and Robyn would need to get Mr Polydorus talking.

And he still wanted to question Mrs Kof about her shadowy past.

Finally, Justin's thoughts drifted to the baffling disappearance of Verity Kiss. Finding and bringing her back home would mean they could get rid of Evelyn Garnet, but, more importantly, there was a good chance Nanny V could help identify Agent X.

'I'll have to get searching through her old poetry book for hidden clues,' Justin reminded himself. 'I know Robyn thinks it's crazy ... but it's a starting point. After all, we've nothing else to go on.'

No, an early night was out of the question. But guessing Miss Garnet might check up on him later, Justin changed into his pyjamas, drew the curtains and then locked his bedroom door from the outside. He could work up in his laboratory by the light of a Bunsen burner, and slide down the fireman's pole if he heard her come snooping.

With the book in one hand and his cocoa mug in the other, Justin hurried up the south tower stairs – but as he reached his lab door he heard the sound of large bare feet slapping heavily on the stone steps down below.

'I'm up here, Mrs Kof,' he called, pressing his right thumb onto the fingerprint recognition sensor above the door handle. With a muffled clunk the deadbolts retracted. Justin pushed his lab door open and strolled over to a workbench, placing the mug and book of poetry beside his computer.

Moments later, the cook ambled in, carrying a large wicker picnic basket which she deposited on the bench with a thud. She grinned broadly at Justin.

'Missiz Kof not lets Nanny Evil starvings you ... or Miss Robbing either.'

She threw the basket lid open, accidentally knocking Justin's mug and sending it clattering across the bench. Justin scooped up the book and dragged his computer keyboard away from the spreading puddle of cocoa.

'Whoops-a-gravy!' laughed Mrs Kof, mopping the sticky mess with her apron. 'I spillikins drinky. No worrits ... plenty more in theremin flask.'

Justin's mouth watered as he peered into the picnic basket; he could see sausage rolls, turkey sandwiches, crisps, chocolate brownies, coconut snowballs and marshmallow cookies.

'Thanks, Mrs Kof,' he said, biting into a sausage roll. 'I'm ravenous!'

Justin ate quietly for a minute or two, wondering how to broach the thorny subject of the cook's past.

Meanwhile, Mrs Kof opened the thermos and poured him a fresh mug of hot chocolate. She handed it to him, peering intently at his troubled face.

'Sum-thinks is botherating you,' she said, looking unusually serious. 'You wants telly me?'

Justin gulped down a large mouthful of sausage, still unsure how to begin.

'A gun's been taken out of Dad's desk,' he explained, deciding straightforward honesty was best.

'And you thinks Missiz Kof stealing it?' asked the cook, sounding faintly tickled.

'Well, no ... not *really* ... but ...'

'But you know I beans in prison.'

She gave a gruff chuckle. Justin felt his cheeks burning.

'I'm sorry,' he mumbled. 'I er ... I guess I'm just curious about your past. I know you've talked to Mum and Robyn ... but ... I ... I'd like to hear about it from you.'

Mrs Kof helped herself to a small chocolate brownie; she tossed it high into the air and caught it in her mouth, chewing it slowly until she was ready to speak.

'Many long time ago, after my papa dyings, ringmaster make me overtake his strongman act,' she said. 'Soon I become famulus star in Bohemian Circus and getting happily marinated to handsome fire-eater called Boguslav Przolwamiczenkof.'

The big cook reached for another brownie. She closed her eyes, inhaling its delicious chocolaty aroma as if her story needed enticing out with food.

'One day, he guzzly too much vodka before show, and get flambéed like a kebabs,' she continued sadly. 'Week after-warts, Vazsilev the bear-trainer and Romolo the Wolf-boy both asking will I marrow them.'

Justin's eyebrows shot up in surprise. 'Go on ...'

'I tells Romolo, I'm a frayed knot ... but I saying ya to Vazsilev. Then, night before weddinks, I see hims whippeting bear-cubby. I gets thundery angerful, and says I artichoke him with my bare handles if he ever doodles this again. Next mornings Vazsilev found deadly straggulated, and policy-men take me to prison. I keep tellings everybodkin I abslutty innocent ... but nobodies are belief me. So,' she concluded, pausing as if half-afraid to ask. 'You thinking Mrs Kof was killing him?'

Justin thought for a moment, wanting to answer truthfully.

'I think you *could've* killed him,' he said. 'But ... well, I'm *certain* you didn't.'

He meant it, too. Although unable to explain why, he sensed there was something intrinsically good about their peculiar cook. If there was one person in the castle he truly wanted to believe, it would be her ... no matter how illogical it seemed.

'That twenty-seven yearlings ago,' sighed Mrs Kof. 'Since then, I got the runs ... through many, many countries. Last six months I liver in Paris – I wok as chef in days and hidey in Notre Damp Cathodical at nights. But when policy-men ketchup with me ... I swimy across channels to Eggland.'

'Amazing!' gasped Justin. 'But I don't understand why've you told us all this. Aren't you afraid we might hand you over to the police?'

'You good peoples,' said Mrs Kof solemnly. 'My first name – Nadezhda – it meaning hope! I am hope you knows truthful when hearing it.'

'Yeah, I'm pretty sure I do,' Justin assured her. 'But I'm no closer to finding that pistol. Anyone here could've stolen it. Except for Miss Garnet; she didn't arrive until *after* Dad discovered it was missing. At least I can rule *her* out.'

Mrs Kof gave another deep guttural laugh. 'Not nessie-celery! Nanny Evil could stollen gun yesterdays. Ya, ya, she could ... you asking Mister Nightie!'

In her room at the top of the west tower, Robyn was sharing the contents of her own picnic basket with Haggis. Hearing her munching through a bag of crisps, the little doddling had woken up and was now busily devouring a pile of crumbled-up fruitcake.

Feeling comfortably full – although surprisingly sleepy – Robyn switched on her computer, planning a little late-night retail therapy to brighten her mood. Mrs Kof had agreed that any shopping could be addressed to her, and she'd smuggle the parcels up to Robyn's room later.

With a jaw-cracking yawn, Robyn scrolled down her fashion favourites, certain that if she really put her mind to it, she could buy new clothes even faster than Nanny Evelyn could confiscate them.

Harpy Nyx first, she decided, wondering if they'd released their neon cashmere collection yet. They had – and within seconds Robyn had chosen at least a dozen must-have outfits. She clicked the checkout button and typed in her credit card number from memory, but to her astonishment a window popped up saying: *payment declined*.

'Oh, crud-crumpets!' she muttered, yawning again. 'I must've muddled the rotten number.' But re-entering it made no difference whatsoever, and ten minutes later she had exactly the same problem at Déshabillé's website.

By the time she logged onto Feckless & Frippets, Robyn was struggling to keep her eyes open. After entering her credit card number again, she clicked BUY – only to have her payment rejected a third time. Utterly baffled, and now almost too tired to think, she flicked the computer off and tumbled into bed, determined to investigate the problem first thing the following morning.

Justin felt discouraged. Although he hated to admit it, it looked as if Robyn was right. Nanny Verity's book of poetry didn't appear to contain any secret messages at all. He'd spent the last two-and-a-half hours wading through page after page of gloomy romantic verse, hoping to spy a few random letters underlined in pencil, or a string of numbers jotted in a margin ... but the only thing he found was a short inscription written on the flyleaf:

To V ~ I'll never forget you ~ Love, X

If anything, this depressed Justin even more. No doubt Nanny Verity's ex husband had given her the book years ago, perhaps when they first met – but the fact she chose to keep it by her bed was decidedly worrying. Why, if she feared him as much as she claimed, would she still cherish this token of his affection? Were they *really* divorced – or had she lied about that too? Perhaps they'd been in cahoots all along, Justin thought, and her tearful confession had been nothing but a smokescreen, buying her some time to escape. Maybe he was wasting his time searching for clues ... because Verity Kiss had no intention of being found.

'No!' he exclaimed, thumping the bench with his fist. 'I'm sure Nan was telling the truth.'

He turned back to the page with the folded-down corner, and read the poem again:

133

When We Two Parted

When we two parted
In silence and tears,
Half broken-hearted
To sever for years,
Pale grew thy cheek
And cold, colder thy kiss;
Truly that hour foretold
Sorrow to this.

The dew of the morning
Sunk chill on my brow —
It felt like the warning
Of what I feel now.
Thy vows are all broken,
And light is thy fame;
I hear thy name spoken,
And share in its shame.

They name thee before me,
A knell to mine ear;
A shudder comes o'er me —
Why wert thou so dear?
They know not I knew thee,
Who knew thee too well: —
Long, long shall I rue thee,
Too deeply to tell.

In secret we met —
In silence I grieve,
That thy heart could forget,
Thy spirit deceive.
If I should meet thee
After long years,
How should I greet thee? —
With silence and tears.

Justin shook his head slowly, wondering if he was on entirely the wrong track. He closed the book, but before he could swivel to face his computer, he heard a faint metallic clattering noise from the direction of the fireman's pole, and turned to see Bugsy scuttling up from the floor below.

The little microbot scurried towards him, its tiny brass feet skittering across the stone floor. It clambered up onto the bench and headed for the computer, plugging itself into a vacant USB port. Instantly, the words BUG ALERT flashed across the screen – then, moments later, a window opened showing a 3D wire-frame diagram of the entire south tower. A bright red light pulsed at one side of the ground floor. Justin moved his cursor over an outline of the library desk and clicked ZOOM. Then, repositioning over the telephone, he kept clicking until its mouthpiece filled the entire screen.

'Nice job, Bugsy,' Justin muttered. 'I'd better go and investigate.'

After selecting a small screwdriver from his tool-rack, he dashed across to the fireman's pole and took a deep breath. Sliding from top to bottom of the south tower was always fairly exhilarating, but wearing pyjamas made the descent even faster. He landed on the library floor with a thud that made his teeth rattle.

Externally, the library telephone didn't look any different – but once Justin unscrewed the grill over its mouthpiece he spotted a micro-transmitter wedged behind the diaphragm. He prised it out with his screwdriver, replaced the grill, and then strolled over to the fireplace. The flames had burnt low, but a huge smouldering pine log crackled in a nest of hot orange coals. Using the poker, Justin split the log open, tossed the bug into its shimmering heart, and watched it melt, hissing and spitting like a wildcat.

As he stared into the fire, Justin tried to work out who could've planted the transmitter. Bugsy usually completed one comprehensive search of the south tower every twenty-four hours – which meant virtually anyone could be responsible. Mrs Gilliechattan must have had plenty of opportunities whilst cleaning; Knightly had been to the library to light the fire; the professor could've sneaked along while they were all at supper; Nanny Evelyn had enough time while Sir

Willoughby was fetching the tranquiliser gun; Grandpa Lyall might have planted it during one of his nocturnal somnambulations; and Mrs Kof could have crept in after delivering the picnic basket. In all fairness, even Sir Willoughby could have done it ... although why he'd want to bug his own telephone Justin couldn't imagine.

Loath to stray from the warm glow of the fire, he stood for a moment, staring at the old Thyme Clock on the mantelpiece. Despite being one of the Thyme family's most valuable heirlooms, Sir Willoughby had always referred to it as *"that Victorian monstrosity"*. Until quite recently, Justin assumed this was simply because it was such an eccentric-looking design, but now he wondered if his father's dislike of it went deeper.

Justin had to agree the clock was ludicrously ornate; its solid gold outer case encrusted with jewelled playing cards and thyme leaves, and flanked by a pair of elaborately carved mechanical figures: Old Father Time on its right side, and a sinister-looking jester on the left. While developing his theory of time, Justin had gradually realised that these two strange characters represented the uneasy balance between the precision of time and the random nature of chance – an eternal equilibrium of order and chaos.

As a small child he'd been fascinated by these clockwork automatons, and had loved to watch Old Father Time striking the bell with his scythe, or the joker twirling his dice. But now they unsettled him – in fact, the words engraved across the clock's golden bell positively gave him the shivers. Its inscription read: *Beware Procrastination*. Justin glanced down at his wristwatch, where the same two word warning encircled the tenth Roman numeral on its dial. An X ... like Agent X, Sir Willoughby's old enemy – who sometimes called himself the Thief of Time, a phrase long associated with procrastination.

Beware the Thief of Time.

The uncanny connections between the clock and watch were clearly no coincidence; in fact, the back of the wristwatch was engraved with the words of Leonardo Da Vinci: *"Everything is Connected to Everything Else"*. As Justin murmured this phrase to himself, he

wondered if both timepieces had been made by the same horologist –
but that was impossible; the clock was dated 1838, whereas the watch
had been left anonymously on his bedside table the day he'd turned
thirteen. True, its casing looked well-worn, but its face featured an
ambigram of his name, so it couldn't be an antique. At the time, Justin
had thought it a peculiar gift for someone who didn't celebrate his
birthday and practically never wore a watch. But whether it was
from some mysterious well-wisher trying to forewarn him of the
perils ahead, or an enemy intent on luring him into danger, he
couldn't be sure.

Justin leaned forward, peering closely at the jester, wishing it
could give him some sign ... some clue to Agent X's identity. The
figure's tiny sapphire eyes glittered back at him mischievously, as if it
knew the answers to all Justin's questions were right there in front of
him, if only he knew where to look.

It was almost midnight. Justin decided to head back to his
bedroom in case Nanny Evelyn came checking; after all, a decent
night's sleep wouldn't do him any harm. He turned, walked across
to the desk and picked up his screwdriver – but as he tucked it into his
pyjama pocket, he heard a muffled click from the phone ... the sort of
click that meant someone had just lifted another receiver on the same
line.

Justin frowned at the phone, wondering who could be making a call
at such a late hour. Curious, he reached for the receiver – then drew his
hand back, not wanting to pry.

'You're not snooping, you're investigating,' he told himself firmly.
'Remember – someone in this castle is a devious bug-planting spy ...
and you need to know who.'

As the second hand of the old Thyme Clock started its final
revolution of the day, Justin lifted the receiver, holding his breath. He
held it to one ear and almost gasped out loud when he heard who was
speaking.

'Wolf-in-Sheep's-Clothing here,' said the familiar voice. 'Listen
carefully: You're right; the old motorbike *must* be the time machine.
Sir Willoughby locked it in his workshop the moment he got back

from Mauritius.'

Justin's mind reeled as he struggled to grasp the painful truth: that someone he'd trusted and respected was, in fact, a vile, rotten traitor. Almost too stunned to process the information, he sank against the desk, hardly aware of the faint mechanical whirring noise behind him as the clockwork figure of Old Father Time gradually drew back his scythe.

'They brought a baby bird back with them,' the voice continued. 'I got a close look at it this evening; it ran right past my nose. I'm fairly sure it's a dodo. So you know what that means? *This* machine *doesn't* alter the traveller's age. He's finally fixed the fault. It's time for the next phase of ...'

DONGGGGG ... DONGGGGG ... DONGGGGG ...

It was the old Thyme Clock striking twelve. Moments too late, Justin clapped his hand over the phone's mouthpiece, but he knew it was futile; any second now the south tower's enormous bell would start chiming, and its deafening clangour couldn't possibly be muffled.

'Got to go,' said the voice. 'Someone's listening.'

Justin heard a click, followed by a peevish buzzing sound. Slowly, as if in a dream, he replaced the receiver, feeling physically sickened by the betrayal. Even without his usual stammering and stuttering, Justin had no problems recognising the voice of his tutor ... Professor Wilfred S Gilbert.

Go Through Time Only When Stationary

Converting a standard road vehicle into a time machine has several advantages. The traveller can conveniently reposition their machine in the present, and will have greater mobility in the past, (as long as they're visiting a time period when motorised vehicles are commonly seen).

However, the chrononaut must NEVER attempt to time-warp whilst moving. Time machines that need to reach high speeds in the present before they can navigate the fourth dimension only exist in fiction.

Because the journey takes a fraction of a second, momentum gained in the present would keep the vehicle moving in the past. Materialising in the unknown is dangerous enough without this added complication, and could result in a serious – possibly fatal – accident.

CHAPTER NINE

Eliza Goes Bananas

That night Justin didn't sleep at all. He lay in bed with his eyes wide open, staring at the ceiling, thoughts zooming round his brain like elementary particles in a hadron collider.

Professor Gilbert – the man who'd taught him more than all his other tutors combined – was a traitor. It seemed impossible, but what other explanation could there possibly be? His soft American accent, nervous twitches and debilitating stammer, were all part of an accomplished act – while the bookish beard and tweedy clothes had disguised him enough to fool even Nanny Verity.

But *had* she been fooled, Justin wondered. Was Professor Gilbert the second spy she'd feared? Or was he Agent X himself? And, if so, could Verity Kiss have known the identity of her ex-husband all along?

Justin tried to reject the idea – but the devoted inscription in Nanny's book of poetry suddenly sprang into his mind, reminding him of something strangely similar: a month ago the professor had dropped a small scrap of paper covered in his spidery handwriting, the last line of which said: "*Do not forget you've married me*". Had *this* message been intended for Nanny Verity too?

After Nanny divorced him, had Agent X skilfully disguised himself as a timid professor and applied for the job of tutor? Was this why he'd warned Nanny that he'd know if she ever tried to double-cross him? And ... was it Professor Gilbert who'd helped her escape?

At first, Justin wanted to believe that his teacher was just a mole, whose job was to report back to Agent X whenever he overheard anything useful – but if he actually *was* X, perhaps tonight's phone call had been to Nanny Verity, telling her how his plans were progressing. Who knows ... perhaps they weren't even divorced.

'Maybe *that's* why Nanny told me not to look for her,' sighed Justin, feeling thoroughly discouraged.

So many questions ... so few answers.

On one point, however, Justin felt slightly reassured. Clearly, Agent X still believed that it was his old colleague, Sir Willoughby, who'd made this latest time machine.

But even *that* seemed odd, Justin decided. If there was one person in the castle who should've guessed that *he* had designed and built the chronopod, then surely it was Professor Gilbert.

Slowly, Justin repeated the professor's exact words: '"*This time machine doesn't alter the traveller's age. He's finally fixed the fault.*"'

Yes, it fitted, Justin thought, suddenly remembering how his father once told him that, whilst testing their prototype, Agent X had almost died. "*Our machine was fatally flawed,*" Sir Willoughby had said. "*Time altered inside the capsule at the same rate as on the outside. The further back he travelled, the younger he became ... until he was just a few months old. Fortunately, although his physical appearance changed, his memory remained intact, so he knew to wait until the automatic safety mode zapped him back to the present. He grew older during the return journey ... but the experience left him so badly traumatised he was afraid to use the time machine again ... unless I could fix it.*"

But Sir Willoughby *hadn't* fixed it ... so Agent X had waited ... and waited ... keeping him under constant surveillance.

Justin frowned, trying to recall the last thing Professor Gilbert said: "*It's time for the next phase of ...*" Of what, Justin wondered; his plan? Would he try to steal the chronopod now he knew it was safe ... or was

141

he planning to abduct Sir Willoughby and force him to fix his original machine?

Either seemed perfectly plausible.

The old tower clock chimed four. Justin groaned, knowing that in an hour's time his alarm would wake him, so he could phone his mother before she left the villa. He closed his eyes and tried to will himself off to sleep – and when that didn't work he tried to relax and empty his mind. But it was useless – he'd never felt *less* relaxed, and one stubborn thought kept swimming round and round his brain like a fish in a bowl: What was he going to do about the professor?

'Don't exaggerate – I'm sure she's not that bad,' groaned Henny. 'Why, the poor woman's not even been with you a full day yet.'

It was nine a.m. in Mauritius, and Lady Henrietta Thyme was just finishing her breakfast. Justin sighed; he could tell his mum was only half listening to him; she was probably learning her script, or jotting notes on her shooting schedule.

'Miss Garnet's been here precisely thirteen hours,' he replied, glancing at his watch. 'Thirteen minutes were enough. She's conned Dad into handing over your tranquilizer gun, and she's threatening to send Eliza to a zoo if we don't behave.'

'I'm sure she's only joking.'

'She wouldn't know a joke if it jumped up and bit her. Last night she confiscated practically all of Robyn's clothes. How's that for funny?'

Justin heard a faint sound, which he hoped *wasn't* a muffled snort of laughter.

'Your sister needs a firm hand,' Henny said. 'And with Nanny Verity still away there's no other choice.'

'But this'll only bring out the worst in her,' Justin continued. 'Look, can't you come home, Mum? You and Robyn need to sort this out before it gets any worse.'

'Sorry, son ... the eggs have just started to hatch. And satellite reports indicate there's a major storm heading straight for Mauritius. Hank and Polly are trying to secure things on the island; I gotta go help them or our equipment could get damaged.'

'But Mum ...'

'Listen up: I get that the new Nanny's a tad strict ... but she's just a temp. If you want Nanny Verity back, the best thing you can do is track down that rotten ex-husband of hers and hand him over to the police.'

Justin sighed. 'Don't worry, Mum ... I'm pretty sure I know who he is now.'

Once he was washed and dressed, Justin decided to head on down to the kitchen, thinking it might be a good idea to rustle up a covert snack before breakfasting with Nanny Evelyn. But first, he decided to stop by the great hall to check if there were any twins on the Thyme family tree.

The old tapestry was rather faded in parts, and its various names and dates not that easy to make out. Realising he'd need as much light as possible, Justin strode across to open the curtains, and tripped over something on the floor beside his father's desk. Whatever it was clattered then made a faint humming noise.

'Flux!' muttered Justin, hopping and rubbing his shin. He fumbled across the desk, snapped the lamp on, and peered down. The telephone lay upended on the floor with the receiver off. Instantly, Justin remembered the abrupt termination of last night's overheard phone call. It looked as if the professor, fearful someone would come to investigate, had knocked it off the desk in his hurry to get out of the room.

After opening the other curtains, and putting the phone back where it belonged, Justin dragged a chair across to the fireplace, and stood on it to get a better look at the tapestry. Carefully, working his way along the branches, he traced his ancestors through several generations, looking for siblings with the same date of birth – but the only twins he found had died almost a century before old Sir Lyall had been born.

Grandpa was certainly a puzzle, Justin thought; at times he seemed so genuine – then he'd say something that simply didn't fit.

143

'No wonder Dad feels confused,' he sighed, stepping down off the chair. 'If it wasn't so clear that Professor Gilbert's the impostor, Grandpa would probably be my main suspect by now.'

The tower clock chimed seven. As Justin stepped into the portrait gallery he heard a loud sneeze, and saw Knightly gliding towards him carrying a teapot on a silver tray.

'Good morning, Master Justin,' he droned as they drew level. 'Breakfast isn't ready yet, but I'm sure Cook can fix you something if you're hungry. I'll set the dining room table as soon as I've taken Sir Willoughby his tea.'

'Wow! Dad's up already?' said Justin, his eyes irresistibly drawn to the glistening dewdrop quivering at the end of Knightly's nose.

'He's ordered the old Rolls to be brought round for nine-thirty,' Knightly explained. He spoke in a hoarse, confidential whisper as if revealing a secret. 'I believe he's planning to take Sir Lyall out for the day. Cook's preparing a picnic.'

'Oh, that reminds me,' said Justin, suddenly remembering what Mrs Kof had told him last night. 'When you interviewed the new nannies, was Miss Garnet ever left on her own?'

If the butler was surprised by the question, he didn't show it; his face remained as bland and impassive as ever. 'There were three applicants,' he said. 'I sat them here in the portrait gallery, then saw them one at a time in the dining room. I called Evelyn Garnet in last, so she would've been unattended for the half hour it took me to interview the second applicant.'

Hmm ... so Mrs Kof was right, Justin thought; Nanny Evelyn *could've* stolen the little pistol. She had a good half hour to snoop – and with the family away, the south and west towers would've been conveniently empty.

'Will that be all?' asked the butler, with an impatient sniff.

'Er, yes – thank you, Knightly.'

Knightly gave a brief, deferential nod, and oozed off to the west tower.

'So, Dad's taking Grandpa out for the day,' Justin murmured to himself. He felt a grim satisfaction at having goaded his father into action. For a moment or two, he wondered whether to tell him about Professor Gilbert's treachery – but decided it could wait. The fact Grandpa was now in the clear didn't relieve Sir Willoughby of his responsibilities; whatever he decided about the old man, the decision *had* to be his alone.

Justin glanced up to his left, realising that, by an uncanny coincidence, he'd stopped directly beneath the gallery's sole portrait of Sir Lyall Austin Thyme. He gazed at it, searching – not for the first time – for any physiognomical similarities to the old man they now called Grandpa. Undeniably, there *was* a certain family resemblance; the line of his nose, perhaps, or the tilt of his right eyebrow – but nothing more substantial.

Hardly surprising given the age difference, thought Justin; the portrait was dated 1951 – nine years before Willoughby had been born – and showed a vigorous young man in his early twenties. Justin always felt it was a picture of a person reluctant to have his portrait painted. There was something about his stance that suggested apprehension, and his eyes had a haunted preoccupied look about them.

Justin had never been able to equate the subject of this painting with Sir Willoughby's descriptions of his father. Young Lyall certainly didn't look like the bold explorer he eventually became. Perhaps his adventures had been a strategy to cope with the loss of a beloved wife and son; a desperate need to escape the tragic memories that surrounded him.

As Justin strode into the entrance hall, he heard voices coming from the kitchen – and to his astonishment, the loudest sounded like Knightly's. Baffled, he crept closer, straining to listen.

'Mr Gilliechattan, the evidence is indisputable,' the voice said. 'Clearly, you forgot to remove your Wellington boots.'

Justin pushed the kitchen door open slightly and put his eye to the crack. He could just see the Gilliechattans and Mrs Kof at the far end of the kitchen. Tybalt the octo-puss was rubbing his head against his mistress's ankles – and Burbage was perched on a fruit bowl, digging his beak into a peach. Unable to see Knightly, Justin eased the door a little further open, but there was no sign of him.

'Honestly, Mrs Kof, I've never been spoken to so rudely,' said Angus Gilliechattan in his booming theatrical voice. 'So I told the old codfish straight.' Then, switching to his fake highland brogue he continued: 'Och, nay ... ye canna pin this on me, Jimmy. A nivva wear ma boots indoors.'

'What did he sayings then?' asked Mrs Kof, chuckling helplessly.

Justin watched as Mr Gilliechattan cleared his throat, stuck his nose in the air and gave a disdainful sniff. His face seemed to change, becoming haughty and sneering, and when he spoke his impersonation of the butler was uncanny: 'So you deny coming into the castle last night, Mr Gilliechattan?' he droned in Knightly's hollow voice. 'When I locked up at eleven, the floor was spotless – look at it now!'

Mrs Kof almost exploded with laughter.

'Aye cairn't see what's soo fanny,' remarked Morag Gilliechattan coldly. 'Angus always takes his boots orf on the bairk dooerstep; he knows what'll hairpen if aye faind mud on my naice clean flooer.'

The gardener nodded vigorously – much to Mrs Kof's amusement.

'Poor Mister Grill-a-kitten,' she chuckled. 'Me sozzy you getting blame for Missiz Kof's footy-mudprints.'

'What?' gasped Mr Gilliechattan.

'Ya, ya ... last night Profiterole Gimlet taking me out walky in Lupin Wood. He showing me where howls nest in big tree. But Missiz Kof all-wiz going everywhere barefeets, so ... cannot takey boot-offs when coming in.'

Burbage raised his sulphur-yellow crest and put his head on one side. '*Tell truth and shame the devil*,' he cackled.

Mr Gilliechattan roared heartily, as if he found the whole misunderstanding a huge joke ... but his little wife seemed distinctly put out, and glared at the muddy marks with her lips pinched tightly together.

'As if I doon't have enough worrk to doo,' she grumbled.

'No worrits! Missiz Kof cleanings it later,' replied the cook, waving her concerns aside with an enormous hand. 'And I telling Mr Nightie they is my footy-prints. Now ... you want I makes you hot coffees and toasty before I gets bizzy?'

The housekeeper, looking reasonably mollified, thanked Mrs Kof politely and settled herself at the kitchen table. 'Aye, corfee would be nayce,' she agreed.

Once they were munching their hot buttered toast, Justin opened the door fully and strode into the kitchen, hoping they wouldn't guess he'd been eavesdropping. In no time at all Mrs Kof was telling him about her owl-watching trip with the professor.

'It very darkly,' she said. 'But he showings me many nice howls by mooning.'

'What time was that?' asked Justin, trying to keep his voice casual as he reached for a slice of toast.

'Most lately. We outgoing at huff-past eleven and come backs about tooth-hurty.'

'But that's impossible!'

'No, no,' laughed Mrs Kof. 'We take plenty sand-wedgies.'

At eight o'clock sharp Mr Gilliechattan donned his boots on the back doorstep and tramped off with his wheelbarrow; Mrs Gilliechattan, (in a surprisingly good mood now), fetched her mop and bucket, assuring Mrs Kof that she didn't mind cleaning the kitchen floor one little bit.

Meanwhile, Mrs Kof packed a huge picnic basket for Sir Willoughby and Grandpa Lyall. She placed it by the pantry door, ready for Knightly to carry out to the old Rolls, then set about making Justin some bacon sandwiches.

Five minutes later Robyn wandered in looking half-asleep.

'Those smell good,' she yawned, swiping one off her brother's plate. 'Thought I'd better come down and grab a quick snack before the dragon woman appears.'

'Me too,' said Justin.

Robyn pulled a chair from beneath the table and flumped down onto it.

'Hey, you don't think Dad's put a stop on my credit card, do you?' she asked, rubbing her eyes.

'It doesn't seem very likely ... but I guess it's not impossible. Why?'

'Last night I couldn't get a single website to accept payment,' mumbled Robyn through a mouthful of sandwich. 'And I *know* I got the number right.'

'Weird,' said Justin. 'Shall I ask him?'

'No way! I wouldn't give him the satisfaction! I'll phone the credit card company later on. Or I might ...'

She stopped. They both heard the sound of brisk footsteps marching across the entrance hall.

'Quick ... it's Sergeant Major Garnet,' hissed Robyn, grabbing a couple more bacon sandwiches. 'Let's go.'

They scurried out onto the back step and pulled the door to behind them, leaving a gap just wide enough to peep through.

Nanny Evelyn stalked into the kitchen looking grumpier than ever. After dumping Albion in his highchair, she pounced on Justin's abandoned plate, pressed a few crumbs onto her fingertips and sniffed them like a forensic expert. Her eyes flashed towards the back door, but Mrs Kof stepped in front of it, grinning.

'Good mornay, Nanny Evil. Diddle you sleeps well?'

'Too well,' snapped Miss Garnet. 'I've got the most *ghastly* headache.'

'You sittings down. Missiz Kof making you special pick-up potion,' the cook insisted. 'Ya, ya ... is just the thing for a rotten haddock!'

Turning her back to Nanny Evelyn, she took an electric blender out of a cupboard and plugged it in. After filling it with two raw eggs, a dozen prunes, a dash of vinegar, a big glob of molasses, some cod-liver oil and a heaped teaspoon of cayenne pepper, she whisked them together then poured the concoction into a large tumbler. With a sly wink in the direction of the back door, she handed the glass to Miss Garnet.

'Best you hold nosey and drinkings in one big guzzle,' Mrs Kof advised her.

'Oh, righto,' said Nanny. 'Bottoms up!'

148

She gulped down the mixture, slammed the tumbler on the table and shuddered. For a moment or two she just sat there, silently gasping like a stranded fish. Then, clutching her stomach, she leapt to her feet and hurtled out of the kitchen, setting a new unofficial world record for the hundred metre sprint.

'Bottoms up indeedy!' chuckled Mrs Kof. 'That should keeps her bizzy-whizzy!'

Justin and Robyn ran through the arched garden gate, across the clifftop and down the stone steps to the lochside, laughing all the way.

'That was brilliant!' said Justin, as they walked to the end of the jetty. He and Robyn sat side by side, their feet dangling just above the water, and munched their bacon sandwiches, confident that even if Nanny Evelyn did emerge from the nursery bathroom and peer through a window, she wouldn't be able to see them.

They gazed out across Loch Ness, watching the pale morning sunlight melt the wraithlike swirls of mist shimmering across its glistening glassy surface.

Between mouthfuls of hastily-swallowed sandwich, Justin told his sister about Professor Gilbert's midnight telephone call, expecting her to gloat that she'd suspected him all along.

'I don't believe it,' she said – then seeing her brother's sceptical expression added: 'No ... *really* .. I just don't buy it. He can't be Agent X – he's got less backbone than a jellyfish. He can scarcely string two words together without getting his tongue in a knot.'

'Well, he wasn't stammering on the phone,' said Justin. 'I guess it's all part of his act.'

'Sorry, but I'd *know* if he was acting,' Robyn insisted. 'His ears go bright pink when he can't get his words out. You can f-f-f-fake a stutter, but you *can't* blush on cue.'

Justin gave an exasperated sigh. 'Look, I heard him ... okay? Although, oddly enough, Mrs Kof claims she and the prof were out owl-watching at midnight; I can't think why she's lying for him.'

'Maybe she isn't. I mean ... *owl-watching*!' groaned Robyn, rolling her eyes. 'If I was going to lie for someone, I'd come up with something a bit more convincing than *that*!'

'Well, you're the expert,' said Justin, dodging a punch on the arm. 'So who do you think our impostor is? Grandpa?'

'No ... Mrs Kof,' replied Robyn decisively.

Justin almost laughed – then, seeing his sister's indignant glare, hurriedly enquired why.

'Because I really suspect Knightly,' explained Robyn. 'And it's always the person you don't suspect.'

'That sounds like something Nanny Verity would say,' Justin chuckled. 'Perhaps you can suggest an equally logical explanation for the prof's telephone call?'

Robyn frowned pensively. 'Hmm ... maybe Mrs Kof persuaded him to do it as a joke,' she said slowly. 'Yeah, that's it. She'll probably bump him off before he can reveal the truth, then forge a suicide note confessing he's X.'

'Seriously?'

'Nah ... not really.' She gazed across the loch for a moment or two, chewing her thumbnail. 'Actually, my gut feeling is that Xavier Polydorus is X. I suppose Mrs Kof *could* be his spy. They were both circus performers.'

'Hey, that reminds me: I'll have to phone Mr P if we're going to visit him this afternoon,' said Justin. 'I do wish you hadn't opened Polly's letter.'

'Don't worry; I can easily forge his handwriting on a new envelope,' Robyn promised him. 'Old Mr Polydorus'll never guess.'

Justin yawned. 'Last night I was convinced Professor Gilbert's our man; now I don't know *what* to think. Maybe if I'd had a decent night's sleep everything would seem clearer ... but I'm so tired my brain hurts!'

'Well, don't tell Mrs Kof you've got a haddock,' laughed Robyn. 'Anyway, what were you doing all night? Deciphering Nanny's old poetry book?'

'I gave it a good couple of hours,' Justin sighed, looking unusually dejected. 'But you were right .... there's nothing!'

'Mmm ... maybe.'

Justin glanced at her sharply. 'What do you mean, *maybe*?'

'I've been thinking. Perhaps the *poem* isn't the *message*.'

'Go on.'

'After you mentioned it yesterday, I googled "*book code key*",' Robyn explained. 'Turns out that years ago spies used to send long strings of numbers to each other – both using the same book as their code-key. The numbers were usually ...'

'Page, line and word numbers,' murmured Justin. '*That's* why Nanny left her key on the book ... to tell us it's the code-key. Nice work, Bobs!'

Robyn grinned. 'We've not cracked it yet; we still need to find a coded message made entirely of numbers.'

'Hmmm ... there was nothing like that in Nanny's room.'

'Then it must be in the nursery,' said Robyn.

'But where?'

'Well, if *I* was Nanny I wouldn't've hidden it someplace hard to find ... I'd've left it right out in the open where everyone can see it.'

At first, Justin thought this sounded like more back-to-front logic – then he suddenly realised Robyn was absolutely right; this was *exactly* what Nanny Verity would have done. '*Hunt the Thimble*!' he gasped. 'Do you remember ... when we were little?'

'Of course! Nanny V used to sit in the nursery rocking chair, sewing – and we couldn't find the thimble anywhere ... no matter how hard we searched.'

Justin laughed as the memory came flooding back. 'Yeah ... the only place we *never* looked was right on the end of her finger!'

Miss Garnet did not come down to breakfast. She sent a note with Knightly explaining that she was temporarily indisposed, and instructing Robyn to care for Baby Thyme as part of that morning's *Domestic Responsibilities* lesson.

'I've even got a timetable,' Robyn explained, seeing her brother's questioning glance. She slid it across the dining table to him.

151

'*Manners and Deportment*,' he read, struggling to keep a straight face. '*Rules of Etiquette ... Ladylike Accomplishments*. Why, I do declare, Miss Thyme, it is a truth universally acknowledged that young ladies can never be too accomplished!'

'Shut it, Dustbin! You've no idea what a psycho that woman is. She's says I have to practice needlework, and insists I always use a proper lace handkerchief. She's even confiscated my mobile. Honestly, I might as well live in the past!'

'Well, at least we're not on starvation rations with her out of the way,' said Justin, as Knightly dished out two large helpings of eggs Benedict. He glanced at the empty chair at the head of the table and frowned, wondering if his father was trying to avoid him. 'Where's everyone else this morning?'

'Sir Lyall and Sir Willoughby breakfasted in their respective rooms half an hour ago,' Knightly informed him. 'They want to be away by nine-thirty sharp.'

Robyn sighed. 'I suppose I'd better fetch Alby then; is he still in the kitchen?'

'You'll be pleased to hear that Cook has persuaded the gorilla to take care of Master Albion this morning; they should be along shortly.'

Sure enough, moments later Eliza strolled in with Albion clinging to her neck – both of them looking decidedly grumpy.

'Phew, that lets me off the hook,' said Robyn, pretending to mop her brow.

'I believe the ape drove a hard bargain,' Knightly whispered. 'Cook had to promise her a dozen banana fritters with toffee sauce and fudge sprinkles.'

By the time breakfast was over, it was clear that Eliza had, quite literally, got the sticky end of the bargain. Albion stubbornly refused to eat his porridge, and whenever Eliza handed him a piece of banoffee fritter he hurled it right back in her face, chortling impishly until the poor gorilla's patience was tested to the limit. Spying trouble on the horizon, Robyn quietly excused herself and melted away from the table, murmuring something about having to feed Haggis. Eliza glared at her scurrying out of the dining room and blew a long, loud raspberry.

Justin, meanwhile, wandered into the entrance hall, checking his watch to see if there was time to phone Mr Polydorus before the mail van arrived. He dialled the number Polly had given him, and waited – then, just as he was about to put the receiver down, he heard a deep mesmerising voice say: 'Xavier Polydorus here, mind-reader extraordinaire. Don't tell me who's calling – let *me* tell *you*!'

Justin laughed ... then waited quietly.

'I sense you are calling from a large old building,' the voice continued. 'I'm getting a distinct water vibe ... you live close to a river ... no, a Scottish loch ... Loch Ness ... and you're phoning from inside a castle. Am I speaking to Master Justin Thyme?'

'That's amazing!' said Justin. 'Or does your phone have *Caller ID* by any chance?'

Xavier Polydorus gave a deep chocolaty chuckle. 'Drat ... you sussed me! I recognised your number as soon as it came up, and couldn't resist a little joke. I know your mum's away, of course – and I ruled your father and sister out the instant I heard you laugh.'

'Sounds as if mind-reading's a lot like being a detective,' said Justin. 'I wonder if you can work out why I'm phoning.'

There was a long pause. 'Hmm ... you're planning a charity gala to launch one of your latest inventions, and you want the world's best illusionist and mind-reader to entertain your clients.'

'Nice try, Mr P. Actually, Polly asked me to bring a letter back for you. I was wondering if Robyn and I could call round with it later on.'

'Great!' said Mr Polydorus, sounding suddenly excited. 'How about coming for afternoon tea?'

'Thanks. What time?'

'Be here by four o'clock ... and prepare to be *AMAZED!*'

As Justin put the phone down, he heard footsteps behind him, and turned to see his father helping Grandpa Lyall across the entrance hall.

Sir Willoughby strode to the castle door then, after opening it, peered uncertainly at the sky.

'Now, have you got your umbrella?' he asked – but noticing the old man's vague expression, muttered, 'Oh, never mind. Knightly, leave that basket for a minute – cut along upstairs and get Sir Lyall's Macintosh, will you?'

'Right away, Sir.'

Knightly, who had been struggling with the enormous picnic basket Mrs Kof had prepared, left it in the middle of the hall floor and traipsed up the north tower stairs, rubbing his back.

After settling Grandpa Lyall in the car, Willoughby stepped indoors and drew Justin to one side, speaking to him in a hushed voice. 'I thought I'd take the old man to a few of your grandpa's favourite haunts ... see if they trigger any memories.' There was a slight aloofness to his tone, as if he resented explaining himself. 'I've got a couple of his highland journals, so I can check any details,' he added, patting his jacket pocket. 'We might even drive by the foot of Ben Nevis, in case he remembers anything about the avalanche; it's a long shot ... but you never know.'

Justin nodded solemnly, trying to think of a supportive reply that wouldn't sound patronising. 'That sounds great, Dad ... I hope everything goes well.'

Sir Willoughby looked directly into his son's eyes and took a deep breath, as if he was about to say something else – then, giving an odd little half-shrug-half-shake-of-the-head, he seemed to change his mind, and muttered: 'Where's that dratted butler got to?'

They waited, side by side, shuffling their feet and making comments about the weather until Knightly returned. Meanwhile, Eliza deposited Albion on a tartan rug, and prowled off to fetch his pushchair from the cloakroom – but as soon as he was alone, Alby hauled himself upright and staggered towards the open door.

Hearing his unsteady footsteps, Eliza turned back and settled him on the rug again. Frowning this time, she prodded his chest with a big black finger then tapped the rug firmly and grunted. Justin could sense her frustration, and silently cursed Nanny Evelyn for taking her laptop.

Albion gave the gorilla one of his cherubic smiles. But the moment Eliza's back was turned, he rose to his feet and toddled across the floor a second time.

'Pag-nik!' he chuckled, reaching for the wicker picnic basket.

Roaring angrily, Eliza raced over to him on all fours – then, to his horror, Justin saw his little brother toppling backwards, crashing into a suit of armour with a harsh metallic *CLUNKKK!* Instantly, the sound of his screaming filled the entrance hall – and Eliza, looking deeply troubled, backed off, shaking her head.

'Great Scott!' exclaimed Sir Willoughby, dashing over to his baby son and scooping him up off the floor. 'Did she hit him?'

'Of course not!' But even as the words flew out of his mouth, Justin realised he couldn't be certain. It had all happened so quickly – and the speed Albion had flown through the air hadn't looked like an accidental tumble.

Justin turned to face Eliza. Her dark brow was deeply furrowed and her lips were pursed in an unhappy pout. Swaying from side to side, she edged slowly forwards, making soft *hoo-hoo-hoo* noises and reaching out to the baby with the back of one hand – but, seeing her, Albion screamed louder than ever, burying his face against his father's chest.

'Nanny Evelyn was right,' Willoughby growled, shooing Eliza away. 'Damned creature's becoming a liability.' Then, glancing round the entrance hall, he asked: 'Where *is* the wretched woman, anyway?'

'In her room, I think; she's not too well this morning,' Justin explained.

Sir Willoughby made several exasperated huffing and tutting noises as he paced back and forth, jiggling Albion. 'Dash it all ... I've a good mind to cancel my outing.'

'Don't worry, Dad ... Robyn and I can look after Alby until Nanny feels better. I know how important it is for you to settle things with ... with Grandpa.'

Sir Willoughby dithered indecisively by the castle door. He looked down at Albion, whose crying had now subsided to the occasional muffled sob, then peered outside at Grandpa Lyall, waiting in the back the old Rolls Royce.

He exhaled forcefully, shaking his head. '*Aarrghhh*! You're right, son – I've *got* to find out who that old chap *really* is ... and I can't delay it any longer; there's too much at stake.' With a regretful grimace he handed the baby to Justin. 'Now, listen,' he said sternly. 'The minute we've gone, take Alby straight up to the nursery ... and don't let that blasted ape anywhere near him. Furthermore, I want you to tell Nanny Evelyn to keep her tranquilizer gun loaded and ready at all times. If that ... that *creature* ... so much as frowns at my little son, she has my permission to use it. Understand?'

For a moment, Justin stared mutely at his father, too shocked by the sudden turn of events to speak. He didn't want to agree ... but what choice was there? After all, he knew he'd never forgive himself if anything happened to Albion.

'Yes, Dad ... I understand,' he whispered. He glanced back at Eliza, cowering at the foot of the east tower staircase with her head in her hands, hoping she hadn't heard. But the look of sorrow in her eyes made Justin feel as if he'd betrayed a lifelong friend.

Sir Willoughby turned briskly on his heels and marched out to the Rolls, his feet scrunching across the gravel. He paused by the car door, checking his mobile phone.

'Call me if there's a problem,' he said. 'One more incident like that and I'll hire a truck and take that ruddy gorilla to the zoo myself!'

156

dentify a Safe Place to Materialise

The time traveller should always aim to materialise in the past somewhere free of humans. Apart from the obvious risk of discovery if their sudden appearance is witnessed, they would want to avoid fatally injuring any innocent passers-by.

Again, careful research is the key. Perhaps you may learn of an abandoned building that has been uninhabited for several decades – or, better still, a remote cave that has remained unaltered for centuries.

If you go back to a time and place you remember well, you might already know of somewhere you will not be disturbed. However, if you travel further back, try to find a secluded spot; a lonely graveyard at midnight would probably be a safe destination.

CHAPTER TEN

The Xtraordinary Xavier

As the tower clock struck nine-thirty, Justin stood at the castle door, watching Grandpa's ruby-coloured vintage Rolls Royce sweep slowly round the courtyard.

Enigma – as the car was affectionately known – had spent the last thirteen years covered in dustsheets. According to Sir Willoughby, the old Rolls had been his father's one extravagance – and as a boy he'd only been allowed inside it on *very* special occasions. Justin thought that even now he didn't look entirely at his ease behind the wheel, and noticed him shooting wary glances at Sir Lyall through his rear-view mirror. Grandpa, however, seemed oblivious, and gazed out of the window wearing a bemused smile.

Justin stared at the Rolls' distinctive number plate – **EN19MA** – as it purred sedately through the castle archway, disappearing into the shadows. Seconds later, he heard the genteel *parp-parp* of its old-fashioned horn, followed by the answering toot of a less dignified vehicle. Then Jock's shiny red mail van trundled into the courtyard and crunched to a halt beside the castle doorstep. Its door creaked open, and Fergus bounced out, scampering over to Justin to demand his daily stick of rock.

Albion shivered. Hearing the little dog's ferocious-sounding bark, he clung tightly to his older brother – eyes wide, bottom lip quivering.

Meanwhile, Jock McRosie clambered out of the van, muttering one of his usual stock phrases – but seeing Albion's puckered little face, he stopped abruptly, peering at him with genuine concern. Behind his spectacles, the corners of his eyes crinkled sympathetically – then, for the first time in more than a year, he said something completely different: 'Is everything okay, little chap?' he whispered, reaching forward and gently rubbing Alby's tearstained cheek with one finger.

Albion brightened immediately, and gave the postman one of his dimpliest smiles.

'Lattah!' he chuckled, sticking his thumb in the air.

'Later?' asked Jock, with a questioning look at Justin.

Justin laughed. 'No ... *letter*, I think.' He pointed to the wad of envelopes in Jock's right hand. 'Alby's probably hoping you've brought one for *him*.'

Unaccustomed to normal conversation, and now getting visibly embarrassed, Jock reverted to his usual monosyllabic reply. 'Aye,' he muttered, thrusting the mail awkwardly into Justin's hands. He climbed hurriedly back in the van, whistling for Fergus – but the little dog followed Justin into the castle.

'Sorry Fergus, I almost forgot,' said Justin, hurrying over to the hall table and taking a stick of Edinburgh rock out of the middle draw. The Scottie trotted after him, his claws tick-tacking across the stone floor. He sat up on his hind legs, whining impatiently – then, after catching it in midair, raced back outside to his master.

Even before Justin had time to close the drawer, he heard the mail van's engine start up, and its tires churning the gravel as Jock accelerated out of the courtyard.

With Albion still nestled in the crook of one arm, Justin flipped awkwardly through the envelopes. The few that were not addressed to him he left on the hall table beneath the old glass paperweight; the rest he stuffed into his pocket – although one envelope looked so alarmingly thick he decided to open it immediately.

It was Robyn's credit card bill. Since becoming Britain's youngest self-made multimillionaire, Justin had paid this like he paid everything else. *No problem*. But today he had to admit the total at the end of the third page made him gulp.

'Flux!' he gasped. Then, grinning at Albion, he added: 'If shopping ever becomes an Olympic event, your sister could win gold, silver *and* bronze.'

Returning the bill to its envelope, he remembered how Robyn had told him that her online payments had been rejected last night. Of course, she'd conveniently forgotten to mention spending nearly three times her authorised credit limit. No wonder the card company had frozen her account.

Before taking his brother up to the nursery, Justin felt compelled to say something to Eliza. He guessed that her frustration with Albion was partly because she longed to have a baby gorilla of her own – but he also knew that sending her to a zoo wasn't the answer.

Henny had promised to help Eliza find a mate as soon as her Mauritian assignment was over. However, previous gorilla blind-dates had been disastrous. When introduced to prospective boyfriends, Eliza always seemed dismayed by their primitive communication, asking why they didn't have computers. After a lifetime of laptops, internet access and cable TV, she had little in common with them – yet despite her unique upbringing, she could never feel fully integrated with the human world either.

Justin was disappointed his father had been so ready to dismiss her as an "unwanted pet" at the first sign of trouble. Okay, she'd lost her temper – but surely everyone deserved a second chance. Clearly, it was the loss of her laptop that had pushed her over the edge; finding herself limited to grunts and gestures, while surrounded by humans who couldn't understand them, must've been exasperating.

With his mother away, Justin knew it was up to him to put things right. Like it or not, it was another responsibility he'd have to shoulder.

He glanced at the dark alcove beneath the east tower staircase where Eliza had tried to hide herself. She was hunched over, swaying to and fro, making soft little grunts of despair. Moved with pity, Justin walked towards her, not the least bit afraid. Hearing his advancing footsteps, the gorilla looked up, and instantly Albion started to whimper and squirm.

'Don't worry, Alby,' Justin whispered. 'Eliza won't hurt you.' He stepped back slowly, giving the baby a reassuring squeeze. Once Albion had settled, he spoke again: 'I'll sort this out, somehow, Eliza ... I promise. But for now, I think it's best if you keep upstairs out of everyone's way.'

The gorilla grunted irritably and banged the floor several times with her knuckles.

'Calm down, Eliza,' Justin continued. 'Look, I won't tell Nanny Evelyn. I know you didn't mean to hit Alb—.'

The rest of his words were drowned by a thunderous roar as Eliza rose suddenly to her full height, beating her chest and baring her teeth. Justin felt a warm wetness seeping through Albion's nappy. Remembering how his mother had told him that wild gorillas felt threatened by direct eye contact, he stared at the ground and edged away, murmuring, 'It's okay, Eliza ... it's okay,' over and over again, while his heart pounded like a pneumatic jackhammer.

But the more Justin tried to reason with her, the more agitated Eliza became. Finally, unable to suppress her feelings a moment longer, she picked up the nearest suit of armour, and dashed it against the panelled wall. Then, with another almighty roar, she bounded up the east tower staircase to her room.

Drawn by the commotion, Knightly came running out of the dining room, and Mrs Gilliechattan rushed down the north tower stairs with Tybalt scurrying after her. Mrs Kof peered anxiously round the kitchen door, wiping her hands on her apron.

'Good gravy! What's harpooning?' she called. 'I thinkings a bum is exploded.'

Justin trudged up the west tower, feeling thoroughly despondent. He'd never seen Eliza get so angry before, and wondered if Albion had been lucky to get away with nothing worse than a small bump on the

161

head. Still, he seemed his usual placid self again now Eliza was out of the way.

'Remember,' Justin told him, as he crept across the landing. 'If Nanny asks, we'll say you fell over Tybalt.'

'Tyb!' chuckled Albion.

'That's right.'

The nursery was empty – and judging from the reverberating blasts and groans echoing from the second floor bathroom, Nanny Evelyn would be bizzy-whizzy for the foreseeable future.

'Better change you, I suppose,' Justin sighed. He settled Albion on the nursery rug, then fetched the chamomile bottiwipes, some talcum powder and a fresh nappy.

Five minutes later Alby was crawling round his playpen, gurgling happily – while Justin, taking full advantage of Miss Garnet's absence, decided to search the nursery, hoping to find Nanny Verity's coded message.

'Strings of numbers ... strings of numbers ...' he muttered, casting around the room.

If Robyn's suggestion was correct, Nanny V had probably left her message somewhere right out in the open. But where? The room was full of toys.

What about Alby's building blocks, he thought. They had a different letter or number on each side; perhaps Nan had arranged them in a special sequence. He knelt to examine the stack of brightly-coloured wooden bricks, but realised Albion must have played with them at least a dozen times since Verity Kiss had left.

Then, straightening up, Justin caught sight of the nursery notice board and, instantly, he knew that *this* was where the code *had* to be hidden. The cork panel was covered in all manner of oddments, some of which had been pinned there for several years: postcards, a calendar, magazine clippings, knitting patterns, a list of phone numbers, two of Albion's finger-paintings, a recipe for *Verity K's Real Bean-Bread*, some long-forgotten homework in Justin's own handwriting, and an origami bird Robyn had made when she was five.

'It's got to be the phone numbers,' Justin whispered, prising the pin out with his thumbnail. He frowned at the small rectangular card, wishing he had time to fetch Nanny's old poetry book and start decoding the message right away.

Dentist: 1854 - 8518189147
Doctor: 6112195 - 20181912
Hospital: 4514 - 5144
Playschool: 1415 - 31221519 - 85185
F.L.U.F.F. 201825 - 171914

But it was almost five minutes to ten; there was scarcely enough time for him to collect his homework and dash to the schoolroom. Justin tucked the card inside his shirt pocket, and crouched beside Albion's playpen.

'I'll have to go, Alby,' he said. 'Will you be okay until Nanny Evelyn appears?'

Albion put his head on one side, and placed a small, chubby finger on his dimpled chin. 'Det sissa!' he said, giving his brother a beguiling grin.

Justin laughed. 'Okay ... I'll get your sister. Maybe she'll let you play with Haggis.'

He hurried out of the nursery and ran up the west tower, yelling for Robyn. Seeing her amble out of her bedroom with the little doddling under one arm, Justin quickly brought her up to speed on events since breakfast, and asked her to keep an eye on Alby.

Robyn pulled a face. 'I was just going to call about my credit card, but Nanny Evelyn's got my mobile.'

'No need to bother. Though you might want to contact *Shopaholics Anonymous*,' teased Justin, handing her the bill. 'Don't worry ... I'll wire payment through later; that'll sort it. Shall I ask them to raise your credit limit, or are you all shopped-out now?'

Robyn's eyebrows flew up as she scanned the first page. 'Crud-

163

crumpets! I've not spent all *that*! Someone must've cloned my card.'

'Flux!' exclaimed Justin, reaching into his pocket. 'Looks like you'd better phone them after all. Here ... borrow mine.'

Five minutes later Justin was racing round his laboratory gathering his homework. High in the rafters, the tower clock's striking mechanism had already started to turn; he could hear the fluttering whirr of a fly fan as the hammer drew back above the old bronze bell. After grabbing Euclid's "*Elements*" and his geometry notebook, he hurtled through the lab door, letting it slam shut behind him. From experience Justin knew that if he ran like the clappers along the upper corridor, he could reach the schoolroom a split-second before the tenth chime rang out.

As he panted up the north stairs, he could hear Professor Gilbert singing: '*Hark, the hour of ten is sounding,*' and arrived to find him hovering by the door, tapping his watch. Justin dashed into the schoolroom and skidded behind his desk.

'Made it!'

'I'd be tempted to say *just in time*, if it wasn't your least favourite joke,' laughed the professor.

Justin groaned silently, masking it with a polite smile. He'd never liked his name, but right now that was the least of his worries. All night long he'd been wondering what he'd say to his tutor – and now that they were facing each other, he was still at a loss for words.

Fortunately, Professor Gilbert didn't notice, and spent the next half hour drawing complex geometric diagrams on the whiteboard, comparing ancient Euclidian theory to modern mathematics. His voice was passionate and animated, and when he glanced at his pupil his dark eyes sparkled with enthusiasm.

Somehow, Justin had expected him to be rather subdued after coming so close to getting caught. To find him so uncharacteristically cheerful seemed odd – but perhaps he thought it best to brazen things out, relying on the alibi he'd arranged with Mrs Kof. Determined to wrong foot him, Justin listened carefully to the professor's monologue,

164

waiting for an opportunity.

'Yet despite being one of history's most influential mathematicians, we know nothing about Euclid the man,' concluded the professor, without any sign of his usual stammer. 'There's no record of his birth ... or death ... and his personal life is unknown.'

'Does it really matter, sir,' asked Justin, spying a potential opening.

'Maybe not. But aren't you at all curious about the personality behind that *incredible* intellect? Haven't you ever wondered what his hobbies were? Whether he liked music, perhaps? Or if he had a wife and children? Trivial I know ... but ...'

'I suppose it *would* be fascinating,' said Justin. 'Actually, he rather reminds me of you, sir. You've lived here at Thyme Castle for over two-and-a-half years ... yet I know even less about you than Euclid!'

'W-w-well, you know I like opera and or-or-orrr-ornithology,' stammered the professor. His eyes had lost their twinkle and now had the glazed look of a cornered rabbit. 'Any-w-way, I'm of no in-in-in-interest. But Euclid ...'

'Oh, but you *are*,' said Justin, wishing he didn't feel *quite* so uncomfortable. 'I've often wondered if *you* were married ... or had a family, or ... or ...' He took a deep breath. '... Or *anything*! But you've never said *a word*.'

Looking directly at his tutor, Justin waited, steeling himself not to weaken. Meanwhile, the professor sank behind his desk, twiddling nervously with his bowtie. He appeared to be sinking into a deep depression, and had the wilted look of a delicate plant that had been doused in weed-killer.

'I ... I ... I'm ...' His eyes flickered closed as he tried to speak, but the words stubbornly refused to come.

Justin felt sick. Last night he'd been convinced his tutor's stammer was an act – now he wasn't so sure. And probing into the professor's personal life seemed horribly insensitive. He watched Gilbert clench his fists and fill his lungs with air, knowing that when speech became impossible, singing opera was the only way he could relax his vocal chords and loosen his tongue.

'Ah ... a-a-ahh ... "*Alone, and yet alive!*"'he sang. '"*Remote the peace *that death alone can give. My doom, to wait! My punishment, to live!*'"

Justin stared down at his desktop, cheeks burning with embarrass-ment. Part of him wished he'd never put Professor Gilbert on the spot – whilst another part wondered if this was some clever ruse to avoid answering questions. But before he could decide, the professor, wearing a defeated expression, spoke again.

'You w-w-want to know about my w-w-wife and f-family,' he stuttered. 'The f-fact is ...'

The schoolroom door crashed open and Robyn stormed in, her eyes blazing. Professor Gilbert glanced up at her, and from his puzzled expression Justin could tell that, for a moment, he didn't recognise her. And no wonder. With her hair in plaits, wearing a long grey smock, and devoid of all makeup ... she bore little resemblance to the lip-glossed psychedelic rock-chick he knew so well.

'IT'S YOU!' yelled Robyn, slamming her brother's mobile phone in front of him. 'It has to be. And all this time I thought you were on *my* side.'

'Excuse us a moment, Professor,' Justin muttered, grabbing his sister's arm and dragging her out of the schoolroom. He waited until the door clicked shut, then hissed: 'What's this about?'

Robyn shook her arm free, and gave Justin one of her best scowls. 'I just phoned the card company; the excessive spending – all online, apparently – triggered an automatic card-freeze in case my account details had been stolen. But *I* think *you're* behind it.'

'That's crazy!' said Justin, suddenly angry. 'What's the point of me using your credit card? It's *me* that pays the bill!'

'I suspect you've got your reasons,' snapped Robyn.

'Such as?'

'You're in league with Mum and Dad ... doing what they say like a good little boy. Once they realised confiscating my card didn't work as a punishment, they asked for your help – and you devised a way to freeze my account instead.'

'But ...'

'Only *you* could think up something so brilliant, only *you* could fund it ... and only *you* have my account details,' she concluded, waving the credit card bill in her brother's face.

Justin gave a short humourless laugh. 'I'm flattered. But I'd need more than your card number to do *that*; I'd have to know your username and passwords. And clearly you didn't notice the date all these purchases began.'

Robyn glared at him, but before she could reply, Justin continued:

'No? I thought not. They started weeks ago ... long before you and Mum fell out. So this has *nothing* to do with them taking your card.'

'*Fffuhhh*! You think this is about one measly credit card?' yelled Robyn. 'Think again, little brother! When I finished phoning, I went online to check my bank account ... and it's been emptied. Every last penny *completely* and *utterly SWIPED*! They claim *I* transferred it to another account. Which I haven't. So who could it be? Personally, I think it'd take a genius to pull *that* off.'

After a long silence Justin shook his head sadly. 'Surely you don't think I'd steal from my own sister? And I'd *never* side with Mum and Dad against *you*. I thought you *knew* that.'

Robyn folded her arms and shrugged her head.

'Well, I can't prove it, but take *my* credit card,' said Justin, taking out his wallet. 'Here ... spend whatever you want; I won't tell them.' He leaned forward and slid his platinum card into Robyn's top pocket. 'Look, Bobs, I give you my word I'll get to the bottom of this – and if I can't, I'll open a new account for you, and replace whatever's been stolen.' Then, turning silently, he stepped back inside the schoolroom and closed the door.

Professor Gilbert was standing beside the window, gazing distract-edly across the loch. Several seconds passed before he appeared to realise he was no longer alone, although Justin knew he must've heard every single word of Robyn's accusation. At length, he turned to face his pupil.

'Now, w-w-where were we?' he said, his manner artificially brisk and breezy. 'Ah, yes ... the geometrical pattern in Ulam spirals – is it a meaningful design or ra-ra-random chance?'

By some unspoken agreement neither student nor teacher acknowledged the abrupt change of subject. Instead, Justin replied with

167

a forced brightness, sensing that as long as he didn't ask any more awkward personal questions the professor would tactfully forget all he had overheard.

As the lesson continued, Justin's thoughts kept wandering – and judging from his faraway expression, he guessed the professor's did too – but neither deviated from their dusty academic theories. After analysing prime spirals they discussed patterns in chaos, then argued about the difference between golden and Fibonacci spirals – until fifty-five minutes later they heard the tower clock chime twelve and Professor Gilbert, looking decidedly relieved, suggested breaking early for lunch.

Justin trickled downstairs, hoping he wouldn't bump into anyone; he wasn't sure his digestive system could cope with any more drama.

The dining room was empty – and as it was such a fine, warm day, Mrs Kof had left sandwiches, redcurrant cheesecake and a jug of homemade lemonade on the sideboard.

After about five minutes, Robyn appeared, looking as sombre as her outfit. She helped herself to a sandwich and glanced sheepishly at her brother as she sat down. Relieved that her anger seemed to have dissipated, Justin gave her a friendly grin and asked if Albion was okay.

'Yeah, he's fine,' Robyn muttered. 'But Nanny Evelyn's still feeling a bit dodgy, so they're staying in the nursery. I sneaked off when Knightly came up with a tray.' She slid Justin's credit card across the table. 'Thanks, but I didn't use it,' she said – then, after hesitating for a moment, took a deep breath and whispered: 'Look, Dustbin ... I er ... what I'm trying to say is ... I'm sorry I yelled at you. I know you wouldn't *really* side against me ... or take my money.'

'I wouldn't dare,' said Justin, giving her an amiable punch on the arm. 'So, you're still coming to visit Mr Polydorus with me?'

'Absolutely! Are we taking Mum's boat?'

'No. The old Brown house doesn't have a jetty, just a narrow shingle beach... so I asked the prof if we could borrow his dinghy.'

'You're planning to row us?' laughed Robyn. 'You? Geek-of-the-week?'

Justin shrugged. 'How hard can it be?'

Altogether too hard, Justin silently admitted to himself, as he sculled "*The Manxman*" towards the shore.

From across Thyme Bay he could hear the distant chime of the old tower clock echoing over the loch. Four o'clock already. Determined to row the last few metres without another jibe from his sister, Justin gritted his teeth, and tried to ignore her infuriating smirk. He knew Robyn had been itching to snatch the oars off him for the last ten minutes at least.

'Shame your arms aren't as well-exercised as your brain,' she said.

'Shame you look like a Victorian scullery maid,' replied Justin.

Robyn glared at him. When Nanny Evelyn had heard they were going out for afternoon tea, she'd insisted that Robyn wore something "modest and ladylike". Dressed in a white smock tied over a long charcoal dress, striped grey socks, plain black shoes, and with her hair tucked beneath a white ribbon, Justin thought she looked like a monochrome version of Alice in Wonderland.

Once ashore, they dragged the professor's dinghy up onto the shingle, and hurried towards the old house Mr Polydorus had rented for the summer.

Number 99, Thyme Bay Road, was a large grey building that had probably once been quite grand – but now, with its crumbling stonework covered in a tangle of briar roses, it reminded Justin of a proud old lady hiding her wrinkles beneath a veil.

A tarnished brass sign with the words "*Sub Rosa*" engraved on it had been fastened to the gatepost. As Justin and Robyn walked forwards, the garden gate creaked slowly open before either of them could touch it.

'Probably on a wire,' Justin hissed, hearing his sister's gasp of surprise.

Walking past flowerbeds choked with nettles and thistles, Justin led the way along a weed-covered path to the front door. As he reached for the knocker, it rose of its own accord, then dropped with a reverberating crash that echoed inside the old house.

Curious, Justin peered at it closely – and noticed a near-invisible nylon thread running up to a first floor window. He was just about to show Robyn, when the door started to open. Gradually, it swung inwards revealing an empty hallway – then, with a sudden explosive crack, Xavier Polydorus appeared in a whirl of smoke.

'Welcome ... welcome!' he murmured in his deep velvety voice.

He was dressed entirely in black, including a shiny top hat and a long black cape lined with scarlet silk. He had unnaturally dark hair, and a rather false-looking moustache. Justin wondered if he dressed like this every day, or had dug out his stage costume especially for their visit.

'Wow! That was amazing, Mr P. I don't suppose you'd tell us how that's done?' Justin nudged his sister sharply, hoping she wouldn't blurt out that they'd both seen his hand dropping a firecracker as he'd stepped out from behind the door.

'Trade secret, I'm afraid,' replied Mr Polydorus, tapping the side of his nose. He stood aside, beckoning his guests to enter. 'Do come in, Justin ... and er ...' He stopped abruptly as he turned to Robyn, and seemed so astonished by her strange costume that, for a moment, he stammered just like Professor Gilbert: 'Ver–ver-*very* kind of you to come, too, Miss Robyn. I do hope you like cucumber sandwiches.'

'Oh, yes ... I adore them.'

Mr Polydorus placed his left palm on Robyn's forehead, closed his dazzling blue eyes, and then sank into a trance. 'You fibber!' he said, after a long silence. 'You absolutely hate them. But don't worry ... I can easily prepare your favourite: Peanut butter and blueberry jam, I believe?'

He led his guests down a long hall decorated with faded posters of his old performances. One showed him fanning out a pack of cards, in another he was levitating a glamorous female assistant, and in a third he was dressed as a butler, presiding over a chaotic chimpanzee's tea party.

At the end of the hallway, Mr Polydorus ushered them into an enormous spartan-looking room. It had the same air of dilapidated grandeur as the garden. The walls were bare plaster; the floor uncarpeted. In each corner there was a huge elaborately-carved candelabrum.

'*Flimflambeau*!' he whispered, and snapped his fingers. Instantly, a hundred candles ignited with an audible *whoomph*, sending a hundred shadows dancing across the ceiling. 'Please ... take a seat.'

In front of a boarded-up fireplace, three high-backed wooden chairs had been placed round a small tea table. Robyn perched politely on the nearest one, then looked about, sniffing.

'What's that gorgeous smell?'

'Jasmine,' said Mr Polydorus, waving to a vase of white flowers on the mantelpiece. 'The greenhouse here is full of it.' He broke off a small sprig and handed it to Robyn, who tucked it in her buttonhole.

The strong, sweet fragrance made Justin's nose itch. As he reached into his pocket for a paper handkerchief, his fingers brushed against an envelope.

'Oh, here's Polly's letter,' he said, handing it to the magician.

Mr Polydorus tore the envelope open, hardly glancing at the writing Robyn had so carefully copied. He read the letter hurriedly, then sighed, clutching it against his heart.

'Such a dear thoughtful boy; always worrying about me.'

Uncertain what to say, Justin gazed round the room. The only other item it contained was hidden beneath a vast dustsheet, no doubt intended to arouse their curiosity. Purposely ignoring it, Justin sat down, wondering how he could weave some sleuthing into the conversation. Meanwhile, Mr Polydorus kept passing his hands over Robyn's head then striking exaggerated theatrical poses to imply deep concentration.

'So, you really can read minds, then?' Robyn asked, after a sly wink at her brother.

'Well, one tries,' murmured Mr Polydorus, with a self-depreciating shrug. 'Of course, some days the vibes are stronger than others. Today, for instance,' he said, massaging his forehead. 'I sense much trouble at the castle; someone who doesn't belong there – an unwelcome guest,

171

perhaps ... spreading anger and despair. Am I close?'

'Very,' laughed Robyn. 'What's your secret? A spy at Thyme Castle?'

Justin flinched, stunned by his sister's sledgehammer audacity. He shot a swift sideways peek at Mr Polydorus, trying to gauge his expression.

'Rumbled again!' the magician sighed, giving Robyn a rueful grin. 'You kids are a tough audience. Actually, I phoned Mrs Kof to ask what your favourite sandwiches are, and she mentioned your new nanny has been upsetting Eliza.' He darted forward, grabbing Justin firmly by the left wrist, then pointed through the window at Thyme castle, clearly visible across the Bay. 'Look! Can you see her on the battlements? I guessed something was troubling her; she's been prowling to and fro all day.'

'So much for mind-reading,' sighed Robyn, looking a trifle disappointed.

'My methods aren't always so mundane, young lady. When we met a few weeks ago I made a genuine prediction – and I still stand by every word of it.'

'Something about travelling to a far-off land and meeting a tall, dark stranger, wasn't it?'

Mr Polydorus frowned at her severely. 'I believe my precise words were: "*You will commit a crime, embark on a hazardous journey and fall in love with a handsome strange*r." He struck another dramatic pose, which was rather spoilt by his moustache coming unstuck and dangling off one side of his upper lip. 'Dratted thing seems to have lost its stickum since I retired,' he grumbled, whisking it off and tucking it in his top pocket. 'Ah well ... I'd better fetch the tea.'

He hurried out, shutting the door behind him with a loud click.

'Well, what d'you think?' Justin whispered, as soon as they were alone.

Robyn smothered a giggle. 'He'd be creepy ... if he wasn't so pathetic. I mean, it's sweet of him to try and entertain us, but if that's what his act was like, it's no wonder he retired.'

'Yeah, wouldn't fool a five-year-old,' Justin agreed. He frowned pensively for a moment or two, then added: 'Unless that's what we're meant to think.'

'Go on.'

'What if it's all an illusion to convince us he's no threat?'

'Fool us into lowering our guard, you mean? Hmm ... I hadn't thought of that.'

'And Polly's letter ...' hissed Justin, sitting bolt upright. 'What if *that's* part of the trick, too? Maybe he *wanted* us to open it ... cos he knew that if we saw how ordinary it was we'd feel safe delivering it.'

'And deliver ourselves, too ... right into the hands of Agent X,' gasped Robyn. 'Oh, *crud-crumpets*! We've walked right into a trap. This place is miles from anywhere; we could scream all day long and no one would hear us.'

They turned towards the door, both suddenly thinking the same thing: had Xavier Polydorus locked them in? Robyn jumped up, raced across the room and yanked at the door handle. The door flew open – and Mr Polydorus stepped in pushing an old-fashioned tea trolley.

'Th-thank you,' he said, looking startled. 'Did you hear my footsteps?'

'Er ... sort of,' Robyn muttered. From the anxious look on her face Justin guessed he wasn't the only one to have lost his appetite.

Mr Polydorus parked the trolley beside the little table, and transferred the tea things.

'I like my tea brewed for a full two minutes,' he said. 'Perhaps you could time it for me, Justin?'

But as Justin glanced down at his wrist he had the shock of his life. 'My watch! It's ... it's gone.' He jumped up, and started scouring round on the floor. 'The catch has been loose for a few days,' he explained. 'It must've broken.'

'Maybe it's in the boat,' suggested Robyn.

'No ... no, I remember checking the time as we walked up to the front gate. Perhaps it fell off somewhere in the garden. I'd better go and look ...'

'Oh, I wouldn't worry, it's bound to turn up,' said Mr Polydorus dismissively. 'Here, have some cake.' He reached over to the trolley and, with a flourish, lifted a silver plate-cover off a large dish, whilst shouting '*Tempus fugit.*' With a sudden clatter of white feathers, a dove launched into the air and flew round the room. As it returned to settle on the magician's outstretched hand, Justin noticed it had something fastened around its body. 'Is this yours?' asked Mr Polydorus, sliding a watch over the dove's head, and handing it to Justin.

Justin gazed at it in dismay. It was nothing like *his* watch. Its face was plain black with just a single diamond at twelve o'clock; it had a dark leather strap; and, strangest of all, its winding crown was on the wrong side of the face.

'No,' he said. 'I think this is for someone left-handed.'

'Aha! Then it must be mine,' said Mr Polydorus. 'Which means I must be wearing yours.' He pushed his right sleeve back and turned his wrist towards Justin, who let out a cry of relief as he saw the ambigram face of his beloved timepiece.

'Phew,' he sighed. 'That's a pretty impressive trick. For a minute I really thought I'd lost it.'

'You will if you don't get that catch fixed,' laughed Mr Polydorus, flicking an inscrutable glance at Robyn. He unfastened the wristwatch carefully and handed it back.

For the next quarter of an hour, Justin and Robyn nibbled their sandwiches dutifully and sipped their tea. At first they felt wary, but after a while they both started to wonder if their imaginations had run wild. Maybe Mr Polydorus was just as harmless as he appeared. However, determined not to waste any more time, Justin tried to steer the conversation round to his mother's kidnap.

'Doesn't Polly e-mail you when he's away?' he asked, hoping this might lead somewhere useful.

'I don't have a computer,' confessed Mr Polydorus. 'Or a mobile phone. All this newfangled technology is bit beyond me.'

'Really?' said Justin, rather surprised. 'Well, if you want me to answer Polly's letter for you, jot something down and I'll copy it into an e-mail.'

'Thank you. I must admit I'd like to know when he's due home.'

'Soon, I should imagine,' said Robyn. 'It's Mum and Dad's anniversary on the twelfth – they'll all be back for the party.'

'I hope there aren't any problems this time,' Justin said. 'Mum got kidnapped whilst travelling back from her last assignment. Did Polly tell you?'

Mr Polydorus nodded solemnly. 'Shocking, absolutely shocking! I didn't hear about it until later, of course. There was an upset at the circus that day. I missed my afternoon performance, and the evening show was such a fiasco I decided to retire.'

'Oh, I'm sorry ...'

'Don't be. It was entirely my fault. I was a bit squiffed, actually. My brother had turned up the night before. Long-lost brother I should say. We fell out more than twenty-five years ago – came to blows over a pretty girl and went our separate ways,' he said, with a sad, sidelong look at Robyn. 'Anyway, he heard I was renting this place, and turned up with a bottle of whiskey. We made things up, then celebrated all night long. I was absolutely blotto the next day.'

Justin groaned inwardly. It was the worst kind of alibi ... impossible to either prove or disprove. Yet surely, he thought, a professional criminal would have come up with a more convincing story than that.

Meanwhile, Mr Polydorus rose to his feet. 'More tea, anyone?' he asked. 'Another slice of cake, perhaps?' When Justin and Robyn shook their heads he gave a short jerky nod, then strode across the room, grinning and rubbing his hands together. 'I'm sure you've been wondering what's hidden beneath this dustsheet,' he boomed, as if now addressing a large audience. 'Well, before you go, I have a special treat for you.'

He whisked the dustsheet aside to reveal a hexagonal Chinese cabinet; it was about the size of a telephone box, and made of shiny black lacquer decorated with red dragons. It looked like an antique – except for the acid-green lights pulsating around its base, and coils of wire spiralling down each side.

'I shall perform my most famous trick – *The Lady Vanishes*,' announced Mr Polydorus. 'However,' he added, bowing deeply to Robyn. 'I will need the help of a beautiful young assistant.'

Robyn smiled politely, then grimaced at her brother as Mr Polydorus turned back towards the cabinet and tapped at a small keypad. With a gentle *shhhlunk* and a sudden hiss of air, its door slid open to reveal an almost blindingly-bright mirrored interior.

Justin wasn't familiar with conjuror's stage props – but as he watched, it occurred to him that this device had an authenticity about it that seemed unnecessary for a mere illusion.

Then, the sight of his reflection inside the cabinet triggered a horrifying chain of thoughts: mirrored panels and an airtight chamber; had Sir Willoughby's old time machine harnessed the Casimir effect? Justin couldn't remember his father ever mentioning it – but he knew it relied on negative energy built up between oscillating reflective plates in a quantum vacuum.

Could this strange oriental cabinet be Agent X's faulty time machine? After all, Sir Willoughby had never described its appearance.

'No, it can't be,' Justin told himself. 'You're letting your imagination run riot again.'

He tried to push the thought out of his mind – but he couldn't. If this *was* the pod that altered time and age simultaneously, Robyn could be in terrible danger. With destination coordinates set to before her birth, she could simply wink out of existence ... permanently! The very fate Agent X had almost suffered at the hands of Willoughby. Perhaps disposing of his daughter the same way was his warped idea of revenge.

As Xavier Polydorus led Robyn towards the cabinet, he gave Justin a mischievous wink. 'Time's running out for your sister,' he whispered. 'She's about to disappear!'

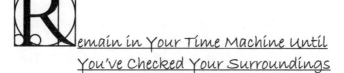

Remain in Your Time Machine Until You've Checked Your Surroundings

Don't leap out of your chronopod the instant you arrive in the past. A few moments of caution could save your life.

If, as outlined in rule 6, your return coordinates were preset before the trip commenced, then keep your hand poised over the launch button whilst looking out of the time machine's windows.

Can you be reasonably confident that you are safe from either natural or manmade hazard? Are you certain your arrival hasn't been witnessed? If there is any sign of danger or discovery, then leave. An instantaneous disappearance will get you out of harm's way faster than light-speed; and any eye-witnesses will probably assume you were an optical illusion or a momentary hallucination.

CHAPTER ELEVEN

Count Ten

Justin's mind raced. He knew he needed to do something, and do it fast – but what? There was no time for planning; Mr Polydorus was already helping Robyn into the cabinet – and if it was the faulty time machine, she could be zapped into oblivion in less time than it took to say *subatomic particles*.

Focus, he told himself. *Identify clear objectives.*

Phase one: get rid of Xavier Polydorus. Phase two: disable the machine.

Desperate now, he blurted out the first thing that flew into his head: 'Is that your front doorbell?'

Mr Polydorus paused, glancing at Justin with one eyebrow raised sardonically. 'There *is* no doorbell ... only a knocker.'

Justin cursed himself silently. *Flux! I should've remembered. That's what happens when you lose a full night's sleep.* He turned away from Mr Polydorus and strode across the room, hoping the magician wouldn't continue without an audience.

'Well, I definitely heard something ringing,' Justin insisted, sliding one hand into his trouser pocket. He opened the door and stepped into the hallway; once out of sight, he whipped out his mobile, rapidly keying in the magician's phone number from memory. 'Yeah, it's your telephone,' he called back. 'Listen.'

'What a nuisance!' groaned Xavier. He turned to Robyn. 'Stay there, my dear ... I won't be long.'

The instant Mr Polydorus was through the door, Justin dashed back into the room and tossed his mobile to Robyn.

'Switch it off as soon as he picks up,' he hissed. 'Then count ten and press redial.'

'What the ...?'

'*Shhhhhh* ... no time for questions.'

Justin raced over to the vanishing cabinet, scanning it at warp-speed from top to bottom. If it *was* a time machine, it looked nothing like his own. But, of course, that didn't prove anything. During the last thirteen years technology had advanced in leaps and bounds; circuit boards were a fraction of the size they used to be, while computers were a gazillion times faster and more powerful. There were probably other differences, too. Sir Willoughby had spent years building his time machine, giving him plenty of opportunity to conceal its internal mechanisms. Justin, however, had been forced to complete his own pod in less than a week, which meant that every nut and bolt was clearly visible, and a network of bare wires snaked between its negative-energy generator and the anti-gravity unit.

He stared at the cabinet's mirrored interior, vividly illuminated from below through a floor of frosted plate-glass. The light was dazzling – yet there was no external power supply. Justin realised he needed to find its core energy source and disable it. He dropped to his knees and peered underneath the cabinet, sliding his hands between its clawed feet. Through a small hole, he found several wires branching out towards the perimeter; ignoring the danger, he looped his fingers behind them and ripped them out. Instantly, the flashing green lights around the cabinet's outer base flickered and died, but whether this was enough to make the contraption safe, he couldn't tell.

Squinting through half-closed eyes, he peered inside the cabinet, running his fingers around the edge of its glowing floor. He could feel a narrow crack where it met the mirrored wall-panels. Justin jumped to his feet and seized the vase of jasmine off the mantelpiece. After throwing the flowers aside, he emptied it inside the cabinet. A few minuscule bubbles appeared as the water trickled out of sight ... then a few more ... followed by a dangerous sizzling noise, a blinding flash, then ... complete darkness.

'That should do it,' Justin muttered. He grabbed a napkin, sprinted across the room and held it over a candle. Once it started to smoulder, he wafted it vigorously beneath a smoke alarm on the ceiling. Then, snatching his mobile phone off Robyn, he just had time to stuff it back in his pocket before Mr Polydorus burst into the room.

'What in the name of Houdini is going on?' he shouted, struggling to make himself heard over the blaring alarm.

'I think your magic cabinet must've overheated,' Justin explained. 'Right after you left, smoke started pouring out of it. Fortunately, I managed to douse the flames,' he said, pointing to the empty vase.

'Thank goodness you're such a quick thinker,' replied Mr Polydorus, eyeing the cabinet with a regretful frown. 'That trick always *was* a bit temperamental. It's an antique, of course – made by the famous Victorian illusionist, Dexter Sleight; I probably should've had it rewired ages ago.' He hurried over to the window, flung it open, and climbed out. 'Come on, you two,' he said, beckoning them into the garden. 'Outside, where it's safe.'

Robyn clambered onto the windowsill, all the time staring at her brother as if he'd gone stark raving mad. Justin caught her eye and shook his head ever so slightly, hoping to discourage any awkward questions.

As they walked down the path to the gate, Mr Polydorus kept up a constant stream of apologies. 'Why is it all my tricks seem to go wrong?' he sighed, after Justin and Robyn assured him they were fine. 'You must be *so* disappointed.'

'Not at all; we've had a great time,' said Justin politely. 'You made us a really excellent afternoon tea. Next time Mrs Kof phones, you can tell her the advice about the sandwiches was spot on.'

Mr Polydorus gave him a sharp sideways glance. 'Your cook has *never* phoned *me*. Not *ever*!'

'Oh, I assumed you were friends,' said Justin, trying to act surprised.

'Why?'

'I thought you knew her from the circus ... and when I rang this morning you said you recognised our phone number.'

Mr Polydorus laughed. 'Of course I do. Polly's phoned me often enough when he's stayed at Thyme Castle – and your number isn't one I'd easily forget.' Seeing Justin's questioning glance, he explained. 'Actually, I'm a bit of a sci-fi fan – especially H.G. Wells. In his book "*The Time Machine*" the year his time traveller visits is 802701 ... exactly the same as your phone number! *That's* why it sticks in my mind.'

'Wow! Weird coincidence,' said Robyn. 'Especially with ...'

'*THAT* reminds me,' Justin interrupted, giving his sister a warning look. 'Do you still want me to e-mail Polly for you?'

'Most definitely,' said Mr Polydorus. He fumbled through his pockets, pulling out a scrap of paper and a pen. After scribbling a few words he folded the paper and handed it to Justin.

'Thanks again, Mr P – and sorry about your vanishing cabinet,' he said, feeling slightly guilty. Now he and Robyn were safely out of the magician's house, Justin began to question whether his actions had been necessary.

I really *am* getting as paranoid as Dad, he thought. Anyway ... I guess the good news is that if Mr P's cabinet *is* a time machine, he won't be using it for the foreseeable future. Although the bad news is that I might just have made him all the more determined to steal mine.

Standing behind his garden gate, Mr Polydorus waved goodbye to his guests. As they trudged downhill to the loch, Justin could tell that his sister was almost exploding with curiosity. She kept glancing over her shoulder, as if trying to decide whether they were far enough out of earshot to start bombarding him with questions.

'I can't wait a second longer,' she finally hissed, jumping down onto the wet shingle. 'What *were* you playing at?'

Leaping after her, Justin pushed the dinghy into the water, not wanting to answer until he was ready. It all seemed pretty far-fetched now, and he didn't want Robyn to laugh.

'Erm ... I didn't think that cabinet looked safe,' he said, helping his sister into the boat. 'And the more convinced I felt that Xavier Polydorus was Agent X, the less I liked the idea of him shutting you inside it.'

'No need to blow it up, though,' Robyn sniggered. She sat down, taking hold of the oars in a brisk no-nonsense way that made it clear it was her turn. After ten minutes of vigorous rowing, she eased up and spoke again. 'So, you're sure he's X, then? What convinced you?'

'Couple of things,' said Justin. 'He must've swiped my watch while he was talking about Eliza; probably took it off my wrist with one hand whilst pointing through the window with the other. That shows he's a master of misdirection and sleight-of-hand ... and whoever released Nanny Verity had to get her handcuff key out of Constable Knox's pocket.'

'Exactly! And he's perfectly positioned to watch us across the bay. All he'd need is a pair of binoculars and he'd know our every move ... even without a spy inside the castle.'

'Also, he reminds me of someone,' Justin continued. 'Though I can't think who. Did you notice he mentioned having a brother? Maybe that's who his contact is at Thyme Castle.'

Now they were almost half way across the loch, Justin offered to take the oars. But Robyn hardly seemed to hear him. Her mood had changed. She shook her head distractedly then drew the oars in and let the boat drift for a while. Guessing she had something on her mind, Justin waited patiently. Finally, after a couple of false starts, Robyn steeled herself to speak.

'Do you think he was telling the truth about not having a computer?' she asked, looking thoroughly uncomfortable. Then, before Justin could reply, she said: 'Don't answer that – I need to tell you something first.' She took a deep breath, and looked directly into her brother's eyes. 'Here's the thing: around the time Mum got kidnapped I was e-mailing a boy – well, I thought he was a boy ... turns out he probably wasn't. Anyway, when I first met him online his user ID was "X". I swear to you, at the time I had no idea Dad's old enemy was called

Agent X; in fact, I didn't discover *that* till *you* told me on the way back from Mauritius – then suddenly all the weird questions he'd kept asking made sense. I don't *think* I gave anything away, but I can't be certain ... and it's been bothering me ever since. What if *I* was the leak? What if Mum's kidnap was all my fault?'

'There's no need to worry,' said Justin, eager to reassure her. 'You didn't tell him anythi—.' Instantly realising his mistake, he slammed on his verbal brakes and skidded to a clumsy halt – but the outraged look on his sister's face told him the damage was already done.

'Excuse *me*! How do *you* know what I told him?' Robyn demanded, her eyes flashing like knives. 'You'd better not've been hacking into my e-mails, little brother.'

As Justin tried to calm her, Robyn's face hardened to a frozen slab of granite. 'Look, it wasn't personal,' he said quietly. 'Dad suspected someone was leaking information, so I agreed to access your computer. That's all. Once I cracked your password, I just printed a few e-mails so Dad could check you hadn't accidentally said anything that might've compromised our security. It's not like we thought you were a spy ... or ... or anything.'

Robyn glared at him with such fierce intensity that it made him shudder. 'You two-faced snake-in-the-grass scumbag,' she snarled. 'All those fine promises about never siding with Mum and Dad ... and now I discover that's what you've been doing all along behind my back. So *that's* how you got the username and passwords to access my bank account. I suppose the three of you planned all this weeks ago. NO! *DON'T* BOTHER DENYING IT A SECOND TIME,' she shouted, as Justin opened his mouth to protest. 'I don't care any longer. I used to think you were my best friend ... but now ... now I ... I just HATE you! And I NEVER want to speak to you AGAIN!'

Silently, with tears coursing down her cheeks, Robyn picked up the oars and started to row. Justin tried to apologise, tell her she'd misunderstood – but Robyn wouldn't even look at him. When they reached the jetty, she leapt out and ran up the cliff steps without looking back. Watching her go, Justin had the strangest feeling that she was running right out of his life, and that their friendship would never be the same again.

If last night's supper had been ghastly – tonight's was a thousand times worse.

Nanny Evelyn – now looking quite chipper – had ordered another frugal meal; but the strained atmosphere made eating it impossible. Sir Willoughby was in the foulest of moods; Robyn refused to speak to anybody; and Justin, staring at his solitary boiled egg, wondered if he'd ever feel hungry again.

Falling out with his sister had been bad enough – but now his father was furious with him too. While he and Robyn were out, Sir Willoughby had phoned home to check everything was okay. When he'd discovered that Justin *hadn't* warned Miss Garnet about Eliza, he'd been annoyed. But once he heard how the gorilla had just stormed into the nursery and Nanny Evelyn been forced to dart her to keep Albion safe, he'd turned the Rolls round and driven straight back to the castle.

The sight of Albion's tearstained cheeks and Eliza slumped unconscious on the nursery rug had made his mind up in an instant. He'd instructed Nanny Evelyn to phone Edinburgh Zoo at once. No matter how much Justin had pleaded with his father, Sir Willoughby refused to back down – and even managed to twist things round, insisting it had all been Justin's fault for not telling Nanny in the first place.

Typically, it was Justin who'd been left to wait with Eliza and then to take her back to the east tower once she'd woken up. He'd guided her along the upper corridor, one hand resting on her huge black shoulders as he'd tried to reassure her that he'd sort things out ... somehow.

Now, faced with food, Justin felt nauseated – as if he was carrying everyone else's problems around inside him, like a big indigestible knot in his stomach.

He glanced down the table at Grandpa Lyall, wondering whether his outing with Sir Willoughby had been a success. Justin had an uncomfortable feeling that if it hadn't been, he'd probably get blamed for that too. Old Sir Lyall – who was sitting next to Robyn – looked unusually miserable, as if the trip had stirred up some distressing memories. Only Baby Albion seemed genuinely happy.

At length, Sir Willoughby pushed his plate aside and excused himself, saying he had an important letter to write. Five minutes later, Robyn, too, threw down her napkin and sloped out of the dining room. Justin thought about following her and trying to patch things up – but after the withering glance she gave him passing his chair, he decided to wait and see if she was in a better mood tomorrow.

'I suppose you two have been stuffing yourselves with cake all afternoon,' grumbled Miss Garnet, frowning at his untouched plate.

'Actually, I'm just really, really tired,' Justin told her, realising it was the truth. 'I hardly slept a wink last night.'

Nanny Evelyn gave him a hard puzzled look. 'Well, an early night for you, then,' she said firmly. 'I'll bring you some cocoa once I've put Baby Thyme to bed.'

Straight after supper, Justin stopped by the kitchen to tell Mrs Kof he was too sleepy for one of her special picnic baskets that night – but she scarcely glanced at him. She was busy rummaging through her little potions cabinet, muttering darkly. After wishing her goodnight, Justin plodded along the portrait gallery. Then, as he past the great hall he peered through the open door and saw Sir Willoughby hunched at his desk.

Remembering his promise to Eliza, Justin wondered if it might be worth talking to his father again; perhaps, by now, he was in a calmer frame of mind – especially without Nanny Evelyn badgering him.

'Goodnight, Dad,' he called. 'I'm turning in early ... for once.'

'Hmmm ... probably,' Willoughby muttered, clearly not paying attention.

This was usually a sign he didn't want to be interrupted, but Justin knew time was short; the van from Edinburgh Zoo was due between half-nine and ten the following morning.

'Have you told Mum about Eliza yet?' he asked quietly.

185

Surely Henny would put her foot down once she found out, he thought.

Sir Willoughby stopped writing. He spoke without turning, but Justin could see his shoulders stiffen. 'I'll remind you that *I'm* the head of this family,' he said, his voice cold and crisp. 'I'm perfectly capable of making my own decisions, despite your belief to the contrary.'

'I didn't mean ...'

'And in case you get any ideas ... *don't* go contacting your mother behind my back. Keep out of this.'

Justin shrugged unhappily. 'Okay, Dad.'

As he turned to go, he spotted the Gilliechattans' scrapbook, still on the coffee table beside Eliza's confiscated laptop. He strode over and picked it up.

'Any luck with Grandpa today?' he asked, hoping to ease the tension.

Willoughby shot a swift glance over his shoulder, then drew a blank piece of paper over the sheet he'd been writing on. 'Complete waste of time.' He gave Justin a reproachful look as if the excursion had been his idea. 'The usual hazy memories interspersed with random drivel. But I won't be beaten. I'm determined to clear this up once and for all. You'll see.'

'He mentioned twin babies last night,' said Justin. 'But when I checked the Thyme family tree it didn't seem to fit.'

Sir Willoughby frowned thoughtfully, murmuring, 'Twins ... twins?' Then he slammed his fist on the desk. 'Great Scott! Who do we know who has twin daughters *and* twin grandsons?'

'Nanny Verity!' gasped Justin. 'Which means Agent X ...'

'... is both father and grandfather to twins!' Willoughby groaned. 'Finally ... he's given himself away.'

Justin placed the Gilliechattans' scrapbook on the edge of the desk. 'I suppose it *could* be a coincidence,' he ventured.

Willoughby shook his head. 'No ... I've got a definite feeling it's him. Anyway, if all goes according to plan, by tomorrow morning I'll know for certain.'

'How?' asked Justin, wondering if it was anything to do with the letter his father was writing.

'Hah ... never you mind,' replied Willoughby. He gave Justin a sudden boyish grin, then glanced down at the scrapbook. 'Now, what's this?'

Justin explained. 'Perhaps it's worth taking a quick look to see if you can rule Mr Gilliechattan out,' he concluded. Then, as he slid the scrapbook across the desk, it brushed against the paper his father had placed so carefully over the letter, giving him a momentary glimpse of who it was addressed to.

'Well, I guess it can't do any harm,' Willoughby agreed. 'Now, off to bed, son ... you look completely exhausted.'

'Yeah ... g'night Dad.'

Justin edged out of the great hall, hiding his anxiety beneath a puzzled smile. As he plodded up the west tower stairs and along the upper corridor, the knot in his stomach seemed to twist and tighten.

'Why, oh why,' he kept asking himself, 'is Dad writing a letter to *me*?'

As tired as he was, there were a couple of things Justin really wanted to do before getting ready for bed. The first – and most important – was to try decoding Nanny Verity's message.

After stopping off at the library to collect his favourite decryption manual – "*Get Cracking!*" *by Marnie X Pagoda* – he hurried upstairs to his laboratory. There, he fetched Nanny's old book of poetry, opened it to the page with the folded-down corner, and placed it beneath the lamp on his workbench. Finally, he searched through his pockets for the little white card he'd found on the nursery notice board, and examined each phone number carefully.

But no matter how he divided the numerical strings – applying them to the lines, words or letters in the poem – he couldn't make them spell anything. Sensing he was on the wrong track altogether, Justin grabbed his mobile phone and dialled the first number.

'Flux!' he muttered, snapping his mobile shut halfway through a voicemail message from Philip McCavity's Dental Practice. 'They're *real* phone numbers.' He tossed the card across his bench, closed the book and pushed it away. 'Admit it ... you're wasting your time. After all, it's not like Nan *said* she'd leave a hidden message – quite the opposite.'

There was just one last hope, he thought, swivelling to face his computer. Maybe ... just maybe ... he'd overlooked something in Nanny Verity's last e-mail.

After accessing his mailbox, Justin worked his way back to Saturday May 17th – searching for the message Verity Kiss had sent on the stroke of midnight. He opened it, scanned briefly through the first few paragraphs, and clicked PRINT. Then, as he waited, he remembered the other thing he needed to do: e-mail Polly.

Quickly, Justin rummaged through his pockets, hoping he hadn't lost the note Mr Polydorus had given him. He unfolded the paper and read it slowly. It seemed just as disappointingly mundane as the letter *from* Polly – although something about the handwriting did look strangely familiar.

Once he'd typed the message and clicked SEND, Justin re-examined Mr Polydorus's note, trying to remember where he'd seen writing like it before; just a few words, he thought – and quite recently.

Then it struck him like lightning. He grabbed Nanny's old poetry book, flipped it open and dragged it under the lamp. The inscription on the flyleaf matched the handwriting on the note perfectly:

Justin leaned back in his chair. It felt good to have the mystery solved ... or at least part of it. Now if he could just prove that Professor Gilbert was the spy, then find Nanny Verity, everything would be back to normal.

But somehow, it didn't feel *quite* as satisfying as he'd expected. It all

188

seemed a little too easy, too convenient. And the more he thought about it, the less convinced he felt.

Had Verity Kiss left her old poetry book hoping he'd spot the inscription? Perhaps – but how could she know he'd find a matching sample of her ex-husband's handwriting?

Casting his mind back to the day of his mother's abduction, Justin suddenly remembered: There'd been a few words scrawled across the envelope Agent X had used to post his ransom note. When Jock delivered the mail that morning, Nanny Verity had been right there in the entrance hall – and had actually opened the envelope.

Justin shivered as the memory replayed itself. Up to that point, life had seemed perfectly normal; then everything went crazy. Minutes later – via Eliza's webcam – he'd watched Agent X kidnap his mother, over 130 miles away at Prestwick Airport.

Swivelling back to his computer, Justin moved the cursor down-screen and opened a folder labelled: X Files. This was where he kept scans of all the clues he and Robyn had found whilst tracking down Henny's kidnapper. He scrolled through the various news clippings, ransom notes and letters ... until he came to a thumbnail showing two envelopes. He clicked MAGNIFY and peered at the screen. The right-hand envelope with its tea-stained stamp was irrelevant; Nanny Verity had sent this, doing a remarkable forgery of Justin's own handwriting. But the other envelope – mailed by Agent X himself – was the one he was looking for.

As Justin remembered, it had two words scribbled beneath its neatly typed address:

Extremely Urgent

The writing was bold and spiky – but although there were some basic similarities, it clearly *wasn't* penned by the same person. Justin felt a wave of disappointment as another promising theory collapsed like a house of cards.

'Maybe X disguised his writing on the envelope,' he told himself. But he knew that wasn't playing fair; a good detective wouldn't bend a clue to fit a preconceived theory. 'Hmm ... Nanny V would know,' he sighed.

It was strange, Justin thought, how everything seemed to revolve around Verity Kiss. Stifling a yawn, he took her e-mail out of the print tray and started to read carefully.

Even by Nanny's standards, it was rambling and oddly-worded – but half way through the second paragraph, he spotted something curious ... something he'd failed to notice when he'd read it onscreen. The word "*hidden*" had been typed in italics.

Then, as he read on, he found a further four italicised words – which when strung together read: *Hidden message in first letters*.

A delicious tingle of excitement shivered over Justin's skin. Taking his pen, he swiftly noted down the first letter of each paragraph: *C* ... followed by *O*, then *U, N, T, E* and *N*.

COUNT TEN! Ten what, he thought. Words? Letters?

Trying words first, he tapped each one with his pen as he counted under his breath. The tenth word was "I". Justin drew a ring round it, his hand shaking. Carefully, he counted another ten and ringed the word "would" ... then he counted the next ten ... and the next ... until, gradually, Nanny Verity's hidden message started to emerge:

To:	justin@thymecastle.co.uk

☺ Dear Justin,

Clearly, I had to escape Thyme Castle. I was terribly afraid that if I stayed, the police would take me to jail. It's crazy; I feel exactly like a fugitive – but of course, I have just myself to blame. It's quite impossible for me to accept your help ... yet.

Once Agent X has been caught and imprisoned, I'll be quite free to return. Meanwhile, I'm afraid to leave this place of hiding, and intend to keep well hidden. Don't attempt to find me, Justin. I left no clues – it would be far too hazardous.

190

'I *knew* it!' exclaimed Justin. 'The question is: *where*?'

But before he could decipher the rest of Nanny Verity's e-mail, he heard a brisk rap on his laboratory door, and a snappish voice telling him to open up at once.

Hurriedly, Justin switched off his computer, folded the e-mail inside the old book, then locked them both in his safe next to the prototype *Hover-Boots*. Before unlocking the door, he took a quick squint through the peephole; Evelyn Garnet was hovering outside with a steaming mug of cocoa.

As he edged onto the landing, Miss Garnet craned her neck, trying to see inside the lab, but Justin pulled the door closed behind him, and pressed his left thumb onto the fingerprint recognition sensor. Evelyn Garnet watched him closely, her eyes burning with curiosity as the deadbolts clunked home.

'Why all the security?' she barked. 'What are you hiding, boy?'

'Oh, nothing,' said Justin airily. 'Homework and stuff ... that's all.'

'Hm ... a likely story. It's high time you were in bed. Downstairs – quick march!'

She handed him the mug, turned sharply on her heels and clacked down the stone steps to the floor below.

Justin sloped after her, half frustrated he hadn't been able to finish decoding Nanny Verity's e-mail; half thrilled he was finally on her trail. Now he was certain she really *had* left a hidden clue, he tried to remember if there was anything else on the nursery notice board with strings of numbers written on it.

Only that old homework, he thought. And that's in my own handwri—

Justin stopped abruptly and gasped.

That's where Nanny Verity hid her coded message, he thought ... *in the homework*. Brilliant! No one else knows she can forge my writing – so I'm the only person who could *ever* suspect it's a clue!

'Nanny, you're a genius,' he murmured.

'Whaaat?' called Evelyn Garnet.

As she glanced back at him, Justin noticed that the hearing aid she'd worn yesterday was now missing. 'I *said* ... THIS COCOA'S

DELICIOUS.' He took an enormous mouthful, hoping to convince her.

'There's no need to shout,' she snapped. 'I'm not deaf.'

Justin wasn't about to argue; he was too busy wondering if he could dash upstairs and finish decoding the e-mail once Miss Garnet left, or sneak over to the nursery and fetch the homework clue – but, much to his annoyance, she followed him into his bedroom, chivvying him to finish his cocoa. Eager to be rid of her, Justin drank it in single gulp, handing her the empty mug as he strolled into his bathroom.

'Goodnight, Nanny,' he said, trying to make it sound like a polite dismissal. But Evelyn Garnet didn't take the hint – and ten minutes later, when Justin returned wearing his pyjamas, she was still hanging around like a bad smell, looking remarkably pleased with herself.

'Now, into bed ... this instant,' she told him, turning back the quilt.

Normally, Justin would've objected to such treatment – but he felt so overwhelmingly sleepy all of a sudden, he simply couldn't muster the energy. He'd been tired all evening; now he was exhausted beyond belief. He felt as if his entire life-force was trickling away like bathwater down a plughole.

I guess last night's insomnia finally caught up with me, he thought as he tumbled into bed. He tilted his left wrist back and fumbled to remove his watch. But although its scythe-shaped catch was now looser than ever, unfastening it seemed as challenging as any Chinese puzzle.

When it finally flipped open, Justin turned the watch over and tried to focus on the worn inscription engraved across its back. For some inexplicable reason, reading it felt desperately important – as if his drowsy, befuddled brain needed to grasp the chain of words like a lifeline.

'Everything is Connec—,' he mumbled. But the rest was lost in a prodigious yawn. He slumped forwards, letting the wristwatch slip between his useless rubbery fingers.

Through a bewildering cloud of fuzziness, he saw Nanny Evelyn swipe the watch off his bedcover; heard her plonk it onto the bedside table; then felt a bony hand shove him back against his pillow.

Justin closed his eyes, allowing his thoughts to drift like soap bubbles. As he sank into a hazy sleep, a slideshow of memories flickered through his dreams: Eliza's strange tantrum, tears streaming down Robyn's face, Professor Gilbert's midnight phone call, the missing miniature pistol, Mr Polydorus's peculiar prediction, the Gilliechattans' scrapbook, a terrified doddling racing through the castle, Mrs Kof rummaging anxiously through her potions cabinet, and Sir Willoughby busily writing at his desk.

As fast as the Laird of Thyme could write, his words spiralled off the page, weaving themselves through Justin's dreams in a never-ending chain: "*Everything is Connected to ... Everything is Connected to ... Everything is Connected to ... Everything Else ...*"

The words whispered over and over inside his head, with the soporific rhythm of a train rattling along its track. Justin felt as if he was hurtling through one long tunnel after another, each deeper and darker than the last.

Then, seconds before spiralling to an endless chasm of stygian blackness, one final image shimmered into his brain: not a memory, this time, but a petrifying subconscious deduction: He saw a gnarled hand stealing Mrs Kof's dreamy-drops then emptying the entire bottle into his cocoa. As the image faded, Justin heard the harsh, braying laugh of Nanny Evelyn – and even though he was now sound asleep, three chilling questions echoed through his mind: How big was the dose? Why had she given it to him? And would he ever regain consciousness?

ecure Your Time machine – Lock it, Hide it.

It might seem obvious, but the scientific genius, smart enough to build their own time machine, yet absent-minded enough to leave it unlocked and in open view, is another classic cliché of time travel fiction.

Unless you want to be stranded in the past, security is something you really cannot afford to overlook. NEVER under any circumstances leave your chronopod without locking it first.

If your time machine will be left somewhere it may seem incongruous, you might also want to consider some form of camouflage-covering or cloaking device as an extra precaution.

Even in the present you mustn't lower your guard for an instant. Never leave a primed working time machine unattended.

CHAPTER TWELVE

Thief of Time

Sir Willoughby signed his full name with a flourish then put down his pen.

It had been a difficult letter to write, as evidenced by the discarded drafts smouldering in the great hall fireplace. Hoping that this time he'd got the wording just right, he read it through slowly, a furrow of concentration creasing his forehead.

'Yes, that should do nicely,' he murmured. 'All perfectly truthful. And if everything goes according to plan, Justin won't read it anyway. I'll dash back here and burn it unopened.'

Willoughby folded the letter and slid it into an envelope. After writing his son's name across the front, he stood it on the mantelpiece where Justin could easily find it if the worst should happen.

'But it won't,' he told himself firmly. 'I'll be back in no time at all.'

Maybe if his palms hadn't been sweating, if his heart hadn't been thumping, and his stomach hadn't felt like it was full of radioactive plutonium, Willoughby might have believed his blustering words. But, deep down, he knew the discovery of time travel had brought him nothing but trouble – and now, thirteen years later, history was repeating itself.

'But there's no choice,' he sighed. 'I *have* to know the truth.'

Sir Willoughby glanced down at his watch. It was ten o'clock on the dot, and he didn't intend going out to his workshop until everyone in the castle was asleep. He strode to the door, planning to watch TV in his room until midnight, but then his eyes lit upon the Gilliechattans' scrapbook. With a wide yawn, he picked it up and sank into the nearest armchair, mentally preparing himself for a half-hour of mind-numbing boredom before heading upstairs.

The news clipping on the first page was almost thirty years old, and showed the cast of "*Arsenic and Old Lace*" taking their final curtain call. Sir Willoughby peered closely at the photograph, wondering which of the blurry faces might belong to their gardener. Then, to his astonishment, he spotted someone he recognised about half way along the line-up. Despite the grainy black and white image, there was no mistaking the charming debonair smile of his old enemy, Agent X.

Robyn threw down her X-Box controller with a frustrated snarl. Usually, a few hours of blasting cranio-zombies took her mind off things – but tonight she couldn't concentrate. Every time she reached level twenty-three, the Encephalophage guarding the Thalamus Vault defeated her in seconds, which meant starting again from level nineteen.

It was all Justin's fault, she decided. Since falling out with her brother, Robyn's resentment had festered and swollen like an abscess. Her tears had dried, but her anger felt as raw and fresh as it had out on the loch.

Despite their differences, she and Justin had always been close – best friends as well as siblings – which was why she felt particularly hurt now. She suspected their father had persuaded him to hack into her computer – but, somehow, that didn't make it any less painful. It felt like a betrayal – and all she could think of was getting her own back.

Apologies weren't enough; she wanted Justin to suffer ... to know what it was like to have his bank account emptied then be fobbed off with a pack of lies. But that was impossible – and anyway, taking money wouldn't hurt him. Some days, when share prices plummeted, he lost more than most people earned in a lifetime – but he'd shrug philosophically, knowing that when the stock market picked up again his assets would soar.

No, Robyn knew she'd need to take something that was important to him; something personal ... something utterly irreplaceable.

But what?

She threw herself back on the bed, leaning against the headboard with her eyes tightly closed. There had to be *something*, she thought.

Meanwhile, Haggis, who had been dozing at the foot of the bed, waddled towards her, poking half-heartedly inside a couple of empty crisp packets on the way. He honked plaintively – and when that failed to get Robyn's attention, nudged her hand.

'Revolting thing,' she said, rubbing the doddling's head affectionately with the tip of one finger.

Haggis made a deep, throaty burbling noise then, after a minute or two, he snuggled on Robyn's lap, pecking at the jasmine in her buttonhole. Its sweet floral scent made her think of Mr Polydorus – his bogus tricks and mysterious predictions. She gave a short, bitter laugh as she recalled how the magician had insisted she would commit a crime.

'And here I am trying to think of something I can steal,' she muttered to Haggis. 'How random is that?'

Then, as her mind replayed their strange afternoon tea, Robyn remembered the stricken look on her brother's face when Mr Polydorus had made his wristwatch magically disappear.

'*That's it!*' she grinned. '*I'll* make it vanish too. Yeah ... and this time it won't be reappearing!'

She checked her bedside alarm clock and sighed. 'Better wait till everybody's in bed, I suppose.' Then, realising she had another hour to kill, she picked up her game controller, ready to zap the toughest cranio-zombies *Dead-Brainz II* could throw at her.

It was ten minutes to midnight – and Robyn hoped that, by now, everyone else would be asleep. She padded across to the window overlooking the courtyard and peered out; to her relief, the castle's other three towers were in total darkness.

Fortunately, Haggis had nodded off half an hour ago. Robyn lifted him gently off her bed and carried him into the bathroom, hoping he wouldn't wake up. After settling him next to his hot water bottle, she peered moodily at her reflection in the bathroom mirror – and for once felt pleased with her drab grey outfit, knowing it would help her blend with the shadows.

She crept down to Nanny Evelyn's room and pressed her ear against the door. From inside she could hear snoring – at least, she *hoped* it was snoring; it sounded more like a pig with hiccups.

'So far, so good,' Robyn told herself.

She made her way down the next flight of stairs – then, as she tiptoed across the landing, she noticed a faint glimmer of light around the edge of her parents' bedroom door, and wondered if her father had fallen asleep while watching TV.

As quietly as possible, she ran the full length of the upper corridor and sneaked into the south tower. All was silent and still – except, of course, for the perpetual ticking of the old tower clock which seemed to pulse through the stone walls like a heartbeat. Robyn crept upstairs to her brother's bedroom, hoping his door wouldn't be locked; it wasn't – in fact, it was slightly ajar. Holding her breath, she pushed it fully open and tiptoed towards the bed.

Justin was sound asleep. A pale beam of moonlight slanted in through a long arched window and shone directly across his face, making his skin look unnaturally pale. To his left, on a small bedside table, lay his watch. Robyn's eyes gleamed with excitement. She edged closer, watching her brother the entire time in case he woke up. But he didn't stir. He remained motionless, lying as stiff and straight as a corpse; his breathing slow and regular.

To her astonishment, Robyn felt a momentary twinge of guilt as she gazed down at him; he looked so trusting ... so vulnerable.

'*Fffuhhh*! Get *on* with it,' she muttered, reaching towards Justin's bedside table. 'Left by one mysterious stranger – now stolen by another. Easy come, easy go.'

Yet despite her bravado, Robyn's fingers hovered momentarily over the watch as if she was reluctant to touch it. 'It's not like you're *really* stealing it,' she told herself. 'You're just moving it somewhere else. Who knows ... I might even give it back to him in a decade or three!'

But still she hesitated.

Then, just as she was about to change her mind, the tower clock began striking, its deafening chimes echoing down from the floor above.

Justin stirred slightly and Robyn smothered a gasp. Terrified he would wake up and catch her red-handed, she snatched the watch, dropped it into her pocket and shot out of the room. Seconds later she was pelting along the upper corridor, laughing breathlessly.

'Done it!' she whispered. 'All I need now is the perfect hiding place!

As the twelfth chime faded, Sir Willoughby rose from his bedside chair and sighed deeply. It had been more than thirteen years since he'd last travelled through time, and his enthusiasm for it had long since waned. He knew only too well the lasting complications it could create. Whilst inventing his own time machine he'd thought only of its potential advantages – but now, with hindsight, he realised these came at an impossibly high price.

He strode purposefully over to the door, then paused, his fingers drumming lightly on the handle. The decision hadn't been an easy one. At one point during the last hour he'd almost talked himself out of taking the trip – but the temptation was too great. He *had* to uncover the truth; *had* to find out whether that frail old man in the north tower guestroom really was Sir Lyall, the 23rd Laird of Thyme ... or not.

Hearing the creak of her parents' door, Robyn shrank back behind an old suit of armour and kept perfectly still. From her place in the shadows she watched Sir Willoughby peer out of his room, listen for a moment or two, then step cautiously onto the landing, his eyes swivelling left and right.

As he crept past, Robyn's curiosity got the better of her. Why was he fully-dressed and sneaking round his own home like a thief, she wondered. Realising there was only one way to find out, she waited until her father slunk downstairs, then tiptoed after him.

Sir Willoughby strode along the portrait gallery, one hand quietly jangling a bunch of keys in his trouser pocket. Robyn followed, darting silently from alcove to alcove, crouching behind marble statues of her ancestors. At the end of the gallery, Willoughby stopped suddenly and glanced over his shoulder. Instantly, Robyn dived out of sight, hoping her dad hadn't spotted her – but he seemed lost in thought. She could see him standing in front of the last window, the moonlight shining through its stained-glass transforming his linen suit into a motley patchwork of red and gold.

With a shake of his head, the Laird of Thyme turned and walked on.

Sir Willoughby wasn't the fanciful type, but the painted eyes of his ancestors stared with such unblinking intensity it really *did* feel like someone was watching him tonight. And those footsteps that stopped whenever he stopped – were they really just an echo of his own?

'Get a grip,' he told himself sternly, hurrying on through the dining room. 'You're imagining things.'

Willoughby loped across the entrance hall and opened the front door. He paused on the step, checking that the castle was still in darkness. For a moment, he thought he saw a pale face pressed against one of the gallery windows – but when he looked again, he realised it was just the moonlight casting shadows across the stained-glass.

Then, as he glanced through the archway he half-glimpsed a flicker of light down by the castle gates. He stiffened, peering into the darkness, waiting to see if it flashed a second time, but nothing happened.

'*Another* figment of your imagination,' he groaned. 'Or probably just the headlights of a passing car.'

Brushing his concerns aside, Willoughby headed for his workshop. He stayed in the long shadows at the base of the east tower, and trod carefully to lessen the crunching noise his feet made on the gravel.

As he crept round the back of the garage, he shielded the left side of his face with one hand so he couldn't see the water. Since returning from Mauritius, he'd been careful to avoid looking at the loch – and he wasn't about to make an exception tonight.

Sir Willoughby unlocked his workshop door and wedged it open. It was pitch-dark inside, and smelt damp and musty. After tripping over an oilcan, he groped in midair until he found a pull-cord. He tugged it, and a single dingy bulb flickered feebly, showing rows of dust-covered tools festooned in cobwebs, and a workbench littered with half-built mechanical gadgets. Then, after moving a couple of moth-eaten deck-chairs, he peeled back a tarpaulin and gazed down at the old Norton motorbike and sidecar with a sad pang of nostalgia. He put the key in the bike's ignition, turning it just enough to prime the chronopod's power cells without starting the engine.

The sidecar looked like a gigantic chrome egg. It had a narrow sloping windscreen at the front, and a small porthole in its solitary door. Bringing the lamp closer, Sir Willoughby opened it and peered inside. The pod was uncomfortably cramped for a fully-grown man. Not wanting to squeeze in until the last possible minute, he hunkered down to examine its control panel. It looked dismayingly unfamiliar – a completely different layout to his own time machine. Instead of nice reassuring dials and switches, it had an inbuilt high-tech computer with a touch-sensitive plasma screen. Wires ran everywhere: welded to its internal door panels, countersunk into the floor – and the ceiling looked like a cross between a giant circuit board and a map of the London underground.

Justin had shown it to him, of course, pointing out the negative-energy generator and the anti-gravity unit stowed beneath its leather-upholstered seat. He'd even demonstrated the computer's virtual simulation of the subatomic-wormhole vortex accelerator, and explained how the countdown sequence was automatically triggered by closing the pod door.

Willoughby hoped he hadn't forgotten anything.

He leaned forward and tapped a small glowing dot in the middle of the computer screen, certain this was how he'd seen Justin activate it. It shimmered politely, displaying the *ThymeCom* logo. When nothing else happened, Sir Willoughby tapped it again. The logo faded and a grid appeared in its place, then a calm digital voice said, 'PLEASE ENTER YOUR SPATIOTEMPORAL DESTINATION COORDINATES.'

'Hmm ... the tricky part,' he groaned. Despite their functional similarities, Willoughby knew that the biggest difference between his time machine and Justin's was how the coordinates were set. Both machines could travel through time *and* space – however, Willoughby was used to adjusting a series of interlocking brass dials to determine his spatial location, whereas his son's pod required digital coordinates like a modern GPS.

Sir Willoughby felt uncomfortable with computers, and wondered if he could get away with entering just the time and date of his destination. He tried to remember what Justin had told him about the computer's default settings. Hadn't he said that if the spatial coordinate grids were left blank the chronopod would automatically transport its passenger *through time* to the precise *place* it had left?

Sir Willoughby gave a long sigh. As it happened, everything he wanted to see was right here on the Thyme estate, albeit almost thirty years ago. The real question was: if the motorbike materialised in this selfsame place in the past, would it be perfectly safe?

He cast his mind back. Originally, the building now used as a garage would have stabled a dozen horses. But when he was a boy, there were just two: reliable old Conway, and Deighton's wild, headstrong colt, Equinox. In those days, Sir Lyall also parked his Rolls in one of the empty stalls. The building that later became Willoughby's workshop was then used as a tack room, storing a few spare saddles and riding crops. Most of the time it was empty – and on the day he was planning to visit, Sir Willoughby knew that his father had driven both him and his brother to Inverness.

He gave a brief satisfied nod. What could possibly go wrong?

Robyn cupped her hands round her eyes and peered through the last window in the portrait gallery, ready to dive back again if her father reappeared. She had an uncomfortable feeling he'd almost spotted her earlier, but a full minute had elapsed since she'd watched him plod round the back of the garage – long enough for Robyn's natural inquisitiveness to overcome her caution.

After running through the entrance hall, she pushed the castle door open and looked out.

'I bet he's in his workshop,' Robyn whispered to herself, suddenly remembering the keys she'd heard jingling in her dad's pocket. She edged out onto the castle doorstep, tempted to follow him. But before she could move, a dark shape scuttled across the garage roof, dropped to the ground and shimmied across the courtyard like a giant black tarantula.

Robyn gasped, not realising at first that it was just Tybalt out hunting for mice. She watched him skulk through the archway – then, as he disappeared down the drive, she spotted a strange flashing light just outside the castle gates.

Using the onscreen keyboard, Sir Willoughby entered the temporal coordinates for his destination in the past. The date – August 30th – was easy enough to remember; but the time needed some consideration. According to servant gossip, the event he wanted to witness happened sometime that afternoon – so one o'clock seemed the logical choice; and if he missed it he could always travel back another hour or so.

Willoughby groaned as he eased himself into the sidecar. It was every bit as uncomfortable as he remembered; hunched on its scarlet leather seat, his head touched the ceiling, his elbows brushed its side panels, and his knees were jammed up against the control panel.

He double-checked the coordinates – then, before reaching to close the pod door, took a moment to mentally prepare himself for the unforgettable stomach-churning lurch of being sucked into a quantum vacuum and catapulted through time.

Robyn froze, staring through the archway. There was a long flash, and another ... then a space ... followed by two more long flashes and a short flicker – clearly part of a coded signal for someone inside the castle. Robyn glared at each of the four towers in turn, wondering who was deciphering it and where they were hiding – but every room was in darkness or had its curtains tightly drawn.

'Dad needs to see this,' she muttered, running towards the workshop. 'But he'll be furious if he finds out I've been spying on him.'

Realising she needed to attract his attention – fast – she scooped up a handful of gravel and hurled it onto the workshop roof, then squeezed behind a huge old conifer growing right beside it.

Sir Willoughby jumped, startled by the sudden clattering noise on the roof. Within seconds, he'd clambered out of the chronopod, leaving its door half-open. He hurried outside. Whatever it was needed investigating – and he had no intention of disappearing into the past without checking it out first.

He ran past his workshop – straight by Robyn in her hiding place – then, as he marched across the courtyard, he noticed the flashes of light outside the castle gates and crunched to a halt.

'I *knew* I didn't imagine it!' he growled.

He glowered through the arch, watching the signal-pattern. A series of long and short flashes with a clear space between each group could only mean one thing: *Morse code!*

Willoughby strode through the archway, muttering to himself angrily.

Once Sir Willoughby was out of sight, Robyn wriggled out from behind the tree and raced silently across the clifftop towards the south tower. She hoped her father wouldn't be mad enough to confront the intruder single-handed, and half-wished she hadn't alerted him.

Perhaps I should've gone back indoors and phoned the police, she thought, cursing Nanny Evelyn for confiscating her mobile.

Robyn picked her way carefully round the base of the tower, sticking close to its ancient stone wall where it curved out, dangerously close to the cliff edge. She could hear her father's footsteps echoing through the archway – and, as she drew level with the front of the castle, saw him emerge, looking every inch the outraged Laird.

Instantly, the light at the castle gates winked out. Sir Willoughby gave a gruff snort, and was clearly all set to march straight down the driveway – but at the last moment he seemed to change his mind. He stepped back into the shadows and started creeping along the front of the castle towards the west tower.

At first, Robyn was mystified; then she noticed another flash of light, this time from inside the great hall. From where she stood – level with the opposite tower – her side-on view of the French windows made it impossible to see who was signalling. In fact, if the light hadn't kept catching on the leaves of a rosebush just outside the window, she might have missed it altogether.

If Robyn had ever doubted there was a spy in Thyme Castle, she didn't any longer. But who could it possibly be? Knightly? Mrs Kof? Surely not the professor? Her mind raced as she watched her father edge closer and closer to the west tower, knowing that in less than a minute he'd discover the truth.

Then, with Sir Willoughby just a few steps from the tower, the flashing stopped. Robyn groaned inwardly. Had the spy guessed something was wrong, or was he simply waiting for an answering signal? Undeterred, Willoughby kept inching his way onwards, silently trampling over Mr Gilliechattan's pansies.

Robyn shot a swift glance down the moonlit driveway. What had become of the intruder down by the castle gates, she wondered. Had he run off ... or was he creeping nearer? The thought made her shiver. She listened carefully, but the only sound she could hear was the thumping of her own heart.

As Sir Willoughby reached the foot of the tower the flashing started again. With his back pressed against the curved wall, the Laird of Thyme shuffled slowly sideways until he was standing right next to the French windows. He paused, clenching and unclenching his long fingers. Robyn stared at him intently, almost forgetting to breathe.

'Come *on*, Dad,' she hissed through tightly gritted teeth. 'Get a *move* on!'

Almost as if he'd heard her, Sir Willoughby jumped onto the terrace outside the French windows, turning sharply to face the spy. He held one hand out in front of his eyes, dazzled by the torchlight shining up at him. Robyn watched as he leaned forward and pressed his face against the glass ... then heard him gasp out loud:

'*YOU?*' he shouted.

At that precise instant, Robyn saw a dark figure wearing a balaclava materialise out of the shadows behind him and raise a black-gloved hand. Oblivious, Willoughby took a half step backwards, pointing down through the window.

'DASH IT ALL ... IT ... IT *CAN'T* BE. YOU'RE JUS—'

'*DAAAAAAD! LOOK OUT!*' Robyn yelled.

But before her father had time to react, the stranger slammed his right fist on the base of Sir Willoughby's skull in a vicious chopping motion; he dropped to the ground like a puppet with its strings cut.

Robyn screamed – and immediately wished she hadn't. The intruder's head snapped round in her direction. After muttering something inaudible to the person behind the window, he stepped coolly over Sir Willoughby's body then sprinted towards the south tower.

'Crud-crumpets – now he's after me.' Robyn turned and fled along the clifftop, her thoughts pounding in time with her feet.

Ahead on the left, she could see the castle door, still slightly ajar. Ahead on her right, a faint gleam of light from her father's workshop.

Castle or workshop ... which?

She needed to be in one or the other before Agent X rounded the south tower.

Castle, she thought, picturing the huge iron bolts on its door. But I'll be locking myself in with a spy.

What about the workshop, then? I can hide until the coast's clear. Once X goes inside looking for me, I could try rousing Dad. And if that doesn't work, I'll run down to the phone box on the corner of Spindle Lane and call for an ambulance.

Or *would* I be safer in the castle?

Robyn kept running, her mind changing with every step.

Left or right?

Castle or workshop ... which?

          ... which?

                ... which?

Workshop, Robyn decided, swerving right at the last moment. Hide first – get help for Dad once it's safe. She threw herself through the workshop door and turned swiftly, pulling it to until she had just the narrowest of gaps to peep through.

The intruder – she assumed it *was* Agent X – hurtled round the south tower, almost slipping over the cliff edge. After regaining his footing, he moved cautiously, glancing round the courtyard. Robyn saw him look off to his left, and guessed he'd spotted the open castle door.

'That's the idea,' she whispered. 'Into the castle ...'

But to her dismay, he shifted his attention to the workshop, then moved directly towards her. Not running this time, but advancing stealthily with the single-minded determination of a predator stalking its prey.

'Oh, shinty!' Robyn muttered.

She shut the door as quietly as possible, and cast around the room for a place to hide. There wasn't much choice. After memorising the position of the old motorbike, she turned out the light. Then, thinking it might be best to remove the bulb, she groped in her pocket for a handkerchief, but as she pulled it out she felt Justin's wristwatch snag on its lace trim.

Robyn groaned, wondering why, whenever time was short, everything seemed to gang up on you. She tore the hanky free. There was a metallic *ping* followed by a soft clatter in the direction of the pod. Something had broken off the watch, but Robyn was too panicked to care. After stuffing it back in her pocket, she wrapped the hanky around her fingers, removed the hot bulb and put it on the workbench. Then, with her arms outstretched, she edged forwards, groping for the sidecar's open door. Quickly, she eased herself inside – then reached out, feeling for the tarpaulin folded back over its roof. She pulled it down, suddenly reminded of childhood games of hide-and-seek as she tried to make it cover the bike and sidecar.

Arranging the tarp with one hand through the narrowly-open door wasn't easy – and by the time Robyn got it to her satisfaction, she heard footsteps enter the workshop and saw the faint flicker of torchlight seeping beneath the tarpaulin.

It was too late to shut the pod door properly now – the slightest noise would give her away – so she gripped it with one hand, leaving a gap of scarcely a millimetre.

Crouched on the pod floor, Robyn kept perfectly still. Although she'd seen Justin's chronopod before, she'd never been inside it. Her eyes darted round, but it was too dark to see much – apart from a single word pulsating dimly in the bottom corner of a small screen: STANDBY.

If she'd had longer to think about it, this might have alarmed her – but right then Robyn had bigger things to worry about, specifically: the unwelcome rustle of the tarpaulin being swept back. She held her breath, expecting the pod door to be yanked open; instead she heard a hoarse chuckle, and a deep voice murmur: 'At last!'

The remark struck Robyn as rather odd given how quickly Agent X had found her – but a split-second later she realised her mistake. He *hadn't* found her ... *he wasn't even looking for her*. He'd been after the time machine all along, and had headed straight for the workshop, assuming she'd gone back inside the castle.

It seemed so obvious now. Sickeningly obvious. But as she'd raced across the clifftop the thought had never occurred to her.

Robyn pressed herself closer to the sidecar floor, glad of her dark clothes. Hearing footsteps walking around the bike, she breathed a little easier, knowing she'd be much less visible from the other side. She tilted her head sideways and peeped up through the windscreen; a gloved hand came into view, moving sinuously along the handlebars and toying with the ignition key.

Suddenly, the chronopod lurched sideways. Robyn guessed Agent X was turning the bike around, ready to wheel it outside. She clutched the pod door tightly not wanting it to fly open.

In less than a minute, the motorbike was out on the clifftop. Robyn felt the sidecar shudder as X bounced onto the saddle. Then she heard old Bessy's engine roar merrily as Agent X revved her engine.

As the bike trundled over the grass and across the courtyard, Robyn tried to come up with a plan. At first, she wondered if Agent X might drive all the way home without noticing her; once he'd hidden the motorbike, maybe she could creep out and phone the police, telling them where he lived.

But then, as they rattled out of the archway, she remembered her father, slumped unconscious by the west tower. He might need medical attention, and leaving him in the rose garden could put his life in danger.

No. Robyn knew she needed to escape – and the sooner, the better. She'd simply have to throw herself out before the bike went any faster. Hopefully, Agent X would be so desperate to escape with the stolen time machine, he wouldn't turn back.

Still on her hands and knees, Robyn tried to shove the sidecar door fully open – but it was harder than she expected; each time she pushed it a little, wind resistance forced it back as the bike accelerated.

Glancing up, she saw an arm stretching across the windscreen, and stifled a cry of dismay. Had X spotted her? Or had he just seen the door swinging open? She shrank down as he leaned over, watching his black-gloved hand thump the door. It slammed shut with a resounding *CLUNK* – and, instantly, the pod's inbuilt computer woke up. Its screen glowed and a calm computerised voice announced: TEN SECONDS TO DEPARTURE.

Departure to where, Robyn thought, pushing herself up onto the seat. Departure to *when*?

'NINE ...'

'No need to panic,' she told herself, scrabbling frantically at the door handle. It wouldn't budge – and a red message flashed across the computer monitor saying: SAFETY-LOCKS ACTIVATED.

'EIGHT ...'

Robyn peered sideways, hammering on the windscreen with both fists – not caring if Agent X saw her now, as long as he let her out in the next eight ...

'SEVEN ...'

... seven seconds. She heard an ominous whirring noise start up beneath the pod's seat, and redoubled her efforts. As she pounded on the glass she noticed the broken catch from Justin's wristwatch vibrating against the outer frame of the windscreen.

'SIX ...'

'It was obvious X couldn't hear. Robyn wasn't sure whether her banging was being drowned by the engine-noise or muffled by his balaclava – but either way, she needed to try something else. 'Just don't ...

'FIVE ...'

... panic,' she shouted, glancing down at the computer. It showed a CG simulation of the pod surrounded by a swirling vortex of rainbow filaments. It looked like something out of an old science fiction movie.

'FOUR ...'

The bike hurtled along the driveway, gathering speed. Robyn rattled the door again, watching faint wisps of iridescent plasma spiralling past its tiny porthole.

'THREE ...'

'Still *NOT* panicking,' Robyn yelled. She threw herself back, planting both feet against the windscreen, and kicked it with all her might. With each jolt, the tiny scythe-shaped catch bounced along the window frame, then ...

'TWO ...'

... as the bike swerved through the castle gates onto Glen Thyme Road, it toppled out of sight. A bad omen, she thought – and leaned forward, pressing her face against the glass, trying to squint through the luminous ripples of snowfire.

'ONE ...'

Just beyond the shimmering veil of plasma, Robyn made out the hazy form of Agent X turning towards her, shielding his eyes. Knowing it was already too late, she screamed for all she was worth. Then two things happened simultaneously:

The computer calmly announced: 'WORMHOLE STABLIZED' ...

And Agent X jumped.

'Okay,' thought Robyn. '*NOW* you can pan—'

X rolled across the ground, hiding his face from the dazzling afterglow. Beneath tightly closed eyelids, glowing phosphenes danced like fireworks, and his ears popped as air rushed into the vacuum left by the vanished chronopod. He lay still, curled like an autumn leaf, trying to make sense of what had just happened.

At first, he'd thought the bike's engine had caught fire, igniting the sidecar ... but the instant they disappeared he knew the truth. His precious time machine had been torn from his grasp.

All that remained was a memory; a split-second glimpse of a blurred ghostly face.

He blinked ... and that faded too.

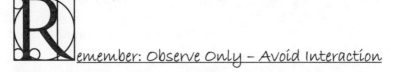

Remember: Observe Only – Avoid Interaction

If you have read part one of my notebook, you will know that changing the past, then finding yourself unable to return to the present, is a fictional contrivance bearing little resemblance to reality.

Events that CHANGE the past create a FORK, which branches off into a parallel universe creating an alternate present. However, some actions merely AFFECT the past, triggering a LOOP which was always destined to happen because it's already a part of the present you left.

However, a visitor to the past should still tread lightly, limiting themselves to observation of events only, and avoiding interaction if possible. Actively interfering with history is unlikely to change it, (in theory), but the potential consequences are too great to risk. Loops CAN become forks, and vice versa!

CHAPTER THIRTEEN

A Rotten Haddock

The voice seemed to come from a long way off – echoing from high, high above him, like someone shouting down a mineshaft.

No, a well, he thought. It must be. He could feel ice-cold water lapping against his shoulders – though it was surprisingly turbulent for a well, tossing him about like a rubber duck in a bathtub.

The voice rang out again, closer this time, and urgent-sounding:

'Wake up, sir ... *please* wake up ...'

Odd, Justin thought – I must be asleep. Concentrating hard, he peeled his eyes open one at a time and blinked; everything looked fuzzy, like a smudged painting. A large transparent globule quivered precariously overhead, but as he tried to focus on it there was a loud snuffling noise and it vanished. He tried focussing a little further away, and made out two cold, clammy hands shaking him by the shoulders.

The voice continued: 'Sorry to wake you, Master Justin – but it seems we've had a break-in, and I can't find ...'

Justin groaned. 'Please don't shout, Knightly, or I think my brain might explode. It feels like a football that's been kicked from Land's End to John o'Groats by a gang of porcupines wearing hobnail boots.'

'A headache, sir?' the butler whispered.

'To put it mildly. What's this about a break-in?'

'Last night I locked up as usual – but when I came down this morning, I found the castle door wide open.'

Justin rubbed his forehead, wondering why Knightly had woken him instead of his father. He tried to remember if Sir Willoughby was away – but a weird mental-fog left him uncertain. 'Have you·told Dad?' he asked irritably.

'Naturally, I went straight to Sir Willoughby to see if he'd like me to summon the police,' Knightly explained. 'But his room's empty ... and his bed doesn't appear to have been slept in.'

Justin sat bolt upright, and instantly regretted it. The room started spinning like a carousel. He closed his eyes and leaned back against the headboard.

'Perhaps he couldn't sleep and went for a long walk,' he said, knowing this was about as likely as him being abducted by aliens. Justin half-opened one bleary eye. 'Has anything been stolen?'

'That's the odd thing, sir. I checked all the ground floor rooms, and nothing's missing. Do you think I should phone Sergeant Awbrite?'

'Flux, *no*!' Justin muttered – then realising his reply might seem a trifle odd, added: 'Dad's bound to be around somewhere. I'll look as soon as I get up. He's probably in his workshop.'

Knightly didn't seem convinced. 'Hmm ... perhaps so, sir.' He hesitated a moment, as if to create a little dramatic tension – then as he continued, Justin sensed he was rather enjoying himself. 'While I was in the great hall I noticed a letter on the mantelpiece; it's addressed to you, Master Justin, in what looks like Sir Willoughby's handwriting. Perhaps you'd like me to fetch it for you?'

Justin frowned. In the deepest recesses of his brain, the fog shifted slightly, revealing a hazy memory of his father writing a letter the night before. He glanced up at the butler, trying to keep the twinge of panic he felt from showing on his face.

'No thanks, Knightly ... I'm sure it's nothing urgent,' he said, giving him what he hoped was a reassuring smile. 'I'll pick it up on my way down to breakfast. Does anyone else know about this?'

Knightly raised a disdainful eyebrow. 'I don't gossip to the staff,' he replied haughtily. 'In fact, I made a particular point of closing the front door before Mrs Kof came down for her morning swim – otherwise she'd tell the Gilliechattans, then by lunchtime half of Drumnadrochit would know.'

'Good thinking,' Justin replied. 'And if Mum phones, not a word to her, either.'

The butler nodded deferentially and turned to leave. Justin closed his eyes and gave a long, groaning sigh, half wishing he'd accepted his offer to bring the letter. But as desperate as he was to read it, he didn't want Knightly guessing anything was wrong – and factoring in his present zombified state, Justin had a nasty feeling things were very wrong indeed.

Gingerly, he sat upright again, swivelling round to put his feet on the floor. The whole room swivelled with him – and kept on swivelling long after he stopped. Justin breathed slowly, trying to remember why his brain felt like it had been pulverised in a blender; he had a vague idea it had something to do with Evelyn Garnet. Then, as more of his internal fog cleared, he remembered the sudden fatigue that had swept over him after drinking his cocoa.

'Nanny drugged me!' he gasped, his eyes shooting to the bedside table. A chemical analysis of the dregs would be his only proof – but the cocoa mug was missing. And it wasn't the only thing; to his complete dismay, Justin realised his wristwatch had vanished too.

Had Nanny Evelyn stolen it, he wondered – or just ensured he slept whilst someone else committed the theft? Either way, she clearly wasn't to be trusted.

Once that particular memory resurfaced, others started to trickle through: Eliza's forthcoming banishment, Sir Willoughby's suspicions about Grandpa Lyall, Nanny Verity's half-decoded e-mail ... and the homework clue she'd left on the nursery notice board.

Knowing he'd need full use of his faculties to sort things out, Justin dragged himself to the bathroom. After splashing some cold water on his face, his head felt a little clearer, though it still throbbed painfully. He washed and dressed slowly, then plodded down to the great hall.

The letter was on the mantelpiece, just as Knightly had said. Uncertain what to expect, Justin tore it open and started to read:

215

Dear Justin,

If you are reading this, then the worst has happened ~ and I am trapped in the past. I am sure you are wondering why, after my repeated warnings about the dangers of time-travel, I have risked it myself.

The fact is I simply had to know the truth about the old man we call Grandpa Lyall. When he first arrived I felt sure he was Pops ~ but while we were in Mauritius you mentioned something that made me doubt his authenticity. You described watching him toss a coin at that fork in the road just outside the castle gates, and said how much he reminded you of Old Father Time.

Well, almost thirty years ago I had an uncannily similar experience. I, too, saw a man tossing a coin at that very same junction. I couldn't tell his age, (he was too far away, and heavily bandaged), but the more I think about it, the more convinced I am we both saw the same person. And, if that is the case, then he cannot possibly be Sir Lyall Austin Thyme, because Pops and I were standing together on the west tower battlements when I saw him.

The scene is so clear in my mind. The school holidays were almost over, and I had been teasing Deighton because he still had another year to wait before he could join me at Gordonstoun.

After breakfast, Pops said he wanted a serious talk with me. He explained that if anything should happen to him, I, as the eldest son, would inherit the estate and become Laird. Somehow, the thought had never occurred to me; I had assumed Pops would live to a ripe old age ~ but the sudden death of his wife had left him acutely aware of his own mortality.

We had been talking quite deeply about Time and Chance, when I glimpsed a distant figure standing just beyond the castle gates. The morning sunlight caught the coin he tossed high into the air, and ... well, you know the rest!

When you told me exactly what you saw, (and how it inspired you), I felt certain our "Grandpa Lyall" must be an impostor. That is why I insisted we returned to Thyme Castle immediately. I fully intended to throw him out ~ but the few random comments he then made planted seeds of doubt, and I started to dither.

Having once made an impetuous decision I later came to regret, I am now, perhaps, overly cautious. I know this frustrates you ~ when I was your age I used to feel exactly the same way about my father. Everything seemed so crystal-clear; either black or white. It is only now that I am older I see life is full of confusing grey areas.

However, I have now made my decision. I will travel back to the day before my original sighting. One of the housemaids, a new girl, witnessed a traffic accident that afternoon. I believe the coin-tossing man was somehow involved, possibly leaving him with amnesia. If my theory is correct, and I can talk to him before it happens, then I am certain to discover his true identity.

But if I do not return and destroy this letter, you will know my plan has failed … and I am lost. Should that happen, I beg you not to give up hope. If I am alive I will try to find a way back ~ if not, then you will be the next Laird of Thyme. Meanwhile, I hereby grant you the authority to take my place as head of the family, knowing you will take good care of everyone in my absence.

Yours affectionately,

Willoughby Homer Gaynor Knott Ivor
Hope Toby Neville Austin Thyme

Justin sank into a chair beside the fireplace, feeling physically sick. It was bad enough discovering his father was trapped in the past – but realising it was entirely *his* fault made it a thousand times worse.

'I practically pushed Dad into it,' he groaned, remembering how he'd told Sir Willoughby to stop asking for advice and make his own decisions.

Justin hunched over with his elbows resting on his knees, trying to think of a practical solution. I suppose I *could* build another time machine, he thought. But I'll need specific date coordinates to find him – "*almost thirty years ago*" is too vague – and that's assuming the pod hasn't malfunctioned. He could be anywhere ... or anywhen.

With a deep sigh, he tucked the letter inside his pocket and tossed the envelope into the empty fireplace. Then, as he straightened up, he noticed some half-burnt sheets of notepaper beside a pair of small brass tongs. It looked as if the fire had gone out before the papers were completely destroyed, and someone had dragged the fragments onto the hearth. Justin scanned through them quickly – recognising them as discarded drafts of his father's letter. They were charred around the edges but, in the centre, a few lines of Sir Willoughby's handwriting were still visible. Fortunately, none of the readable bits mentioned time travel.

He paced across the room, wondering who'd been reading the half-burnt pages. Knightly, perhaps? It would explain his sceptical attitude – but why leave them behind? Then, as Justin passed his father's desk, he spotted a torch lying on the floor directly in front of the French windows. He picked it up and turned it over in his hands, trying to remember where he'd seen it before.

Hoping Robyn might recognise it, he wedged the torch into his other pocket and trudged quietly out of the room. Straight after reading Sir Willoughby's letter, Justin had instantly decided to patch things up with his sister no matter how hard it was. He knew his dad wouldn't want *anyone* knowing the truth about his disappearance, but he was determined not to keep any more secrets from Robyn.

As he passed the window at the top of the west staircase, Justin glanced across at the old tower clock. It was very early – barely ten minutes to seven – but he knew this was far too important to wait. He crossed the landing and knocked on Robyn's bedroom door; when there was no reply, he pushed it cautiously open.

Robyn's bed was rumpled, yet it clearly hadn't been slept in; the curtains were closed and her bedside lamp was lit. Justin felt an icy shiver of foreboding; something was very wrong indeed. He searched round the room, hoping to find an explanation for her mysterious absence – another letter, perhaps – but there was nothing.

Justin perched on the end of his sister's bed, wishing his wits felt sharper. It was hard enough trying to grasp this bewildering turn of events without a pounding headache making things worse. For a moment, he wondered if Robyn had felt so upset she'd run away – though that seemed unlikely; and she wouldn't get far without any money.

Then a terrible thought struck him: if Willoughby had already taken the time machine by the time Agent X broke in, maybe he'd kidnapped Robyn instead, planning to ransom her.

There was a certain chilling logic about it – but if Willoughby *had* crashed the machine somewhere in the past, there'd be no way of getting Robyn back.

For once in his life, Justin felt overwhelmed by the problems he faced. When his mother had been kidnapped, he'd had Robyn to help with the sleuthing whilst he'd built the chronopod; now he was completely alone. Both his time machine and wristwatch were missing; he needed to rescue his father and sister, despite having no idea where either of them were; he wanted to capture Agent X and unmask the second spy; not to mention working out what Nanny Evelyn was up to. And all this before Henny flew home for her and Willoughby's anniversary party ... in one week's time!

'And just in case that isn't enough to cope with,' Justin sighed to himself. 'I need to come up with a plan to keep Eliza out of Edinburgh Zoo.'

Well, one thing's certain, he thought. Tracking down Nanny Verity will have to be put on hold. Dad and Robyn are the priority now.

Justin leaned over and switched Robyn's bedside lamp off, then he turned her bedclothes back and thumped a head-sized dent in her pillow. It seemed wise to conceal her absence for the time being. If anyone discovered she was missing, they'd insist on calling the police – and that would seriously complicate things. Justin knew it was all very well Willoughby putting him in charge – but when you're thirteen years old, adults tend to think they know best and just take over.

After opening Robyn's curtains and checking Haggis was okay in the bathroom, Justin dashed along to the north tower. There'd be no time for lessons – so he crept into the schoolroom and left a note for Professor Gilbert, explaining that he felt unwell.

The prof won't mind – and anyway, it's true, he thought. Then he hurried downstairs to the kitchen, feeling as if every footstep rattled his skull.

Justin could hear Mrs Kof's deep voice as he opened the kitchen door.

'Stop fussying, Mr Nightie ... I gettings changed after-warts.'

Knightly pursed his lips and remained silent, eyeing the wet foot-prints trailing across the kitchen floor with disapproval. The cook – still damp from her morning swim – was wearing an enormous robe and had a tartan towel knotted round her bald head. She was sifting powdered sugar over a huge mound of banana fritters – a special last treat for Eliza.

'There!' she said, handing her the entire plateful. 'You wanting toffee sauce?'

Eliza shook her head, grunting softly. She seemed strangely dimin-ished without her computerised voice. Her eyes, usually sparkling with good humour, looked downcast – but as she spotted Justin she ambled forwards, offering him a banana.

'Thanks,' said Justin, taking it from her. He took a small bite, not wanting to hurt the gorilla's feelings.

'Did you find Sir Willoughby's letter, sir?' Knightly enquired.

'Yes ... and it explained everything,' Justin told him, trying to sound perfectly at ease. 'Mum e-mailed him late last night, asking him to fly back to Mauritius immediately. There's been a big tropical storm, and she needed his help fixing some damaged equipment. Robyn decided to go too.'

It had seemed a convincing enough story when he'd rehearsed it on his way downstairs, but now he had to admit it sounded pretty lame – and judging from the butler's sneering expression, he didn't believe a word.

'Ya, I seeing them go,' remarked the cook, helping herself to one of Eliza's fritters.

Justin tried to hide his surprise. 'What time was that, Mrs Kof?'

'Was just after middlenight. Somebody stollen Missiz Kof's dreamy-drops. I worrit so much I not sleepings ... so I get up to go tiddlywinks. When I looking through window I see man walky cross clifftop. At first I think it Grandpa Liar doing sleepy-walk ... but this man was wearing nice baklava. Then he riding off on motto-bike, and I guess it must be Sore Will-berry.'

'Er, yes ... I suppose,' Justin muttered, trying to fit this startling piece of information in with what he already knew. He rubbed his forehead and closed his eyes, wishing for the umpteenth time he didn't feel so lousy.

The cook peered at him, looking genuinely concerned. 'You got a haddock?' she asked. 'You want Missiz Kof make you special pick-up potion?'

'Oooh, no thanks,' shuddered Justin. 'I saw what the last one did.'

Mrs Kof roared with laughter, showing the gap in her teeth. 'No, that special bizzy-wizzy drink for Nanny Evil. I make you something extra-good.' She leaned forward, fixing Justin with her clear blue eyes. 'You truss Missiz Kof, ya?'

Justin nodded solemnly. The cook grinned back at him, then started rummaging through various cupboards and drawers, muttering to herself as she gathered ingredients. Finally, she unlocked her little potion cabinet ... and gasped out loud.

'Somebody has returning dreamy-drops.' With a puzzled frown, she held the tiny glass phial up to the light and shook it. 'Hhmph ... it nearly empties now,' she said, putting it back inside the cabinet and

222

choosing a different bottle.

Five minutes later, she placed a tall glass in front of Justin, which she filled with an ice-cold ruby-coloured concoction. It smelt of liquorice, cherries, ginger, honey, rosehips and vanilla – and was the most delicious thing he had ever tasted. As he sipped it, he could almost feel it trickling into the darkest, dingiest corners of his brain, gradually soothing away all traces of his headache.

'You feelings butter now?'

'Yes, thanks, Mrs Kof,' Justin replied. He thought for a moment or two, then, after Knightly left to set the dining room table for breakfast, he said: 'D'you think Nanny Evelyn might've taken your drops? I'm pretty sure my cocoa was drugged last night.'

The cook's eyes flashed angrily. 'She is *very* bad womans. I think she was puttying dreamy-drops in your cocoa night-before-last, too.'

'Really?'

'That why I knocking mug overs when I bring pig-nick basket up to your lavatory. I try doing same for Miss Robbing, but she already drunken hers.'

Justin could hardly believe his ears. Part of him wanted to fire Evelyn Garnet immediately. But if she was in league with Agent X – which seemed highly likely – it might be better to keep a close eye on her; watch her movements; see who she contacted.

'Now she sendings poor Eliza to Edin-burger Zoo!' grumbled Mrs Kof, patting the gorilla's arm. 'Bad, bad womans. I hopes you make her payings for this one day ... indeedy I do!'

'Yeah, one day,' said Justin. 'But not yet; I need her to look after Alby until Mum gets home. But we've got to stop Eliza being sent to the zoo, haven't we?'

'We serpently haves!' said Mrs Kof, slamming her fists on the table.

'Great! Okay then – listen up, you two. I've got a plan.'

Ten minutes later, (after checking Nanny Evelyn's curtains were still closed), Justin, Mrs Kof and Eliza went out to Sir Willoughby's workshop, each carrying a large cardboard box.

'Wow, it's dusty in here,' said Justin, peering through the open door. 'We'll leave your things outside, Eliza; Mrs Gilliechattan'll unpack them once she's cleaned up.' He glanced uncertainly at Mrs Kof. 'You *are* sure we can trust her?'

The cook nodded grimly. 'Ya, Mrs Grill-a-kitten is okey-dokey.'

'Good,' said Justin.

Mrs Kof hurried back to the kitchen, leaving Eliza to stare broodingly across the loch. Meanwhile, Justin stepped inside the workshop. He glanced round, looking for anything that might help him understand what had happened last night. The tarpaulin, under which the motorbike and sidecar had been stored, lay in a crumpled heap – and marks on the dusty floor showed where the bike had been turned and wheeled outside.

So far, the evidence matched with Mrs Kof's eye-witness account – yet neither quite fitted with Sir Willoughby's letter. Justin couldn't work out what his father had been doing. Why, if he'd planned to travel into the past, had he moved the motorbike outside? Had he changed his mind and driven off somewhere in the present? And, if so, why was he wearing a balaclava?

Justin was fairly sure his dad didn't even own a balaclava – but he remembered his mum telling him that Agent X had worn one to obscure his face when he'd kept her prisoner. But that didn't explain what had happened to Robyn and Sir Willoughby? If X had stolen the time machine, surely he wouldn't need two hostages.

Justin cast around the workshop, looking for clues. Amongst several half-finished rusty gadgets on the cluttered bench, he spotted a lace-trimmed handkerchief wrapped round a light bulb. He picked them up. The hanky had three initials in one corner: R.A.T.

'Robyn Anastasia Thyme,' Justin murmured. 'Bobs was in here ... and probably hiding if she took the bulb out. But I wonder how the lace got torn.'

There was nothing else of interest, so he rolled the tarpaulin up and stuffed it under the workbench.

'Come on, Eliza,' he said. 'Let's take a walk round; I want to see if I can work out what happened.' They both wandered outside, and Justin shut the workshop door behind them, wishing he had the key.

Out on the clifftop there were clear marks where the bike had churned up the turf. They followed these to the edge of the courtyard, then walked along the tyre ruts in the gravel through the archway. Justin gazed down the castle drive towards the gates; it was clear that whoever had taken the motorbike was long gone.

He turned right and headed for the west tower, thinking about the torch he'd found in the great hall. The person who had used it must have been standing at one of the windows overlooking the rose garden.

As Justin got closer, he noticed a row of trampled pansies beside the castle wall. Had someone signalled to the intruder then let him in by the French windows?

However, on a closer examination, he noticed footprints in the soil – a few of which were so deep that the letters SP were just visible on the heel. Unless the thief bought handmade shoes from *Skipdew & Paxby* – which Justin doubted – these were his father's footprints.

Directly outside the French windows a couple of miniature rosebushes had been completely squashed, as if someone had been lying on them. Eliza sniffed the flattened ground, grunted anxiously and pointed. Justin knelt down beside her – and there amongst the bruised rose petals was the missing workshop key.

'Why was Dad lying in a flowerbed?' he murmured, trying to piece the clues together in his mind. He jumped to his feet and stepped back from the castle, visualising the scene. 'Perhaps he took the bike out of the workshop, drove it through the archway ... then noticed a light flashing from the west tower,' he said slowly. 'If Dad stopped to investigate, someone could've crept up behind him, knocked him out, then put him in the sidecar and driven off.'

Justin shook his head, not entirely convinced. The man Mrs Kof had described seemed more like Agent X than Sir Willoughby – and Robyn's disappearance wasn't explained by this scenario either.

For a moment, Justin wondered if his sister had been so angry she'd somehow sided with Agent X and let him in through the French windows. 'No – that's ridiculous,' he told himself, feeling guilty the thought had even occurred to him. 'Robyn would *never* betray the

Thyme family.'

Justin sighed and beckoned Eliza to follow him. He walked through the topiary arch and turned right, keeping close by the castle wall – looking for any further clues. Then, after skirting the north tower, they went round behind the Gilliechattans' cottage, eventually ending up at the arched gate leading back into the kitchen garden.

Before Justin could push the gate open, Morag Gilliechattan bustled out onto the clifftop carrying an armful of mops and dusters.

'Oh, hi Mrs G,' he said. 'Did Mrs Kof explain our plan?'

'Good morrrning, young sair,' Mrs Gilliechattan simpered. 'Aye, she did. I've been a hankering to get in that worrkshop an' give it a good doo – but Sair Willoughby would nivva allow it. I'm sure it'll be a *disgraceful* mess.'

Despite her grumbling, Justin got the impression she was looking forward to poking and prying somewhere new. Her cheeks were flushed and her eyes gleamed like two newly-minted pennies.

'Thanks, Mrs G,' he said. 'Just do the best you can ... and remember: don't tell Nanny Evelyn.'

He watched her trot off round the east tower, and wondered why Tybalt wasn't following her as usual. But as he stepped into the kitchen garden, he saw the octo-puss lurking half way up an ancient pear tree. Beneath him hung a web as big as a fishing net, its long sticky filaments glistening in the morning sunlight. Tybz sat with his paws resting on the topmost strands, staring greedily at a flock of sparrows twittering amongst the redcurrants.

Justin heard the tower clock strike eight, and glanced automatically as his left wrist. He felt a sudden pang, realising he still hadn't the faintest idea where his watch was. But before he could give it any further thought, the back door flew open and Mr Gilliechattan strode out. He grinned through his beard at Justin, then stooped to put on his Wellington boots. Meanwhile, Burbage flew off his shoulder, swooping across to the small patch of lawn beneath the pear tree. He raised his sulphur-yellow crest and barked like a dog. As the frightened sparrows scattered up into the air, Tybalt glared at him and hissed. Burbage stared back boldly, bobbing his head up and down and cackling with laughter.

'*The web of our life is a mingled yarn,*' he remarked, doing a remarkable impersonation of Professor Gilbert's well-educated voice.

Angus Gilliechattan chuckled. 'Och, yer a canny old bard' he told Burbage, as the cockatoo landed on his shoulder. He turned to Justin. 'Is Morag off a-cleaning yon wee shed, Jimmy?'

'Er ... yes,' Justin replied cautiously, still concerned the Gilliechattans might want to side with Evelyn Garnet. But he needn't have worried.

Angus Gilliechattan rose to his full height and folded his thick arms across his singlet. He spoke again in a resounding stage whisper, quite forgetting his Scottish accent. 'Your secret is safe with us, fair Eliza,' he said, addressing the gorilla directly. 'That dreadful woman ... she wants to ban poor Burbage and Tybalt from the castle next. We must stand together against this foul tyrant!' he concluded dramatically, raising a clenched fist in defiant salute.

'*Once more unto the breach*,' shrieked Burbage, standing straight and tall with his crest fully erect. '*Stiffen the sinews, summon up the blood!*'

'You'd better stay in your room, Eliza,' Justin whispered, once they'd returned indoors. 'I'll come for you later.'

The gorilla gave him a thumbs-up sign and prowled off.

On his way back to the south tower, Justin checked quickly through the ground floor rooms – but, as Knightly had already assured him, nothing was missing. The gallery was intact, the dining room had its full quota of silver, and every priceless timepiece along the upper corridors and stairways seemed to be ticking away in its usual place.

Clearly, it was the time machine the thief had been after.

Justin's final call was to his parents' room, where he hoped to find some answers to the innumerable questions now tormenting him. Feeling thoroughly uncomfortable, he searched methodically through his dad's belongings – but the only thing he found was the larger of the two antique pistols that had once belonged to his great grandfather. It was at the back of Sir Willoughby's bedside drawer, wrapped in an old sock.

'So, that's Dad's idea of somewhere very safe,' Justin groaned, putting it back and slamming the drawer. With a shake of his head, he decided to give up. It seemed that the letter Sir Willoughby had written to him was the only help he was going to get.

Back in his lab Justin tried, once again, to get a clear picture of all that had happened whilst he'd slept. Over the next half hour or so, he came up with several plausible scenarios, but there was always something that didn't quite fit. And if there was one thing Justin now firmly believed, it was that everything had to connect to everything else.

Thinking unhappily of his wristwatch, he glanced up at the huge back-to-front face of the tower clock. It was almost ten minutes to nine, and he needed to hide his *Hover-Boots* downstairs before Nanny Evelyn took Albion down to breakfast.

Having kept the prototype boots a secret, the thought of using them in full view of others bothered him – but this *was* an emergency. As he lifted them out of his safe, Justin caught sight of Nanny Verity's book of poetry with the half-decoded e-mail folded inside. It didn't seem so important now that his father and sister were missing. Still, he thought, I suppose I'd better get that homework clue off the nursery notice board – I might need it later.

After leaving his *Hover-Boots* wedged behind a suit of armour in the entrance hall, Justin hurried up the north tower stairs. At the end of the upper corridor, he crouched behind a large oak chest and waited, listening for footsteps on the west staircase. A minute later, Evelyn Garnet marched down carrying Albion.

Once he was certain the coast was clear, Justin crept up to the next floor and tiptoed across the landing. The nursery door was open, and the sheet of arithmetic homework was still pinned to the notice board.

Justin sighed, hoping it wouldn't be another false trail – but on closer inspection he felt more optimistic. It was indeed a genuine page of old schoolwork. The last few sums were ridiculously easy, yet unanswer-

228

ed; he suspected *these* four lines had been added by Nanny Verity.

He tore them off, then took out a pencil, doing some rapid mental calculations.

$$15 + 6 + 17 - 9 - 12 + 2 - 17 + 1 =$$
$$1 + 6 - 20 + 7 + 13 + 14 + 8 - 17 =$$
$$5 + 10 \times 3 - 7 - 12 - 1 - 9 + 5 =$$
$$1 \times 5 + 2 \div 1 \div 7 + 5 + 16 - 17 =$$

The answer to the first line was 3, the second line came to 12, and the third and fourth lines were 21 and 5. Justin gasped, instantly realising that the third, twelfth, twenty-first and fifth letters of the alphabet were: C – L – U – E.

'Wow!' he breathed. 'I'm *finally* on the right track!'

He pushed the paper and pencil into his pocket, beside the torch he'd found earlier, and suddenly remembered where he'd seen one just like it. 'Under Nanny Evelyn's bed,' he whispered to himself. 'I should probably check to see whether it's missing.'

The connecting door was unlocked. Justin opened it and walked in, thinking how cold and characterless the room now looked. The only personal item he could see was Miss Garnet's hearing aid on top of the writing bureau. He knelt beside the bed, but before he could turn back the quilt cover, the door to the landing creaked open and Grandpa Lyall stepped in. He seemed almost as surprised to see Justin, as Justin was to see him.

'Is this the physiotherapy department?' he asked vaguely. 'I ... I seem to be lost; all these hospital corridors look the same to me.'

Justin jumped up, his face flushing. 'No, Grandpa, you're at Thyme Castle,' he spluttered. Then seeing Sir Lyall's confused expression, added, 'You live here. I expect you were on your way down to breakfast and took a wrong turn. Just go to the bottom of those stairs,' he said, taking hold of his arm and pointing. 'If you walk right through the gallery, the dining roo—'

'I can find my own way, thank you,' Grandpa interrupted, his voice now coldly distant. 'I'm not senile, you know.'

Justin's cheeks burned an even deeper shade of red – but then he thought of his father's letter, and how Sir Willoughby had been certain the old man was an impostor. Frowning pensively, he watched Sir Lyall wander off, then shut the door and returned to the bed. As he peered beneath it, he remembered how Haggis had sent the torch clattering across the floor as he'd wriggled past Nanny Evelyn's slippers.

The slippers were still there; the torch, however, was not.

Justin shivered. Suddenly, everything made sense. Nanny Evelyn was the spy – and she'd drugged him last night so she could signal Agent X to come and steal the time machine. Clearly she was a very dangerous woman indeed.

Then, as Justin moved the slippers, he realised just *how* dangerous – for behind them, right under the bed, he spotted something small, shiny and made of metal. Although he'd never seen it before, Justin knew at once it was the missing miniature pistol.

He stretched his arm out, trying to reach it – but as his fingers edged closer he heard the creak of the bedroom door again, and groaned inwardly.

'I'll show you the way, Grandpa,' he muttered, shuffling hastily backwards.

But it wasn't Sir Lyall, this time ... it was Evelyn Garnet herself.

mergency Routine – Plan Ahead

Should the time traveller want to explore somewhere in the past, it's almost inevitable that they'll need to leave their time machine occasionally. If it is securely locked and well-hidden this needn't be a problem – however, as it is their only means of transport back to the present, a sensible chrononaut would avoid straying too far away from it.

When travelling by aeroplane, passengers are advised to familiarise themselves with the locations of the emergency exits, and plan out their escape route ... just in case. Likewise, a traveller in the past should think of their time machine as the only emergency exit back to their own time. At any given moment, they must always know the fastest and most direct route to where it is hidden.

CHAPTER FOURTEEN

Memento Mori

Justin felt a cold, iron-like hand grip his collar. Nanny Evelyn dragged him roughly to his feet, then yanked him round to face her. She looked white with fury and her eyes stabbed at him like knives.

'What *precisely* are you up to?' she growled.

Justin's mind raced. It was vital Miss Garnet didn't guess he suspected her. If Agent X was holding either Robyn or Sir Willoughby captive, it could put them in even more danger – and make it twice as hard to rescue them. But the thought of saying nothing at all sent a wave of anger surging through him.

'I felt ill,' he said, looking directly in her eyes. 'I woke up with the most dreadful headache; then I remembered Nanny Verity used to keep some painkillers in her room.'

'Under the bed?'

'I dropped my ... erm ... pencil,' he said. Then seeing Nanny Evelyn's look of disbelief, he fished it hurriedly out of his pocket.

She gave a barking laugh, and Justin realised this tack wasn't working; he'd have to divert her – catch her off guard before she continued her interrogation.

'Did you put anything in my cocoa last night?'

'WHAT?' roared Nanny Evelyn.

232

Justin knew this was a risky strategy, but he decided to press on. 'I fell asleep so fast, I wondered if ...'

'You impertinent boy! I only *brought* you the cocoa; your *cook* made it, not me.' She said the word *cook* with a distaste usually reserved for words like cockroach or traffic warden.

Justin shrugged. 'I just wondered. You er ... seem to be rather fond of tranquilisers,' he added, with a pointed look at the dart-gun still tucked in the broad leather belt fastened over her apron. His eyes returned to Miss Garnet's face and remained firmly fixed there.

After a moment or two, her gaze faltered and she stepped back, perhaps realising that if she asked any more awkward questions Justin might too.

She jerked her head towards the open bedroom door. 'Get down to breakfast, and don't let me catch you in here again.'

Justin sloped past her and trotted meekly across the landing, relieved she hadn't spotted her torch bulging in his trouser pocket. He took a swift glance back from the top of the staircase and saw Nanny Evelyn collect her hearing aid off the bureau.

She turned to follow him, her lips pinched tightly together and a steely glint in her eyes.

Down in the dining room, Grandpa Lyall was making loud chuff-chuffing noises, as if Albion's spoon was a train and his mouth was a tunnel. The tunnel, however, was clamped tightly shut.

Nanny Evelyn frowned disapprovingly. 'I'll feed Baby Thyme, if you don't mind,' she said, snatching the spoon.

Justin slumped down in his usual seat, not feeling the least bit hungry. He nibbled a dry oatcake, trying to work out how he could trace the whereabouts of his father and sister. In the absence of any other clues, keeping a close watch on Nanny Evelyn seemed the best bet – although questioning everyone in the castle might help; maybe Mrs Kof wasn't the only eyewitness.

'Your sister's late this morning' grumbled Miss Garnet, interrupting his train of thought. '*And* Sir Willoughby.'

233

Justin felt his stomach twist. He was certain she knew *exactly* where they were. Struggling to keep the anger out of his voice, he gave her the same explanation he'd given Knightly, watching her face closely for any flicker of amusement – but she remained as sour as vinegar.

'I shall miss Robyn,' Grandpa remarked wistfully. 'I sometimes think she's the only person who really wants me here.'

Justin glanced up sharply, surprised by the old man's unusually lucid comment.

'I'm sure she'll be back in a day or two,' he said, trying to sound convinced.

The door flew open and Knightly glided in with tea and coffee pots.

'Ah, Miss Garnet,' he droned. 'I've left a clean apron and cuffs on your bed, as requested. And Master Justin,' he continued, lowering his voice. 'There's a frightful commotion coming from Miss Robyn's bathroom; I thought you'd like to know.'

'Flux!' exclaimed Justin, grabbing a plate of scrambled eggs and a kipper. 'I'd better go and feed Haggis.'

As Justin raced up the west tower, he was tempted to dash into Nanny Evelyn's room to remove the pistol – but the shrill, skirling cry of the hungry doddling was too loud to ignore.

Haggis ate for almost ten solid minutes before his hunger subsided. Meanwhile, Justin swilled out the bathtub, made a new nest with dry blankets, and refilled the hot water bottle. Eventually the little dodo settled down next to it, looking comfortably replete; it closed its eyes, hiccupping softly.

'That's one less thing to worry about,' Justin muttered to himself as he locked the bathroom door. 'Now, I'd better get that pistol.'

But there wasn't time.

A quick glance at Robyn's alarm clock told him it was twenty-five past nine; the mail van would be here any minute. Panicking slightly, he dashed across to his sister's desk, searching for a spare sheet of paper; the only one he could find was candyfloss pink. Too flustered to care, Justin took out his pencil and scribbled a hurried message.

234

Jock –

I urgently need your help. Eliza (our gorilla) is being taken to a zoo this morning, and I absolutely <u>must</u> rescue her. Please create an obstruction along the narrowest part of Spindle Lane in about fifteen minutes ... then distract the driver. Leave the rest to me!

With grateful thanks.

Justin.

Justin folded the note and tucked it in his top pocket, then ran along the upper corridors to Eliza's room at the top of the east tower. He pushed her door open, and found the gorilla huddled on her bed, swaying unhappily.

'Come on, Eliza,' he hissed. 'It's time to go downstairs.' He took hold of her huge black fist and gave it a gentle tug. 'You do understand why I've got to hand you over to the zookeeper, don't you?' he asked. 'Nanny Evelyn's *got* to believe we're cooperating; if you run off and hide *now*, she'll search everywhere, then shoot you with Mum's dart-gun again.'

Eliza grunted quietly. Justin could tell from her troubled expression that this simple deception bothered her more than anything else. She always found dishonesty of any kind distressing. Just hearing a lie would thoroughly unsettle her– and the more untruthful someone was, the angrier she became.

'We're not *really* lying, Eliza,' Justin assured her. 'Think of it like evading a predator.' But that's the problem, he thought; gorillas don't have any natural predators – only deceitful gun-toting humans.

As Justin had expected, Nanny Evelyn was waiting in the entrance hall when he and Eliza got downstairs. She'd fetched Albion's push-chair from the cloakroom, and was busy settling him in it, pretending she hadn't noticed their arrival.

Justin wasn't fooled for a moment. He knew she'd keep strict watch on the two of them until Eliza had been driven right off the estate. Technically, with Sir Willoughby gone, Justin had full authority to overrule Miss Garnet – but he feared that could lead to her contacting his mum. If that happened, Henny might discover her husband and daughter were missing – and once the police were called in, Knightly would doubtless mention Willoughby's letter.

Justin groaned quietly. He knew his dad wouldn't want *anyone* reading about the time machine. I've *got* to sort this out myself, he thought. That's what Dad would want.

From outside, he heard the sound of tyres on gravel, followed by the honk of a horn. He grabbed a stick of rock out of the hall table draw, opened the front door and stepped outside. Eliza prowled slowly behind him. Then, much to his dismay, Nanny Evelyn wheeled Albion onto the castle doorstep and stood watching them with her arms crossed.

Justin kept the note folded tightly next to the Edinburgh rock, hoping he could deliver it without Miss Garnet noticing. But even if he did, there was no guarantee the postman would help; Jock was hardly the adventurous type.

The mail van rattled to a halt, and its door creaked open. Fergus jumped out, barking for his daily treat, closely followed by his master, smiling blandly as he rummaged in a large canvas postbag.

'Grand weather,' he remarked, handing over the usual wad of about forty envelopes. Then, as Justin took them, he added diffidently: 'Parcel for you today, too; Special Delivery.' He leaned back inside the van and took a clipboard off the passenger seat. 'Sign here, please.'

Justin scribbled his name in the square Jock indicated, then, after a quick glance over his shoulder, slid his note under the bulldog clip at the top. He handed the board back in exchange for a mysterious-looking brown paper package.

''E pacs!' called Albion, holding both hands out and wriggling his fingers.

'Sorry, Alby, this one's for me,' Justin told him. He looked down at the parcel and frowned. It was about the size of a pencil case and knotted tightly in old string. The wrapping looked dusty and tattered, and the address, inked in rough capital letters, had faded. Its stamp, however, was quite new, and the postmark showed it had been mailed locally, yesterday. Burning with curiosity, Justin shook the package gently – but he had no intention of unwrapping it until he was completely alone.

Fergus snuffled up his last few crumbs of rock and leapt back inside the van. Jock climbed in after him, and sat for a moment or two staring pensively at his clipboard – then, after turning the van round, he gave Justin a discreet nod, winked at Alby and tootled his horn as he drove off.

Jock must have driven past the zookeepers on his way down the castle drive, because Justin scarcely had time to toss the mail on to the hall table before a truck trundled through the archway and stopped with a loud hiss of airbrakes.

Eliza's eyes widened and her hair bristled – but she stood her ground resolutely. Justin waited beside her, one hand resting on her shoulders. He took a swift glance back at Nanny Evelyn's infuriatingly smug face, and decided he'd never hated anyone so much in his entire life.

Two burly men clambered out of the truck's cabin and ambled slowly forwards. Justin thought they looked a bit like gorillas themselves; blonde gorillas with buzz-cuts and ugly crimplene uniforms.

'I'm Cark,' said the first one, who seemed to be in charge. He pointed to his companion with a flick of his thumb. 'This 'ere's Maggot; 'e don't talk much.'

Maggot had a deep scar down one cheek, and carried what looked like a cattle-prod. Justin had no desire to talk to him whatsoever, but when the prod made a sudden crackling noise and emitted a shower of sparks, he felt he had no choice.

'You won't need that,' he said quickly. 'Eliza's completely tame.'

'Yeah, so wiv 'eard,' laughed Cark. 'Gentle as a lamb ... til she starts wallopin' babbies. You flippin' posh kids! Pesterin' yer parents for these fancy pets – an' nobody finks about 'ow dangerous they is.'

Justin's blood boiled inside him. He stepped round the other side of Eliza, and positioned himself between her and Maggot, determined not to lose his temper.

'There's no point me arguing with them,' he whispered to Eliza. 'Let's just keep calm and stick to the plan.'

The rear half of the zoo-truck was just a long cage covered in khaki-coloured tarpaulin. At the back, the tarp had been rolled up and fastened with leather straps. Cark took a key out of his pocket, unlocked a huge brass padlock, then opened the cage door. Justin was glad Eliza wouldn't have to be inside it long; the bare wooden floor looked damp and smelt nasty.

Eliza wrinkled her nose and glanced uncertainly at Justin. He motioned her in with a slight tilt of his head, hoping she hadn't forgotten her part of their plan. She stalked ponderously inside, and the door clanged shut behind her.

Maggot climbed back into the cabin, looking disappointed he hadn't got to use his cattle-prod. Cark, meanwhile, snapped the padlock shut – then, as he turned round, two things happened at once:

Justin, who had been chatting to him about the journey back to Edinburgh, started giving him directions, whilst Mrs Kof came rushing out of the castle, carrying a huge armful of bananas. She pushed past Nanny Evelyn and ran towards the back of the truck, where she stumbled, dropping the fruit round Cark's feet.

'Whoops-a-gravy!' she bellowed, standing next to Justin. Between the two of them, they had Cark backed right up against the cage – hiding him completely from Nanny Evelyn's watchful gaze.

'... The main road's always blocked solid in the season,' continued Justin. 'But Spindle Lane bypasses all the traffic ...'

'I must giving bananas to Eliza for eats on trip,' Mrs Kof explained to Cark. She made as if to bend over – then groaned loudly, clutching

238

her back.

Justin pointed through the arch. 'Just turn right at the castle gates ... then ...'

'Please help with pick-upping, Mister Zoo-man ...'

Reluctantly, Cark bent forwards, gathering bananas whilst simultaneously trying to follow Justin's directions. Meanwhile, using the pick-pocketing skills she'd learned from Hank and Polly, Eliza reached through the bars and slid her fingers into his pocket, nimbly removing the padlock key.

'... Then take the next right,' Justin concluded. 'It'll cut an hour off your journey.'

'Thanks,' muttered Cark. He helped Mrs Kof toss the bananas inside the cage, then reached up to lower the tarpaulin. Instantly, Eliza started banging on the cage door with her firsts, roaring and hurling the bananas back at him. Cark laughed as he buckled the tarp, completely impervious to Eliza's tantrum. Then he climbed into the driver's seat and started the engine.

Once the truck disappeared through the archway, Nanny Evelyn wheeled Albion's pushchair along the clifftop, wearing a self-satisfied smirk. As soon as she'd turned past the Gilliechattans' cottage, Justin and Mrs Kof began picking up bananas and tearing them open, one after the other.

'Got it!' hissed Justin, easing the key out where Eliza had pressed it through the yellow skin. He wiped it clean, then gasped as he saw the words embossed across the top:

'Oh, FLUX!' Justin yelled. He sprinted back inside the castle and fetched his *Hover-Boots* out of their hiding place. 'Eliza's in *real* danger,' he told Mrs Kof, flumping down on the doorstep to put his boots on. 'That vile woman didn't phone the zoo at all.'

He pulled the Velcro-tabs tight and jumped up. The instant his feet hit the step, the boots' antigravity units fired up – and with a sudden woomphing noise, he was hovering about ten centimetres above the ground. Once he'd got his balance, Justin clicked his heels together to activate the propulsion-thrusters, then leaned forward, pressing the accelerator buttons with his toes. He caught a quick glimpse of Mrs Kof's gobsmacked expression, then he was zooming across the courtyard and through the archway.

Once he'd zapped past the rose garden, Justin swerved off the castle drive and cut diagonally across the estate. He was cruising about a metre off the ground now, weaving dangerously through pine trees and gorse bushes. As the castle boundary drew closer, he triggered the acceleration-boosters and soared over the wall with an exhilarating WOOoooOOSH!

To his relief, the road ahead was empty. Justin hurtled along it, gathering speed. He'd purposefully sent Cark down a quiet stretch, away from the swarms of tourists along the lochside – but he kept a sharp lookout, ready to zip over a hedge if a car appeared.

After five minutes he turned right; then about halfway along Spindle Lane he cut his speed, rising amongst the treetops to give himself more cover. Two hundred metres ahead he could see the truck – and beyond that, Jock's mail van completely blocking the road.

Jock was flat on his back with his head under his van; Fergus sat close by, guarding an open toolbox. As Justin glided down to the back of the zoo truck, he saw the Balm brothers climb out of their cabin and walk towards the postman.

'Havin' trouble, mate?' Cark called.

Fergus jumped up, barking gruffly. Maggot pointed to him and nudged Cark in the ribs. Meanwhile, Justin eased back on the anti-gravity buttons, unbuckling the tarpaulin as he descended.

'It's me, Eliza,' he whispered. 'Keep quiet now. I'll have you out in two ticks.' He took Cark's key out of his pocket and unlocked the cage door. The gorilla climbed out, making soft little *hoo-hoo-hoo* noises through pursed lips. 'Squeeze through that bush and stay out of sight,'

240

Justin told her. He refastened the padlock, and secured the tarp, wondering what Cark would think when he discovered the gorilla had vanished out of a locked cage.

After checking the Balm brothers were still talking to Jock, Justin edged round to the cabin door and opened it quietly. Cark's jacket was draped over the back of his seat. Justin reached over and slipped the key back inside the pocket. Then, just as he was about to close the door, he spotted the cattle-prod wedged under Maggot's seat.

Justin wasn't accustomed to taking things that weren't his, but he couldn't bear the thought of it being used on some other poor creature. Carefully, he hauled it out, then zoomed silently over the hedge, landing beside Eliza. Together they crept past the truck, keeping out of sight behind the hedge. Once they came to a gap, Justin crawled through and found himself immediately behind Jock's van. He crouched low, peering cautiously between its back wheels.

'Well?' whispered the postman.

Justin gave him a thumbs-up sign. 'Mission accomplished!'

Ten minutes later Jock was driving them back to the castle. Justin sat in the front with Fergus on his knee, whilst Eliza stayed hidden in the back amongst the mailbags.

The inside of the van was dusty and old-fashioned. It smelt of dog and pine air-freshener; the seats had worn tartan covers; and a pair of faded, fluffy dice hung from the rear-view mirror.

Justin took a sideways glance at Jock. There was a spark about him now; only a faint spark, but a spark none-the-less. He looked more alive than he had in years. And he was talking ... laughing, too; telling hopeless old jokes, or pointing out landmarks Justin had known his entire life.

For once, it was Justin who felt tongue-tied. He wanted to thank Jock, but couldn't think how to begin. He sensed it would embarrass him; turn him back into the quiet grey man he'd always seemed.

Justin looked round, searching for something to talk about. On the dashboard he noticed a stack of files, all with neatly-typed tabs:

PAPER – STAMPS – INK – NO I.D. and so on – and beneath them, in a cubby-hole labelled *route maps*, a well-chewed rubber ball and a dog-eared paperback. Justin pulled the book out; it was the latest Madigan Axrope thriller: "*Nine Evil Tasks*".

'Are you into whodunits, Jock?' he asked, half wishing he could tell him about the mystery at Thyme Castle.

'Aye, that I am,' replied the postman shyly. 'Read near every one in the village library.' He paused for a moment, then added: 'I'd like to have been a detective; I notice things ... people ... and I never, *ever* forget a face.'

'Really?'

'Aye,' Jock continued, warming to his subject. 'Like that butler of yours. First time I handed him the mail, I knew I'd seen him somewhere before ... I just canna think where.'

'According to his references he's worked for royalty,' said Justin.

Jock chuckled softly. 'Well, wherever I met him, it certainly wasn't Buckingham Palace.' He clicked his indicator, and pulled up just past the castle gates. 'Well, here you are,' he mumbled, looking suddenly uncomfortable again. 'Where you goin' to hide Eliza?'

'Dad's workshop.'

'Won't it be a bit cramped for her?' asked Jock, glancing back at the enormous gorilla wedged amongst his mailbags.

'It's only till Mum gets back next week – she'll sort things out.'

As Justin opened the door, he realised he still hadn't said thank you. He followed Jock to the back of the van, and watched Eliza step out into the sunlight. For a moment she stood upright, looking the noble and powerful wild creature she truly was – then she leaned forwards, wrapped her arms around Justin and hugged him.

'We did it,' he said, hugging her back. 'Thanks to you, Jock ... if you hadn't ...'

'Stop right there,' interrupted the postman. 'I don't need thanks.' He took a deep breath. 'Most people barely notice me. But you ... you've always been so nice; always had a treat for Fergus. And this morning you've given me an adventure! This has been the best day I've had for ... for longer than I can remember.' He took Justin's hand and shook it

242

firmly. 'No,' he said, looking a little dewy-eyed. '*I* thank *you*!'

After waving Jock and Fergus off, Justin and Eliza had to go their separate ways.

We can't risk Nanny Evelyn seeing you,' Justin explained. 'You'll have to keep outside the walls until you reach the cliff edge; climb down, then head along the shore to the steps up from the jetty. I'll meet you in Dad's workshop in about quarter of an hour.'

Justin watched Eliza prowl away, then headed towards the castle gates. It was a fresh, breezy day, and he hoped that a few minutes walk alone might help him get his thoughts in order; work out what he needed to do next. He was still wearing his *Hover-Boots*, but as they were heavy to walk in, he decided to take them off and cut across the grass in his stocking feet. Jock had loaned him a spare mailbag to carry the cattle-prod; the boots could go in that.

He stopped just outside the gates and bent over. But as he tugged at the Velcro fasteners, he saw a half-hidden glimmer of gold directly in front of his feet. Curious, he crouched right down, trying to prise it out of the gravel with his fingertips.

'Ouch!' He drew his hand back quickly and looked at his forefinger. There was a tiny gash across the tip, as fine as a paper-cut, but deep enough to bleed profusely. Justin sucked his finger, picking the object up carefully with his left hand.

He looked at it closely and gasped again – this time not from pain but from sheer astonishment. It was the scythe-shaped catch off his wristwatch, its tiny sickle blade now stained with his blood. As he stared at it, a dark cloud drifted across the sun, and he felt an icy shiver trickle down his spine. Goose bumps erupted over his bare arms and, for a moment, he was overwhelmed by an inexplicable sense of foreboding.

Suddenly, a crack of thunder exploded out of nowhere, as terrifying and unexpected as a gunshot; huge, heavy drops of rain came spattering down, drenching Justin in seconds. He hurriedly refastened his boots and activated the antigravity units, then skimmed across the lawn as fast as the propulsion-thrusters would allow.

By the time he reached his father's workshop, Justin was soaked to the skin. He pushed the door open and glided inside – and for a moment almost wondered where he was. The transformation was incredible; Mrs Gilliechattan had scrubbed, polished, mopped and cleaned until the whole place positively sparkled. But that wasn't all. Tartan blankets had been draped over the walls and ceiling, so that it looked like a cross between a highland croft and a Bedouin tent. Shelves that once stored tools were filled with fruit and bottled water. There were rugs on the floor; Eliza's extra-large beanbag in one corner, and a portable television on the workbench.

Justin took his *Hover-Boots* off, wrapped them in the mailbag, and stuffed them out of sight under the bench. The cattle-prod he had other plans for, though he'd need to make some minor adaptations to it first.

It was quite some time before Eliza arrived. Justin guessed she'd probably had to shelter from the rain – although none too successfully judging from her bedraggled appearance. She stalked inside looking cross and wet, shook herself, then sat down on her beanbag with her back to Justin.

'It won't be so bad once the weather brightens up,' he told her. 'You'll only need to sleep in here. During the day you can hang out in Lupin Wood. No one'll see you there; it's right across the estate.'

The gorilla reached for a blanket and pulled it over her head. Justin sighed; even without her computerised voice, it was perfectly clear Eliza wanted to be left alone.

The downpour stopped as abruptly as it had started. Shivering now, Justin dashed back inside the castle, wanting to change out of his damp clothes. He grabbed the mail off the hall table and ran up the north stairs two at a time.

As eager as he was to unwrap the parcel, without scissors its tightly knotted string defeated him, so he tucked it under one arm and flipped routinely through the envelopes instead. They were mostly junk mail and a few business enquiries – but one stood out from the rest, making his heart pound against his ribs. It wasn't the typed address that alarmed him, but the words "*extremely urgent*" scrawled across the bottom in Agent X's unmistakable handwriting. The envelope looked almost identical to the one that had arrived when Henny was kidnaped. That, too, had been mailed ahead of the actual abduction.

With a horrible feeling of déjà vu, Justin tore it open and pulled out two sheets of paper. The first said:

The Laird of Thyme is my prisoner,
(proof enclosed). I had no Choice but
to abduct him. I'd intended to steal
his time machine – but someone went
time-travelling in it. Once they
return, park it outside the castle
gates (keys hidden in exhaust pipe).
Do not contact the police. You have
until Monday at noon or your father
will die ... and I'm not joking!

The other – a brief note probably written under duress – read:

Dear Eldest Son,
They require obedience. Yield that infernal machine
entirely. Must advise cooperation henceforth is now
essential. No objections! Willoughby

Justin felt sick. Rescuing Eliza had distracted him for a couple of hours– but now the reality of the situation hit him hard. Once again, his family were in terrible danger – and all because of that wretched chronopod.

'No wonder Dad calls it *that infernal machine*,' he muttered. 'It's brought us nothing but trouble.'

He stopped dead, half way along the upper corridor and read both notes a second time. On the plus side, there was no mention of Robyn – which meant she wasn't in immediate danger from Agent X. However, it now seemed fairly definite that *she* was the one who'd vanished in the time machine, and not Willoughby as he'd initially thought.

But otherwise, the two notes left Justin feeling extremely confused. Whereas the ransom note for Henny had been prepared beforehand – this time, X's letter mentioned things he couldn't possibly have known in advance. His abduction of Sir Willoughby hadn't been premeditated, and he referred to it in the past tense – so how could the letter have been posted yesterday?

Puzzled, Justin re-examined the envelope, and an obvious explanation occurred to him. The postmark was on the stamp, but *not* the envelope. That could only mean one thing: the stamp had been steamed off another envelope, then stuck on this one to make it look as if it had been delivered with the mail. Then, while he and Jock had been rescuing Eliza, someone must have slipped it amongst the envelopes on the hall table.

But who? Nanny Evelyn? Professor Gilbert? Knightly? Anyone in the castle would have had ample opportunity.

Justin stared at the envelope again, wondering why the sender hadn't bothered to ink in the missing bit of postmark with a black pen. It would've taken seconds – and made it virtually undetectable. The professor wouldn't have made such an obvious mistake, Justin thought; he's too meticulous.

Justin walked on again, rereading the note from his father. This bothered him in an entirely different way. Its vocabulary seemed strangely out of character; his dad never used words like "*yield*" or

246

"*henceforth*". And why did it start "*Dear Eldest Son*" instead of *Dear Justin*?

For a moment Justin considered the possibility it was a forgery – but after comparing it to the letter Willoughby had left on the mantelpiece, he felt convinced the note was genuine. Then, as he poured over it, the solution suddenly jumped out at him. It was a simple acrostic – a message hidden in the first letters of each word:

D-E-S-T-R-O-Y—T-I-M-E—M-A-C-H-I-N-E—N-O-W.

Clearly, Sir Willoughby had no idea the chronopod had vanished.

As Justin headed across the west tower landing he glanced out of the window. In the courtyard below, Miss Garnet was talking to Mr Gillie-chattan. Seeing them, Justin suddenly remembered the little pistol hidden in Nanny's bedroom. This seemed the perfect opportunity to retrieve it.

He hurried up to the next floor and cut through the nursery. Albion – snuggled next to his old teddy bear – stayed sound asleep as Justin tiptoed past his cot to the connecting door.

Once in Nanny Evelyn's room, Justin dropped to the floor and squirmed beneath the bed ... but the gun was no longer there.

After grabbing a dry shirt out of his bedroom, Justin hurried up to his laboratory. He threw the mail onto the nearest workbench, then fetched a pair of scissors so he could finally open the mysterious parcel. As he snipped through the string he tried to guess what was inside – but nothing he imagined came anywhere close to the truth.

He tore off the brown paper and cardboard packaging, folded back several layers of thick cotton wadding, and pulled out something small but heavy wrapped in tissue paper. Seeing a glint of gold through a tear, he ripped it apart and found ... his stolen wristwatch!

Hardly able to believe his eyes, Justin turned the watch over and over in his hands, staring at it as if he'd never seen it before. Then, as he ran his fingers over the bracelet, a startling thought occurred to him. Carefully, he fished the tiny golden scythe out of his top pocket and held it close to the last card-shaped link. The two broken ends fitted together perfectly.

'That's impossible,' he murmured, rummaging through the discarded brown paper to find the stamps. He peered closely at the postmark; it looked completely genuine. 'But it *can't* have been mailed yesterday. I was wearing it ... and it *wasn't* broken then!'

Determined to fix the catch immediately, Justin opened the bench drawer and took out his horologist's toolkit. The watch was showing the wrong time – twenty-five past ten – and, as he examined it again, he realised the second hand had stopped. Carefully, he prised off the back panel to find out why it wasn't working.

He discovered the problem at once: a minuscule scrap of paper had been jammed in the mainspring. Using a pair of tweezers, Justin winkled it out and unfolded it beneath a magnifying glass.

At the bottom was a tiny drawing of what looked like a mouse – and above it a short hand-written verse made up of just thirteen words:

Time ran out;
Heed this rhyme.
Seek the Truth
To find the
Thyme!

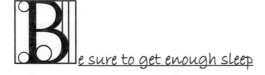

Be sure to get enough sleep

As unlikely as it sounds, this is extremely important. Despite returning to the present seconds after leaving it, the time traveller cannot discount the hours spent in the past. If several consecutive visits are made, these will add up to a long tiring day.

An extra hour or two in bed once safely in the present might help – but this isn't always possible if the chrononaut needs to keep his or her adventures a secret. The solution is to rest in the past, aiming for at least one hour of sleep for each four spent awake. If you don't feel safe napping in the distant past, stop off at a more recent location, somewhere you know your sleep won't be disturbed.

Remember: exhaustion can lead to mistakes – and time travellers cannot afford to be careless.

CHAPTER FIFTEEN

The Truth is Out There

It was uncanny, Justin thought; no matter how events twisted and turned, no matter how lost and confused he felt, everything always came back to Verity Kiss, like the needle of a compass steadfastly pointing due north.

Seek Verity – seek the truth!

Justin had no doubt that was what the minuscule note was telling him to do. The word *truth* was capitalised like a name – and verity, of course, meant truth. Somehow, wherever (or *whenever*) Robyn was, she believed Nanny Verity held the key to finding and rescuing her.

And Justin was *certain* the note was from his sister; it was the little sketch at the bottom that convinced him. At first he'd assumed it was a mouse, which made no sense at all. Then he'd realised it was Robyn's way of concealing her name that only *he* would be likely to grasp. Her initials: R.A.T – Robyn Anastasia Thyme.

Justin felt a sudden surge of excitement. It felt good to have a plan at last – and, best of all, the clues Nanny Verity had left for him were already at his fingertips. All he had to do was decode them, and he'd know exactly where to find her.

But first things first; before he did anything else he needed to fix his watch.

Hardly able to keep his hands from shaking, he took a pair of micro-pliers out of his toolkit, and started to reattach the gold scythe to the watch's bracelet.

As his fingers moved deftly, Justin allowed his mind to sift through the clues he'd found. He felt sure there were now enough facts to formulate a clear summary of last night's events.

'The tiny note I found in my watch proves Robyn took it,' he said, thinking out loud as he squinted through his horologist's eyepiece. 'I guess she was still angry about our argument. When she returned to the west tower, she probably saw Dad sneaking out and decided to follow him.

'According to Dad's letter he was going to use the time machine. I know he got as far as his workshop, because he left the door unlocked. In his ransom note, Agent X says *somebody* went time-travelling. If it wasn't him or Dad, it must've been Robyn ... but *she* didn't know how to set the coordinates. Perhaps Dad set them for *his* trip ... then noticed a light flashing in the great hall and decided to investigate. That explains his footprints by the west tower, and Evelyn Garnet's torch inside the French windows. The flattened bushes make me think someone knocked Dad out – and his acrostic message shows he was *still* unconscious when the time machine vanished, because he didn't know it had gone.'

Pausing momentarily, Justin opened a miniature bottle, and shook a single drop of oil onto the bracelet's catch-coupling. He worked it to and fro, trying to deduce what had happened next.

'Maybe Robyn saw Dad get attacked, then ran to the workshop. That's where I found her hanky – and the fact it was wrapped round a light bulb suggests she was hiding. If she hid in the sidecar, X could've stolen it not realising she was inside. Yeah, that fits with what Mrs Kof said. She saw a man in a balaclava driving the motorbike away just after midnight.

'But how did the scythe-catch end up outside the castle gates?' he muttered to himself.

'I suppose Robyn snagged it on something. Maybe it got wedged on the bike, then fell off as it swerved through the gates. The time machine probably vanished seconds later – and once X realised what'd happened, he must've come back and carted Dad off before he regained consciousness.'

Justin nodded to himself; it all seemed to fit. Admittedly there were a few gaps, but it was a decent working hypothesis.

After checking the little golden scythe hooked snugly through the hourglass, he fastened the bracelet round his wrist. Then, as the tower clock struck twelve, he set the watch to the correct time and wound it up.

He stared pensively at the ticking second hand, wishing he'd patched things up with Robyn last night. The realisation that her disappearance could, perhaps, have been avoided, left him in no mood for lunch – and anyway, tracing Nanny Verity's whereabouts seemed far more important.

Justin opened his safe and pulled out Nanny's old book of poetry and her half-decoded e-mail. Then, after rummaging through his trouser pocket for the homework clue, he placed all three on the bench next to his open copy of "*Get Cracking!*"

Justin decided to finish solving Nanny's e-mail first. He'd already decoded the start of her message: *I would like to help. I'll leave hidden clues.* Now all he needed to do was continue circling every tenth word:

Until quite recently you thought I was just your dizzy old Nanny. Events will have changed your mind I expect. However, I did need help to escape – though I've no idea who rescued me To my utter astonishment, a mystery saviour turned up shortly after you locked me in.

Naturally, it was quite unexpected I'd simply decided I'd give up and accept whatever disaster awaited me. It served me right. All the brazen lies I'd been telling the Thymes were finally getting their just reward. I knew I deserved whatever punishment lay immediately ahead

Justin gasped. Had Verity Kiss known her ex-husband was planning to steal the time machine? Suddenly, a hot wave of guilt swept over him. He'd had her e-mail for two-and-a-half weeks; maybe if he'd decoded it sooner he could've prevented last night's events from happening.

With a regretful sigh he picked up his pencil and carried on counting.

Then, amazingly, I sensed that somebody was behind me. When I asked who it was, a deep voice said: "You must heed this *message*: Do not look back. You need to escape quickly, so I've fetched you the key to those handcuffs." A key was tossed onto my lap. "Find a safe place to hide in," the voice said. "The job you have done will be continued by the next agent."

There was no chance to ask questions. The person had vanished just seconds before I could turn around to say thank you. It was very puzzling. I'd better vanish too, I thought. *In* a taxi!

Even now, I find it quite impossible to identify the person who rescued me. I didn't get enough time to scrutinize the evidence. First I hurried to my room to collect some money for the journey. Then I "borrowed" Robyn's computer; it's the only thing I could think of. She'll be utterly furious I expect – but writing *letters* is much too risky – so will you tell her I'm sorry.

Now Poppet, you must be very careful. My husband's a wonderfully talented actor, perfectly able to masquerade as anyone at Thyme Castle. You'll want to amaze everyone and unmask Agent X, but Nanny can't help – that would be just too dangerous. Don't try to locate me. Remember that Nanny has always loved you from the "heart of her bottom!" Look after Robyn and Alby.

☺Missing you already! Love, hugs and kisses to all the Thyme Family,

Mrs Verity Kiss, (Nanny).

253

As Justin ringed the final word, he felt a cold stab of panic.

How could Nanny Verity have known another family member would vanish? She couldn't have guessed about Robyn hiding in the chrono-pod, he thought – but perhaps she'd known Sir Willoughby would be kidnapped if the theft didn't go according to plan.

Did that mean she was still in league with Agent X?

Justin shook his head. Despite all she'd done, he simply *couldn't* believe Verity Kiss was a traitor. He remembered her impassioned words as she'd begged for his forgiveness: *"I'd never do anything to harm the Thymes; you're my family."* No, Nanny had been a victim, just like the rest of the family; forced to obey her manipulative, bullying husband. The only thing Justin didn't understand is why she'd put up with him for so long.

Still, one thing was certain: he had to find Verity Kiss as soon as possible.

Fiercely determined, Justin opened her poetry book to the page with the folded-down corner, and studied the poem carefully. It had four verses, each with eight lines – which corresponded perfectly with the four mathematical equations, each containing eight numbers.

According to *"Get Cracking!"* most book-code decryptions involved nothing more complicated than counting words or letters. The first number was fifteen – so, as the lines were never more than six words long, Justin logically assumed the code-numbers indicated individual letters.

The poem began with the line *"When we two parted"* – which meant the fifteenth letter was D. Justin jotted it down, then moved to the second line; the sixth letter of which was E.

By the end of the first verse, he had: D-E-D-O-C-N-E-S ... which looked utterly incomprehensible, until he noticed that, apart from the last letter, it was ENCODED spelt backwards.

Five minutes later, Justin had the complete string of thirty-two letters:

DEDOCNES-THGILFYM-NIHTIWSE-ILHTURTA

Which, when written in reverse said:

A TRUTH LIES WITHIN MY FLIGHTS ENCODED

After his struggle finding both halves of the code, solving it had been surprisingly easy – but at first, Justin felt slightly disappointed by the message.

He'd imagined the letters would spell something like: *Ivy Pane, Thirty Snuck Street, Boscombe* – or some other bogus name and address. But Nanny Verity hadn't taken any chances with her new identity; she'd hidden the clues extremely thoroughly, and was simply telling him where to look next.

Justin grinned as he remembered Sergeant Awbrite's bewildered face when he'd called at the castle to see Sir Willoughby a couple of days ago. "*Mrs Kiss booked and paid for nine different international flights,*" he'd told them. "*But according to our investigations she didn't catch* any *of them.*"

At the time, Justin had assumed the multiple bookings were nothing more than a smokescreen designed to misdirect the police whilst Nanny Verity had travelled somewhere else entirely. But it was now clear they'd had a double purpose.

The truth about her destination was somehow encoded within those flights.

Justin reached for his mobile and scrolled through its contacts menu looking for the number Sergeant Awbrite had given him. As the phone rang, Justin thought about what he was going to say. After Nanny had disguised her trail so skilfully, he wasn't about to reveal his findings to the police.

'Awbrite here; Inverness Constabulary,' said an efficient voice.

'Oh, hello Sergeant. It's Justin ... Justin Thyme.'

The policeman's tone changed instantly, sounding much friendlier. 'Aha, young Master Thyme. You're not ringing to report another kidnapping, are you?' He laughed to show he was teasing.

Feeling thoroughly uncomfortable, Justin forced himself to join in, then said: 'Actually, I'm phoning about ... erm ... our Nanny.'

'The redoubtable Mrs Kiss? Have you got a lead on her where-abouts?'

'Well, er ...'

Awbrite sensed his hesitation. 'You *have*, haven't you?' he pressed eagerly. 'I bet it's something to do with all those blinkin' flights she booked.'

'Possibly. I'd er ... rather not discuss it on the phone.' said Justin, choosing his words carefully. 'Perhaps you could fax the details through to me – assuming you've still got them on file.'

'Of course we have. Look, I'm going to Fort Augustus later this afternoon. I'll call in on my way back and bring you a copy. How's that?'

'Thanks, that's great.'

Justin sighed as he switched off his phone. He had an uncomfortable feeling the sergeant had guessed he was on to something, and that was the *real* reason he was calling in person. He, too, wanted to discover the truth about Verity.

Shortly after one o'clock, Justin headed downstairs. Despite Mrs Kof's insistence, he still didn't feel like eating – but he knew Haggis would be as hungry as ever. He foraged in the refrigerator, filling a bowl with tuna fishcakes and venison pâté topped off with a scotch egg.

As he hurried out of the kitchen, he bumped into Professor Gilbert returning his empty lunch tray. He slammed it down on the table and gave Justin a long reproachful look.

'Feeling better?' he asked crisply.

'Yes, thank you, sir,' said Justin. 'You got my message, then?'

'Yes ... and straight after I read it, I glanced through the schoolroom w-window and saw you roller-skating.'

Justin felt his cheeks growing hot. 'Actually, I was ... er ... road-testing my latest invention,' he muttered.

'Well, if you're quite cer-certain you've recovered, I'll expect you at two o'clock sharp. Bring your Newtonian mechanics essay, and don't forget your trigonometry ho-ho-homework.'

Less than an hour later, Justin knocked on the schoolroom door and stepped inside looking penitent. He knew he could've insisted on missing lessons – he paid the prof's wages, after all – but tracking Nanny Verity was at standstill until Sergeant Awbrite called with her flight details. And anyway, he wanted to ask his teacher if he'd seen or heard anything last night.

As the afternoon progressed, Professor Gilbert thawed a little – but it was almost the very end of the lesson before the conversation turned in a useful direction.

'Do I take it your sister won't be joining us again now she has her own governess?' the professor asked, looking hopeful.

'She's away, actually,' Justin told him. 'Dad and Robyn went back to Mauritius late last night. Perhaps you heard their taxi; they left shortly after midnight.'

'No, I was in Lupin W-wood from about eleven o'clock onwards ... owl-watching,' replied Gilbert. He seemed oddly discomfited. 'I didn't get b-back till dawn.'

'Did you take Mrs Kof again?' asked Justin, wanting to check the cook's story.

The professor's ears turned a deep shade of pink. 'No, th-th-thank goodness. She was busy looking for something.'

'Why *thank goodness*? I thought you were friends.'

'La-la-last time she seemed to th-th-think we were rather more than f-f-friends.'

'Oh?'

'She th-thought I'd invited her on a romantic moo-moo-moonlit date,' stammered the professor, looking completely mortified. 'I've never been so em-embarrassed in my entire life. She actually tried to k-k-kiss me!'

Once lessons were over, rather than hanging around waiting for Sergeant Awbrite to arrive, Justin decided to use the time before supper to continue his investigation. He chatted to each of the remaining castle residents in turn – discreetly steering the conversation round to the previous night, and whatever they might have noticed.

Grandpa Lyall claimed he'd been in bed by ten-thirty, and couldn't remember whether he'd heard anything or not.

The Gilliechattans insisted they were both asleep long before midnight – although Mrs G said she'd heard footsteps heading past their cottage around eleven o'clock, (which appeared to corroborate Professor Gilbert's story).

Finally, Justin went out to his dad's workshop to question Eliza – but she grunted irritably and waved him away. He considered fetching her laptop from the great hall, then decided it was too risky; if Nanny Evelyn noticed it missing she might get suspicious. Anyway, it was unlikely Eliza had noticed anything useful; she liked to rise early and was often in bed by sunset.

As he left the workshop, a police car purred through the castle archway and pulled to a halt outside the portrait gallery. Sergeant Awbrite jumped out and strode briskly across the courtyard towards Justin, unbuttoning his top pocket.

'Well, here's the flight info you wanted, young man,' he said, taking out a folded sheet of paper and handing it to him.

'Thanks, Sergeant.'

As he scanned through the list of destinations Justin could almost feel the intensity of Awbrite's gaze.

'That's the order she booked them in,' the policeman explained. 'Not that it matters.' He rubbed his hands together. 'So, what's your theory?'

'I er ... just wondered if knowing the places Nanny *didn't* go ... might give me an idea where she actually *did* go.'

Awbrite lifted one eyebrow and rubbed his moustache. 'Well, I guess there's *some* logic in that.'

Justin cringed, certain the sergeant had guessed he was being deliberately evasive. He *had* hoped the initials of each country might spell something – but the code couldn't be *that* obvious or the police would have seen it already.

FLIGHT NUMBER	DESTINATION	IATA CODE	DEPART TIME	GATE
V-07-13	Marseille, France.	MRS	00:18	3F
52-16-X	Frankfurt, Germany.	FRA	21:02	2I
I-06-19	Marrakech, Morocco.	RAK	05:03	4B
S-49-52	Nice, France.	NCE	21:12	9C
86-85-C	Sofia, Bulgaria.	SOF	01:00	1D
53-08-O	Spartanburg, USA.	SPA	15:19	6E
D-06-02	Washington DC, USA.	IAD	03:21	5A
06-18-E	Porto, Portugal.	OPO	12:21	8G
R-15-57	Las Vegas, Nevada, USA.	LAS	13:00	7H

Then he spotted it: irrefutable confirmation that Nanny Verity *had* encoded something within the flights. He turned away, not wanting his face to betray his discovery – and when he spoke again he tried to make his voice sound dull and dispirited.

'I'm sorry, Sergeant. I hoped something would leap right out at me ... but ...' He shook his head and shrugged.

'Never mind, it was worth a try,' said Awbrite. He held his hand out for the paper.

Justin shot a guarded glance at him, sensing this was a test. If he seemed too desperate to keep the paper, the policeman would immediately know it contained vital information.

'Thanks – but it looks like you've had a wasted journey,' he said, surrendering the page as if it held no further interest to him. Then keeping his voice as casual as possible, he added: 'Unless I er ... show it to the rest of the family.'

Awbrite gave Justin a long penetrating look before handing it back. 'If you *do* come up with anything you *will* let me know, won't you?'

Justin nodded.

'Remember, you can call me any time – night or day,' the sergeant continued, looking deadly serious. 'And please ... *please* don't do anything reckless; your nanny's ex-husband sounds a pretty nasty piece of work.'

When Justin remained silent, Awbrite gave him a cursory salute and returned to his squad car.

'Back to HQ, Knox,' he muttered as he opened the passenger door.

The young constable waiting in the driver's seat nodded vacantly and started the engine.

The instant the police car disappeared through the archway, Justin sprinted back inside the castle. He could hardly wait to get to his lab and start decoding the message properly. As he hurried across the entrance hall, he looked again at the clue he'd spotted in the left-hand column. Each flight number contained a single letter.

Carefully, Justin checked them a second time, reading from top to bottom: V-X-I-S-C-O-D-E-R. Surely that *had* to mean "*Verity Kiss is coder*!" She'd cleverly booked the flights in a specific order to verify she'd hidden a coded message. But where?

With his eyes still glued to the sheet, Justin strode through the dining room, only half registering the smell of food.

'You, boy ... I mean ... Master Justin,' called a saccharine-sweet voice. '*Do* come and sit down; supper's getting cold.'

Justin glanced up, momentarily puzzled – and saw Evelyn Garnet giving him an artificial smile from across the table; Knightly hovered beside her, ladling soup into Albion's bowl, whilst Grandpa Lyall seemed to be talking to his bread roll.

'I'm not really hungry,' Justin muttered, suddenly realising he was.

'Nonsense, dear! With your parents away, proper nutrition is my responsibility; I won't have you skipping meals.'

Justin thought this was a bit rich considering she'd spent the last few nights trying to starve him. Perhaps confronting her about the drugged cocoa had been a good move. She appeared to have undergone a complete personality transplant – although her attempt at chumminess came over as just plain creepy.

Justin stuffed the flight details into his shirt pocket and sat down. The delectable aroma of Mrs Kof's triple-cheese soufflé *was* tempting. A few mouthfuls wouldn't take long – and anyway, he reminded himself, brains work better when properly fuelled.

Nanny Evelyn beamed her approval. She turned to Albion and tickled under his chin with a long, bony finger. 'Now my little precious ... *you're* hungry, *aren't* you?'

Alby nodded happily. ''Es,' he chuckled, then he reached up, grabbed her hearing aid and pressed it into his mashed potatoes.

'Oh ... *isn't* he *adorable*?' gushed Miss Garnet. Then she laughed, like someone who'd once read an article about laughing but never got around to trying it herself.

Half an hour later, after shutting himself in his laboratory, Justin placed the sheet of paper on his desk and stared at it broodingly. The IATA codes looked the most promising place to find a hidden message, he decided. He knew all major airports were assigned a unique three-letter abbreviation by the International Air Transport Association. Perhaps Nanny Verity had chosen destinations that formed a sort of puzzle-anagram revealing her whereabouts.

MRS, the abbreviation for Marseilles seemed the logical place to start. Apart from spelling "*Mrs*" – which could be the first part of an assumed identity – it was also the earliest of the nine flights. Struck by a sudden idea, Justin took a pair of scissors, cut the sheet into nine horizontal strips, then rearranged them in chronological order:

V-07-13	Marseille, France.	MRS	00:18	3F
86-85-C	Sofia, Bulgaria.	SOF	01:00	1D
D-06-02	Washington DC, USA.	IAD	03:21	5A
I-06-19	Marrakech, Morocco.	RAK	05:03	4B
06-18-E	Porto, Portugal.	OPO	12:21	8G
R-15-57	Las Vegas, Nevada, USA.	LAS	13:00	7H
53-08-O	Spartanburg, USA.	SPA	15:19	6E
52-16-X	Frankfurt, Germany.	FRA	21:02	2I
S-49-52	Nice, France.	NCE	21:12	9C

The airport codes now spelled out a name and location:

MRS SOFIA DRAKOPOLAS, SPA, FRANCE.

Justin reached over to his computer and googled the last two words. The search came back with a gazillion page hits, and a quick glance at the first one told him there were more than fifty spa towns in France.

He groaned. There had to be more information ... a more detailed address. On a whim, he shuffled the paper strips again, arranging them numerically by the gate number:

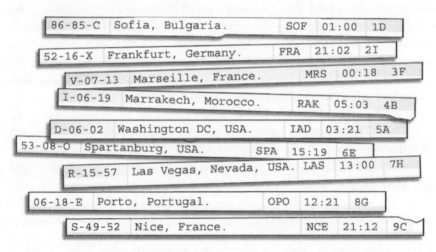

86-85-C	Sofia, Bulgaria.	SOF	01:00	1D
52-16-X	Frankfurt, Germany.	FRA	21:02	2I
V-07-13	Marseille, France.	MRS	00:18	3F
I-06-19	Marrakech, Morocco.	RAK	05:03	4B
D-06-02	Washington DC, USA.	IAD	03:21	5A
53-08-O	Spartanburg, USA.	SPA	15:19	6E
R-15-57	Las Vegas, Nevada, USA.	LAS	13:00	7H
06-18-E	Porto, Portugal.	OPO	12:21	8G
S-49-52	Nice, France.	NCE	21:12	9C

The triple-letter IATA codes became random gibberish again – but Justin swiftly spotted the word "DORES" spelled out in the last five flight numbers.

Weird, he thought. Dores was tiny village on the southern shore of Loch Ness. On a fine day he could actually see it across the water.

Was Nanny Verity in France or Scotland?

'It's probably just a coincidence,' Justin told himself. 'Or a red herring.'

He jotted down all nine letters: C-X-V-I-D-O-R-E-S – but they didn't make sense ... unless ...

Unless the first four letters were Roman numerals: CXVI. Could *116 Dores* be a house number and street name?

Justin typed *dores spa france* in his computer's search box; this time it found only a handful of web pages – all referring to Mont-Dore, a tiny French spa town by the Dordogne River, with a population of just a few hundred. It was known for its thermal springs – and, apart from a few rustic guesthouses, had just one hotel: Château Dores, an exclusive sanatorium that specialised in pampering rich celebrities with its luxurious detox treatments. Just the kind of place Nanny Verity dreamed about.

He found the telephone number onscreen then picked up his mobile – but before he could dial, he heard a familiar scuttling noise ... and Bugsy scrambled onto the desk top. The little microbot plugged itself into a USB port and, once again, the words BUG ALERT flashed across the computer screen, accompanied by the usual 3D wire-frame of the south tower. To Justin's immense surprise, it showed *two* bugs ... both of them in his laboratory.

For a moment, Justin half wondered if Bugsy was malfunctioning. Surely no one could've broken into his lab. The door remained permanently locked unless his right thumb touched the fingerprint sensor. But now that he glanced around, a few things *did* seem fractionally misplaced; his copy of Newton's "*Principia*" – which he'd left open – was now closed; and his digital-theodolite certainly hadn't been next to the spare incubator bulbs.

Justin leaned towards his computer and clicked the zoom function. The first bug was beneath his desk, and appeared to be another listening device identical to the one he'd found in the library. The second was a micro-camera – and had been positioned directly opposite his safe.

His initial instinct was to destroy them both – but cool logic prevailed. After making his travel arrangements silently on the internet, he pretended to phone his mother, telling her he'd be flying over to Mauritius first thing the following morning.

'Okay. Bye Mum,' he concluded. 'No, don't worry. I won't forget my passport. I'll get it right now.'

He switched his phone off, strode over to his safe, and turned its combination lock, whilst muttering, 'fifty-seven, twenty-two, seven,' clearly enough for the bugs to transmit. Then, with a big show of yawning and rubbing his eyes, he switched his laboratory lights off and went to bed.

The flight to Paris was uneventful and landed punctually. Of course, it would have been a great deal more comfortable using the private jet – but Justin knew he couldn't risk that; if his mother found out she'd ask too many awkward questions.

Charles de Gaulle Airport was seething with tourists and Justin had an hour to kill before his short flight to Auvergne. As he wandered round the transit lounge sipping bottled water and staring up at the ever-changing timetables, his unquestioning belief that Nanny Verity would be in Mont-Dore suddenly seemed incredibly foolish. The world was a big place for a game of hide-and-seek. In fact, as he waited for his flight, Justin counted planes jetting off to thirteen different countries around the globe: Cambodia, Italy, Germany, Netherlands Antilles, Portugal, Peru, Indonesia, Sweden, Morocco, Israel, Malta, Austria, and Norway. By now, Verity Kiss could be anywhere.

Perhaps the whole thing's been a trick to get me out of the castle, he thought; or lure me into a trap. After all, Nanny Verity once told me her ex-husband's name was Valentine. VX could just as easily stand for Valentine Kiss.

Justin felt a dark cloud of pessimism descend upon him. Eager to cheer himself up, he wondered if anyone had tried to reach his safe yet. If so, they'd have had a nasty shock. He couldn't help grinning as he remembered Maggot's cattle-prod, now fastened to the back of the south tower door, with newly added wires running into the keyhole.

Lunch on the internal flight was inedible – plastic food on *small white oval plates*. Even Haggis would've rejected it, Justin thought, poking it with his fork. Right now, the little doddling was probably enjoying an absolute feast. Justin had decided to leave Mrs Kof in charge of feeding him – in fact, she was the only person who knew his real destination and how he was hoping to find Nanny Verity. He realised a professional detective would *never* confide in a suspect – but all Justin's instincts told him Mrs Kof could be trusted.

The last leg of the journey was in a dilapidated French taxi. Justin sat in the back clutching his overnight bag, feeling evermore anxious the closer he drew to Mont-Dore. Hoping to take his mind off the bevy of butterflies fluttering in his stomach, he pulled out Nanny Verity's e-mail and examined it one last time.

Since finding the secret message hidden in every tenth word, he'd been plagued by an uncomfortable feeling there was something he'd missed ... *something important*. But no matter how many times he'd reread it during the trip, the answer still evaded him.

Nanny's vocabulary seemed oddly out of character, and reminded Justin of his father's acrostic note instructing him to *DESTROY TIME MACHINE NOW*. Why, for example, had she chosen words like *brazen*, *hazardous* and *scrutinize*, which she wouldn't normally use? Apart from all containing the letter Z, they had practically nothing in common.

Justin scanned though the e-mail checking initial letters – but there was no simple acrostic in this message. Then suddenly, the text's subtle peculiarity struck him so forcibly he gasped out loud: not only did the letter Z appear in all eight paragraphs, but other rarely-used letters – like J, Q and X – were there in each paragraph too. Justin suspected that when writing conventional English it would be statistically impossible for this to happen by chance. There had to be a reason.

He glanced out of the window as the taxi rattled past a battered-looking road sign; Mont-Dore was only one kilometre away; Justin knew he had just minutes left to crack the e-mail's final secret. Hurriedly, he fished a pencil out of his pocket, jotted the entire alphabet down one side of the page, then re-examined each paragraph carefully. Maybe ... if he could just work fast enough ... maybe ...

'Voici le Château Dores,' announced the taxi driver gruffly, waving towards a magnificent turreted building that looked like something out of a fairytale.

'Too late,' Justin groaned, crumpling the e-mail in his fist.

Time had run out; he'd reached the moment of truth.

'Ah, oui, the fabulous Madame Drakopolas! She is friend of yours, non?'

The concierge flashed Justin his most obsequious smile as he turned the guestbook round and offered him a pen. If the Château Dores was unaccustomed to welcoming solitary thirteen-year-olds, Justin's platinum credit card had swiftly removed any misgivings.

'La belle actrice Grecque booked in under 'er real name, of course,' the concierge continued, shooting a cool questioning glance in Justin's direction.

'Oh ... er, yes ... yes, of course ... Mrs Kiss,' Justin muttered quickly. He slipped the concierge a generous tip. 'She's my aunt ... Aunt Verity.'

'You 'ave a Greek aunt?'

'Half-Greek,' Justin muttered. 'Half-aunt, I suppose. Is she still in room 116?'

'Oui monsieur – though at this time of day you'll probably find 'er relaxing by the pool.'

As the concierge turned away to summon a bellboy, Justin flipped back through the guestbook, suddenly worried there was some ghastly mix-up.

'La belle actrice Grecque,' he murmured to himself. He could imagine Nanny using a fake name, but passing herself off as a beautiful Greek actress was a bit of a stretch.

But then, half way down the page, he found her full signature, *Verity Peripetia Kiss*, dated May 17th – just a few days after she'd disappeared from Thyme Castle.

Nanny was definitely here; her handwriting was unmistakable.

Five minutes later, Justin strolled outside to the swimming pool, but there seemed to be no sign of Nanny Verity anywhere. In fact, just six of the Château Dores' exclusive clientele were soaking up the afternoon sun: a military looking gentleman sipping tomato juice through a huge walrus moustache, two tiny Chinese ladies playing mah-jong, a tall African-American lying on a colourful towel, a chic woman in a black swimsuit – positively dripping with diamonds, and a bald, fat man wearing a thong.

Perhaps Nan's in her room, Justin thought. But then, as he turned to leave, he noticed something strangely familiar: the woman in the black swimsuit was wearing a cameo. When Justin looked closer, he saw it was fastened around her throat with a broad band of petersham ribbon, and looked strangely incongruous next to her fabulous diamond jewellery.

Slowly, tentatively, he walked towards the woman, taking in every detail of her stylish appearance. Her eyes were hidden behind costly designer shades; her sleekly coiffed dark hair had been swept into an elegant French pleat; and as for her legs ... *well!* Nanny's legs had always been primly imprisoned in thick grey stockings beneath her starched uniform. If forced at gunpoint, Justin would have imagined them as pale as ivory, probably covered in a mauve map of varicose veins – whereas these tanned specimens looked as if they'd been stolen from a retired supermodel.

'It can't be,' Justin muttered under his breath. 'It's ... it's imposs—'

He froze in his tracks and stared opened-mouthed as the woman sat up and gave him a dazzling smile of recognition.

'Och, hello Poppet,' said a familiar gentle voice. 'It's about time!'

'*Nanny!*' gasped Justin. 'Is it ... is it *really* you? You look, well ... *incredible!*'

He stepped forward, wanting to give her a hug – but her new-found aura of sophistication made him feel shy and awkward. Verity Kiss laughed, slid gracefully to one side and patted the sun-lounger with a well-manicured hand.

'Come on ... sit next to Nanny and tell me what's to do.'

Justin backed off and lowered himself into a vacant chair opposite, studiously avoiding all eye contact with Nanny's impossible legs.

'I knew you'd track me down sooner or later,' she continued, removing her sunglasses. 'I left enough clues.'

'Yeah ... it just took me a while to find them all.'

'Hmm ... something tells me you might've missed one or two.'

Justin grinned, feeling more comfortable now Nanny's merry, twinkling eyes were visible. The strange spell she'd cast was broken, but there was still something different about her; a self-assured inner confidence the old Verity Kiss had never possessed.

'What've you got to tell me?' she asked quietly.

Justin sighed. 'So much has happened since you ... you *left*; I hardly know where to begin. Robyn's vanished ...'

'Mm-hm.'

'Dad's been kidnapped.'

'Oh ... *that* I didn't realise,' said Nanny, raising her eyebrows in genuine surprise. 'Though I suppose ...'

'And my time machine's gone,' Justin interrupted. With a wonderful sense of release, words started tumbling out of his mouth. 'I think Robyn might've taken it; she took my watch too ... but she mailed it back with a weird cryptic note telling me to find you. Well, actually, it said *find the Truth* ... but I guessed that meant you. So I looked in your e-mail and found a hidden message, then another in that old book of poems by your bed ... then I tracked you down by decoding all those flights you booked, and ... and ...'

'And here you are,' Nanny laughed. 'Desperate to find your sister.'

'You *know* what happened to her?'

'Everything.'

'And where she is now?'

'Yes.'

'Then, let's get going!' Justin shouted, bounding to his feet and grabbing her hand.

'*Please*,' said Nanny reprovingly, sounding more like her old self.

'*Pleeeeeeeease*! Come *on*!'

'No,' replied Nanny, firmly extricating her fingers from Justin's vice-like grip and reaching for her old Victorian cameo.

Justin could scarcely believe his ears.

'*No*? But ... but why *not*?' he begged, utterly bewildered.

'There's no need to.'

Then, with a calm smile, Verity Kiss untied the petersham ribbon around her throat and lowered it slowly to reveal a faded tattoo of a robin carrying a sprig of thyme.

'You see, Dustbin,' she whispered, 'I'm already here!'

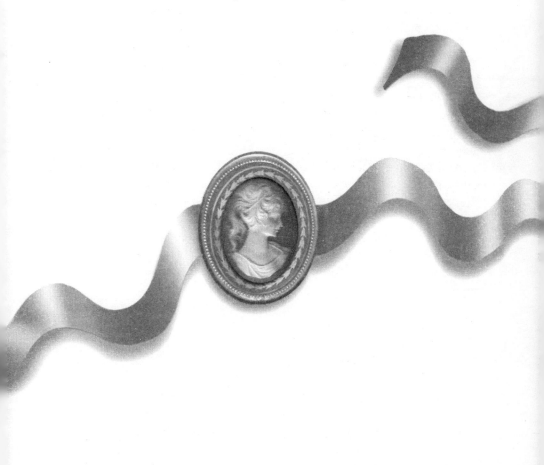

Meeting Your Younger Self – When & How

Many sci-fi writers suggest that meeting oneself is dangerous – but the truth is stranger than fiction.

To begin with, unless you already remember meeting your older self several years ago, it's unlikely you'll meet your younger self when you travel back in time. You could, of course, conceal your true identity, but even then, as you adopt your chosen disguise the memory of a past encounter will probably resurface.

Bizarrely, time travel allows for two or more versions of the same person to exist concurrently (as part of a time-loop), and if their ages are significantly different, the younger might not recognise the older duplicate.

Ideally, it's best to limit intentional self-encounters to a time AFTER you've started time-travelling so as not to shock your other self.

CHAPTER SIXTEEN

Back in Thyme

Justin stared at the faded tattoo with his mouth hanging half open, a substantial part of his brain steadfastly refusing to accept the evidence in front of his eyes. The truth seemed impossible, yet he had to admit his time travel theories *did* allow for such paradoxical anomalies; he just hadn't guessed he'd been living with one his entire life.

'But ... but ...' he faltered, rubbing his forehead. He had the stunned look of someone who'd just walked into a plate-glass window.

The woman he'd always called Nanny Verity laughed – though not unkindly – and when she spoke again, her voice was gently teasing. 'So you never twigged? Not even the teensiest inkling?'

'How ... how could I *possibly* ...?' Justin murmured.

'The clues were always there. When you and Robyn were little, didn't you ever wonder how I always knew what mischief the two of you were planning? That's because I still remembered my part of it.'

'Oh? ... I er, hmm ...' Justin muttered, still in shock. Suddenly, so many little things made sense. Like those nursery games of *Hunt the Thimble*; Nanny had already known where they *wouldn't* look! Then another memory flashed into his mind: Verity Kiss telling him, '*When I first came to work at Thyme Castle I wasn't much older than your sister.*'

'Och, I often thought you'd guessed, but weren't letting on,' she continued, smiling at Justin's moonstruck expression. 'Especially when Lady Henny – I mean, *Mum* was kidnapped; that's when I almost gave myself away.'

'How?'

'Copying your handwriting was my first silly mistake; your sister was always the forgery expert. And I used to pretend I knew nothing about computers, yet I e-mailed you from Robyn's address; to do that I needed to know her passwords, though fortunately I ...'

Justin sat bolt-upright and gasped. 'Robyn's *passwords*! It ... it was *you*! *You* emptied her bank account – *you* stole her money!'

'Och, I didn't *steal* it exactly,' Robyn replied, turning very prim and nannyish all of a sudden. 'It *is* my money, after all. When your poor old Nanny went into hiding she soon ran out of cash – but with Robyn's card number I was able to shop online. And why not? After years of starched pinafores and thermal stockings, I was ready for some decent designer outfits ... not to mention a bit of bling!'

'And you still remembered the card number after all these years? That's amazing!'

'Not really. Once I guessed Dad was going to confiscate the card I decided to memorise it. I tried changing the numbers to corresponding letters of the alphabet to see if they spelt anything, and by the weirdest coincidence I got: N-Y-B-O-R-M-A-I ... which is *I am Robyn* spelt backwards. Freaky – but impossible to forget!'

'Dad says nothing happens by chance,' Justin whispered. He cast his mind back to breakfast just three days ago. 'That morning, Robyn ... I mean, *you* told me your credit card number. Grandpa Lyall was dozing at the other end of the table. I thought perhaps he'd overheard you, and *he* was the thief.'

'Me too ... until just a week or two ago. I assumed the old fraud was about to empty Robyn's bank account ... *my* account.'

'But Bobs always believed Grandpa was genuine,' Justin reminded her.

'I *did*,' said Robyn, with a disdainful snort that reminded Justin of his sister. 'But once I got trapped in the past, I met the old laird in person. I'll admit this impostor looks astonishingly like him ... but he's a fraud, none-the-less. And the idea of him stealing my money made me *so* furious I decided to open a Swiss bank account in the name of Verity Kiss and transferred every last penny. Then a few hours later it struck me like a thunderbolt: nobody else *would've* taken the money – it was me all along.'

'Well, at least you finally know *I* wasn't the culprit,' said Justin.

Nanny's ... or, rather, Robyn's eyes filled with tears, and for a while she was unable to speak. 'That's plagued me for thirty years,' she finally gulped. 'I felt so terrible about blaming you, Dustbin – none of this would've happened if we hadn't fallen out.'

Justin shrugged. 'Maybe it would; maybe it was meant to happen.'

They both sat for a minute, silently pondering this thought. Justin gazed pensively at his much older sister. She still looked and sounded exactly like Verity Kiss – albeit after a radical makeover – but now he knew the truth, he kept catching the occasional glimpse of Robyn: a flash of the eyes, a turn of the head; little mannerisms they shared, that he'd mistakenly assumed Robyn had picked up off Nanny Verity.

'You've acted the part brilliantly,' he said.

'Och, I only acted at first – this is who I *am* now,' Robyn told him, smiling through her tears. 'That's why Eliza never sensed any dishonesty. Thank goodness for Mrs G's acting lessons. She always said: "*Don't portray – BE!*" It took me a while ... but once I realised you weren't coming to rescue me, I threw myself heart and soul into *being* Verity Kiss. Bit by bit, I managed to let go of Robyn – until she was little more than a distant memory. I even started my robin collection so I wouldn't forget my true identity. I bought one for every year I couldn't be myself ... gradually counting my way back to the present.'

'But how come you ended up so different to her?' asked Justin, still struggling to make all the pieces fit.

'People change, Poppet,' Robyn explained in her most nannyish voice. 'Our characters aren't carved in stone; we constantly grow, develop ... learn to see things differently depending on what life throws at us. When I was Robyn, I didn't believe in the Loch Ness Monster, but after hand-rearing a dodo, and getting zapped into the past, I was ready to believe just about anything ... no matter how impossible.'

Justin nodded uncertainly. 'Yeah, I can see how your outlook might change, but not your personality; surely that's hard-wired in our DNA. I just don't get how my feisty, confident sister could grow up to become ...' He stopped short, not wanting to say: *a dithering ineffectual Nanny obsessed with photographs of her grandchildren.* Whether Robyn or Nanny – he had no desire to hurt her feelings.

Seeing his discomfort, Robyn chuckled softly. 'Och, your sister wasn't *quite* as confident as she appeared. Having a younger brother who did *everything* a gazillion times better was bound to leave her feeling a wee bit insecure. All that sarcasm and rebelliousness was her way of getting attention, and making sure you never guessed how she *really* felt. She didn't want you getting too big for your *Hover-Boots*!'

'I think you'd better tell me the whole story,' Justin murmured. 'Right from the beginning.'

'Hmm ... I'm not sure when that *is* exactly,' said Robyn, frowning. 'Probably after we argued? No ... before then; the day Miss Garnet arrived ...'

'Evelyn Garnet wasn't hired until two-and-a-half weeks *after* you vanished,' Justin pointed out.

'Och, you're still muddling me with Nanny Verity,' said Robyn, patting his arm. 'I know it must be terribly confusing – even for a genius! Perhaps you should keep your eyes closed and picture your sister talking ...'

'But ...'

'And no more interruptions.'

Justin leaned back in his chair and did as he was told. Then, after taking a deep breath, Robyn started her story – but this time, her voice seemed subtly different; her gentle homely lilt replaced by a self-assured tone that conjured up in Justin's mind the image of his sister as a middle-aged woman remembering her youth.

'I suppose it all started with the tattoo,' said Robyn. 'That led to my row with Mum. Then we got stuck with that dreadful Garnet woman and everything got a thousand times worse ... though I have to admit, if she hadn't confiscated my mobile phone and dressed me like a scullery maid, things might've turned out quite differently.

'But ...' she continued, checking Justin's eyes were still closed. 'Stealing your watch was probably the final trigger. On my way back from the south tower, I spotted Dad creeping off somewhere. I followed him out to his workshop ... and that's when I noticed a light flashing down by the castle gates. I thought Dad ought to know about it, so I threw some gravel on the workshop roof to attract his attention. He dashed through the archway to investigate and saw someone signalling through the great hall window.'

'I *knew* it,' Justin began, shooting up and opening his eyes. 'I found a tor—'

Robyn silenced him with a firm stare. As he sank back and closed his eyes again, she continued: 'Someone – Agent X, I guess – crept up behind Dad and knocked him out. Then, when I screamed, the intruder turned and started chasing after me. I ran into the workshop and ended up hiding in the sidecar.'

Justin pulled a face, but before he could speak, Robyn said: 'Yes, I know it was a dumb place to hide ... but I panicked, okay? I didn't realise he was going to steal the bike with me still in it. But he did – and about half way down the drive a computer countdown started; then seconds after we turned through the castle gates everything went crazy. I mean *totally* crazy – like one of those warp-speed theme park rides where your stomach gets left in the middle of last week. Only this was about a trillion times worse. I felt like I'd dematerialised, got sucked through the eye of a needle, and then vomited into a hurricane ... all in a fraction of a second. And craziest of all, the bike was *still* zooming along Glen Thyme Road, only now it was brilliant daylight.'

'Dad mustn't have set the spatial coordinates,' remarked Justin, unable to stop himself. 'If he only specified a date and time, the computer would've chosen a point in space parallel to the one you were leaving, auto-adjusting for earth's axial rotation ... otherwise you could exit a wormho—'

'Can we skip the quantum physics lecture?' said Robyn impatiently.

'Sorry, it's just that using a time machine while it's moving is incredibly risky ... especially on a main road. You can't predict traffic conditions in another time period. You could ...'

'Crash? *Yeah*, been there; bought the four-dimensional tee-shirt,' Robyn interrupted, sounding more than a little peeved. 'May I continue?'

Justin nodded meekly.

'So, there I was ... stuck in a sidecar attached to a driverless motorbike, hurtling along the road. If that wasn't bad enough, I was heading straight towards a car – and between the two of us was a teenage girl, screaming. The computer announce: SAFETY-LOCKS DEACTIVATED then, somehow, I managed to kick the sidecar door open and throw myself out onto the grass verge.

'It all happened so fast I can't remember much. I must've rolled over and tumbled into a ditch. Then I heard this almighty crash and felt a blast of searing heat blow over me. I noticed a faint acrid smell, like singed hair ... then everything went dark and fuzzy.

'The next thing I remember was someone shaking me gently, and a deep voice asking if I was hurt. When I opened my eyes I saw a man crouched beside the ditch, peering down at me. For moment or two, I lay still, wondering if this was all part of some freaky nightmare – but, if so, it was incredibly real.

'"*Well, it looks like you're all in one piece,*" I heard him say. "*Just a few scrapes and bruises*; *a heck of a lot better than the other two, anyway.*"

'He slithered down into the ditch and lifted me gently onto the verge. Now that I could see him properly, I realised he was extraordinarily good-looking. He had the most dazzling blue eyes imaginable, and gazed at me with a fierce, almost hungry intensity. I muttered something idiotic about aching everywhere, hoping that would explain my flushed cheeks.

'"*You'll live,*" he said, sounding faintly amused. "*But I'm afraid your bike's a total right-off.*"

'He moved to one side and I saw Dad's old motorbike – now a twisted, mangled heap of scrap metal. The car it had smashed into was even worse; the bonnet looked like it had exploded; one door was hanging off, and its windscreen was shattered. Both vehicles were in flames and a plume of thick black smoke hung over them like a thundercloud.

'"*Are* you *okay?*" I asked.

'"*Me? Never better!*" he said, with a disarming chuckle.

'"*But ... your car ...*"

'"*No, no ... I was just walking by – sightseeing. The driver's over there*," he said, pointing across the road. "*Unconscious. I dragged him out first. The other girl's in rather a mess, I'm afraid; broken leg by the look of it; I didn't like to move her. I left you till last, seeing as you had the good sense to roll into a ditch.*"

'He gave me a breathtaking smile, which seemed oddly inappropriate considering two people were seriously injured. To avoid returning it I leaned sideways, trying to peer round him. The driver was face-down on the opposite verge; the girl – the one I'd heard screaming – lay in a crumpled heap a few metres to my left; she had one leg buckled beneath her, and half her hair had been scorched off.

'"*Don't worry,*" the man continued, taking hold of my hand and giving it a reassuring squeeze. "*I'm sure it wasn't your fault. Now, what happened? Brake failure? Or did the front wheel lock?*"

'It suddenly hit me: he thought I'd been driving the bike. Telling him the truth was completely out of the question, of course, so I muttered: "*Yeah,*" hoping that would satisfy him.

'"*Which?*"

'"*Both ... wheel failure and erm ... the other thing ... broken front locks.*"

'The man eyed me closely then shook his head, giving me a sympathetic lopsided grin. "*Fibber ... I bet you're not even old enough to drive!*"

'Ignoring his comment, I rose unsteadily and staggered towards the injured girl. Mercifully, she was unconscious. "*We need to call an ambulance,*" I told the man. "*Police too, probably.*"

'"*There's a phone box about half a mile back ... I could ...*"

'"*Haven't you got a mobile?*" I asked, without thinking.

'"*Mobile what?*" He gave me an odd, sharp look then, after a pause, added: "*Hmm ... you're not from round here, are you?*"

'"*I ... I live right there*," I told him, pointing towards the castle gates.

'"*What? Thyme Castle?*" he laughed. His eyes flickered over my clothes, and his grin widened. "*Well, what are you waiting for? Go and phone from* there *then!*"

'It was obvious he didn't believe me; he looked so infuriatingly smug I could've slapped him. But as I turned to leave, he grasped hold of my wrist and stared deep into my eyes. "*Hey, you really* do *live there, don't you?*" he whispered. "*Look, if anyone asks, don't tell them you were driving; just say you* saw *the accident, or you'll get in the most frightful trouble.*" Then seeing my puzzled frown he asked: "*Do you trust me?*"

'I nodded, not really sure why.

'"*Good girl – just leave everything to me,*" he said. "*I'll square things with the police. You've got to forget you were ever on that bike, okay?*"

'"*Okay.*"

'He pushed me gently. "*Go!*"

'I ran along the edge of the road. At the castle gates I glanced back, wanting to thank him, but he was leaning over the unconscious driver, reaching inside his jacket – probably checking the poor man was still breathing.

'As I hurried up the driveway, I tried to work out what had happened to me ...'

Justin half-opened one eyelid. 'Didn't you realise you were in the past?'

Robyn sighed. 'Hmm ... I did, and I didn't. Denial, I suppose. I knew I'd been inside a time machine, but my brain refused to believe I'd left the present. If I accepted *that*, then I'd have to accept I was trapped in the past and had crashed my only means of getting back to the future. I told myself I must've banged my head during the accident, and the computer countdown, the time-warp sensation, and the sudden switch from night to day, were all part of some weird hallucination. They *had* to be.

'But as I got closer to the castle, my theory seemed less and less convincing. The grounds looked oddly different; trees and shrubs were smaller, and there was a croquet lawn outside the west tower instead of the rose garden. When I entered the courtyard and found a liveried chauffer polishing Grandpa's Rolls Royce, I couldn't deny the evidence any longer.

'I was in complete shock, frozen to the spot as the enormity of the situation dawned on me. I tried to convince myself that you'd build another time machine and rescue me ... but I soon realised I couldn't depend on that happening. The last time I saw Dad he was out cold; until he regained consciousness you wouldn't know what coordinates I'd been zapped to. And for all I knew he might not have survived.

'"*Don't think that about it now,*" I told myself sternly. "*Just take things one step at a time. Phone for an ambulance – worry about the rest later.*"

'I guess the chauffer must have heard me muttering. He looked up and shouted: "*Hey ... you, girl; you'd better scarper round to the kitchen before old Tredwell sees you.*"

'I had no intention of scarpering anywhere. I gave him a cool glance and walked through the castle front door. The second I was inside, I dashed to the telephone, but before I could dial I felt a bony hand on my shoulder.

'"*You're late,*" said a frosty voice.

'I turned to find an elderly man dressed in a butler's uniform. He had a pale, hard face that looked as if it had been carved out of alabaster.

'"*Ah, Tredwell, I presume, I need to pho—*"

'"*Mr Tredwell to the likes of you, girl,*" he growled. "*And don't ever take that insolent tone with me again.*" He surveyed me with a cold, critical eye. "*Most unsuitable! I've a good mind to complain to the agency.*" Then propelling me briskly towards the kitchen, he called: "*Mrs fforbes-Fettlesham – the new girl's arrived.*"

'I started to explain about the accident, but he shushed me brusquely as a little old woman in grey approached.

'"*Ah, you must be Miss Hawkins,*" she said, giving me a kindly smile.

'"*Obviously!*" Tredwell snapped, before I could explain. "*Get her smartened up, sharpish, before the Master gets back – and cover that obscenity on her neck. A tattooed housemaid is NOT something I wish to see!*"

'The housekeeper bustled over and took hold of my arm. "*Where're your things, Dearie?*" she asked, leading me towards the east tower staircase. "*Still at the station?*"

'I suddenly realised that the girl I'd crashed into must've been expected at the castle. Part of me wanted to tell Mrs fforbes-Whatser-name the truth, but I knew that was impossible; so I decided to play along, still hoping for a miraculous rescue. I told her about the accident – but kept my promise to the blue-eyed man, saying I'd seen the crash as I was walking along the road.

'Tredwell was listening. "*Why didn't you say so before, you silly girl,*" he snapped. He turned smartly on his heels and hurried over to the telephone.'

'Do you think he suspected anything?' Justin asked.

'I doubt it,' said Robyn. 'Though he *was* a rather stickler. Fortun-ately the housekeeper could handle him, and *she* was a sweetie. She took me straight up to her room and sat me down in front of an old-fashioned dresser.

'"*I don't approve of maids wearing jewellery,*" she said, opening a little wooden box. "*But I expect this old cameo on a nice plain ribbon won't look too ostentatious. If anyone asks, say it's covering a birthmark.*" She tied it round my throat and it hid the tattoo completely. "*Now,*" she said brightly. "*When old Tredwell's around I'm Mrs fforbes-Fettlesham – but off-duty, you may call me Fluff – everyone does. And I shall call you Verity, of course. You'll be sharing a room with Becky; she's rather a scatterbrain, so I hope you'll set her a good example.*"

'Then she told me what my household duties would be, and that I'd get every second Wednesday afternoon off ... but I wasn't listening. I'd just realised that the girl whose place I'd taken was called Verity. At first I thought it was a coincidence; then I remembered Nanny V had started work at the castle almost thirty years ago ... as a trainee housemaid. I felt a sudden sickening fear that I'd changed history; that I'd stopped Verity Kiss from becoming our nanny. Yet that didn't make sense ... because the girl I'd seen outside the castle gates had

280

ginger hair and freckles – whereas Nanny had dark hair ... like ... like *mine*!

'And that's when it hit me. I hadn't changed history ... I'd simply fulfilled my predestined part of it. '

'A loop in time!' gasped Justin. 'I've been researching those. In some parallel universe that red-haired Verity probably *did* come to work at Thyme Castle – but in *our* universe, it's always been you ... even though you didn't know it.'

'I tried to remember what Nan had told us about being a maid,' Robyn continued. 'But she never spoke about it much ... only the barest facts ...'

'Just enough to help you grasp the truth when *her* past became *your* present,' said Justin, his voice sounding awestruck.

'Yeah, but the *really* strange thing is: I have a double set of memories for those conversations. I remember *listening* to Nanny when she mentioned how the housekeeper gave her an old cameo ... but I also remember *telling* Robyn the very same thing myself, thirty years later ... although I never revealed what the cameo was hiding.'

'Of *course* not! Nanny – I mean *you* – wanted to keep the loop consistent; make sure what *had* happened, still *did* happen. You probably thought if you revealed too much – accidentally said *anything* that could stop Robyn getting a tattoo – then she might not travel back through time and complete the loop. But I think it couldn't *not* happen ... because, for you, it already *had*. Wow! You've got to admit that's pretty cool!'

'Ffffuhhh! Theory's one thing, Dustbin – but let me tell you: *living* in a loop drives you completely loopy. For ages I was afraid to do almost anything in case I erased the future.'

'I'm not sure that's possible,' Justin reflected. '*Your* future was already part of your past. Even if you *tried* to change things, your actions would probably *cause* them to happen – like how you ended up stealing your own money.'

'I came to that conclusion eventually,' said Robyn, her voice sounding weary. 'But it was too late by then; continually living on a knife-edge destroyed my confidence. I'd swither over the most trivial

of choices – and big decisions were a nightmare. I was always terrified
of doing the wrong thing.'

'Well, it's time to stop worrying,' said Justin. 'You've come full
circle, Bobs. From now on, your life's whatever you choose to make it;
a fresh start ... a new page.'

He leaned forward, taking his sister's tensely clutched hands in his.
Now that she'd stopped talking, there seemed little of Robyn in the
woman sitting before him; she was Nanny again ... dear, sweet Nanny
Verity. Free, at last, to let go of the burden she'd carried her entire
adult life.

Silent tears trickled down her face – only this time, they were tears
of relief.

Justin knew there was a great deal more he hadn't been told, but he
realised it would have to wait. Nanny – or Robyn, (he still found it
strange to think of her as his sister), had promised to resume her story
later; right now she seemed physically and emotionally drained, and
had retired to her room for an hour's rest before dinner.

After unpacking his overnight bag, Justin went for a solitary swim.
He rarely used the pool back at Thyme Castle; good weather and
afternoons off seldom coincided. After a few dozen laps, he wrapped
himself in a huge, soft towel and found a quiet corner to sit and think.

He had an uncomfortable feeling that the next part of his sister's
story would involve the mysterious blue-eyed stranger who'd so
chivalrously come to her aid. Out of loyalty to Verity Kiss, he'd never
told Robyn that their beloved nanny had once been married to Agent X
– but now he found himself questioning his judgement. Despite all his
theories to the contrary, he couldn't help wondering if he might have
saved her from a lifetime of unhappiness.

Back in his room, Justin had half an hour to kill before he and Robyn
went down for their evening meal. Rather than waste it, he flattened
out Nanny Verity's crumpled e-mail and settled down to crack its final

code.

Using a pencil, he worked methodically through the first paragraph, ticking off each letter of the alphabet. As he'd suspected, it contained every letter except one: the letter N. The next paragraph used the entire alphabet apart from Y; and in the third, only the B was missing.

When all eight paragraphs had been decoded, he had N-Y-B-O-R-M-A-I ... or *I am Robyn* written backwards!

Later, as he walked downstairs to the Château Dores dining room with his sister, Justin praised her remarkable encryption skills.

'And to think – I've had the truth at my fingertips almost three full weeks! Weren't you worried I'd crack the code too soon ... or show your e-mail to Robyn?'

'Well, maybe just a teeny bit,' she admitted. 'But, like I said before, after thirty years I'd learned that things would probably happen pretty much as I remembered. And if my memory serves me correctly, your sister never saw that e-mail – and before she vanished, *you* were still looking for clues in one of Lord Byron's poems.'

Justin stopped abruptly, grabbing hold of her wrist. 'I've just realised: as Nanny, you *knew* to hide the code-key in that particular book, because Robyn remembered that's where I thought it was hidden. And when Robyn told me to look for your coded message on the nursery notice board ... you remembered that too.'

'True! Your poor Nanny didn't have much time the morning she mysteriously disappeared; knowing where to leave the codes in advance made it much easier.'

They walked side by side into the dining room where a waiter greeted them with a deep bow. As he guided them to a secluded table, Justin noticed how his sister drew admiring glances from every corner of the room. And no wonder, he thought proudly – she moved with the easy grace of someone who belonged on a Hollywood red carpet. Her outfit – a perfectly cut, though disconcertingly short, little black dress – oozed sophistication and elegance; and instead of her old cameo, she wore a broad diamond choker with a matching bracelet and earrings.

Once they were both seated, Robyn spoke again: 'Of course, I was fairly sure you'd overlook the easiest clue of the lot.' Ignoring her brother's questioning glance, she fished her reading glasses out of her clutch bag, muttering, 'I told your sister that computer would ruin her eyesight,' then peered at a menu.

'So, what did I miss?' asked Justin, trying to sound indifferent.

Robyn wasn't fooled. Enjoying an all too rare moment of triumph, she made him wait a little longer. 'The sole marinière looks good,' she remarked casually.

'*Pleeeease*, Nanny!'

'Oh, okay, Dustbin,' she laughed. Then unable to restrain herself any longer, Robyn leaned across the table and whispered: 'Tell me ... what's *Byron* an anagram of?'

By mutual agreement they decided not to talk about the past whilst eating. Robyn kept the conversation bright and impersonal; the weather, fashion, books. She waved to people at other tables and flirted with the waiters. Everyone called her Sofia or Mrs Drakopolas, and she spoke to them fluently in their own language.

She seemed happy, Justin thought – but it was a fey happiness; a surface gloss of merriment masking the sad realisation it couldn't possibly last.

Once the meal was over, they carried their coffees onto a deserted balcony overlooking the mountains, and watched the setting sun shroud everything in a dusky blanket of pink. Gradually, the sparkle in Robyn's eyes faded, and Justin sensed she was reluctant to resume her story. He decided to ease her back into the past with a safe question.

'I was thinking,' he said quietly. 'You must've known Dad when he a boy. What was he like?'

'Very like you in many ways,' Robyn answered. 'Although to be honest I rarely saw him. Shortly after I arrived, he went back to boarding school and he didn't come home until the following summer. I knew little Deighton much better. He got so terribly lonely when Sir Lyall went off on his travels, he'd sneak into the servants' quarters for company. I used to play snap and happy families with him.'

'Did you ever find out what happened to the real Verity?' asked Justin, hoping she was now ready to continue.

Robyn nodded and took a deep breath ...

'Later that night I phoned the local hospital. Poor girl; her leg *was* broken, but her parents were travelling up from Yorkshire to take her back home. I remember breathing a huge sigh of relief, knowing it was safe to continue my charade! The nurse I spoke to said the driver of the car had concussion and was being kept under observation overnight – but the motorcyclist didn't have so much as a scratch. However, she told me he'd been arrested for dangerous driving and carted off to Inverness Police Station.

'That night, in my tiny east tower bedroom, I couldn't sleep a wink. I kept worrying about how long I could keep up the pretence without slipping. And another thing bothered me: Why would a complete stranger willingly take responsibility for an accident that wasn't his fault?'

'I bet he saw the motorbike appear out of nowhere,' said Justin. 'If so, he must've known all along you hadn't been riding it.'

'Yeah, it should've been obvious, I suppose,' Robyn sighed. 'But the following morning I jumped to another conclusion entirely ...

'It was a pretty stressful day. I was woken up at dawn – and my first job was to clean out all the fireplaces, set the kindling, then refill the coalscuttles. Next, I had to scrub the kitchen floor. Then, once the dining room was empty, I was sent to clear away the breakfast things. That's when I came across Sir Lyall's morning paper; the crash was headline news. Scanning through the article, I discovered the blue-eyed man had been ordered to pay a fine and imprisoned for one month. I was horrified – but then, right at the bottom of the page, I read something so mind-blowing my legs turned to jelly: his name was Valentine *Kiss*.

'At first, I just thought: *what a lovely romantic name* – and wondered if he was related to Nanny Verity. Then I remembered: *I* was called Verity now. If I remained in the past, maybe this was the man I was destined to marry.

'*That* was the ridiculous conclusion I jumped to: that Mr Kiss had gone to prison in my place because he'd fallen madly in love with me. I remembered his attentive concern, his oddly flirtatious manner ... and how his fabulous blue eyes had devoured me so hungrily. What other explanation could there possibly be, I thought.'

'Hmm ... that he'd fallen madly in love with the idea of owning a disappearing-reappearing motorcycle,' Justin murmured, reaching over and giving his sister's arm a sympathetic squeeze. 'And if he guessed it was a time machine, he probably intended to claim the wreckage once he got out of jail, hoping someone in your future would know how to repair it.'

Robyn sighed. 'You're right, of course. What a silly, romantic little fool I was – but daydreaming about him *did* help me through that first month when I was missing you all so terribly. I couldn't help it; he was the handsomest man I'd ever met.' She sighed again, with a wistfulness that worried Justin slightly. He raised one eyebrow and shot a quizzical sideways glance at his sister.

'Don't worry,' she told him. 'I eventually discovered his darker side. But back then, he was my knight in shining armour. I was the envy of all the housemaids when he wrote to me from prison. He told me not to worry – and promised to take me out for tea as soon as he was released.

'Sure enough, on my third afternoon off he was waiting outside the castle gates. We caught the bus to Inverness, and went for a quiet stroll through the Pleasure Garden. He was all smiles and flattery, brushing my thanks aside – insisting any gentleman would've done the same. Then, after our tea, he suggested calling at the police station, to find out what had become of the motorcycle ...'

'Told you,' Justin whispered.

'That's when his mood changed,' Robyn continued. 'Once the desk constable informed him the bike had been sold as scrap to pay his fine, he turned quite nasty. He shouted and swore until we were both thrown out. I told him it didn't matter ... that I didn't mind a bit ... but that only seemed to infuriate him more. In the end, he stormed off, leaving me to make my own way back to the castle.'

'I cried all the way home, certain I'd changed the future and that Nanny Verity's children and grandchildren would never exist.'

'But it wasn't your fault,' Justin insisted.

'Ah, but it was,' said Robyn, shaking her head. 'While he was still in jail, I phoned the police station pretending to be his sister. I asked about the fine, wondering if I could pay some of it out of my wages. When they suggested the scrap value of the bike would cover the debt, I gave them permission to sell it. After all, it was totally wrecked.'

Justin laughed. 'Serve him right.'

'That's as maybe,' said Robyn, sounding prim and nannyish all of a sudden. 'But I was distraught; my mind was in a complete turmoil. From then on, every decision I faced made me a dithering wreck.

'Several months passed before I saw Valentine Kiss again. I spent the long winter nights trying to reassure myself we were destined for each other, and our parting was temporary. I was scarcely fifteen, after all – I had plenty of time to put things right.

'Then one fine spring morning, whilst running an errand for Cook, I spotted a poster in the butcher's window. It was advertising Shakespeare's "*Romeo and Juliet*" at the Pygmalion Theatre – and half way down the cast list I noticed Valentine Kiss would be playing the part of Benvolio.

'As I walked back to the castle, I felt strangely uplifted. I was still missing you and Mum and Dad ... but I figured if you'd been coming to rescue me, you'd have done it already. Clearly I was stuck as Verity – so maybe this was my opportunity to give fate a helping hand.

'On my next afternoon off, I headed straight to Inverness for the matinee performance, buying the best ticket I could afford. Shortly after the curtain rose, my heart sank; I didn't know who was playing Benvolio, but it obviously *wasn't* Valentine Kiss. I'd spent a full week's wages for nothing. However, my dismay soon turned to delight when minutes later he strolled onstage as Romeo.

'After the final curtain call I hurried round to the stage door, hoping to catch him when he left – and I wasn't the only one; there was a crowd of at least two dozen other girls. When Mr Kiss appeared they all started screaming and waving their autograph albums, but the

287

instant he spotted me, he swept past the whole lot of them, grabbed my arm and hailed a taxi. You should've seen their faces!

'"*To Bunbury's, my good fellow*," he called to the driver. Then, after opening the cab door and flashing me one of his most dazzling lopsided smiles, he said, "*Hop in, Angel-face – I want you to meet my brother.*"

'It was most peculiar. He acted as if we were old friends, and barely a week had gone by since out last meeting. I tried to apologise about the motorbike mix-up, but he didn't seem interested; he was too busy explaining how he'd landed the starring role.

'"*Splendid bit of luck*," he said, grinning roguishly. "*When I auditioned, the lead had already been cast, but – by a remarkable chance – the chap who* should've *played Romeo fell downstairs and broke his arm. He'll be off work for months, so the director's just asked me to tour with the company.*"

'He laughed like it was a terrific joke ... but I could tell something was bothering him. After a minute or two, he leaned closer, locked his sky-blue eyes onto mine and whispered: "*I say, would you do me an enormous favour?*"

'"*I suppose,*" I said, edging back slightly.

'"*Look, I'm going to be perfectly honest with you – I can tell you're a decent sort. This younger brother of mine – the one I want you to meet – he'll probably say he's been working away or travelling or some nonsense. But he hasn't; he's just got out of clink ... and for something a lot worse than crashing a motorbike.*"

'That got my attention.

'"*Don't panic,*" he continued hurriedly. "*He's not dangerous – he just fell in with the wrong crowd, tried a few idiotic money-making scams and ended up in debt ... then before I could help him out, he graduated to petty theft and blackmail. He's easily led, that's his trouble; tells everyone he's innocent – but the only person he really fools is himself. I've always had to watch out for him ... but he's going straight now; turned over a new leaf. He's got this crazy idea he wants to be a magician. The problem is I need someone to keep an eye on him whilst I'm touring with the play; someone he can talk to – make*

288

sure he's not slipping back into his old ways."

'"*Me?*" I asked, perfectly horrified.

'"*Only if you don't mind,*" he assured me. "*You mustn't feel obligated just because of ... well, you know ...*" He shrugged, looking horribly embarrassed. "*On second thoughts, forget I asked ... it was wrong of me to put you on the spot...*"

'He looked so thoroughly ashamed and unhappy I couldn't help myself. "*Of course I'll help out; it's the least I can do,*" I muttered, wondering what I was letting myself in for.

'His gloomy expression vanished as if he'd wiped it off – and instantly, a boyish grin lit up his face. "*You'll like him, I'm sure,*" he said. "*And I just* know *he's going to adore you.*"

'A sudden unsettling thought occurred to me: what if the Mr Kiss I was destined to marry wasn't the charming, debonair Valentine ... but his wayward younger brother?

"*Yes,*" laughed Val, rubbing his hands together. "*I bet you and Xavier will get on like a house on fire!*"

Unless unavoidable, Limit Your Stay in the Past

As mentioned in rule thirteen, the amount of time a chrononaut spends in the past is quite different to the length of their absence from the present.

It would be perfectly possible to spend weeks, months or even years in the past, yet not be away from the present for more than a few seconds.

However, what the time traveller must never forget is that they will still grow older whilst visiting the past. If they stay away from the present for too long, their increased age will be obvious to friends and family when they return.

Unless some unavoidable disaster occurs, trapping the traveller in the past, they would be well advised to always return within twenty-four hours.

CHAPTER SEVENTEEN

Robyn's Return

'Xavier?' gasped Justin. 'You ... you *don't* mean Xavier Polydorus?'

Robyn nodded. 'Of *course*. In those days he was still Xavier Kiss; he legally adopted his stage name after he and Val went their separate ways. But that's jumping ahead a few years ...'

'Hang on a tick,' Justin said, looking puzzled. 'Right up to the night Robyn – I mean, *you* – disappeared in my time machine, the two of us were almost certain Mr Polydorus was Agent X, right?'

'He *did* seem the most likely candidate,' Robyn agreed. 'Unfortunately, that rather coloured my view of him when we met in the past.'

'So you recognised him, then?'

'Sort of. People change a lot in thirty years – as you've discovered. But it was remembering the present-day Xavier that convinced me. When Val told me his brother's name, I suddenly thought of old Mr Polydorus's prediction: *You will commit a crime, embark on a hazardous journey and fall in love with a handsome stranger.* He wasn't mind-reading – he *knew*! Which meant the young Xavier I was about to meet was almost certainly the same person ... and he'd get to know me pretty well. And that wasn't the only thing. The day you and I had afternoon tea with Mr Polydorus, he *nearly* called me Verity. Didn't you notice?'

Justin shook his head.

'At the time, I thought it was just a slip of the tongue – but once I was trapped in the past it all made sense,' Robyn continued. 'Of course, Evelyn Garnet had me dressed like a scullery maid, so it was no wonder I shocked him. Although I think he *first* recognised me a few weeks earlier ... the day Polly brought him round to the castle.'

Justin frowned thoughtfully. It was hard to believe barely two days had elapsed since he'd visited Xavier's home with his sister. As he replayed the magician's conversation in his mind, he remembered something: '*Hey*, when Mr Polydorus said he and his brother fell out over a girl, he ... he was looking *straight* at you.'

Robyn turned away without replying, but Justin noticed her blush.

'Were *you* that girl?'

'I wasn't going to tell you about *that*,' Robyn replied, sounding a tad defensive. Then, after a moody silence she added: 'That afternoon, I thought he was just being creepy – but years later, when I'd broken his heart, I sometimes wondered why he hadn't warned me not to ... for both our sakes.'

'He told us he was a sci-fi fan,' said Justin. 'Perhaps he's read about temporal loops, and guessed that interfering probably wouldn't change anything.'

'But he *did* interfere ... even if he didn't mean to; it was actually his "*You will commit a crime*" comment that made me think about stealing your watch.'

'You can't deny there's a certain inevitability about all this,' Justin remarked, with a quiet chuckle. 'Well, that's one of my best theories up in smoke. I thought Mr Polydorus was your ex-husband in disguise ... but it turns out they're two separate individuals.'

'Very much so,' said Robyn. 'And worrying about which one I was supposed to marry nearly drove me insane. Fortunately, you never told Robyn that her trusty old Nanny had been married to Agent X.'

'Why fortunately?'

'Because there's a good chance it would've made me pick the wrong brother. You see, the wrong brother would've been the right one, and the right brother wasn't ... which, bizarrely, meant the incorrect choice was the correct one.'

'Now you've lost me.'

'*Fffuhhh* ... that's *nothing*! Imagine living in that kind of muddle!' Robyn screwed her eyes up and squinted like someone concentrating on untying a knot; after a deep sigh she leaned back and gazed at the starlit mountaintops. 'When I landed in the past I was certain that Xavier Polydorus was Agent X – and when Val told me his brother was a convicted criminal that only convinced me more.

'Our first meeting was pretty awkward. Val had reserved a table at a fancy teashop. When we arrived, Xavier was already there; he was trying to impress one of the waitresses with a card trick, but the moment he saw us he knocked over an entire plateful of fondant fancies.

'As we walked towards the table, Valentine whispered: "*You mustn't let on you know he's been in trouble. He'll only deny it and insist he was wrongly imprisoned.*"

'I had absolutely no intention of embarrassing him, so I nodded in silent agreement.

'Given my prejudices, what surprised me most about Xavier was how much I liked him. He had none of his brother's easy charm, and wasn't half so good-looking. Ordinary ... that's how he seemed; and just a little too eager to please – like an abandoned dog, desperate for some little sign of approval. There was a warmth and openness about him ... a naivety, I suppose. If Val hadn't warned me, I'd have thought him incapable of dishonesty.

'It was clear he idolised his older brother; he combed his hair the same way and dressed in similar clothes – but he lacked the personality to pull it off. What looked slick and stylish on Valentine looked all wrong on poor Xavier.

'As we ate our tea, he told me how he'd tried acting for a while, but it hadn't worked out.

'"*Kept fluffing my lines,*" he said ruefully. "*I let Val down completely.*"

'Valentine gave him a glowing smile and slapped him on the back. "*Nonsense, Xav,*" he said. "*That improv of yours was inspired.*

'Friends, Romans, countrymen, lend me a few quid,' – brilliant! They should never have sacked you."

'He cast me a meaningful sideways glance that implied his brother had been fired for something else entirely.

'Anyway,' Robyn continued. 'I kept my word. Val bought a little second-hand caravan; while he was touring with the Harlequin Players I stayed in contact with Xavier. We'd meet up on my afternoons off and picnic by the loch, or go to the cinema if the weather was bad.

'Valentine kept in touch too; he wrote to me almost every week, telling me what play he was in, often sending theatre programs or photographs of himself as different characters. He had the most astonishing chameleon-like knack of being able to transform himself into anyone – and in full costume and makeup he was unrecognisable.

'Lucky Val, he always got the starring role; the leading men in his company were an accident-prone lot. If the theatre wasn't too far away, he'd send tickets for us. I saw him in "*Spider's Web*", "*Othello*", "*No, No, Nannette*" ... and I remember Xavier taking me to see "*The Admirable Crichton*"; Val played a butler in that one.

'When he wrote, he always asked what was happening at the castle, and insisted I replied with all the latest gossip. I didn't guess he was already using me as his spy. Once every few months he'd turn up at the castle gates and whisk me off for tea, but he never stayed long.

'For the next few years our lives ticked by without much change. Looking back, I realise Val was biding his time ... and I strongly suspect he'd instructed Xavier to keep an eye on *me*.

'Then, one winter, everything changed. Sir Lyall bought that old Norton motorbike for young Master Willoughby. He couldn't drive it on the road until he was seventeen – but during the school holidays he enjoyed zooming around the estate with Deighton in the sidecar. Obviously, I'd no intention of telling Val about it – or anyone else for that matter – but he saw it the next time he called to take me out.

'"*Isn't that bike like the one you crashed,*" he asked.

'I shrugged and said mine had been quite different. He gave me a long, hard look ... but by then I'd got pretty good at acting myself.

'Up to that point his interest in the Thymes had centred mainly on Sir

294

Lyall, but from that day on his focus changed. He immediately wanted to know where Willoughby was being educated, and if he had a particular interest in science.'

'Didn't that ring any alarm bells?' Justin asked.

Robyn gave a long, tired-sounding sigh. 'I suppose it should've done, but I'd been blinded by our suspicions of old Mr Polydorus in the 21st century. I was certain young Xavier was destined to become Agent X, which meant Valentine was just the dutiful older brother. Even my friendship with Xavier didn't sway me – and by then I'd become *very* fond of him indeed.

'With practice, his conjuring skills had improved considerably, so he applied to a circus, hoping to become their resident magician. Unfortunately, all they needed was a chimpanzee trainer. Poor Xavier ... he kept pestering me to leave my job at the castle, certain the best way to advance his magical career was to have a glamorous female assistant.

'I have to admit it *was* tempting. I was tired of skivvying from dawn till dusk – so I decided to talk to Val about it on my next afternoon off.

'We met at *Bunbury's*, and I could tell at once from his earnest expression he had something important to say. To my astonishment, he presented me with a single red rose, went down on one knee and asked if I would marry him. But before I could reply, Xavier burst in, shouting furiously at Val, and in no time at all their quarrel turned into a fight.

'I discovered that Xavier had confided in his older brother ... not only about me becoming his stage assistant, but also how he intended to ask for my hand in marriage. He called Val a despicable cad for proposing behind his back – then begged me to marry him instead, showing me the diamond solitaire he'd already bought.

'I'd never been so utterly bewildered in my entire life. I *knew* I married one of them – but which? It seemed an impossible choice. Over the years I'd grown closer to Xavier than I ever expected – but how could I choose someone destined to become our most hated enemy. I wondered if, by marrying him, I could change his future, stop him from becoming the Thief of Time ... but I wasn't convinced that was possible.

'I knew Valentine was the sensible choice; a handsome, successful actor, always looking out for his wayward younger brother. True, he *had* proposed to me behind Xavier's back – but didn't that prove how much he loved me?

'I said I needed time to think it over, and promised I'd give them my decision by mid February – but the following day Xavier was arrested. It turned out he'd bought the engagement ring with money he'd stolen. He denied it, of course – but the evidence was overwhelming; he'd been seen by several eyewitnesses.

'You'd think that would've simplified things – but even though I felt sure Nanny wouldn't have married a crook, I was terrified of making the wrong choice. I combed though my memories of her, searching for some little clue to guide me. Then I suddenly remembered the names of Nanny's twin daughters: Hathaway and Henslowe. They had a distinctly theatrical sound to them, like something an actor might choose.'

'Good thinking,' said Justin. 'But once you were Nanny V, couldn't you have given your younger self a few hints? Made it easier?'

Robyn shook her head. 'I didn't because I knew I hadn't ... and by *then*, I was fairly sure she *would* pick the right person, because *I* already had. Valentine was the man I was *meant* to marry; although I didn't realise he'd only proposed so he wouldn't lose his spy at Thyme Castle.

'I wrote to Xavier while he was in prison, telling him about my engagement to Val. His reply was brief and courteous – accepting my decision, and promising that when he was released he'd stay out of our lives completely; he never wanted to see his brother again.

'From then on I was determined to bury my feelings for Xavier. After all, a rotten apple doesn't change its spots. I married Valentine Kiss three months later. It should've been the happiest day of my life – but it was marred by tragedy.

'The morning before, young Deighton had been thrown from his horse; he broke his neck and never regained consciousness. On the day Val and I got married, the hospital switched off Deighton's life-support system. Sir Lyall was devastated – but poor Master Willoughby was inconsolable; he kept wishing he could turn back time and save his little brother.'

Hearing a muffled sob, Justin glanced up at his sister; she was dabbing her eyes with a lace handkerchief and seemed suddenly older and more nannyish.

'Och, sorry,' she gulped. 'I didn't think this would upset me so much. I'm exhausted.'

Justin made a sympathetic face, and waited until she stopped crying. He didn't want to distress her, but there was still so much he needed to know.

'Just one last question before you go to bed,' he said after a minute or two. 'How long was it before you realised you *had* married Agent X?'

Robyn cleared her throat and whispered huskily: 'Not for a while – though I soon discovered he wasn't the gallant gent I'd always thought; he had quite a temper. There were *some* happy times,' she insisted, as if trying to convince herself. 'And the children, of course; Kitty first, then the twins the following year. With Val away so often, they were my whole world. He'd tell me he was off touring with a play, but I had my doubts.

'When the girls were little he got a permanent job in Edinburgh, and I moved there so we could be a family. He wasn't acting then ... although I suppose he *was* in a way. He said he'd started a drama school called "Tutor of Thespians" or *TOT* for short – but I think it must've been when he...'

'... first started working with Dad!' gasped Justin. 'But *TOT* really stood for *Thief of Time*.'

Robyn gave a tired nod. 'It was all very *hush-hush*. Years later – shortly after you were born – Valentine admitted he'd been working for a top secret organisation inventing a time machine, and I finally realised Agent X simply stood for Agent Kiss. He said Sir Willoughby had been his lab assistant, and he'd stolen the only blueprint. Knowing all I did, I strongly suspected Val was lying – but I *had* to pretend otherwise. That was when he bullied me into applying for the job of Nanny, so I could tell him if I ever overheard the words "*Time*

Machine!'"

'Of *course*!' Justin exclaimed. 'It all makes sense now. *That's* why X faked Dad's memory-wipe; he was expecting him to secretly convert his motorbike cos he'd already seen it in action. He never imagined it would be left under an old tarpaulin for thirteen years.'

Justin's face fell as a sudden unsettling thought occurred to him. 'If I hadn't adapted the bike,' he said slowly, 'you couldn't have travelled into the past. And if Agent X hadn't seen you arrive he might never have become the Thief of Time.' He glanced down at his wristwatch and took a sharp breath as he remembered the words engraved across its back. 'Everything is connected to everything else,' he whispered, staring wide-eyed at his sister. 'Oh *flux*! Everything that's happened ... it ... it's all *my* fault!'

Justin's bed was comfortable, and his turret-top room in one of the Château Dores' towers should have made him feel right at home – but he couldn't sleep a wink. His mind was full of constantly shifting thoughts, weaving and tumbling over each other like maggots in a tin.

He kept remembering how angry he'd felt when he'd discovered his father's deception, and felt hot with shame.

'Dad wouldn't have needed to lie if I'd never built a time machine,' he told himself for the hundredth time. Sir Willoughby's reproachful face flashed into his mind, and Justin wondered if his father had guessed the truth.

Robyn had insisted he wasn't really to blame – but Justin couldn't shake the feeling her voice lacked conviction. He reminded himself that Nanny Verity had always been somewhat hesitant and insecure – although perpetually living in fear of making a wrong decision would probably do that to anyone, especially with life-changing consequences at stake. Even her obsession with family photo albums made sense now. Keeping them constantly to hand reassured her she'd made the right choices so far, and that her loop in time hadn't deviated into a fork.

Yet despite knowing the truth about Verity Kiss, there was still one thing that bothered Justin enormously. While he could accept *Verity* had been bullied into becoming Agent X's spy – he couldn't comprehend *Robyn's* disloyalty. He knew X had threatened to harm her grandchildren if she disobeyed him – but the Thymes were her family too. How could Robyn have sided with him against her own flesh and blood, Justin wondered – and though he despised himself for considering it: could he be certain she'd remain loyal in the future?

'Of *course* she will,' he told himself firmly. 'I trusted her as Nanny Verity; now I know she's Robyn, I've got twice as many reasons to believe her.'

He thumped his pillow and turned over, wishing things were really that simple. Trying to shelve any doubts, Justin switched his thoughts to Valentine Kiss instead, imagining his frustration the night he'd stolen the time machine. After waiting thirty years to get his hands on it, the bike had probably disappeared right in front of his eyes.

Then, as Justin chuckled quietly, another thought occurred to him; a thought so startling, he groaned out loud.

Had Agent X worked out where the time machine had gone to?

Justin frowned, trying to remember how the ransom note had been worded. It was something like: "*I tried to steal the time machine, but somebody disappeared in it. Once they return, park it outside the castle gates. You have until Monday at noon or your father will die.*"

Clearly, when he'd written the note, X had seen *someone* inside the chronopod ... but he *couldn't* have guessed who. However, once he realised the place it vanished precisely matched where it had crashed thirty years earlier, he'd know two things – both of them bad.

If he hadn't guessed already, he might work out his ex-wife's true identity ... and worse than that, he'd know the time machine had gone for good. Sir Willoughby would be a worthless hostage – and if Agent X treated him with the same callous indifference he had Lady Henny, then his life now hung by the flimsiest of threads.

Justin woke early, intending to phone the airport and book seats on the first available flight back to Scotland. However, on a sudden whim he decided to call his mother before she left the villa. He knew she'd be home next week for her and Willoughby's anniversary party – and with his dad still missing, Justin wanted to know exactly how much time he had left to find and rescue him.

Lady Henny answered her cell phone on the first ring, but her voice sounded so despondent Justin half wondered if he'd pressed the wrong speed-dial.

'Mum, is that you?'

'Yeah.'

'What's wrong?'

Henny sighed. 'That storm I told you about; it hit last night and was far worse than we feared. A tidal wave flooded the island; all our equipment was either destroyed or swept out to sea.'

'What about the incubators? The generator?' Justin asked.

'All ruined,' replied Henny, gloomily. 'Not that it mattered by then. Every specimen died within twenty-four hours of hatching. We're not sure why yet – but we're doing tests.'

Justin didn't know what to say.

Henny continued: 'How's the little dodo you took home? Is *he* okay?'

'Fine ... last time I saw him,' said Justin.

'And your sister? Behaving herself?'

Justin hesitated a moment before replying. 'She's really changed, Mum' he said, choosing his words carefully. 'Honestly, you wouldn't recognise her.'

'Not before time. And what about you? Are you any closer to finding Nanny yet?'

Justin laughed uneasily. 'Actually, I tracked her down yesterday – to a château in France. That's where I'm phoning from.'

'Wow, great news. Did you take the jet over?' Henny asked.

'Er ... no, Mum. I didn't want to drag the pilot all the way from Mauritius for a quick hop across the channel.'

'But he's not in Mauritius. After flying you all home he phoned to say his altimeter was faulty and he needed a few days to get it fixed. I assumed he'd told you.'

300

'No – not a word,' said Justin quietly. 'Ah well, it should be mended by now; I'll get him to zip over and fetch us. When are *you* heading back, Mum? I imagine Mrs Kof'll want to know.'

'I reckon it'll take two or three days to clear the debris and see what we can salvage. Send the jet on Tuesday. And you'd better get word to Polly's dad or he'll worry.'

Justin smothered a gasp; he'd forgotten his mum knew Xavier Polydorus. 'Hey, did you know he and Nan were once an item?'

As soon as the words slipped out, Justin regretted them, instantly realising he might have betrayed a confidence. After a long silence Henny replied.

'Hmm ... that kinda explains something I never understood. I first met Xavier shortly after we rescued Eliza. When poachers killed her mom she was so tiny we couldn't get her to eat *anything*. Polly said his dad had once hand-reared some orphaned chimps and might be able to help us. He came to the castle and got Eliza eating in no time; I truly believe he saved her life.'

'Wow! That's so cool ... but ... I don't remember ...'

'Ah, Willo took you and Robyn out for the day; I was certain Eliza wouldn't make it, and I didn't want you watching her die. Darling Nanny stayed behind; she'd been helping with Eliza – getting her to sleep, changing her diapers. Anyway, when Xavier arrived she acted real strange and couldn't get outa the room quick enough. Later, when he left, I saw her hurry down the driveway after him, and give him a small brown-paper package. I never asked her about it, but I always wondered ...'

Justin was pretty certain he knew what the parcel contained, but he decided not to say anything.

'Hey, gotta go,' drawled Henny. 'The guys'll be waiting. Give my love to Nanny – and if your Dad hasn't decided on my anniversary present yet, you might drop a few hints about that bracelet I saw at Spiffany's.'

'Okay, Mum.' Then, getting a sudden idea, he added: 'Hey, hang on a tick. Could you do something for me?'

'Sure thing.'

'If you get chance, I want you to think carefully about when you were kidnapped. I know we've talked about it before, but this time relax and empty your mind ... visualise everything just as it happened. I'm hoping there's some insignificant little clue you've overlooked that'll help us identify Agent X.'

'Yeah, I'll do that,' replied Henny gravely. 'But don't get your hopes up. I'll call if I remember anything new.'

'That's great! Bye, Mum.'

Justin pressed END CALL then scrolled through his contacts menu until he came to JET PILOT. For a moment his finger hovered over the call button – but, as curious as he was to hear the taciturn pilot speak, he chickened out and sent a text instead.

Hi, Plz brng jet 2 AUVERGNE airpt ASAP.
Advise ETA. Rgrds, Justin Thyme.

After packing his overnight bag, Justin went down to breakfast. The croissants didn't look nearly as good as Mrs Kof's, so he helped himself to toast and marmalade instead. Half way through his second slice, Robyn appeared and walked slowly towards his table. She wore a brightly coloured dress and had her hair loose, making her look quite modern and Robyn-like.

Justin waited until she'd poured her first cup of coffee before speaking. 'I phoned Mum – told her I found you.'

'Hmm ... me-Robyn or me-Verity?' She sounded tired, and Justin guessed he hadn't been the only one worrying all night.

'You-Nanny V,' he said quietly. 'She thinks Robyn's still at home, remember?'

Robyn gave her brother a wry smile. 'Mum's pretty laid-back, but discovering she's got a forty-four-and-a-half year-old daughter won't exactly brighten her day.'

'I've got a plan,' said Justin. 'But it involves catching Agent X first. So, here's the deal ...' He leaned back in his chair, fixing his sister with a firm stare. When she glanced up, he continued. 'Look, Bobs ... I hate asking this, but I need to be absolutely clear where you stand ...'

302

'With the Thymes, of course – my family.' She gave Justin a reproachful look as if bewildered by his question. 'Och, you still think I betrayed you,' she said, with a sad shake of her head. 'I thought once you knew my true identity you'd understand.'

Now it was Justin's turn to look baffled.

'When Valentine persuaded me to become your nanny, do you think I *wanted* to put you in danger? Quite the opposite; I only agreed to be his spy so I could protect you. Don't forget, even before you were born I knew *you'd* be the one that converted Dad's motorbike. Val's instructions were very clear: "*Tell me if you ever overhear SIR WILLOUGHBY mention the words TIME MACHINE.*" And that's precisely what I did; I purposely withheld the truth so he wouldn't discover *you* were the inventor.'

Justin frowned. He wanted to believe her, but it wasn't easy. 'That still put *Mum* at risk,' he pointed out.

'Mm, but *I* knew she'd be rescued,' said Robyn, a defensive edge creeping into her voice. 'Her abduction was inevitable; it *had* to happen because I remembered it had. I played along, knowing ...'

'*Played along?*' Justin growled. He felt a bubble of anger growing inside him as he remembered how Nanny had helped him and Robyn. 'So you *knew* we wouldn't stop Mum being kidnapped ... or catch Agent X? You were just pretending the *whole* time?'

'Yeah, *that's* life in the loop,' snapped Robyn. 'You have to keep acting like you don't know what happens next, when most of the time you do – and it's not as easy as it sounds. My memory of events was entirely from Robyn's perspective ... so it was often incomplete, and occasionally quite misleading. I felt like I was in some bizarre theatrical performance where I knew the general plot, yet had to improvise my lines. And that's pretty scary when you're afraid of changing the future.'

'But even after you admitted being a spy, you *still* kept lying,' Justin sighed. 'I remember your exact words: "*I never guessed Val was going to kidnap Lady Henny.*"'

Robyn's eyelashes glistened wetly. 'Of *course* I lied; I didn't dare reveal the truth until I'd completed the loop. What if you told Robyn?

What if she didn't go back in time? Maybe I'd lose my children ... my grandchildren. I couldn't take that risk. Believe me – I've lived through stuff you've only theorised about. You can't even begin to comprehend the mental strain. My one pleasure was caring for you, Robyn and Alby, but ... but ...' She paused, trying to gulp back a sob. 'But if you seriously think I'd've done *anything* to harm you, then you don't know me at *all*.'

Justin stared at his plate, giving Robyn a moment to compose herself. He could see now that she'd been trapped in an impossible situation – with one family endangered if she obeyed X, her other family threatened if she didn't ... and possibly both families at risk if she accidentally altered the future. Even though the logical part of Justin's brain doubted this was possible, he couldn't prove it – it was *just* a theory. Faced with the same choices, Justin had to admit he'd have probably done the same rather than risk losing those he loved. Clearly, Robyn had done the best she could – and Justin knew if they talked all day long he'd never truly understand the anguish she'd suffered.

'I'm sorry, Bobs,' he whispered. 'Thing is, you've had years to get used to this; I'm still trying to adjust. Give me time.'

'Time!' murmured Robyn, laughing through her tears. 'Spelt T-I-M-E it's one of my least favourite words.'

'I can't say I blame you,' said Justin, giving his sister an awkward grin.

Robyn leaned across the table. She placed her hand on Justin's arm and whispered solemnly. 'But spell it T-H-Y-M-E and that's an entirely different matter. I'll *always* be true to the Thyme family; never doubt that for a moment.'

By twelve-thirty, Justin and Robyn were settled in their seats aboard the Thymes' private jet, watching the pilot load the last of Robyn's enormous new suitcases into the luggage hold. As he swept past them, his long black robes swirling out behind, Robyn called to him in fluent Greek, pointing to a small travel bag. He turned and glared at her, then, with a sardonic arch of one eyebrow, slammed the bag down beside her and disappeared through the cockpit door.

'I always did like the strong silent type,' Robyn sighed, fanning herself with a magazine.

Justin waited until the jet was taxiing along the runway before he replied, hoping the engine noise would keep their conversation from being overheard. 'What's in the bag?'

'My uniform,' said Robyn, pulling a face. 'Can't go home dressed like this, can I?'

'Hmm, I suppose it *would* prompt some rather awkward questions. I guess you'll have to play the part a little longer ... until I can sort things out.'

Robyn glanced up quizzically, but Justin avoided her gaze, not sure his plan would work. He decided to change the subject.

'I meant to ask you something yesterday,' he began. 'You said the night X stole the chronopod, Dad saw someone signalling from the west tower just before he was knocked unconscious. Did you get an impression of who it was?'

'At the time I assumed it was you,' Robyn told him.

'ME?' asked Justin, genuinely shocked. 'That's impossible; Evelyn Garnet drugged my cocoa that night; you must've seen me sleeping when you took my watch.'

'Yeah ... but it's not *impossible*, though, is it?' said Robyn. 'You might've come from the future.'

Justin's eyes widened. 'Flux! I hadn't thought of that.' He considered the possibility for a minute or two, then said: 'What made you think it was me?'

Robyn frowned pensively; although it was only three nights ago from Justin's point of view, it was three decades ago from hers. 'I ... I don't know. Everything happened so fast, I can't remember.'

'You probably *do* – subconsciously,' said Justin. 'Or you wouldn't be so certain. Hypnosis might help.'

'Like you did when Grandpa Lyall first arrived?'

Justin nodded. He'd studied enough to know the basics of trance induction: calm voice, monotonous tone, rhythmic speech pattern.

'Close your eyes,' he whispered. 'Relax ... empty your mind. Breathe slowly and deeply. Feel yourself unwind. With each breath drift further into the past ... back through the years ... until the night you saw your father knocked unconscious. When you find that memory, step into it – notice every little detail. Now, tell me what you see ...'

Robyn mumbled incoherently, then answered slowly in a thick, muffled voice. 'I see Dad,' she said. 'He ... he's standing outside the French windows ... there's a dazzling beam of light shining right up into his face. He's shielding his eyes ... pointing down through the glass. He's stepping back, shouting: "*YOU? ... DASH IT ALL ... IT ... IT CAN'T BE. YOU'RE JUS—*" AAARRGHHHH!' Robyn screamed. Her eyes remained closed, but her fists clenched tightly and her whole body shuddered.

Justin snapped his fingers, instantly bringing his sister out of her hypnotic trance. She blinked her eyes a few times then sat up straight.

'I ... I remember it now,' she said, her voice hushed and breathless. 'A man ... a man wearing a black balaclava ... he crept up behind Dad and hit him just as he was saying your name.'

Justin stared through one of the jet's tiny windows, gazing absently across an endless skyscape of marshmallow clouds. Despite analysing the situation from every angle, he couldn't fathom why his future self would have signalled out of the great hall windows. It simply didn't make sense.

He sighed deeply, then, hearing the soft click of his flight-lab door, turned to see his sister step back into the main cabin.

She didn't look like Robyn any longer. Gone were her high-heeled shoes, glamorous clothes and expensive jewellery; instead she wore a pearl-grey nanny's uniform with starched collar and cuffs, thermal stockings, and a crisp, snowy-white apron. All traces of lip-gloss and fingernail polish had been washed away, and her hair was pinned up neatly beneath a stiff lace cap.

She paused for a moment, carefully adjusting her cameo so that its broad band of petersham ribbon covered her faded robin tattoo. As Justin watched, he felt a sudden rush of affection for her ... this gentle motherly soul who'd cared for him since birth, witnessed his first steps, taught him the alphabet, nursed him through measles, and forgiven him when he'd accidentally blown out the nursery windows with his first stick of homemade gelignite. His shyness of the day before evaporated in a flash, and he couldn't resist jumping up and giving her a boisterous hug.

'Och, what's that for, Poppet?' she asked, pretending to fend him off.

'For being you,' said Justin. 'For being the best sist—'

'Hhrrmph ... best *Nanny*, if you *don't* mind,' she said, with a stern frown. 'Let's start as we mean to go on ... or there'll be *such* a muddle back home.'

'Yeah, I'd better call you Nanny Verity even if we're alone,' Justin agreed. 'Just in case someone's eavesdropping.'

Fortunately, Robyn now looked so completely and utterly nannyish, it probably wouldn't be too difficult.

She perched primly on the edge of her seat, clasping her hands in her lap. 'Well now,' she said, sounding unusually decisive. 'The last time we were together on this plane, we talked about catching Agent X. I assume that's *still* the plan?'

'Yes,' said Justin. Then seeing the sharp glint in his sister's eyes, muttered: 'Yes, *Nanny*.'

'Splendid. Well, this time we have three things in our favour.' She counted them off using her fingers. 'First of all, having been married to X, I understand a *lot* more about him. Secondly, we can rule out our chief suspect, Xavier Polydorus. And thirdly, I know the identity of our resident spy!'

'*YOU DO?*'

'Of *course*. Who do you think brought me the key for Awbrite's handcuffs the day I escaped? I've been expecting you to ask,' she added, sounding a little disappointed. 'I thought you'd be *desperate* to know.'

Justin frowned at her. 'I didn't think you *saw* anybody. Your e-mail said you just heard someone telling you not to look back.'

'True,' said Nanny. 'And I didn't. But when the spy spoke I had no problems *whatsoever* recognising her voice!'

Never Leave Anything Modern Behind

Care must be taken that nothing from the present is ever accidentally left in the past.

This rule isn't limited to twenty-first century technology. While it would be disastrous to lose a GPS or an iPod in medieval times, it would be equally catastrophic to leave anything in any historical period that doesn't belong there.

Apart from the obvious fork-creating possibilities of leaving a digital camcorder in the Victorian era, imagine the complications that could ensue if palaeontologists discovered a fossilised house key from the Jurassic period.

A chrononaut should carry as little as possible – and always check they have all their personal belongings before retuning to the present.

CHAPTER EIGHTEEN

A Web of Deceit

'*HER* voice?' Justin exclaimed. 'You mean the spy at Thyme Castle is ... is Mrs Gilliechattan?'

'Och, *no,*' said Nanny Verity, shaking her head impatiently. (She was so completely back in character by now that Justin couldn't think of her as Robyn any longer). 'I know Mrs G pries into *everything,*' she continued. 'But that's just plain nosiness, not espionage. Mrs Kof is the spy.'

'No *way*!'

'I'm afraid so,' said Nanny. 'I promise you, her deep voice was quite unmistakable, even without all that bogus mispronunciation – and I distinctly heard her bare feet on the wooden floor.'

'But how did she get in? ' asked Justin. 'Sergeant Awbrite made me lock the sitting-room door.'

'I imagine she climbed up the fireman's pole,' Nanny explained. 'Simple enough for an ex-circus strongwoman. She threw the handcuff key onto my lap ... then, before I could turn round to thank her, she slid back down to the library.'

Justin pictured Nanny Verity as he last saw her that day: sat facing the south tower window, with her right wrist handcuffed to the grand piano's carved wooden leg.

'Well ... I suppose ...' he muttered half-heartedly. Deep down, he realised Mrs Kof had always been a possibility, but that didn't make it any easier to accept.

Nanny snorted irritably. 'Hhrrmph ... the way she mangles the English language ... it's simply *too* ridiculous for words. Didn't it make you at *all* suspicious?'

'Maybe at first,' Justin admitted. 'But then I thought surely no one would act *that* badly; she's got to be genuine ... unless it's some bizarre double bluff.' He frowned a moment, as if puzzled. 'Your husband said he'd planted a second spy in the castle, didn't he? Can you remember *when* he told you?'

'Er ... about a year ago,' replied Nanny, looking slightly uncomfortable. 'Maybe a wee bit longer.'

'But Mrs Kof's only worked at the castle for the last five weeks. That's why I assumed you meant Mrs G.' Justin narrowed his eyes as he thought. 'Hmm ... I'm not convinced *she* fits either. The Gilliechattans have been with us three years; if X employed them as his spies, why wait so long before telling you?'

'Truth be told, Val never mentioned spies at all,' Nanny confessed. 'He just warned me not to double-cross him because he'd know if I did.'

'So he might've been planning to infiltrate the castle himself,' said Justin. 'Which means he's either Mr Gilliechattan, Professor Gilbert, Grandpa or Knightly.' He gave an exasperated groan. '*Urrghh*, we've been over this a dozen times before, but we're still no closer to identifying him.'

Nanny pulled a sympathetic face. 'Well, he's not Knightly,' she said. 'And the professor looks shorter than Valentine. Actors can put lifts in their shoes to appear taller, but they can't shrink.'

'But I overheard Professor Gilbert on the phone, remember? He knew all about Dad's time machine.'

'You didn't see him, though, did you?'

'No,' said Justin, sounding dejected. 'That leaves Grandpa and Angus Gilliechattan. Hey, d'you think Mr G could've mimicked the professor's voice? I once heard him pretending to be Knightly.'

'Well, he *is* about the right height, and that shaggy beard keeps his face well hidden – but I'm not convinced he's Agent X. Mr and Mrs G came to the castle at least a full year before Val and I divorced.'

'Maybe they weren't married then,' Justin remarked. He was about to tell Nanny how, shortly after she'd disappeared, Robyn had discovered the Gilliechattans were actors, then he realised she must know already. 'Remind me to look at their scrapbook once we get home,' he said. 'I'd like to do a thorough background check on Oliver and Ariadne Marsh.'

'Hmm,' said Nanny, pressing her lips tightly together. 'I still think your so-called grandfather's the most likely impostor. Val could impersonate him easily; he saw the old laird often enough to study his appearance and mannerisms. But *he's* only been at the castle a few weeks *too* ... just like Mrs Kof.'

'Maybe X lost faith in his spy and decided he could do a better job himself,' Justin suggested. He thought for a moment. 'Unless ...' he continued, his voice sounding somewhat sceptical. 'Unless Mrs Kof isn't the *spy*. What if she's Agent X himself?

Nanny considered his question seriously. 'Val *did* do a couple of seasons as a pantomime dame,' she said, unable to conceal a faint smile. 'He was brilliant, of course ... and *quite* hilarious. You know, I think he'd rather enjoy playing Mrs Kof – she'd appeal to his warped sense of humour; he'd get a real kick out of being utterly outrageous.'

'But can he cook?'

'Och, Valentine can do *anything*.'

There was an odd wistfulness about her tone that made Justin glance sharply in her direction – but he decided not to pursue it. He cleared his throat. 'Well, this might explain why Mrs Kof helped you; I used to think Mr Polydorus had made you vanish!'

'I know; Robyn thought so too,' said Nanny. 'That was one of the times her memory misled me. I knew *when* I was going to disappear, but I didn't know *how*. When Xavier turned up that day, I assumed *he'd* be my mystery saviour. That's why I wanted Robyn to distract the constable – so Xav could steal the handcuff key; then I sent you searching for Lady Henny to give him chance to rescue me ... although that wasn't the main reason, of course.'

Justin looked thunderstruck. 'You knew I *had* to leave immediately or I wouldn't reach her in time. *You saved Mum's life.*'

'Quite possibly!' Nanny agreed. 'I had Robyn's memory of you telling her what a close call it was. Though you can't imagine how confusing her memories were at times. Like when she was e-mailing Agent X. I mistakenly thought Knightly would disable her computer before she could leak anything. I kept waiting ... and waiting. Then, at the last possible moment, I realised *he* wasn't the saboteur – *I* was! So I cut the plug off and planted it inside his wardrobe where I knew your sister would find it.'

Nanny leaned forward and lowered her voice 'But that wasn't the worst muddle,' she continued. 'Robyn had a particularly vivid memory of me lying injured in the kitchen garden. She never knew the truth about what *really* happened that day, so neither did I. Oddly enough, it would've been my twenty-sixth wedding anniversary if I'd still been married. That, coupled with Robyn's misconceptions, made me think my ex-husband was planning to kill me. Finally, fearing violence or arrest I decided to take matters into my own hands, and faked the attack to get me safely into hospital. After a couple of near misses with the paperweight, the dints it left in the lawn triggered another of Robyn's memories, and I suddenly realised *no one* wanted to kill me – I was merely fulfilling another part of my time-loop. Fortunately, I knew I'd survive – and I'd given your sister first aid lessons beforehand just to be on the safe side.'

'Wow ... you probably saved *your own* life too,' said Justin. 'How cool is that?'

'Cool? Hhrrmph!' Nanny snorted. 'All I can say is thank goodness the whole looping muddle is finally over!'

The sky in Scotland was a depressing gunmetal-grey. A harsh wind blew from the east, and black smudges of cloud scudded along the horizon, threatening rain.

Within minutes of landing, the pilot transferred their luggage into a taxi, then stood glaring down at Justin with his arms folded across his chest.

'Thanks, erm ... Horace,' Justin mumbled, steeling himself to keep steady eye contact. 'Mum says she'll need you back in Mauritius by Tuesday ... okay?'

The pilot said nothing – and apart from the merest sneering twitch of one nostril his face remained as expressionless as a stone statue. However, when Verity Kiss walked past, he swept forwards and held the taxi door open for her – then, after a curt bow, he stalked wordlessly back inside the hangar. Nanny gave an *if-only-I-was-twenty-years-younger* kind of sigh, opened her handbag and helped herself to a peppermint.

During the drive home, Justin brought her up-to-date with everything at the castle.

'I suppose that dreadful Garnet woman's still in my room,' she muttered, bristling with indignation.

''Fraid so,' said Justin. He grimaced awkwardly. 'Perhaps you could sleep in Robyn's room for the time being. Just until we get things sorted out ...'

Nanny made a tutting noise with her peppermint.

'The thing is ...' Justin went on, 'Evelyn Garnet *did* drug me the night X tried to steal the time machine; I can't sack her until I know what she's up to.'

'Well, from now on I can help with the investigation,' said Nanny. 'I used to be pretty good at that ... when I was Robyn.'

Justin gave a long sigh. 'I sometimes think you and I are the *only* ones who *aren't* spies!'

'Hmm,' said Nanny, looking pleased. 'I take it that means you've finally decided to trust me again?'

'Absolutely,' Justin grinned. 'We're still the Thyme-team; brains and action.'

'Yeah ... and don't you forget it,' laughed Nanny, giving him a sudden Robyn-like punch on the arm.

The first thing Justin noticed as they drove into the castle courtyard was a large pair of muddy Wellington boots on the front doorstep. Seconds later, Knightly rushed outside and tripped over them.

'Dratted gardener,' he muttered, looking unusually harassed – then opening the cab door, he droned in his usual hollow-sounding voice: 'Welcome home, Master Justin. You should have phoned; I could have collected you from the airport.'

'Oh, er ... we didn't want to bother you, Knightly.'

Justin shot a quick glance at Nanny Verity as he paid the driver; he'd chosen a cab so they could talk freely until the last possible moment.

Meanwhile, Knightly marched round to the rear of the taxi, opened the boot and smothered a groan. 'Ah, *Mrs* Kiss,' he said, wondering which of Nanny's enormous suitcases to tackle first. 'You've had a pleasant holiday, I trust?'

For a moment, Nanny looked rather put out by the slight emphasis he'd placed on the word *Mrs*, but she replied smoothly, giving the butler one of her brightest smiles.

'Och, indeed I have, Mr *Knightly* – but it's good to be home.'

Knightly gripped the largest case and hauled it out, his knees almost buckling under the weight. As Justin hurried to help him, Nanny took hold of his arm.

'Leave those to Knightly, Poppet,' she said firmly. 'After all ...'

But the rest of her admonition was drowned by an ear-splitting screech, as Burbage swooped through the castle door and alighted on the taxi roof. He peered at Nanny Verity with his head on one side, then raised his crest, cackling with laughter.

'*Age cannot wither her, nor custom stale her infinite variety*,' he remarked.

Knightly dropped the suitcase and shooed the cockatoo away with a dignified sweep of one arm. But Burbage dodged him easily, and flapped in a wide arc right round the courtyard, squawking, '*The wheel has come full circle*,' as he flew back indoors.

Ignoring Nanny's instructions, Justin grabbed a couple of small cases and followed her into the entrance hall. Mr and Mrs Gilliechattan were huddled together by the kitchen door, engaged in a furtively whispered conversation with Mrs Kof. Burbage, now perched on his master's shoulder, muttered: '*Pitchers have ears*,' and immediately the gardener stopped talking and nudged his wife. He turned, smiling broadly, then strode forward, making a big show of welcoming Nanny Verity home. Abandoning his Scottish accent he called out in his most booming theatrical voice.

'My dear, dear lady ... you have been sorely missed. That foul termagant hired in your absence has made our lives a perpetual misery.'

He tried to take hold of Nanny Verity's hands, but she tucked them inside her apron pockets, looking embarrassed.

Justin groaned. 'Urghh, don't tell me Miss Garnet's spotted Eliza.'

'No – the noble beast has kept wisely offstage,' said Mr Gilliechattan, striking a dramatic pose. 'We think she slept in Lupin Wood last night – in the old folly – don't we, Nadezhda?'

Mrs Kof nodded. Justin glanced up at her uncertainly, the thought of her being a spy still fresh in his mind.

'This mornings I taking her whole wheely-barrow of bananas,' she told him. 'But Eliza staying hids ... far away from Evil Incarnate.'

'And now that nairsty woman's got it in for ma pooer wee Tybs,' grumbled Mrs Gilliechattan, her green eyes flashing angrily. 'She claims he scrairtched her hand.'

'No doubt Burbage will be her next target,' added her husband. He shook his head and looked grave. 'We've seriously considered tendering our resignations. My agent just phoned offering me a lead with the Royal Shakespeare Company. Their *Hamlet* got knocked down by a double-decker bus and they need a last-minute replacement.'

'You're going away?' Justin gasped. He was genuinely shocked – and a sideways squint at Nanny Verity told him he wasn't the only one. 'Both of you?'

'I suppose I *could* take some time off – but the thought of leaving my wife behind at the mercy of that evil crone ...' The gardener gave an exaggerated shrug. 'Perhaps, now that our dear Mrs Kiss has returned, you can dispense with the understudy.'

'Well, er ... I guess that's the plan,' said Justin, wondering how this strange turn of events affected Angus Gilliechattan's status as a prime suspect. 'When d'you need to leave?'

'Monday,' he replied, flashing a satisfied look at the castle cook. 'I'll have a week of rehearsals, then ...'

'*The play's the thing!*' cackled Burbage.

'And you needn't werry aboot the gairden,' said Mrs Gilliechattan. 'We've arranged for my nephew to help oot. He's arriving Thairsday.'

Then, moving with almost clockwork precision the little group disbanded at lightning speed: Mr Gilliechattan donned his Wellington boots and hurried outdoors; Knightly plodded off lugging one of Nanny's suitcases; Mrs Gilliechattan scuttled up the east tower brandishing her feather duster; and Mrs Kof slid back into the kitchen, chuckling to herself.

'Very niftily done,' whispered Nanny Verity, once she and Justin were alone. 'Quite masterfully stage-managed and acted, don't you think?'

'What?' asked Justin.

'The way they all worked together to hustle you.'

'Hustle me?'

'Och, quite definitely. I'm certain those two had *no* intention of resigning. Mr Gilliechattan – or whatever he's called – wants a few weeks off to pursue his acting career ... supposedly. Not only did he wangle your consent, they even arranged for some relative to fill in for him ... *and* suggested you fire Evelyn Garnet.'

'Well ... it's not like we want her to stay, is it?' said Justin. 'And as for Mr G ... I was too busy trying to work out whether this makes him more or less likely to be Agent X.'

'And ...?'

Justin made an exasperated noise. 'I'm not sure,' he said. 'But one thing's certain ... we've got to get this mystery solved before he leaves.'

'So, what *are* you going to do about Evelyn Garnet?' Nanny enquired, as she climbed the west tower staircase. Justin, who was a few steps behind her (helping Knightly with a final gigantic suitcase), didn't reply immediately – but waited until he reached the second floor landing.

'Haven't decided yet,' he panted.

'Well, get thinking – *quick*,' said Nanny. And before Justin could stop her, she rapped smartly on the nursery door, which was such a Robynish thing to do he felt an instant flash of exasperation. When no one replied, Nanny opened the door and stepped inside.

'Hmm, not as tidy as I'd like,' she remarked acidly. 'Still ...'

She trotted past Albion's empty cot and through the connecting door into her bedroom. Justin heard her give a loud disapproving tut, and hurried after her. He watched as Nanny did a one-finger dust check along the top of her writing bureau, almost knocking Miss Garnet's hearing aid on the floor.

'What about Robyn's room?' hissed Justin. 'Like we said. Once Nanny Evelyn's gone, you can move back down here ... unless ...'

He paused by the open window, peering through a gap in the lace curtains. Down below, he could see Evelyn Garnet wheeling Albion's pushchair along the clifftop. Justin watched her stop beside Mr Gillie-chattan; she appeared to be arguing with him. After pointing to a bandage wrapped around her right hand, she marched past him towards the kitchen garden, wearing a superior expression.

As Justin stepped away from the window, Knightly materialised in the doorway behind him and coughed discreetly. 'Shall I move Miss Garnet's things to one of the guest rooms, sir,' he murmured.

Justin sighed. 'I'd like to speak to her first. Tell Mrs Kof to serve afternoon tea in the great hall. Maybe we can sort this out amicably.'

'Very good, sir.'

Knightly headed downstairs, his shoes squeaking as usual.

Justin waited until he was out of earshot then turned to Nanny Verity. 'Didn't your husband play a butler once?'

'Och, yes ... but ...'

'*AAAAAAAAAAAARRRGGHHHH!*' A sudden blood-curdling scream echoed across the courtyard.

For a split-second, Justin froze; but as the screaming continued –

now accompanied by the high-pitched cry of a baby – he dashed out of the room and down the west staircase, checking anxiously through one window after another. He saw Mr Gilliechattan scrambling to his feet, then hurrying towards the walled kitchen garden.

Justin raced along the portrait gallery, only half aware of Nanny Verity trotting breathlessly behind him. Then, as he turned into the entrance hall, he overtook Knightly, hurtled through the kitchen, and out onto the back step.

And there was Evelyn Garnet dangling from the old pear tree, fighting to free herself from one of Tybalt's enormous sticky webs. She thrashed about, limbs flailing wildly, but the harder she struggled, the tighter its silken threads wrapped themselves around her body.

Justin took a few faltering steps forward, uncertain what to do. To his right, Angus Gilliechattan leaned in the arched gateway, looking half furious, half tickled pink; to his left, Mrs Kof was lifting Albion out of his overturned pushchair. She had her back to Miss Garnet, as if deaf to her screams. Alby clung tightly to the cook's apron, then, with a dry hiccoughing sob, pointed over her shoulder. Justin followed his gaze, and saw Tybs prowling silently along the top of the garden wall, his eyes locked intently on the human wriggling in his web.

A moment later, Justin noticed the sound of clattering footsteps from the kitchen, then Knightly stepped through the back door, closely followed by Mrs Gilliechattan and Nanny Verity.

'What's to do?' Nanny panted.

Justin heard her gasp before he could reply, and felt her hand clutch his sleeve.

Meanwhile, as Tybalt edged closer, Evelyn Garnet managed a final shuddering twist, freeing her right arm just enough to reach the tranquilliser gun still tucked in her belt. She released the safety-catch, raised it to one eye, took aim ... and fired.

Mrs Gilliechattan made a strangled squawking noise and staggered across the lawn; her husband bellowed: '*NOOOOOOO!*' and Burbage shrieked with unmitigated fury. But it was too late; Tybalt toppled off the wall and landed, unconscious, in a bed of newly-planted lettuces.

For the next two minutes chaos reigned supreme.

'Ma poooer wee Tybby ... he wouldna harm a fly,' wept Mrs Gillie-chattan.

'It's not flies I'm concerned about,' snapped Evelyn Garnet, still hanging in the web like a tangled marionette. 'What if it'd caught the baby? It might've eaten him.'

'Nonsense, woman,' roared the gardener. 'He's just ... just ...'

'*A harmless necessary cat*,' Burbage concluded.

Albion began crying again. 'Nan ded'n 'im,' he howled, pointing a chubby finger at Tybalt, now slumped in his mistress's arms.'

'Och, he's not dead, Poppet,' said Nanny Verity reassuringly. 'He's just having a wee catnap.' She took Alby from Mrs Kof and tickled him under his chin.

Professor Gilbert arrived, drawn by the commotion. He dithered, stammering: 'W-w-w-what's ha-ha-happened?' but no one explained.

Determined to keep a cool head, Justin fetched a bread knife from the kitchen and cut Evelyn Garnet down from the web. Then, with the professor, he helped her indoors.

'Is serving her rights,' Mrs Kof remarked confidentially to Knightly. 'I hope it givings her anoraknophobia!'

After her third cup of tea, (laced with brandy), Evelyn Garnet was looking her steely-eyed self again. A few string-like strands of gossamer still clung to her arms and hair, but she was too busy reliving her misadventure to care.

'There's no doubt whatsoever,' she said for at least the sixth time. 'That horrid cat tripped me up on purpose.'

Mrs Kof rolled her eyes and leaned over a wicker basket brandishing a kipper. Haggis, who'd been snuggled inside on a tartan blanket, jumped up and snapped it out of her fingers.

'I've never been so terrified,' Miss Garnet went on, casting the dodo a look of acute distaste. 'I honestly thought ...'

Nanny Verity, who'd listened patiently at first, was now bristling with suppressed irritation. She jiggled Albion on her lap and glared poisonously at Miss Garnet over the top of her spectacles.

'Me, me, me,' she muttered. 'Alby got tipped right out of his pushchair, but you haven't even *asked* if *he's* alright.'

'Oh, he's fine,' said Miss Garnet, with a dismissive wave of one arm. 'Anyway, he's your job now.' She held her empty cup out to Mrs Kof, who looked momentarily tempted to brain her with the teapot. 'I realise I'll be given my marching orders now Mrs Kiss has returned,' she told Justin airily. 'But just so long as you know: I expect a full month's pay to compensate for the trauma I've suffered working in this menagerie!'

Nanny Verity spluttered explosively – but Justin nudged her with his foot.

'Oh, I insist on three months,' he said. 'And please consider yourself our guest until you feel well enough to travel. Meanwhile, I'll have Knightly move your things to the north tower, so you can recuperate well away from the nursery.'

Looking suitably mollified, Evelyn Garnet helped herself to a finger of shortbread. Justin winked at Nanny Verity, glad that at least one thing had gone smoothly.

After helping himself to a cup of tea and a slice of Mrs Kof's Dundee cake, Justin excused himself, leaving the two nannies to talk. Now that Verity Kiss had her room back she was chatting quite amiably with Evelyn Garnet – although Justin guessed this was merely part of her investigation. At least, he *hoped* it was.

He heard Nanny rummaging through her handbag. 'I must show you some photos of my three grandchildren,' she prattled. 'The youngest, wee Beowulf, turned one on April Fools' Day ...'

Justin shut the kitchen door quietly behind him, unable to fathom where this particular line of inquiry was heading. He plodded across the entrance hall and along the portrait gallery, munching cake and thinking deeply.

Time really *was* running out. Agent X's ransom note had set Monday as the deadline – which left just one more day to discover his true identity. And Justin had an unpleasant feeling he already had all the clues he was ever going to get. He needed to review the evidence carefully, working out how each piece of the puzzle fitted with all the others. Everything *had* to connect to everything else.

Half way along the upper corridor, Justin stopped in front of an antique long case clock. He removed a filigreed side panel, reached inside and pulled out a pair of thick rubber gloves he'd hidden there early Friday morning. After putting them on, he inserted the key in the south tower door; sparks fizzed out of the keyhole but the gloves kept him safe. Once inside, Justin disconnected the cattle prod, pleased his makeshift security measures had worked so well.

Up in his lab, he flumped onto a stool and switched his computer on. Ignoring the dozens of business e-mails waiting to be answered, Justin moved his cursor to the bottom of the screen, clicked the folder labelled X Files, and spent the next few hours reviewing his notes.

Somehow, by tomorrow night, he *had* to find all the answers! But search as he might, one terrifying question kept dominating his thoughts: *What would happen to Sir Willoughby once Agent X realised the time machine had vanished for good?*

'I *knew* it!' Nanny Verity declared triumphantly. 'That woman is an impostor.'

Justin was in the nursery, waiting for her to finish tucking Albion in his cot. Supper was over, (though he'd felt too stressed to eat much), and the tower clock had just struck eight-thirty.

'A *real* childcare professional would've taken more interest in my baby photos,' Nanny insisted. 'Why, she never asked about teething, sleeping patterns, or baby formula or ... or *anything* nannyish. She just kept on about how clever you are ... and wanting to know about your inventions.'

She leaned over and kissed Alby's forehead, then motioned Justin through the connecting door into her room. Spying her photo albums back in their usual corner, he picked one up and flipped through it absently.

'As a last resort, I told her about the wee foundling left on Hathaway's doorstep last spring,' Nanny continued. 'Even an *abandoned* baby didn't interest her.'

'D'you mean Milo?' asked Justin, lowering himself into Nanny's rocking chair.

Verity Kiss gazed at him in astonishment. 'How do you know about Milo?'

'I was looking through your albums a few days ago. I couldn't understand why there were four different babies when you've only got three grandchildren. It was almost like you'd forgotten one.'

Nanny gave a snort. 'Hardly! Hathaway found him a couple of days after little Wulfi was born. There was a note pinned to his blanket: *"Please take care of my precious little Milo – love Bethany."* I suppose Hathy should've called the authorities, but she couldn't bear the thought of him being put in an orphanage. She made us all swear to keep him a secret.'

Justin shrugged, wondering why he was chatting about babies when there were far more important things bothering him.

'I got a text from Mum just before supper,' he muttered, eager to change the subject. 'She's remembered something about her kidnapper, but she says it doesn't make any sense.'

'How come?'

'She didn't have time to explain properly, but she's going to phone tomorrow night, 'bout eleven-thirty. I hope it's something totally mind-blowing cos I'm getting nowhere.'

'Och, what you need is an early night,' Nanny told him, peering narrowly over her spectacles.

Justin gave a wide yawn. 'I'm fine ... *really*! Anyway, I've got too much to ...' He stopped mid-sentence, and glanced up at the ceiling. 'Hey ... can you hear footsteps?'

'No.'

'It sounds like there's someone in Robyn's room.'

Justin opened the door and stepped onto the landing. He peered up the west staircase; all seemed quiet and still, but a faint light shone down the stairwell.

'I'm going to investigate,' he whispered.

Nanny Verity tiptoed after him, frowning anxiously. As they reached the third floor landing they both heard a muffled sob, and the shadow of someone sitting on Robyn's bed became visible through her half-open door. Together, they edged into the room, and found Grandpa Lyall staring at the photograph on Robyn's bedside table, tears streaming down his pale, wrinkled cheeks.

'You okay, Grandpa?' Justin asked quietly.

The old man looked up, then, smiling sadly, he turned the picture frame towards Justin and tapped it with a gnarled finger. It was Robyn's treasured photo of herself, aged one-and-a-half, sitting on her grandpa's shoulders.

'I remember that day so well,' Sir Lyall murmured. 'Little Robyn toddling across the clifftop, wanting to be in the shot. And you,' he added, suddenly noticing Nanny Verity hovering in the doorway. 'You were there too; yes ... I saw you ... hiding in the archway.'

Verity Kiss took a sharp breath, then backed onto the landing, looking discombobulated.

'D'you want me to take you back to your room, Grandpa?' Justin asked.

The old gentleman nodded. 'May I ... may I take the photo?'

'Well ... er ...' Justin glanced uncertainly at Nanny Verity, hoping for some sign of consent – but she turned away briskly and bustled downstairs without looking back. 'I'll, scan it for you, Grandpa,' he whispered, slipping the frame into his pocket. 'Then you can have your own copy.'

After settling Sir Lyall in his bedroom, Justin returned along the upper corridor. He paused momentarily outside Nanny Verity's room, tempted to knock and ask what was troubling her – but something told him she wanted to be left alone. With a deep sigh, he headed back to the south tower and trudged upstairs.

His lab was in complete darkness, although his computer's screen-saver – a perpetually toppling hourglass – cast a faintly shimmering nimbus of light over his desk. Deep in the shadows, scores of mechanical contraptions whirred and puttered, their soft chatter punctuated by the ponderous ticking of the old tower clock.

Justin strode over to the clock face and pressed his nose against one of the sixty clear panes of glass around the edge. He peered down at the loch. Dark ripples raced across the water, chased by the buffeting wind and lashing rain. He hoped Eliza was safe in Sir Willoughby's workshop and not still skulking around Lupin Wood. Now Miss Garnet was leaving there was no reason for her to remain outdoors.

'I *must* find her tomorrow,' he whispered to himself. 'Ask her again about the day Mum was kidnapped.'

He returned to the desk, and switched his scanner on. As it warmed up, he opened the back of Robyn's picture frame and prised out the photograph – or, rather, *half* a photograph. The left side of the picture had been neatly torn off.

The following morning, Nanny Verity had her and Albion's breakfast sent up to the nursery. Justin suspected she was trying to avoid talking to old Sir Lyall – but, as it happened, he'd already asked Knightly to serve *his* breakfast in bed.

Almost straight away, Justin realised it was going to be one of those days when nothing went according to plan. Practically everyone he wanted to speak to managed to avoid him. The Gilliechattans were busy packing for Mr G's departure the following morning; Evelyn Garnet spent the entire time locked in her room; Knightly drove on an errand to Inverness; and, despite the torrential rain, Professor Gilbert went sailing in his little boat.

Mrs Kof remained at the castle, but refused to let Justin set one foot in the kitchen.

'Bizzy-bizzy,' she bellowed from behind a steaming saucepan. 'I making scrumpity foods for Sir Willberry and Lady Any's annihilation party.'

When Justin pointed out their anniversary wasn't until Thursday, she went very red in the face and shooed him vigorously into the entrance hall, muttering, 'Well begunned is half done-in.' She spent the rest of the day singing boisterously whilst clattering her pots and pans. In fact, the kitchen was in such chaos she almost mistook Haggis for a plucked chicken, and would have popped him in the oven if he hadn't sneezed.

At lunchtime, Nanny Verity was still being evasive. She helped herself to a plate of chicken sandwiches from the dining room then scuttled back to the nursery before Sir Lyall could glance up from his soup bowl.

Justin sprinted after her along the portrait gallery. 'Hey, Nan – we need to talk.'

'Not now ... I've got to get back to Alby,' she grumbled.

'Look,' said Justin, 'if you can rule Grandpa out of the investigation it's only fair you say so.'

Verity Kiss stared at him for a long moment with her lips pinched tightly together; when she finally spoke it was with obvious reluctance. 'Och, very well; I suppose you want the story behind that old photo.'

Justin nodded. 'Yeah, I er ...'

'He was right,' said Nanny, cutting him off abruptly. 'I *was* there. I'd brought Kitty and the twins to Thyme Bay for the Easter hols. It was the last day of March, and we'd walked into Drumnadrochit to mail some postcards. On the way back we stopped at the castle; I wanted to show the girls where I used to work. As we crept through the archway I heard voices coming from the clifftop. When I peeped round the corner I saw Sir Lyall having his photograph taken; I suppose that's when *he* saw *me*.'

'So ... he really *is* Grandpa, then?' Justin asked.

Nanny paused for a split-second, then made a small shrugging gesture with one hand. 'What other explanation could there possibly be?'

Justin glanced at her questioningly, guessing she probably knew who was in the missing half of the photo, but she turned and walked away, signifying she had nothing further to tell him.

'There's one other thing,' he said, hurrying after her. 'I'm trying to tie up as many loose ends as possible, and ...'

'*WHAT?*'

'Well, er ...' Justin hesitated, a little surprised by her snippy retort. 'I've been trying to work out how you managed to mail my watch back once you were trapped in the past.'

A faint look of relief crept across Nanny Verity's face.

'I think you kept it hidden,' Justin continued. 'Then years later – when I was about five – you asked Mr Polydorus to mail it to me.'

Verity Kiss gasped. 'Och, how'd you guess that? You weren't even home that day.'

'It was something Mum said. Tell me about it.'

'Well, I knew the older me went into hiding three weeks before the younger me stole the watch,' explained Nanny. 'So I realised *I* couldn't post it. But who could I trust? Once I'd worked out my husband was Agent X, I started to wonder if poor Xavier had been framed for the crimes Val had committed. By then I hadn't seen Xav for years – then one summer he turned up at the castle looking quite different; he seemed a lot more confident and was wearing dazzling blue contact lenses. He told me they were for his new hypnosis act, but I suspected he was still trying to copy his older brother.'

'You mean his eyes aren't really that colour?' asked Justin.

'Erm ... *no*,' said Nanny, suddenly flustered. 'Is it important?'

Justin considered this for a moment. 'Maybe. When X e-mailed Robyn a few weeks ago, his address was blueeyedboy@nine.com. I'm guessing you forgot, otherwise you'd have *known* which brother to trust.'

Nanny Verity's mouth dropped wide open. 'That *completely* slipped my mind,' she said, looking mortified. 'Of course, it was *years* ago for me.'

'Perhaps it's as well,' said Justin. 'You *had* to marry Agent X to complete the loop.'

'I suppose,' Nanny sighed. 'Now, where was I?' She gathered her thoughts. 'Ah, yes ... the instant Xavier spoke I realised everything Val had ever told me about him was a lie. I just *knew* I could trust him. So I packed up the watch, addressing it to you, and wrote Xav a letter with instructions when to mail it.'

'Brilliant,' said Justin. 'And hiding that tiny note inside it was a stroke of genius – especially the little rat-drawing to represent Robyn's initials.'

'Hmm ... but you missed the other half of the clue,' Nanny told him, with an indulgent shake of her head. 'I purposely jammed the watch hands pointing to five and ten to give you two other initials: V and X for Verity Kiss!'

As the afternoon wore on the rain showed no sign of stopping, and Justin realised if he wanted to talk to Eliza, he'd have to brave the elements. He found a long waxed-jacket of his father's and stuffed the pockets with bananas. After checking inside Willoughby's workshop – which, as he suspected, was empty – he tramped across the estate towards Lupin Wood.

The old folly, now half tumbled-down and covered in ivy, stood atop a small hillock – but, although there were signs Eliza had slept there, the gorilla was nowhere to be seen.

Justin took shelter in a ruined archway and waited, making use of the peace and solitude to review the conglomeration of evidence. Normally, he'd have relished the challenge – but learning he'd overlooked the ridiculously obvious VX clue had badly dented his confidence. *What if I've missed something else*, he thought; *something a lot more important?*

Eliza didn't turn up. Eventually, after the distant tower clock struck seven, Justin left the bananas in a dry corner and returned gloomily to the castle.

Feeling depressed and frustrated with himself, he had supper up in the nursery with Nanny and Albion – although he scarcely ate anything, and spent most of the time grumbling about the lack of evidence that would help them identify Agent X.

'You should talk to Xavier,' Nanny Verity advised him. 'He's the one person we can definitely trust ... and he knows Val even better than I do.'

'Yeah ... maybe,' said Justin, half-heartedly. 'I might call him tomorrow if I'm still stuck. Mum's phoning later; I'm hoping this clue of hers will make everything else slot into place.'

After lights-out time in the nursery, Justin headed to the library. A full-blown thunderstorm now raged outside, so he drew the long tapestry curtains, and tossed a generous handful of pinecones on the blazing log fire.

Determined to try a new approach, he fetched a packet of post-its from the desk drawer and wrote a different clue or suspect on each sheet. He sprawled on the hearthrug with them scattered round him – rearranging them as different theories sprung to mind. But there was always one exasperating piece of evidence that didn't quite fit.

Above him, on the mantelpiece, the old Thyme Clock ticked relentlessly. Time had almost run out, and Justin could've sworn it was passing by at an accelerated pace. As the clock struck eleven-thirty, the library phone rang; he jumped up to answer it.

'Hi, Mum,' he said. 'You're up late.'

'Yeah,' Henny replied. 'I'm still trying to get everything wound up so we can fly home Tuesday or Wednesday.'

'So, er ... what's this clue you've remembered?' asked Justin eagerly.

Lady Henny sighed. 'I sure hope you won't be disappointed; it's not much. And like I told you ... it doesn't make sense.'

'Don't worry, Mum – things that *seem* trivial often turn out to be quite important.'

'Well, okay, son,' said Henny. 'You remember I told you how the kidnapper drugged me with chloroform?'

'Yeah.'

'Well, when he grabbed me I noticed his watch. It was very distinctive: plain black with no numbers on it – just a single diamond at twelve o'clock. I'd kinda forgotten about it until ... '

'Hey!' Justin exclaimed, interrupting his mother. 'I've seen one just like that ... *somewhere* ...'

'But here's the really weird thing,' Henny continued. 'It sorta looked as if he was wearing it upside-down.'

'The watch?'

'Yeah ... but that's impossible,' said Henny. 'Cos the time was absolutely correct.'

Justin put the phone down and stared at it, transfixed, trying to remember where he'd seen a black numberless watch quite recently. Within three seconds he had the answer: Mr Polydorus had worn one that matched Henny's description perfectly.

But why did Mum think it looked upside-down?' Justin muttered to himself. 'She's right ... it makes no sense at all. Unless ... *unless* ...'

The phone made a muffled clicking noise. The very same noise it had made a few nights earlier when he overheard Professor Gilbert dialling out from great hall. Holding his breath, Justin lifted the receiver and put it carefully to his ear. But instead of the professor's educated tones, he heard the deep hypnotic rumble of Xavier Polydorus.

'... you shouldn't have phoned, darling – it's too risky.'

'Och, don't fret, Valentine,' said a familiar voice. 'We're perfectly safe.'

Justin smothered a gasp of dismay. It *couldn't* be true ... *surely* it couldn't.

Xavier spoke again: 'So, the boy-genius believes your web of lies?'

'Of course he does,' replied Verity Kiss. 'Everything went splendidly. He doesn't suspect a thing!'

Going to the Future is Not an Option

Travelling forwards through time, though theoretically possible, should not be attempted as it is both futile and dangerous. Visiting the past, the traveller can set precise coordinates and know what they'll find there – but the future is always uncertain.

Heading into the past, the timeforks we negotiate in life are reversed, converging into a single route back through solitary possibility-planes – however, the future is not ONE timeline, but an ever-expanding web of limitless possibilities. There is not one future but an infinite variety, and the further one travels, the more diverse those possibilities become.

One set of future spatiotemporal coordinates would cover countless possibility-planes, so our destination would be a matter of chance. This makes travelling to a definitive point in the future out of the question.

CHAPTER NINETEEN

Precious Little Thyme

Justin didn't recall putting the phone down; neither did he remember rising unsteadily to his feet and staggering towards the fireplace. The shock of what he'd just overheard wiped everything else clean out of his mind.

The room seemed to be spinning round; whirling and undulating ... giving him a nauseous dizzy feeling like vertigo. He grabbed hold of the mantelpiece and clung to it tightly, as if he was about to fall.

He could still hear those two traitorous voices echoing inside his head – and realised he was trembling with anger. For Nanny Verity to have betrayed him once was bad enough, but to do it a second time was unthinkable ... especially now he knew her true identity.

But *was* she Robyn, Justin wondered ... or was that another of her lies? What if Nanny's entire time-loop story had been one huge fabrication designed to prevent him searching for his sister? Maybe the real Robyn had been abducted ... or worse.

Justin shuddered. He felt numb – empty inside, as if his heart had been torn out. Verity Kiss wasn't just X's spy – she was a double agent who'd tricked him into trusting her again. And Xavier Polydorus was simply another of her husband's many aliases.

Yet even now, with the painful truth staring him in the face, Justin

331

struggled to accept it. Part of him wanted to find a loophole; to believe Nanny Verity was still loyal – only pretending to side with her husband so they could catch him.

'Urrghh, get real,' he muttered bitterly, knowing that if Nanny had meant to help she wouldn't have phoned behind his back. He remembered the promise she'd made only yesterday: "*I'll always be true to the Thyme family.*" Her voice had sounded absolutely sincere ... then Justin realised it would be if she was as skilled an actor as her husband. But on the other hand, the evidence she and Robyn were the same person had been extraordinarily compelling. Would an impostor have gone to such elaborate lengths merely to fool him?

Justin groaned, wishing – yet again – that he'd never built the time machine. Creating it had opened a Pandora's box of trouble right from the day he'd first mentioned time travel to his father. Of course, whenever there was a family crisis, Justin knew it was always left to him to sort things out – but this time he felt the burden of responsibility rested fairly and squarely on his shoulders.

He took a few deep breaths, trying to find some inner strength. The thought of having to confront Nanny the following morning turned his stomach over. And there was still so much he didn't understand ... pieces of the puzzle he couldn't get to fit.

A soft metallic whirring noise broke his concentration; he glanced up at the clock on the mantelpiece, realising it was about to strike twelve. Slowly, the mechanical figure of Old Father Time drew back his scythe, then swung it forward, hitting the bell with a sharp *TING!* Perhaps it was a trick of the light, but Justin thought his carved face looked jaded and weary; the jester, however, had a malicious gleam in its sapphire eyes, and wore a mocking lopsided grin. For a split-second Justin had the urge to snap off its ivory head and hurl it into the fire.

The storm still raged furiously; the library windows rattled and loose branches of ivy tapped against them like skeletal fingers. High above, the deep reverberating toll of the tower bell echoed the delicate chime of the library clock. Then, as the twelfth note of each rang out in unison, a deafening clap of thunder exploded overhead. The window beside the desk crashed open, its curtains billowing inwards; lamps toppled, a newspaper scudded across the floor, and all Justin's neatly arranged post-its swirled into the air like a swarm of moths.

Justin raced to the window and slammed it shut; he redrew the curtains and wiped the rain off his face with his sleeve.

Turning round, he saw the last few post-it clues fluttering towards the floor. Some had come to rest on the mantelpiece; others lay scattered across the chesterfield armchairs; several lay in the hearth; and one was stuck to the old Thyme clock, close to the jester, half over the miniature playing cards bordering the left side of the clock face, half over the Roman numeral X.

As Justin reached for it, he remembered the uncanny connections between the creepy-looking jester and Agent X: the theatrical mask; the cards and dice; and the cryptic warning engraved across the bell ... *"Beware Procrastination"*. Again, he wondered if these were just a coincidence, or all part of some centuries-old feud linking the Thief of Time to the Thyme clan.

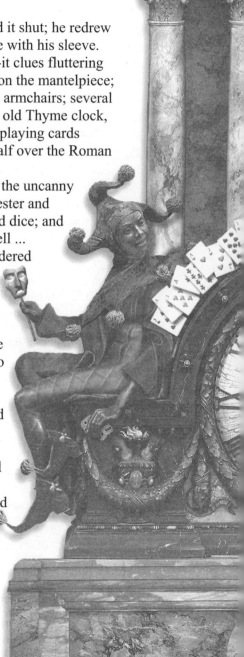

Suddenly, Justin was reminded of the card design Robyn had once spotted on the kidnapper's socks, and how it turned out to be a simple alphanumerical code. The old Thyme clock had stood in the library his entire life, and never once had he imagined its sequence of cards to be anything other than random – but now a curious thought occurred to him: what if these, too, formed a secret message?

Justin knew it was illogical; the clock had been made more than a hundred years before Agent X was born. The Victorian craftsman who'd set each little ivory card with rubies and jet, couldn't possibly have

333

known about him. But once the idea flashed into Justin's mind, he simply *had* to check it out – after all, with time travel in the picture, it wasn't impossible.

He peeled the post-it off the clock face and took a pencil out of his pocket. There were ten miniature cards, as if to subtly emphasise the X. The first card was the three of spades, followed by the ace and five of diamonds, the ace and nine of clubs, and the ace and three of hearts. Justin noted them down carefully on the back of the post-it. Next came the nine of spades and three of diamonds. The last card was a tiny enamelled joker.

Using the same code as before, Justin rewrote them as a number sequence: 3-15-19-13-9-3, then converted them into six letters: C-O-S-M-I-C. However, his excitement at finding an actual hidden word soon faded when he crossed the library and hauled out a huge dictionary to double-check its definition:

Cosmic – *adj* 1) of or relating to the entire universe.
2) originating beyond the vicinity of earth.
3) immeasurably extended in time and space.
4) harmonious (*rare*).

Disappointed, Justin flopped back into an armchair, unable to see how this tied in with the clock ... the jester ... Old Father Time ... or anything. He wasn't sure what he'd hoped for, but something a bit more specific would've been handy – like the cards spelling X-A-V-I-E-R – or something that confirmed the jester's connection to Agent X.

Then Justin realised he'd forgotten the tenth card ... the joker. Adding the letter J to the sequence didn't reveal anything, so perhaps the hidden message was two words: *Cosmic Joker*.

Justin narrowed his eyes thoughtfully; the phrase *did* sound familiar. He jumped up, climbed the rolling library-ladder, and scooted along the upper shelves, peering at the rows of leather-bound books. At length he pulled out an amber-coloured volume with "*Myths & Legends*" *by Daedalus Hap* embossed on its spine. He thumbed through it until he found the right page:

> The COSMIC JOKER is mythology's archetypal trickster. His stories have been told since the dawn of mankind, weaving through the folklore of every civilization and culture. (*Compare Hermes, Anansi and Puck*).
>
> He is a consummate deceiver, capable of lying effortlessly – fooling many with his undeniable wit and charm. Sometimes an impostor; invariably a thief; he is a prank-player, revelling in bizarre coincidence and random chance. He makes the improbable possible, and the more preposterous his tricks are, the better they suit him. Diametrically opposed to the strict confines of time, he employs chaos and folly, seeking to undermine all that is orderly and precise.*
>
> However, despite frequently altering his appearance, and a fondness of ambiguous pseudonyms, he can seldom resist "signing" his misdeeds or leaving cryptic hints to his true identity. He is, indeed, a paradox, wrapped in a puzzle, inside an enigma!
>
> * SEE OLD FATHER TIME, PAGE 80.

'Wow,' Justin murmured, pleased how this tied in with his own theories about the interconnectivity of Time and Chance. 'But surely Agent X doesn't believe *he's* the Cosmic Joker? That's ... *crazy!*'

He thought for a moment, chewing his lower lip. 'Hmm ... maybe he does; this description certainly fits him. And he signed himself *Procrastination* and the *Thief of Time*, as if he particularly *wanted* Dad to know *he* was the kidnapper. Perhaps he thinks the Lairds of Thyme are like ... time-lords or something ... and sees himself as our sworn enemy.'

Justin gave a mirthless laugh. 'Mad as a box of snakes,' he muttered, shaking his head. *But was it quite that simple*, he wondered, remembering the strange holographic image he'd seen of Old Father Time the day he turned thirteen; it had shimmered around Grandpa Lyall who, it had to be admitted, did rather resemble him. Then another unsettling memory flashed into his mind: whilst rescuing Henny, his watch had stopped at a time that spelt J-O-K-E-R ... surely a coincidence worthy of the Cosmic Joker himself.

'But a few coincidences don't prove the modern-day existence of an ancient myth,' Justin told himself firmly. 'No matter *how* uncanny they are.'

He knelt by the hearth and began gathering up the post-it notes, trying to work out whether this latest revelation altered anything. Clearly Valentine Kiss was deluded – but would that make it any easier to trap him tomorrow? Possibly – if his personality truly matched that of the mythical Joker, a subconscious craving for recognition might be his Achilles heel. One overheard phone call, an upside-down black watch, and an alias starting with the letter X would never convince Sergeant Awbrite, but if he *had* left his "*signature*" – irrefutable evidence of his involvement – then a watertight case might just be possible.

Justin knew he needed enough credible evidence to trick Agent X into giving himself away – which meant he'd have to re-examine his clues yet again. And not only that, he wanted to make sure he hadn't missed any; after all, he'd overlooked the two most obvious clues that Nanny Verity had left hinting she was Robyn.

Clues! The problem with clues, Justin thought to himself, was that the most important ones didn't look like clues at all. Usually, they seemed quite ordinary – or, even worse, they resembled red herrings whilst the real red herrings masqueraded as genuine evidence. It was all very well knowing Xavier Polydorus was Valentine Kiss, but that didn't explain the professor's midnight phone call, why Miss Garnet had drugged his cocoa, or who'd stolen the miniature pistol – and why, after going to such elaborate lengths to fool him, Nanny Verity had risked discovery by phoning her accomplice. There had to be a logical explanation for absolutely everything.

Justin felt a fresh perspective was called for; a new starting point. On

336

a sudden whim he turned the post-it clues face down, shuffled them like a pack of cards and picked one out at random. He flipped it over and read:

What made Eliza so angry?

It seemed as good a place as any to start, Justin thought, trying to consider the question from a different angle. Initially, he'd blamed Eliza's tantrums on her resentment of Albion; she'd so clearly wanted a baby gorilla of her own. But had he perhaps overlooked her innate ability to sense dishonesty? What if she'd overheard someone lying the day she lost her temper?

Justin frowned, trying to recall the precise sequence of events that morning. Who else had been there? What had they said or done? Then, after a minute or two of intense concentration, a startling idea occurred to him. At first he dismissed it – but, as he carried on exploring other more plausible theories, it refused to go away. Intrigued now, he decided to analyse the scenario properly, testing it against every item of evidence ... and, as impossible as it first appeared, it turned out to be a perfect fit. The unlikeliest bits of evidence made sense, each clue interlocking with adjacent puzzle pieces until Justin understood *all* that had happened.

Then, as he stared up at the Cosmic Joker leaning against the old Thyme Clock, he saw that Agent X had indeed left an unmistakeable "signature" – and, finally, absolutely *everything* connected to everything else.

It was past three in the morning. Justin had stayed in the library until the storm had blown over and the fire had almost burnt out. He'd been going over his plans – and with a deadline of noon the following day, there was little margin for error. Though if all went smoothly, he hoped Sergeant Awbrite would make his two arrests by ten o'clock at the latest.

Justin felt exhausted, but he still had several things to arrange before going to bed. Somehow, he needed to persuade Xavier Polydorus to visit Thyme Castle straight after breakfast; fortunately Nanny Verity had already suggested contacting him.

After burning his post-it clues, Justin settled himself at the library desk, and wrote her a brief note:

> Nan, I think you're right. If we're going to catch X we'll need Mr Polydorus to help us. Can you invite him over first thing tomorrow morning – nine o'clock. I have a plan!
>
> Justin.

That should do it, he thought, folding the note in half. If Nanny asks him, he's *bound* to come.

Next, Justin hurried to the top of the south tower. The two bugs he'd discovered in his lab were still in place – and, as far as he could tell, still functioning. However, now he'd worked out who'd planted them, it made better sense to turn them to his advantage. Carefully, he disconnected the micro-cam and disabled its transmitter. Then, after fetching a screwdriver, he took it down to the entrance hall where he fastened it to the wall beside a suit of armour.

As Justin tightened the last screw, a hollow voice hissed softly in his ear:

'Can I help you with anything, sir?'

Justin leapt up, cracking his head on an iron gauntlet, and turned to find Knightly wearing a plaid dressing gown and slippers.

'Flux!' he gasped, glancing sharply at the butler's feet. 'I didn't hear you coming.'

'Sorry to startle you, sir,' Knightly whispered. 'I thought I heard a noise downstairs, and wondered if the old gentleman was sleepwalking again.'

'Er ... no,' Justin muttered, stuffing the screwdriver in his pocket. 'Just me – doing a bit of ... er ... nocturnal maintenance.'

The butler nodded solemnly. 'Yes, sir. I thought it best to check. Since Sir Willoughby and Miss Robyn vanished I've been decidedly edgy at night.'

'Vanished?' asked Justin.

'There's been gossip amongst the servants,' Knightly continued. 'I've tried to quash it – but no one believes they returned to Mauritius. Cook thinks something sinister happened ... like her Ladyship's abduction last month.'

'Well, she's right,' said Justin grimly. He frowned, then added: 'Actually, I'm glad you turned up, Knightly; I need to talk to the entire staff about this. Could you arrange for everyone to gather in the entrance hall at nine o'clock tomorrow morning? And you'll need to tell Mrs Kof to serve breakfast half an hour early.'

'Very good, sir,' the butler droned, his bland face showing not one flicker of surprise. Then, after a resounding sniff, he glided silently away.

On his way back to the south tower, Justin stopped off at the great hall, hoping the Gilliechattans' scrapbook was still on the coffee table. Although Agent X's identity was no longer a mystery, he knew it would be foolish to leave a prime piece of evidence unexamined.

He felt his way across the dark room, trying not to make any noise. The book was next to Eliza's laptop, right where Sir Willoughby had left it. Justin tucked it under one arm, then snuck upstairs to leave his note for Verity Kiss. Not wanting to wake her, he tiptoed through the nursery and propped it in front of Albion's Nessie-nightlight, knowing Nanny would switch it off the instant she woke up.

As he crept back towards the nursery door, Justin peeped at Alby sleeping soundly in his cot. He smelt sweetly of baby milk and talcum powder, and seemed so small and vulnerable just looking at him gave Justin a strange mixture of emotions he'd never felt before. He leaned over and lifted Albion's favourite teddy bear off his blanket, then, after a few moments, tucked it gently in bed beside him.

The tower clock chimed four. Justin yawned and turned to leave, realising he desperately needed to get at least a couple of hours sleep; tomorrow was going to be a very busy day.

The nightmare started as it did before, with Old Father Time standing just beyond the castle gates, tossing his coin – but this time it ended quite differently. The old man dissolved in a cloud of oily-grey smoke which blew towards the castle. It swirled in through the open window, solidifying into a man wearing a jester's costume – the Cosmic Joker, Justin thought – yet his face was obscured by a strange theatrical mask covered in dark feathers and with a cruel, sharp beak.

The Joker crept slowly forwards. As he reached the foot of the bed, he lifted his right hand, aiming a gun directly at Justin's chest. There was a loud *BANG*; its muzzle flashed; and Justin awoke, rocketing bolt-upright. Then, realising it was just a dream, he gave a half-strangled groan and flopped back against his pillow, heart pounding furiously.

Justin glanced sideways at his bedside clock – its alarm, set to wake him at six-fifteen, was due to go off in a couple of minutes. He lay still and closed his eyes, wondering why this seemed vaguely familiar – but he was too tired to remember. Instead, he tried to analyse his nightmare. The logical explanation, he decided, was that it subconsciously reflected his plans to unmask Agent X later that morning ... but that didn't explain his glimpse of one narrow silver feather half-hidden amongst the glossy black plumage.

Once Justin was washed and dressed, he took the Gilliechattans' scrapbook over to the window so he could see it in the daylight. The most recent news clippings were from just a few years ago, and showed Oliver and Ariadne Marsh in a variety of Shakespearean bit parts. However, when Justin flipped to a random page near the front of the book, he found precisely what he was looking for.

It was a photograph from an old theatre programme – a group of three actors in full costume and makeup. The first, dressed as a farmer, was, according to the credit line, Oliver Marsh. He was clean-shaven, though wearing rather too much greasepaint to be easily recognised. Next to him was someone called Templar Tercel wearing a sailor's uniform – but the third member of the group was Valentine Kiss. He wore a top hat, a long black cloak, and sported a magnificent waxed moustache; this, combined with his gothic makeup, gave him the look of a dashing Victorian villain.

The write-up beneath the photo was entitled: *A Ruddy Good "Ruddigore"* – and unless both the journalist and photographer had been completely duped, it was clear Oliver Marsh and Valentine Kiss were two distinct individuals.

'Just as I thought,' Justin whispered to himself. 'Irrefutable evidence that Angus Gilliechattan cannot possibly be Agent X.'

At seven-thirty Justin slid down to the library. Bugsy had spent the last half-hour scanning the room for micro-transmitters. It was now perched on the library desk, the digital readout on its exoskeleton flashing: BUG-FREE ZONE.

Justin picked up the telephone and dialled the number Sergeant Awbrite had given him, hoping the invitation to call him any time, night or day, had been genuine.

After several rings, he heard a sleepy voice mutter, 'Awbrite here,' followed by a protracted yawn.

'Hello, Sergeant. It's Justin Thyme. I'm sorry to bother you so early, but ...'

'What's happened?' Awbrite cut in, sounding suddenly alert. 'Tell me.'

'Well, er ... last Wednesday night Dad was kidnapped, and ...'

'WEDNESDAY?' barked the sergeant, clearly annoyed. 'And you wait till Monday to call me. How come you never mentioned it when we spoke last week? Slip your mind, did it?'

'Erm ...'

'I specifically warned you not to do anything reckless – but it appears your recent deductive exploits have led you to think the police are superfluous.'

'No, no ... not at all ...'

'Really? So things haven't proved as easy for you this time? Bitten off more than you can chew, eh?'

'I must apologise, Sergeant,' said Justin, trying to placate him. 'I know I should've contacted you immediately – but I delayed, believing that's what my father would prefer.'

'So he'd prefer to remain kidnapped?'

'No, Sergeant. That's why I called you. I'm pretty sure I know where Dad's being held ... *and* I've identified his kidnapper.' There was a long silence. 'Are you still there, Sergeant?'

'Yes,' replied Awbrite, sounding thoroughly deflated.

'Look, he'll be coming to the castle later this morning,' Justin continued. 'And I thought you'd want to be on hand to arrest him. Thing is ... the evidence ... it's sort of ... well ... I'll need to trick him into revealing himself. But I've got a plan. First you'll need to arrest our resident spy, then ...'

'You mean Mrs Kiss has turned up?'

Justin sighed. 'I suppose I'd better explain ...'

On his way down to the dining room, Justin stopped off at the nursery to check whether Nanny Verity had got his note. Knightly had just informed her that breakfast was being served half an hour early, so she was hurrying around looking flustered. As she scooped Albion out of his cot, he leaned over and grabbed hold of his teddy.

'Ret Sami,' he said decisively.

Nanny frowned. 'Och, can't we leave Sammy Bear upstairs for once? You can play with him later.'

But Albion was in an uncooperative mood; he hugged the saggy old teddy bear tightly, and scowled at Verity Kiss with his bottom lip quivering.

'Very well,' Nanny sighed, not particularly wanting a major tantrum

342

before breakfast. 'Have it your own way.'

This was such a very un-nannyish thing to say, Justin peered at her closely. Her face looked pale and drawn, and her brow deeply furrowed.

'Did you get chance to phone Mr Polydorus, Nan?' he whispered, as they stepped out onto the landing.

Verity Kiss gave him a tired smile. 'Of course, Poppet. He'll be here by nine.'

'Great.'

'Dear old Xavier; we haven't spoken properly for years,' she continued. 'He was dreadfully surprised to hear from me.'

'Yeah, I bet he was,' said Justin. 'Not much of a mind-reader, is he?'

Once Knightly had cleared the breakfast things away, he carried the dining room chairs into the entrance hall and arranged them in a wide semicircle. Meanwhile, Justin, who hadn't managed a scrap of food despite Nanny's wheedling, paced up and down, mentally rehearsing his speech.

'The staff should assemble momentarily,' droned the butler, checking his watch. 'Will that be all, sir?'

'Thank you, Knightly. Perhaps you could fetch Sir Lyall.'

'Certainly, sir.'

Justin peered through one of the narrow windows overlooking the courtyard. Xavier Polydorus, who'd just stepped out of a taxi, was heading towards the castle door. He was wearing a neat charcoal suit, and looked somehow smaller and less imposing without his stage costume and false moustache. Justin opened the door and welcomed him in politely.

'Hi, Mr Polydorus. Thanks for coming at such short notice. Did Nanny explain?'

'Erm ... not exactly,' he murmured. 'Something about identifying the person who kidnapped your mother – but I don't see how I can possibly help.'

'Oh, I'm sure you can,' replied Justin.

Xavier's eyes widened for a moment, then flicked nervously towards the row of chairs. Justin noticed that he wasn't wearing his dazzling blue contact lenses today. Without them, his eyes were a lacklustre grey – but they brightened when he caught sight of Nanny with Albion on her knee.

'Verity,' he said, bowing deeply. 'Always a pleasure.'

Nanny smiled, patting the seat next to her; Mr Polydorus sank onto it, muttering: 'Why do I have a bad feeling about this?'

'Because you're one of those unfortunate people whose toast always lands buttery-side down,' said Nanny. 'But maybe this time it'll be different.'

They chatted quietly while the rest of the staff filed in. The Gilliechattans came through from the kitchen; Mrs Kof followed them, wiping her hands on a dishcloth; and Evelyn Garnet tramped down the north staircase, grumbling loudly, with Professor Gilbert a few steps behind. They each sat down, casting sideways looks at one another.

Mr Gilliechattan – wearing tweeds instead of his usual kilt – seemed particularly fidgety; he kept flattening his unruly red hair and straightening his tie. 'I hope this won't be a long scene,' he boomed theatrically. 'I've a train to catch at ten-thirty.'

'Me too,' barked Miss Garnet. 'I call this an outrageous liberty.'

A faint squeaking heralded the return of Knightly; he guided Grandpa Lyall to a vacant seat and sat beside him, looking as if he'd much rather stand. Only one chair remained unoccupied, and everyone was staring at it.

Then, as the tower clock struck nine, there was a sharp rap on the castle door prompting several muffled gasps. Justin strode across and opened it wide.

'Come in, Sergeant,' he said, gesturing to the last seat. 'We're ready to begin.'

Awbrite removed his cap, and nodded at the assembled group. As the policeman settled on his chair, Justin let his eyes wander along the row. Knightly looked bored and cynical; Grandpa appeared to be nodding off; Xavier Polydorus flexed his eyebrows at Nanny Verity in an I-told-you-so sort of way; and Mrs Kof slid her chair back into the shadows, holding a large recipe book up to obscure her face.

Justin positioned himself at the centre of the semicircle and cleared his throat.

'Good morning everyone,' he said, astonished at how calm his voice sounded when his heart was racing. 'Thank you for your cooperation.'

Evelyn Garnet made a huffing noise and folded her arms.

Justin continued. 'I know there's been some talk about the recent disappearance of my father and sister. These rumours are, in part, quite true.' There was a chorus of whispers and a few hurriedly exchanged glances. Justin ignored them. 'Robyn is quite safe – but Sir Willough-by has indeed been kidnapped. The night it happened someone drugged me – and I've been analysing the clues to determine who. [1]

'I had two main suspects: Miss Garnet who brought my cocoa, and Mrs Kof who made it. I tried to work out if anyone else could've tampered with it – then Mrs Kof told me she *thought* she'd seen Evelyn Garnet putting drops in my drink the night before.' [2]

'She's lying!' snapped Miss Garnet, jumping to her feet. 'I won't stand for it ...'

'Then I suggest you sit down and keep quiet,' said Awbrite forcefully. 'You'll get your chance to speak presently.'

'Fortunately,' Justin went on, 'I didn't drink my cocoa that first night. Mrs Kof knocked it over, [3] but she was too late to stop Robyn drinking hers, which explains why she was so sleepy the next morning. [4] You also slept very heavily, didn't you, Miss Garnet? [5] Perhaps you wondered if you'd mixed up the mugs. Anyway, you were determined there'd be no mistakes the second night, so you broke into Mrs Kof's herbal cabinet and stole her bottle of sleeping potion. [6] This time you gave me a much larger dose, and even stayed to watch me drink it.' [7]

---

[1] If you want to check the clues later, these footnotes will direct you to the right pages.
[2] Page 223.
[3] Page 130.
[4] Pages 132/133, 147, 223.
[5] Pages 148.
[6] Pages 185, 222.
[7] Page 191-193.

'She very bad womans,' Mrs Kof interrupted. 'I telling you she was stealing my dreamy-drops.'

'Nonsense! How could I possibly get them out of a locked cabinet?' demanded Evelyn Garnet.

'Using your skeleton keys,' Justin replied calmly. 'Robyn saw them the day you arrived.[8] You'd brought them hoping they'd open my lab door. I heard you dash upstairs while Dad was fetching Mum's tranq-gun ... right after you bugged the library phone.'[9]

'That's a scurrilous accusation,' growled Miss Garnet, looking furious.

'I've warned you once,' said Awbrite. 'No more interruptions.'

Justin returned to his case summary. 'The south tower is scanned daily. My bug-seeker soon traced your device and I destroyed it, but that didn't stop you planting more. When you brought my cocoa the second night, you saw how my fingerprint-recognition lock operates, [10] so once I was completely unconscious, you carried me upstairs over your shoulder and pressed my thumb on the print-sensor. Then, after a fruitless search of the lab, you planted another two bugs.[11]

'Wh-what did she use to listen in?' asked the professor.

'A micro-receiver disguised as a hearing aid,' Justin explained. 'She thought no one would guess[12] – but her hearing was absolutely fine without it.[13] In fact, she gave herself away when she told me *"There's no need to shout – I'm not deaf."*'[14]

Mr Gilliechattan roared with laughter.

Justin took a deep breath and spoke directly to Miss Garnet: 'After all your trouble, I doubt the bugs were much use. The first thing you probably overheard was my phone call to Sergeant Awbrite.[15] I said I was calling about our nanny. At supper that evening you were

---

[8] Page 122.
[9] Page 117, 135.
[10] Page 191.
[11] Page 263.
[12] Page 119.
[13] Pages 229, 232/233, 317.
[14] Page 192.
[15] Page 256.

unusually friendly,[16] and later I realised you thought I was talking about *you*.

'The second thing you heard was the combination to my safe, the only place in my lab you *hadn't* been able to search. By then, I knew someone was spying, so I said the wrong code number,[17] and set a trap, running an electric current to the keyhole of the south tower door.[18] It must've given you quite a shock!'

'Lies ... all lies,' hissed Evelyn Garnet, looking at the others for support.

'Then prove it,' said Justin. He pointed to her right hand. 'Remove your bandage. If Tybalt really *did* scratch you, you're innocent[19] ... but I suspect you're hiding some badly scorched fingers.'

'I *knew* Tybs wouldn't hurt her,' declared Mrs Gilliechattan, her eyes flashing angrily. 'I bet he didn't trip her into that web either.'

'Of course not,' said Justin. 'She hoped to drive you and Mr G out of the castle before you noticed what she was up to. That's the real reason she got rid of Eliza; she ...'

Evelyn Garnet leapt up and darted at him, her arms outstretched and face contorted with rage. 'I wish I'd got rid of the whole pukin' lot of yer ... especially that messy, stupid baby, talking his gibberish. He's ... he's positively *BACKWARDS!*'

Justin stumbled over, fending her off – but Sergeant Awbrite grabbed her wrist and spoke in his official policeman's voice:

'Evelyn Garnet – you're under arrest. You have the right to remain silent ...'

'Like hell I will,' she snarled. 'This is a set-up; I had nothing to do with Sir Willoughby's disappearance ...'

'Really?' said Justin. 'Then how do you account for your torch being used to signal Dad's kidnapper ... and the stolen pistol I saw under your bed?'

'But ...'

---

[16] Page 260/261.
[17] Pages 263/264.
[18] Page 264.
[19] Pages 315, 317, 321.

'*The Lady doth protest too much, methinks*,' Burbage cackled in Mr Gilliechattan's ear.

'Come along,' said Awbrite, snapping a pair of handcuffs on Miss Garnet's wrists. He propelled her firmly towards the door. 'You'll get the opportunity to make a full statement once we're at the station.'

Under his watchful gaze, Evelyn Garnet tramped out to the squad car, still proclaiming her innocence. Meanwhile, Justin turned to the assembled group.

'Thanks for your patience, everyone,' he said. 'With a little police persuasion I'm sure she'll soon reveal Dad's whereabouts.'

No one seemed sorry to see her go; there was a general murmur of approval, Mrs Gilliechattan muttered, 'Good riddance,' and even little Albion stopped chewing his teddy and chuckled.

Justin hurried outside and watched Awbrite assisting Miss Garnet into the back of his squad car. Then, as the sergeant walked round to take his seat beside Constable Knox, Justin whispered. 'Phase one complete. All set for phase two?'

Sergeant Awbrite gave him a slow, solemn wink.

Once the police car had purred through the archway, Justin glanced up at the tower clock and stepped back inside, leaving the front door wide open. Mrs Kof and the Gilliechattans had returned to the kitchen, Professor Gilbert was scurrying upstairs, and Knightly was helping Grandpa back to the great hall.

Only Verity Kiss and Mr Polydorus remained behind, both looking somewhat bemused.

'Hmm ... that didn't go *quite* as I expected,' remarked Nanny. 'All very convenient ... and just a wee bit *too* obvious.'

Justin grinned. 'Yeah ... absolutely! I needed something the rest of the household would swallow without any awkward questions. You see, Miss Garnet *is* a spy ... but *not* for Agent X. She's a corporate spy, planted here by some big multinational business conglomerate desperate to rip-off my latest inventions. We've had them trying to

348

break in before,[20] though this is the first time one's applied for a job. Fortunately, the night she drugged me and raided my lab,[21] my *Hover-Boots* were locked in the safe.'

'I thought you said she was in league with your father's kidnapper,' said Mr Polydorus, staring uneasily at the open front door.

'No ... I didn't *say* it exactly; implied, perhaps. I'm afraid I had to misdirect Awbrite a little; the real spy's someone he can't actually arrest.'

'But who?' Nanny asked. She jiggled Albion, who was starting to get fractious. 'Mrs Kof, I suppose. I still say she brought me that handcuff key.'

'I know, said Justin. 'She spoke to you ... and you heard her bare feet. But what if some other bare-footed individual mimicked her voice?'

Nanny gasped out loud. 'Oh, *crud-crumpets*, it's Mr Gilliechattan, isn't it? He always leaves his boots on the doorstep ... and he's brilliant at impersonating people.'

'True – but if he'd *really* wanted you to think he was Mrs Kof, wouldn't he have copied her mispronunciations? [22] You said she was word-perfect. At first I didn't grasp how significant that was – but think about it: Who *never* wears shoes and can replicate any human voice *flawlessly*[23] ... including yours?'[24]

Nanny wore a puzzled frown. 'Burbage?'

'No, Verity' murmured Xavier Polydorus in his deep, velvety voice. 'He's talking about Eliza.'

'Spot on, Mr P,' said Justin. 'I thought you'd guess; you've got a rapport with primates. Mum says you worked as a chimpanzee trainer for a while, and saved Eliza's life when she was a baby. At first I thought Eliza was spying for *you* – that her outbursts were triggered by conflicting emotions because she felt obligated to help you ... despite

---

[20] Pages 2/3, 102.
[21] Page 191.
[22] Page 309.
[23] Page 31/32, 54, 65.
[24] Page 73.

her aversion to deceit.'[25]

'I doubt Eliza remembers me,' said Mr Polydorus. 'She was just a few weeks old. And from what Polly's told me, I'm sure she'd never be *willingly* dishonest. When he and Hank taught her my old pick-pocketing tricks [26] they had to convince her it was just a joke.'

'But that's how she must've got my handcuff key out of the Constable's pocket,' Nanny insisted, trying to stop Albion wriggling off her knee.

'Well, one thing's certain,' said Justin. 'Climbing my fireman's pole would've been simplicity itself for a gorilla; she'd just jump up and haul herself through the hole.' He gave a long weary-sounding sigh. 'But Mr Polydorus is right; Eliza *isn't* the spy – she was an unwilling accomplice *forced* to rescue you at gunpoint.'

'*GUNPOINT?*'

'Yes. That's why she's been acting so strangely these last few weeks.[27] Someone she's loved and cared about started threatening her; it's no wonder she's been confused and unhappy. Eliza's never liked guns; she saw poachers shoot her mother.'

'Why didn't she tell someone?' asked Mr Polydorus.

'She did – in a way,' said Justin, looking a little shamefaced. 'But none of us picked up on it.[28] Then her laptop was confiscated, silencing her completely. Though, as it turned out, by using it *afterwards* to impersonate Professor Gilbert, the spy inadvertently put Eliza in the clear.'

Justin walked over to the hall table and lifted Eliza's computer out of the middle drawer. He placed it on the tabletop and opened it. Meanwhile, Nanny turned Albion to face her and spoke to him firmly. 'Och, *do* stop fidgeting, Precious. Nanny's busy; we'll go upstairs in a minute.'

Once the computer screen lit up, Justin continued speaking. 'Last night, afraid I was getting closer to the truth, the spy tried one final

---

[25] Page 235.
[26] Page 239.
[27] Page 32.
[28] 33/34, 79, 108.

350

desperate trick to fool me ... and it very nearly worked. Listen ...'

With a few swift keystrokes he accessed the laptop's memory[29] and a deep voice spoke: "*So, the boy-genius believes your web of lies?*"

Then another voice answered: "*Of course he does. Everything went splendidly. He doesn't suspect a thing!*"

Mr Polydorus looked deeply depressed. Nanny Verity, however, turned pink, and her eyes flashed with indignant fury.

'WHO *IS* IT,' she snapped, glaring at Justin. 'I'll ... I'll ... *spifflicate* them!'

Justin raised his hand and pointed one finger accusingly in her direction. 'Here's our spy,' he said. 'Albion Thyme. Or perhaps I should say: Agent Beowulf – codename: *Wolf-in-Sheep's-Clothing!*'[30]

---

[29] Page 32.
[30] Pages 137, 88.

Never Tell Anyone About Time Travel

Time travel MUST remain a secret. If word of it got out, some corrupt organisation would inevitably want to misuse this technological breakthrough.

Time machines cannot ever become commercially available to the masses. The precautions needed to keep just one time traveller safe would have to apply to everyone. A world database of ALL travel coordinates would need to be kept — and constantly updated to prevent fatal accidents. Without it chaos would ensue.

Hiding the chronopod, never leaving anything in the past, and dressing to blend with the era visited are all excellent precautions — however, the most important rule is: TELL NO ONE. No matter how much you think you can trust someone, you cannot guarantee their confidentiality. If they tell someone else the secret will be unstoppable!

CHAPTER TWENTY

Cosmic Retribution

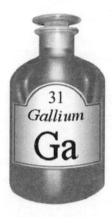

Right up until the moment he said it out loud, a small part of Justin's brain had struggled to accept that a fourteen month-old baby *could* be a spy – but the flash of pure hatred in Albion's eyes removed any doubt. No one else saw it – and, a split-second later, Alby returned to chewing his teddy bear's ear, gurgling mischievously.

Justin wasn't surprised. He'd assumed Albion would brazen it out; after all, they both knew it would be impossible to prove without hard evidence. He glanced at Nanny Verity, expecting a barrage of objections – however, it was Xavier Polydorus who spoke first.

'You can't be serious,' he said, shaking his head in bewilderment. 'Tell him, Verity ... it's insane ... impossible.'

Nanny didn't reply straight away, but stared broodingly at the baby on her lap; Albion beamed back at her, a picture of wide-eyed talcum-scented innocence. After several seconds she glanced up and fixed Justin with a quizzical stare.

'A spy? He can't walk or talk properly yet; I seriously doubt he'd be able to follow an adult conversation.'

'That's what makes him the perfect undercover agent,' said Justin. 'We talk in front of him as if he doesn't understand – but he does!'

They all looked at Albion playing happily with his teddy bear. He was making contented cooing noises and seemed oblivious of their attention. Nanny took a handkerchief out of her apron pocket and wiped a glob of dribble off his chin.

'Hmm ... go on ... I'm listening,' she said to Justin.

'Ohhh, *surely* you don't believe him,' groaned Mr Polydorus. 'It's preposterous ... a crazy farfetched fantasy ...'

'But not impossible,' Nanny insisted. 'Not once time travel's in the mix. Believe me, I know.'

Xavier gasped. 'So ... it's true, then? ... You? ... Robyn?'

'*Shhhh*!' hissed Nanny. Then, seeing his startled expression, a sad, softness crept into her voice: 'I thought you knew ...'

'*Knew*? No, nothing so clear-cut. I always sensed there was something different about you – something special ... but when I saw you in the present, looking as young as the day I first met you ... well, what other explanation could there possibly be?' He gave a deep sigh and rubbed his forehead. 'But this ... spy-baby theory ... I just don't see how it fits in.'

'Me neither, but it will,' muttered Nanny. She turned to Justin with a look of grim resignation. 'You'd better start right at the beginning.'

Justin nodded, and took a deep breath. 'Don't worry, Nan,' he said. 'Once I explain everything properly I'm sure it'll make sense. I knew you wouldn't believe me.' His brow furrowed pensively. 'I guess I'll have to start with Dad's original time machine. It's got a fault he never eliminated: it alters time *inside* the capsule at the same rate it passes on the outside, so anyone travelling to the past gets younger. It sounds impossible, but Dad actually saw it happen to Agent X. He discovered whatever age a time traveller eventually ends up, their memory always remains intact – which probably means that, mentally, they're an adult, however they're now trapped in child's body.[31] I suspect X used this improbable effect to his advantage. Despite hating Dad's machine, he must have vowed that, one day in the future, his adult grandson would be trained in the art of espionage and then sent back through time to the day of his birth. It's all theory, of course, but it's as close to the truth as we're ever likely to get.'

---

[31] Pages 10, 141.

Nanny sighed. 'You've lost me, I'm afraid.'

'It's exactly how I rescued Mum last month,' Justin explained. 'I planned a *future* trip knowing it would shape the *present*. I imagine it happened something like this, Nan: One evening, let's say five minutes to ten – Agent X decides that when his grandson has grown up, he'll send him back to precisely ten o'clock that very night. As the hour strikes, the time machine appears, complete with its tiny age-regressed passenger. He lifts Beowulf out, then the pre-programmed machine vanishes back to the future, leaving him with the perfect spy!'

'An intriguing idea,' murmured Mr Polydorus. 'But if it's just guess-work, how can you be sure it's true?'

'Because when literally *dozens* of clues point directly to one person they *can't* be brushed aside,' said Justin. 'No matter *how* bizarre they seem.'

'Clues?' asked Nanny Verity. 'Such as?'

'Well, for a start, I noticed *this* baby looks exactly like one of those in your photo albums,' said Justin.[32] 'Which I eventually realised meant there are two Beowulfs; one from the present and one from the future.

'I always assumed that was just family resemblance,' said Nanny.

'Then there's their matching ages,' Justin continued. 'The real Albion was born on the second of April[33] – Beowulf was born the day before.[34] X must've known Mum's baby was due about the same time as his third grandson, and *that's* what gave him the idea.'

Nanny looked suddenly dismayed. 'I expect it was my fault. I'd planned to be with Henslowe when Wulfi was born – but your mum was so poorly I didn't want to leave her. I phoned Kitty; I guess she told her father.'

'Probably,' Justin agreed. 'I wonder ... how soon after Alby's birth did your husband hint there might be another spy in the castle?'[35]

Nanny groaned. 'Almost straight away.'

---

[32] Page 89.
[33] Pages 22/23, 33.
[34] Page 320.
[35] Page 310.

'I thought so. Every other castle resident came here either ages before of after[36] – only Albion's arrival fitted perfectly with X's veiled threat.'

'But when did he swap the babies over? And how?'

Justin noticed Albion stiffen, and knew he was listening.

'I'll get to that in a moment,' he said, surreptitiously checking the time. 'Right now I want to appeal to *you*, Alby ... I mean ... Beowulf.' Justin lowered his voice and spoke pleadingly. 'You know I'm right, so why not admit it? You needn't feel any loyalty to your grandfather; he put you in this mess; he's afraid to use the faulty time machine himself, yet he risked *your* life, sending you dangerously close to the point of non-existence. If you cooperate – help us trap Agent X – I'll do everything I can to return you to your own time and age. Think of it: no more mushed food and smelly nappies. What d'you say?'

The baby *said* nothing – but he burped loudly, then giggled. Nanny gazed down at him, and Justin could tell she still doubted his story. She glanced uncertainly at Mr Polydorus, who rolled his eyes then looked away.

'Well, there's plenty more evidence,' Justin assured them. 'The missing miniature pistol for instance. Any adult would've taken the full-sized weapon, but Alby – I'd better call him that to avoid confusion – could only manage the toy-sized one.[37] He'd seen Dad showing the guns to Grandpa,[38] so he knew they were kept in the bottom drawer he could easily reach.[39]

'The following day – after you'd been rushed off to hospital, Nan – he must've sneaked down to the great hall and stolen it. From then on, Eliza had to do whatever he said.

'Once you got home, Alby forced her to pinch the handcuff key out of Knox's pocket then deliver it to you in my sitting room. I bet he was clinging to Eliza's back the whole time, holding the gun to her head. That's why the message he prepared in Mrs Kof's voice started by

---

[36] Page 310/311.
[37] Page 105/106.
[38] Page 107.
[39] Page 103.

telling you not to look back.'[40]

Nanny Verity shook her head. 'He *sneaked* downstairs? *Told* Eliza what to do? You make it sound like he could walk and talk already.'

'That's right!' replied Justin. 'Obviously, when he was just a few months old, he was limited by his small size and physical weakness – but he's not *quite* the slow-developer we all assumed. He's been able to walk for several weeks – and I bet he's been talking even longer.'[41]

'Och, how d'you know that?' asked Nanny.

'Like I said before; Eliza told me,' explained Justin. 'On our last day in Mauritius she got angry and said: "*Bad baby walk and talk already*".[42] At the time I didn't realise how literally she meant it. Poor Eliza – when Mum dismissed her words as jealously it upset her even more.[43] Albion thought it was hilarious; I think he purposely fuelled the conflict between the two of them,[44] knowing that if Eliza got too angry to use her computer she'd be less likely to give him away.[45] He couldn't threaten her with the pistol; he'd had to leave it behind because of airport security.

'On the flight home I mistakenly thought Eliza was listening to our conversation about Agent X – but her focus was actually on the real spy, Albion. She tried to distract him with her computer game, and when that didn't work, she turned the volume up so he couldn't hear us ... much to his irritation.[46]

'Back at the castle, Eliza still kept insisting he was a "*bad baby*"[47] – pistol or not. I think at that point Alby decided she'd become a serious security risk. However, when Evelyn Garnet arrived and took an instant dislike to the gorilla – even threatening to banish her to a zoo[48] – he saw an ideal opportunity to get rid of her.

---

[40] Pages 253, 307.
[41] Page 34.
[42] Page 33.
[43] Page 34.
[44] Pages 34/35, 47/48.
[45] Page 40.
[46] Pages 65/66.
[47] Pages 79, 108.
[48] Pages 109/110, 112, 114.

'Later that evening, when Haggis escaped, Alby got a close look at the little bird as it ran past his playpen.[49] Realising it was a dodo – which meant the new time machine *didn't* alter age and time concurrently – he decided to contact Agent X.

'However, he had no idea whether the new Nanny was a light sleeper or not – and knowing he'd have to unlatch his cot and creep downstairs alone, he foresaw a problem; but after supper a solution presented itself. Like Mrs Kof, Albion noticed Miss Garnet putting sleeping potion in two of the cocoa mugs and leaving a spoon in her own drug-free drink so she wouldn't muddle them.[50] After creating a diversion, (by dropping his bottle), Alby switched the spoon to another mug whilst everyone was searching beneath the kitchen table.[51] When Mrs Kof came up to my lab, the mug she knocked over must've contained nothing but cocoa. Meanwhile, Miss Garnet slept solidly, making it safe for Albion to sneak out of the nursery shortly before midnight.

'Rather than risk speaking himself, he used Eliza's confiscated laptop, which Miss Garnet had left on the great hall coffee table.[52] He chose Professor Gilbert's voice from its vocal menu – but forgot the computer wouldn't replicate his stuttering.[53] He also made a silly mistake, saying the dodo "*ran right past his nose*" – whereas *I'd* seen Haggis dash through the professor's legs.[54] Apart from Albion sitting in his playpen, Haggis couldn't have *PAST anyone's* nose,[55] although he did run right *under* Mr Gilliechattan's as he knelt by his vegetable patch – and for a while I wondered if Mr G had impersonated the professor.

'The following morning I found the great hall telephone upended beside the desk,[56] and assumed Professor Gilbert had knocked it off as he left. In fact, Albion, who couldn't reach that high, must've tugged

---

[49] Page 121.
[50] Pages 126/127.
[51] Page 127.
[52] Pages 112, 186, 258, 339.
[53] Page 137/138.
[54] Pages 138, 121.
[55] Page 121/122.
[56] Page 143.

the phone's wire until it fell on the floor, then dragged the receiver over to Eliza's laptop.

'Miss Garnet was unwell that morning and, once again, Eliza had to care for the baby she'd started to fear and dislike. Albion saw an opportunity to get her evicted from the castle ... so, at breakfast, he did his utmost to annoy her.[57] Next, while she was trying to fetch his pushchair, he goaded her into charging at him, then threw himself backwards with such perfect timing it looked as if Eliza had hit him.[58]

'To ensure the attack looked completely authentic, Alby cracked his head on that suit of armour and screamed in genuine pain. Dad was furious – which only added to Eliza's distress. I couldn't believe she'd ever hurt a baby, but there seemed no other explanation; and without her laptop she couldn't tell us the truth.

'Poor Eliza,' remarked Mr Polydorus. 'I know exactly how she must've felt.'

'Once Dad left, I tried to comfort her,' Justin continued. 'But I probably made things worse. When I said "*I know you didn't mean to hit Albion*," Eliza roared at me – though with frustration, I now realise ... not anger.[59] Alby whimpered and wet himself; whether he was acting or genuinely frightened, I'm not sure – but either way, he soon returned to his placid self, no doubt delighted his foul plan was working.[60]

'Later, while we were having tea with you, Mr P, I think Eliza got so desperate, she went to the nursery and tried to explain. I imagine Alby acted up again. This time Miss Garnet used Mum's tranquiliser gun, then Dad authorised her to contact Edinburgh zoo ... although the horrible woman actually phoned a couple of taxidermists. That night at the supper table only Albion looked happy ... and I think we can guess why![61]

Nanny Verity gave a regretful shake of her head. 'I remember that

---

[57] Page 152.
[58] Page 154/155.
[59] Page 161.
[60] Pages 161/162.
[61] Page 185.

meal vividly,' she sighed. 'Thirty long years ago, but I'll never forget how miserable I felt after we quarrelled. I've often wondered how different my life would've been if we'd patched things up.'

Justin shrugged. 'Life has a habit of unfolding along well-worn creases,' he said quietly. 'Few things – including our mistakes – are entirely original.'

Xavier Polydorus, who had been gazing out of the castle door, gasped suddenly as if someone had punched him. Verity Kiss reached for his arm – but the magician didn't notice. He glanced nervously at his wristwatch then frowned as if lost in deep thought.

Slowly, Nanny drew her hand back and pretended to straighten her apron. She turned to Justin and spoke briskly. 'Go on, Poppet ...'

'Where was I? Ah yes ... the night of Dad's abduction.' He frowned for a moment, then continued: 'When I hypnotised you the other day, you remembered two significant clues that convinced me of Albion's guilt. After describing how Dad went to confront the mystery person signalling from the great hall window, you said he pointed *DOWN* through the glass, and the torchlight shone *UP* into his face.[62] Clearly the spy was extremely short! Also, when Dad got knocked out you thought he was shouting my name – but he wasn't yelling "*It can't be you ... you're Justin,*" I think he was *trying* to say "*It can't be you ... you're JUST a baby!*"'[63]

As he spoke, Justin watched Nanny Verity's expression gradually change, and felt she was finally starting to believe him.

'The following morning, I discovered the torch Alby had used just inside the window. It was the same torch I'd seen when Haggis squeezed under Miss Garnet's bed a couple of days earlier.[64] I guess Albion must've noticed it too – and left it in the great hall hoping I'd recognise it. When I checked under Nanny Evelyn's bed, he'd temporarily put the miniature pistol in its place hoping to implicate her further.[65]

---

[62] Pages 306, 206.
[63] Pages 306, 206.
[64] Page 121, 219, 229.
[65] Pages 230, 247.

'I also found a letter from Dad on the great hall mantelpiece. Most spies would've simply opened the envelope – but instead, someone had dragged a half-burnt discarded draft of his letter onto the hearth while leaving the out-of-reach envelope untouched. Yet another indication the spy wasn't of adult height.[66]

Nanny Verity gazed down at Albion with thin-lipped disapproval. 'You must've been rather annoyed to see me back again,' she said, addressing him directly.

Alby put his head on one side and made a goo-goo-goo noise, which didn't convince anyone.

Justin replied for him: 'Actually, your unexpected return might've played right into X's hands; Miss Garnet was a useful diversion, nothing more. I think he'd always planned to frame you and Mr Polydorus ... but it became a certainty this last weekend because of three things Albion overheard:

'First of all, he heard me asking about the abandoned baby left on Hathaway's doorstep two days after Beowulf was born,[67] and feared I might guess the truth.'

'Milo!' cried Nanny, putting one hand to her mouth. '*He's* the *real* Albion!'

'Of course,' said Justin. 'I wouldn't mind betting his Thyme Streak's starting to come through by now ... whereas *this* Alby'll never get one![68] In all fairness, I think your ex-husband would've swapped the babies back by now ... if his plans had worked.'

'What else?'

'The second thing our spy overheard was that Mum had remembered a clue that might identify her kidnapper, and she was going to phone me.[69] I suspect he panicked and contacted Agent X that night to warn him. I *also* suspect Mr Kiss wasn't particularly bothered, and probably said he'd been waiting for something like this to happen.'

A momentary flicker of surprise crossed Albion's face, and Justin

---

[66] Page 219.
[67] Pages 321/322.
[68] Page 33.
[69] Pages 322, 328.

new he'd scored a point. Without appearing to do so, he observed the little spy move Nanny Verity's left cuff slightly, then take a sideways peek at her watch.

'And the third thing?' asked Nanny.

'The following evening you advised me to ask Mr Polydorus to help us identify Agent X. Your husband once warned you he'd know if you ever tried to double-cross him – and, sure enough, his spy overheard every word you said.[70] Last night Alby crept down to the great hall where he used Eliza's laptop to prepare a fake conversation framing you and Mr P – then, after dragging the phone off the desk, he waited patiently for Mum's call. Once he heard the clicking sound that meant we'd finished talking, he lifted the receiver and placed it beside the computer, hoping the same clicking noise would convince *me* someone was dialling out on the other line. It did; his trick fooled me completely – but not for long.'

Justin leaned back in his chair. 'Taken individually, I guess the clues are pretty insubstantial – but piece them all together and the picture is unmistakable.'

Nanny Verity nodded decisively. 'Well, *I'm* convinced. What about you, Xavier?'

'It's a compelling theory,' sighed Mr Polydorus, hurriedly checking his wristwatch. 'And I'm close to believing it – but it's still just guesswork; you've got no *real* evidence.'

'Oh, haven't I?' said Justin with a sudden grin. He jumped to his feet and walked across the entrance hall. Glancing over his shoulder he saw Nanny and Xavier watching him intently; little Beowulf, however, kept playing with his teddy bear, fiddling with a loose seam along its back. 'While we were in Mauritius,' Justin continued, 'I had the castle security system upgraded; twenty-four hour CCTV with micro-cams installed throughout all the main rooms and passageways. I've got recordings of our spy-baby toddling round the castle and making his phone calls – but it's this camera, here,' he said, pointing to the wall beside a suit of armour, 'that recorded the most dramatic footage: a gorilla charging towards a defenceless baby ... but stopping several

---

[70] Page 327, 328, 310.

centimetres short whilst the baby hurls itself backwards.'

As Justin turned to face the trio, he saw baby Beowulf move with a sudden fluid rapidity that reminded him of a cobra. Reaching inside his teddy he whipped out the miniature pistol, then rammed its muzzle up Nanny Verity's left nostril, forcing her head back against the wall. When he spoke, his voice had the high-pitched cuteness of a fourteen month-old, but his vocabulary was chillingly adult.

'Don't anyone move,' he snarled. 'Or I'll blast the few brains she's got right across that repulsive tapestry.'

Nanny froze with shock. One glimpse of her wide, terrified eyes and Justin took an involuntary step forward. In the same instant, Xavier Polydorus reached out towards the gun.

'I *MEAN* IT,' snapped Beowulf.

The pistol clicked menacingly as he released its safety catch.

Justin froze. 'Please don't hurt her,' he whispered, stepping back slowly. He flashed a warning look at Mr Polydorus, then resumed eye contact with the baby. 'She's your grandmother,' he said, keeping his voice low and calm.

'Yeah, that's why I helped her last time – but now she's turned traitor.' Beowulf kicked his old teddy onto the floor, where it lay with its back gaping wide open. 'So here's the deal: the Boss'll be here soon ... so we're all going to wait quietly.'

'Val's coming?' whispered Nanny from behind the pistol, scarcely daring to breathe.

'Yes,' said Justin. 'Though Mr Polydorus could've told you that. You've worked everything out, haven't you, Mr P? That's why you've been checking your watch. You're expecting his mail van to come trundling through that archway any minute now.'

Nanny Verity's eyes grew wider. 'Mail van? You mean ... Valentine's that ... that dreary little postman? Jock McSomething-or-other? But that's impossible; he was delivering our mail the same time Lady Henny was kidnapped.'[71]

Nanny winced as Beowulf shoved the pistol further up her nose and ordered her to keep quiet. In the tense silence that followed, Xavier

---

[71] Page 189.

Polydorus shuffled uncomfortably, clearly struggling with some internal conflict. Finally, too ashamed to face Nanny, he bowed his head and spoke in a deep melancholy rumble: 'No, Verity ... I'm afraid that was me.'

Justin stared at Nanny's befuddled face. Afraid to defy Beowulf, she said nothing – but her eyes showed the shock and confusion she so clearly felt.

'It's not like it sounds,' Xavier continued. 'Val tricked me into giving him an alibi. I see it now. In fact, when Justin spoke about our lives unfolding along well-worn creases, the truth flashed before me with a sudden devastating clarity. He's been setting me up the same way my entire life.' He slumped forwards, putting his head in his hands.

'Don't feel bad,' said Justin. 'It's often hard to see the truth about those we're closest to. When Nanny told me about you and Valentine, I soon saw the pattern[72] – but I'm not personally involved.'

'I still can't quite believe it,' groaned Mr Polydorus. 'When we were young, Val was my hero; he once saved my life. We were always incredibly close, until ... until ...' He stopped, glancing awkwardly at Verity Kiss. Nanny closed her eyes and a single tear trickled down one cheek.

Justin sighed. 'I'm afraid your brother was conning you long before you first met Verity. You'd already been imprisoned for at least one crime you hadn't committed,[73] and that pattern never changed. Somehow, I think Valentine always hoodwinked you into giving him a cast iron alibi, whilst setting you up should things go wrong. Finally, when your relationship with Verity threatened his long-term plans, he framed you for theft then married her himself.'[74]

Mr Polydorus nodded gloomily. 'You're right. He always used to say he knew I was innocent and vow to do everything in his power to see I got justice – but that was all part of his act. It's obvious now; I feel such a fool.'

---

[72] Pages 285-296, 326.
[73] Page 288/289.
[74] Pages 295/296.

Justin peered out of the castle door and through the archway; in the distance, he saw a small red van turn in through the gates. 'You've just got time to tell us what happened when Mum was kidnapped,' he said quietly.

'I swear I had no idea what he was up to,' Mr Polydorus began. 'The night before, he turned up on my doorstep with a bottle of whiskey, saying he wanted to patch things up.[75] He told me he and his wife were divorced, so there was no reason we couldn't put the past behind us. His apology seemed sincere enough, and he even offered to help me get back together with Verity. I hadn't seen her for years, and wasn't sure I could face reopening old wounds – but Val had a plan. He said he'd retired from acting and was now a postman. As a special favour he offered to let me do his delivery the following day; that way I could call at Thyme Castle, and if I caught a glimpse of Verity I could see whether my feelings for her were unchanged without revealing my identity. I wasn't sure ... but after a few drinks he managed to persuade me.

'We celebrated all night, so my memory of the next morning is a bit vague. I think we raided Polly's spare makeup box to make me look more like Val.[76] There was enough of a family resemblance for us to work with, and he always was a dab hand with greasepaint.[77] His hair's gone quite grey, but we put some chalk-pomade on mine where it showed beneath his cap. Then, once I was decked out in his uniform and spectacles, the transformation was complete ... and as Valentine said: "*No one ever really looks at a postman.*"[78]

'Did he loan you his wristwatch by any chance?' asked Justin.

'Yes!' exclaimed Mr Polydorus, looking surprised. 'I'd forgotten about that. He was quite insistent. Last of all, he gave me his routemaps, and told me exactly what to say when I knocked on the castle door. But the whole thing was a complete waste of time; I didn't see Verity at all. Though Val was right about one thing – you grabbed

---

[75] Page 175.
[76] Pages 22, 64.
[77] Page 294.
[78] Pages 242, 24.

the mail and shut the door without giving me a second glance.' He gave a short, angry sigh. 'Of course, I realise now it was just a scam to provide him with his usual alibi.'

Beowulf sniggered.

'That's not all,' said Justin. 'When he kidnapped Mum he wore your dark suit and false moustache[79] ... and he only made you take *his* watch because *he* wanted to wear *yours*. He hoped Mum would remember its distinctive black face – but fortunately he made a silly mistake that put you in the clear. In his hurry, he didn't notice it was a special watch designed for someone left-handed.[80] Instead of wearing it on his right wrist as *you* do[81] – being right-handed[82] he automatically put it on his left wrist, which meant the winding-crown was on the wrong side of the face. That's why Mum thought it looked upside-down even though it wasn't.[83] She didn't say it was on the *wrong wrist*, which she would've done if *you'd* abducted her ... so I realised your brother had tried to frame you yet again.'

Justin expected the magician to react angrily – but Xavier Polydorus looked a broken man with not one spark of hostility left in him.

'When I finally got home,' he said, sounding almost too depressed to speak. 'Val was waiting with another bottle of whiskey. He must've made me drink the whole lot, because I've had no recollection of that morning – just a blurred foggy muddle, until your prompting brought it back into focus.'

From outside, Justin heard a car horn tooting, and turned to see the shiny red mail van rattling to a halt in front of the castle doorstep. The van door creaked open and Jock McRosie clambered out.

'Grand weather,' he called, as Fergus scampered past him and headed indoors.

Beowulf jiggled his gun up Nanny's nose. 'On yer feet, *now*,' he hissed. 'Out to the boss ... slowly, mind ... and no funny business.'

---

[79] Page 172.
[80] Page 170.
[81] Pages 174.
[82] Page 159. 206.
[83] Pages 328/329.

'No, stay where you are,' said Justin, holding his hand, palm out, towards her. Then, as Verity Kiss widened her eyes questioningly, he spoke again in an urgent whisper: 'If you trust me, do *exactly* as I say.'

Nanny remained seated, casting terrified glances down her nose at Beowulf's furious face. Meanwhile, Fergus trotted to the hall table, and sat on his hind legs until Justin tossed him his daily stick of Edinburgh rock. Once he'd retired beneath the table to gnaw his treat, Justin beckoned to the postman hovering outside.

'Come in, Jock. We're having a family reunion, of sorts ... and you're the guest of honour.'

Jock froze in the doorway, staring at the three figures seated opposite. Determined to keep in character, he smiled blandly and touched his cap, muttering, 'G'morning Ma'am, Sir,' in his usual shy voice.

'Why so formal?' asked Justin. 'Surely you recognise your ex-wife ... your own brother? And you *can't* have forgotten your youngest grandson – the one you smuggled upstairs last spring hidden inside your mailbag.[84] Asking to see Mum's new baby was the very first time you said something different; I suppose that should've made me suspicious. You swapped the babies over when I went to fetch Nanny, then hurried off before the real Albion woke up.'

Jock shot an icy glance at Beowulf, still sat with his pistol crammed up Nanny Verity's nostril.

'The game's up, Gramps,' said the baby. 'You've got to get me out of here; they've caught me on security video.'

Justin laughed. 'Truth be told, I was bluffing. There's no CCTV; I fixed that micro-cam there myself last night, because I knew you'd never drop the act unless you thought I had proof.'

Jock swore angrily – a cold, hard voice replacing his usual rural accent. Then, with a few subtle movements his appearance altered. He dropped his timidly clutched hands and stood straighter, looking suddenly taller and with the strength and vitality of someone ten years younger; his bland face burned with a fiery rage, vaporising all traces of the shy, diffident postman in an instant. Beowulf shuddered ... and

---

[84] Pages 98.

367

Justin realised that Agent X terrified the little spy far more than Eliza on the wildest rampage.

'WULFI, YOU *IDIOT!*' Jock roared, hurling his mailbag to the floor. 'What did I tell you? Never ... *EVER* drop your cover, no matter *what* the provocation. It's the first rule of espionage.'

'An excellent rule,' murmured Justin. 'And one you ought to have kept yourself, Mr Kiss. When I used Eliza's laptop earlier, I activated her webcam; so I now have incriminating footage of both of you ... and I promise: that's *not* a bluff!'

Jock glared at him with a cold venomous hatred.

'I must admit you've been very clever,' Justin continued. 'You made sure that everything appeared to incriminate your brother. You probably even chose your codename hoping people would think the X stood for Xavier. But once I knew Alby – I mean Beowulf – was our resident spy, it didn't take long to work out who'd switched the babies.

Three or four times every week, you'd tell me you'd been delivering mail round Loch Ness for almost twenty years. Perhaps you thought if you repeated it often enough I'd believe it was true. But the morning before the attempted theft, you abandoned your usual daily remarks and asked Wulfi if everything was okay. In reply, he gave you a thumbs-up sign to confirm it was and that he'd signal you *later* once the coast was clear.[85]

'That night things went badly awry – but the following morning you winked at your accomplice, reassuring him that by kidnapping Sir Willoughy you were back on track.[86] You delivered the ransom note with the morning mail, hoping I wouldn't notice you'd stuck a used stamp on the envelope. I *did* ... though I wrongly assumed someone had slipped it amongst the mail *after* I left it on the hall table.[87]

'Despite the change of plans, you were in high spirits after we rescued Eliza[88] – rightly assuming I'd never've asked for your help if I thought you were a suspect. However, that made you careless – and

---

[85] Page 159.
[86] Page 237.
[87] Pages 236, 237, 244-246.
[88] Page 241.

when I told you she was going to hide in Dad's workshop, you said: *"Won't it be a bit cramped for her?"'* which you couldn't possibly have known unless you'd seen inside it.'[89]

While Justin was speaking, Agent X had edged slowly towards the hall table. He now lurched forward, grabbed Eliza's laptop and dashed it against the wall; it left an ugly dint in the oak panelling then clattered to the floor. Fergus shot out from beneath the table, his last bit of rock gripped firmly between his teeth.

'Nice try,' said Justin. 'But you won't destroy the evidence that way; the casing's specially reinforced to be gorilla-proof.'

'If you ever hope to see your father alive again, you'll erase it this instant,' growled Jock, folding his arms and giving Justin an arrogant smirk. 'Which reminds me: I finally realised his motorcycle won't be coming back, so you can fetch his toolbox; he's agreed to fix my old machine ... if I promise to let you live.'

As Justin stared calmly at Agent X a tall shadowy figure stepped into the open doorway behind him.

'I'm afraid you're in for a disappointment,' said Sir Willoughby.

Jock wheeled round to face him. The Laird of Thyme looked tired and unshaven, but his voice sounded remarkably chipper.

'The police raided Dores Post Office shortly after you left on your round this morning,' he continued. 'I believe my son phoned them earlier; he suggested they might find me imprisoned there. They're waiting outside the castle now; you can't possibly escape.'

'Oh can't I?' Jock snarled. 'I still hold one last ace ... or, rather, my grandson does,' he added, gesturing towards Nanny Verity. 'We'll take my traitorous ex-wife as hostage – and if the cops try to stop us, Wulfi, you have my permission to give her a terminal headache!'

'Over my dead body,' said Xavier Polydorus, jumping to his feet. He positioned himself protectively in front of Verity Kiss.

'As you wish,' sneered Jock. 'Finish him off, Wulfi; he's outlived his usefulness.'

Beowulf glanced uncertainly at his grandfather.

Sensing his hesitation, Agent X roared at him with a wild diabolical

---

[89] Page 242.

fury: 'KILL HIM, YOU PATHETIC LITTLE RUNT!'

Slowly – reluctantly – Beowulf withdrew the pistol from Nanny Verity's nose and pointed it at Xavier's back. He took a deep breath and closed his eyes, his tiny hand shaking as he psyched himself to pull the trigger ... but after a long, tense moment, he lowered his hand.

'I can't,' he said quietly. 'I've spied for you, Gramps, but I won't kill.'

'Give it here, you idiot,' Jock muttered. He marched over and snatched the little gun out of Beowulf's hand. Without a second's hesitation he held it to Xavier's head and squeezed the trigger. The pistol clicked feebly.

'No ammunition,' Justin explained. 'Late last night, when I finally guessed why Wulfi never lets anyone touch his teddy bear,[90] I checked inside it while he was asleep. After finding the pistol, I removed all the bullets then put it back.'[91]

'So, old chap' said Sir Willoughby, his voice light and conversational, 'it appears you're not holding any aces after all.'

Agent X spun round on his heels, threw the gun down and snatched up Eliza's laptop. He sprinted towards the door, then shoving Willoughby aside raced out to his van and leapt in. Its engine roared, and a blur of bright red swerved round the castle courtyard, tyres churning long ruts in the gravel.

'Something's gone wrong,' said Justin. 'Awbrite was meant to hide beyond the gates, then tail Jock back and block the archway with his squad car.'

He rushed out of the castle, ignoring the turmoil behind him: Beowulf screaming with rage, Fergus howling ... and Sir Willoughby shouting, 'Leave it to the police.'

Justin hurtled round to his father's workshop, threw the door open and dragged his *Hover-Boots* out from under the workbench. Seconds later he was zooming across the clifftop.

Jock was already half way down the drive. As Justin dodged round a gorse bush he peered towards the castle gates and was pleased to see a

---

[90] Pages 77, 79, 87, 113, 342.
[91] Page 339/340.

police car parked just outside – though why Awbrite and Knox were standing behind it, arguing, he couldn't imagine. When they finally noticed the mail van hurtling towards them, they scarcely had time to dive out of the way before it ploughed through the gateway, catching the squad car a glancing blow to its left bumper which sent it spinning across the road.

Once Jock's van turned right, Justin activated his boots' acceleration-boosters and rocketed over the castle walls. From this height he could see Sergeant Awbrite crawling out of a ditch with his cap askew, but he zoomed on, keeping two metres above the ground so X wouldn't see him.

Jock was heading northeast along the far edge of the Thyme estate; normally, Justin would have swooped down behind the wall if he saw any other vehicles, but the mail van was pulling too far ahead to risk losing it. He swerved to avoid an enormous lorry, then pressed his toes firmly on the boots' accelerator buttons, taking full advantage of the wide, straight road to gain speed.

Almost as if he'd guessed, Jock veered right again down a narrow tree-lined lane – and, in no time at all, Justin found himself having to weave through trunks or duck under branches. He groaned, remembering the road past Lupin Wood was bordered by densely-growing trees for the next mile or two. After coming perilously close to cracking his head a few times, he eased back on the propulsion-thrusters then swept down to ground level, knowing the mail van would leave him behind unless he moved faster.

As he sped gradually closer, Justin wondered how he could ever hope to stop Jock's van even if he *did* catch up with it. This, he told himself sternly, was the trouble with spontaneous action without rational thought first.

Then, about twenty metres ahead, he glimpsed a dark shadowy shape in the overhanging foliage. For a moment or two he lost sight of it ... then a huge gorilla swung out of the leaf-canopy and dropped in front of the oncoming vehicle.

Eliza stood in the centre of the narrow lane, roaring and beating her chest. There was a sudden squeal of brakes, and Jock's van skidded across the road, crashing into a tree.

Justin glided slowly to a halt.

Meanwhile, Eliza prowled over to the crumpled mail van, wrenched its door open and leaned inside. She hauled Agent X off his seat and dumped him unceremoniously on the ground; he lay there, groaning – a narrow trickle of blood seeping through his grey hair.

Then, with a look of satisfaction on her face, Eliza reached into the van a second time, and took out her laptop. She opened it carefully, and ran her fingers over the keyboard.

'Bad man take Eliza's computer,' she said, using her favourite royal voice. Then grinning happily at Justin, she prodded her keyboard again: 'We go home now ... Eliza want plenty bananas!'

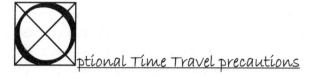

ptional Time Travel precautions

Although not essential, here are a few additional safety measures:

1)   In case the time traveller becomes unconscious during the trip, consider programming your chronopod to automatically return to the present if the pod door is not opened within one minute of arrival.

2)   If you visit the very recent past, (less than 24 hours ago), don't risk a return trip; simply remain in the past until it loops back to your present.

3)   Take your time. Be thorough; double-check everything. Hurrying in the present won't get you into the past any quicker. Past emergencies will wait. Remember: you're in a time machine; you can never arrive late at your chosen destination, but will ALWAYS be just in time!

And finally, remember ...

CHAPTER TWENTY-ONE

The Family Crypt

Eliza pushed the castle door open and wrinkled her nose; following the delicious aroma of Mrs Kof's cooking, she prowled towards the kitchen, making contented little grunting noises. After dropping his *Hover-Boots* on the front doorstep, Justin hurried after her, suddenly realising he felt properly hungry for the first time in days.

They had walked home across the estate rather then accept Awbrite's offer of a lift. The police car would've been cramped for Eliza, and Justin had wanted to explain about Albion before they got back; he particularly wanted to reassure her that everyone finally knew she *hadn't* hit the baby.

Justin paused in the kitchen doorway, his hand resting on Eliza's huge muscular shoulders. He'd expected to find everyone in high spirits – but the atmosphere in the room was somewhat strained. At the far end of the table, Sir Willoughby – now washed, shaved and wearing a long silk dressing gown – was describing his ordeal ... but no one appeared to be listening. Xavier Polydorus stared into his coffee mug; Beowulf was sitting in Alby's highchair, chewing a rusk and looking glum; and Nanny Verity sat with her arms folded, watching him like a hawk. Even Mrs Kof seemed oddly preoccupied, though when she saw Eliza she stomped over and gave the gorilla an enormous hug.

'Aha, you're back,' called Sir Willoughby, giving his son a sudden boyish grin. 'Did Awbrite catch the bounder?'

'Actually, the police made rather a mess of things,' said Justin. 'Miss Garnet made a run for it, apparently. They found her skeleton keys and handcuffs on the back seat. Awbrite blamed Knox for not searching her, but Knox said he hadn't been told to. They were still arguing about it when Jock rammed their squad car and got past.'

Willoughby pulled a scornful face. 'Poor old Awbrite; that's the second handcuffed Nanny he's lost. Did X escape too?'

'No. Eliza caught him,' said Justin. 'She's been hiding out in Lupin Wood,' he added, seeing his father's quizzically lifted eyebrow. 'When the van turned down Spindle Lane she spotted her laptop on its dashboard and dropped onto the road. Jock swerved and crashed into a tree.'

Sir Willoughby roared with laughter. Eliza, who'd been devouring a large plateful of banana fritters at the opposite end of the table, broke one in half and handed the piece to Justin.

'Was he hurt?' asked Mr Polydorus quietly. 'Val, I mean.'

'Just knocked out for a while,' Justin told him. 'He was starting to come round by the time Sergeant Awbrite arrived to arrest him.'

'What about Miss Garnet?' Nanny chimed in.

'He left Knox searching for her on foot; she won't get far.' Justin helped himself to a large slice of Dundee cake and sat down. 'The important thing is they got *you* out safely, Dad. Where were you being held?'

'Cellar,' replied Willoughby. 'Nasty damp place. Had me chained to a wall most of the time ... but I never worried for a moment; not even with the deadline looming. Knew you'd get me out of there somehow.'

'It was nothing, really,' Justin muttered. He could feel his cheeks starting to burn. 'Anyway, it was my fault you were kidnapped; if I hadn't built the *you-know-what* none of this ...' He felt a foot prod him sharply under the table. 'I suppose Nanny's told you everything already,' he sighed.

'*Almost* everything,' said Nanny Verity, staring at him pointedly.

375

Justin shot a hurried sideways glance at his father and changed the subject. 'How's Fergus coping?' he asked, noticing the little Scottie whimpering by the back door.

'Blighter's been howling like a dashed timber wolf,' grumbled Sir Willoughby. 'What d'you plan to do with him?'

'Well, someone's got to look after him,' said Justin. 'I er ... thought I might ... er ...'

Willoughby groaned. 'More animals! Well, I'm sure your mum'll approve.'

'Yeah, perhaps I do take after her, after all,' Justin laughed.

For a moment, Sir Willoughby looked as if he was about to say something else – but the hall telephone rang and he jumped up to answer it. Once the kitchen door swung to, Mr Polydorus spoke in a low voice:

'I'd better go. Your father isn't comfortable with me being here. Unwittingly or not, I still played a part in your mother's kidnap.'

'I'm sure Dad doesn't feel like that,' said Justin. 'You've both got equally good reasons to hate Agent X.'

'But that's the problem; I don't hate him. Despite all Val's done, he's still family.'

'He pointed a gun at you and pulled the trigger,' Justin reminded him.

Mr Polydorus shook his head. 'He must've known it wasn't loaded; he wouldn't *kill* me.'

Justin shrugged. 'You're too nice, Mr P,' he said, pushing his chair back. 'Okay, let's sneak you out the back way while Dad's on the phone.'

They filed out through the kitchen garden. After opening the arched gate, Mr Polydorus glanced back at Nanny Verity.

'You'll think about ... about what I said,' he murmured.

'I will,' said Nanny solemnly.

Mr Polydorus took a half step towards her, dithered, then turned and walked off briskly with his head down. Justin glanced sideways at Nanny Verity, as he closed the garden gate.

Nanny caught his eye and blushed. 'Xavier's still got that engagement ring he once bought for me,' she said, trying to sound nonchalant. 'He says I married the wrong brother last time, so ...'

'You're going to *marry* him?' gasped Justin. He hadn't meant to sound so surprised.

'I'm considering it,' said Nanny primly.

Justin wasn't sure how he felt about that – especially knowing her true identity. He *had* hoped to get his dad's old time machine back, make a few minor modifications and then try reversing her age.

'Well, whatever you decide I think you should see this,' he said, taking a sheet of notepaper out of his pocket. 'I found it in Jock's van before Awbrite turned up – along with a bottle of sleeping pills.'

Nanny read the note quickly:

> To Whom it May Concern:
> I can't live with the guilt any longer. Before ending it all, I hereby confess to kidnapping Sir Willoughby and Lady Henrietta Thyme.
> Yours sincerely, Xavier Polydorus, (Agent X).

'But this is Xavier's handwriting.'

'No ... a clever forgery,' said Justin. 'I think Valentine Kiss planned to kill his brother then leave this note beside the body. He'd have got away scot-free – while poor Mr P, with his criminal record and all the clues pointing in his direction, would've been the perfect scapegoat.'

'Why didn't you tell him?' Nanny asked.

'He's not ready to handle the truth yet,' said Justin. 'You can show him the note later. That's partly why I didn't leave it for Awbrite to find.'

'Partly?'

'The other reason is the police might've asked Mr Polydorus too many awkward questions. He's the only person outside the family who knows about the time machine; we can't risk him mentioning it.'

Back inside the kitchen, Fergus was by the pantry, sniffing round Haggis's basket. The little dodo stuck its head out from beneath a quivering mound of tartan blankets and honked at him morosely. Justin called Fergus – and when that didn't work, he grabbed a piece of short-bread off the table and lured the little dog away.

Meanwhile, Nanny Verity stood staring down at Beowulf. 'What am I going to do with *him*?' she asked.

'Put him in Alby's playpen for now,' suggested Justin. He lowered his voice so Mrs Kof wouldn't hear. 'Don't be too hard on him; he may be a spy, but he's not a murderer!'

'Och, that's easy for you to say,' whispered Nanny. 'You weren't the one with a gun up your nose.'

As they stepped into the entrance hall, Sir Willoughby was just putting the telephone down.

'That was Sergeant Awbrite,' he said. 'Miss Garnet got away – but our old friend Agent X is safely in police custody.' He rubbed his hands together and grinned. 'Better still, Awbrite says he's been authorised to return my mail-sorting invention. I'm guessing he means the *you-know-what*.'

'Yeah, that was the best cover-story I could come up with this morning,' Justin explained. 'I told him it was a top-secret device commissioned by the Post Office; Jock stole it, then kidnapped you to show him how it worked.' He shrugged awkwardly. 'A bit lame, but he seemed to swallow it.'

'Brilliant,' said Willoughby, slapping his son on the back. 'He's bringing it round this evening. That was the one thing still worrying me; I should've known you'd got it covered!'

'Well, I knew we'd need to use it for ...'

'*Use* it?' Sir Willoughby interrupted, his face suddenly clouding over. 'Dash it all! You won't be *using* that damned machine ... *EVER!* I intend to dismantle it before it causes any more trouble.'

'But ...'

'Forget it!' snapped Willoughby. 'My mind's made up.' He turned sharply and marched off upstairs.

Justin and Nanny exchanged glances.

'I'll talk him round later,' Justin whispered. 'We've got to return Haggis for a start; there's no point keeping him here now all the other dodos have died. And don't worry, Wulfi, I'll get you back to your own time too ... somehow. I'll explain everything once we're in the nursery,' he hissed, seeing Mrs Gilliechattan emerge from the dining room. 'I'll catch up with you in a minute, Nan – I just need to grab my *Hover-Boots*.'

He dashed over to the front door and hauled it open – but to his enormous dismay the boots were no longer there.

'It's obvious,' said Justin. 'When Evelyn Garnet escaped she must've headed back here, thinking it would be the last place the police would look for her.'

He stood at the nursery door watching Nanny Verity deposit Beowulf in his playpen.

'I bet she couldn't believe her luck when I left my boots on the front doorstep,' he groaned. 'She'll be miles away by now. Serves me right for being so careless.'

'Och, don't be so hard on yourself,' Nanny told him. 'You've had a lot on your mind.'

'That's no excuse,' said Justin, shaking his head. 'Those boots could've made us millions ... billions, possibly.'

'But you've resolved a problem that's dogged this family for decades; that's got to be worth something.'

Justin brightened a little. 'Yeah, I suppose.' He walked across the nursery and stood beside the playpen; Fergus plodded after him, ears down, tail drooping.

'So, what's the plan?' asked Nanny Verity. 'I suppose I'll have to fetch the real Alby from Brighton.'

'Absolutely. I've phoned Horace; the jet's on standby. I'm afraid you'll need to go this afternoon; he's flying to Mauritius tomorrow. We've got to get this sorted out before Mum gets home.'

Nanny looked sceptical. 'I know she's not the most maternal of mothers, but she's bound to notice a different baby.'

'Maybe – and we'll tell her the truth if absolutely necessary – but I'm hoping the real Alby won't look too dissimilar; he is Beowulf's great-uncle, after all. Perhaps that's why Mum didn't notice the initial changeover.'

'She was too ill to notice anything,' said Nanny. 'But I'm surprised *I* didn't realise!'

'It never occurred to you, that's why,' Justin explained. 'Even if the baby *had* seemed slightly different, you'd have dismissed it as impossible.'

'*Hmmph* ... I'd better start packing.' Nanny bustled through the connecting doorway into her bedroom; Justin could hear her opening and shutting drawers. 'What are your plans for Wulfi?' she called.

'Ideally, I'd like to send him back to his own time and age,' said Justin. 'If I can persuade Dad to let me use his machine.'

Beowulf chuckled. 'Sounds good to me.'

'I should warn you though, it might not be straightforward.' Justin knelt beside the playpen and talked to him through the bars. 'There are so many potential futures, travelling forwards in time is highly impractical ... possibly dangerous.'

'But it's only the future for *you*,' said Wulfi. 'For *me* it's the present I left behind.'

'That's why I'm hoping it'll work,' said Justin. 'We'll be using the same time machine too ... although that probably won't help.'

'Why not?' asked Nanny, popping her head round the door. 'Won't it have the return coordinates?'

'No. Even if Dad's machine has a memory function, it can't store the coordinates of a trip it hasn't taken yet. We'll have to rely on Beowulf for those. Wulfi – can you remember the time and date you travelled back from? Think carefully; the closer we get to the exact coordinates, the safer you'll probably be.'

'It was noon ... the day I turned sixteen.'

'See,' said Justin, turning to Nanny Verity. 'The time machine from Jock's cellar won't make that trip for another fifteen years. Which raises another worrying question: Could bringing Dad's old chronopod *here* alter *that* future? I know it *shouldn't* ... but ...' He paused a moment, his brow furrowed in concentration. 'Hmm ... if we'd changed anything, surely Beowulf couldn't have travelled back ... but he *has* because that future trip's already in *his* past. Wulfi, where was the time machine in your present? Still at Dores Post Office?'

'No. Gramps took me to a sort of creepy hidden cave.'

'Fascinating ... *absolutely* fascinating!'

'Why?' asked Verity and Beowulf together.

'I think it's another loop. If so, we're not changing anything. The good news is we can be sure the machine *won't* be dismantled; the bad news is Agent X is likely to steal it back sometime in the next fifteen years. Flux! I'd better not tell Dad, or he'll smash it to bits; it's going to be hard enough persuading him as it is.'

'What if he won't cooperate?' sighed Nanny.

'I'll tell him we need it for you,' grinned Justin – then seeing the look of shock on Nanny's face, he explained quickly: 'I've got an idea. Instead of fixing the old machine so it *doesn't* alter age, I'll adapt it to be dual-function. That way, I can pre-program it to reverse your age by taking you thirty years into the past, then automatically return you to the present while keeping you young. Once Dad knows it's the only way to get his daughter back, he's bound to agree.'

Justin waited, expecting an enthusiastic response, but Nanny Verity turned and walked out of sight. 'What's up, Nan?' he called, jumping to his feet and hurrying through the connecting door. 'Don't you see? You can be Robyn again ... finally get your life back ... and you won't have to marry Mr Polydorus.'

'Maybe I want to,' she said quietly.

'More than being young again?' asked Justin.

Nanny flumped down on the bed and seemed to crumple before his eyes. '*I don't know!* Part of me does; what middle-aged woman wouldn't want her youth back? But it's a big decision. I spent years hoping you'd rescue me and put things back the way they were; but I eventually made a life of my own. This is who I am now. Even if you change me on the outside, I won't ever be the sister you lost ... and I'm

381

not sure I'd want to be.'

Justin didn't know what to say. He'd grown accustomed to his brain handling any problem life threw at him – but he suddenly realised there were some conundrums cool logic couldn't resolve.

'That's why you *mustn't* say anything to Dad,' Nanny continued. 'He'll tell Mum ... then the two of them will pressure me into doing what *they* want. And they'll be so determined to get their daughter back, they'll forget I've got children of my own to think about. I can't just vanish out of *their* lives.' She gave a muffled sob and rummaged though her apron pocket for a hanky.

Justin sat on the bed beside her. He wanted to tell her how much he missed Robyn; how the thought of never seeing her again gave him an empty aching feeling inside; and how he'd never forgive himself for building the time machine that had taken her out of their lives ... but he said none of those things.

'Sorry, Bobs,' he whispered. 'You're right. I didn't see the big picture. I won't say a word to anyone.' He took a deep breath. 'Think it over while you're away fetching Alby. Whatever you decide I promise you'll have my full support.'

Straight after lunch, Knightly drove Verity Kiss to Inverness Airport. Meanwhile, Justin collected some schoolwork from the professor and took it to the nursery so he could keep an eye on Beowulf.

Despite gnawing his way through several sticks of Edinburgh rock Fergus was still missing his master – but he seemed content to tag along with Justin, never straying far from his side even when Tybalt scuttled past.

Mrs Kof was busier than usual – and appeared to be preparing enough food for a royal banquet instead of a small anniversary party. By the end of the afternoon her pantry shelves groaned beneath the weight of cakes, pies, scones, biscuits and puddings. Yet, instead of being her usual ebullient self, she seemed strangely subdued.

Half an hour after supper, a big police van rattled into the courtyard. Justin, who'd been getting Beowulf ready for bed, peered through the nursery window.

'That must be Dad's old time machine,' he said, watching Sergeant Awbrite and Sir Willoughby manoeuvre a large sheet-covered contraption out of the van and carry it into the castle.

Beowulf leaned forward in his arms, trying to get a better look. 'I can't wait to get back,' he sighed wistfully.

'I guess you've missed your family,' said Justin.

The little spy grinned. 'Yeah, but not half as much as I've missed controlling my bladder!'

After Awbrite left, Sir Willoughby fetched an old trolley; by the time Justin got down to the entrance hall, he and Mrs Kof were lifting the machine onto it. Together, the three of them wheeled it carefully along the portrait gallery, with Fergus trotting after them.

'Where are we heading, Dad?' Justin asked, relieved his father hadn't taken the time machine straight out to his workshop and started dismantling it immediately.

'Library,' replied Sir Willoughby curtly.

Justin was surprised; with the south tower only accessible over the archway, the library was the last place he'd expected. He kept quiet, hoping this meant his father had changed his mind, and might allow him to hoist the machine up to his lab.

Negotiating the stairs was every bit as awkward as Justin anticipated, and without Mrs Kof's help it would've been impossible. Again, the cook seemed unusually quiet. After helping them push Sir Willoughby's time machine into the library, she wished them a cursory 'Good-nits,' and plodded off.

Willoughby waited by the door, listening for the sound of Mrs Kof's bare feet along the upper corridor. Once he was certain she was out of earshot he turned to Justin and winked.

'Could do with a torch,' he said. 'Got one handy?'

'Yeah, I've still got Miss Garnet's; I'll be back in two ticks.' Justin

383

ran up the south tower steps two at a time, wondering why they needed a torch in a well-lit room. Then, as he unlocked his lab door, he heard a deep grinding noise from below, like huge stone blocks sliding over one another. He grabbed the torch off his workbench then slid down the fireman's pole, landing in the library with a soft thud.

Sir Willoughby was standing in front of what Justin had always believed was an arched stone alcove; for as long as he could remember it had housed a life-size statue of Sir Seymour Thyme looking at his pocket watch – but now, both the statue and the entire stone wall behind it had swivelled back to reveal the entrance to a dark tunnel.

'Wow!' gasped Justin. 'Where does that go to?'

'The family crypt,' Willoughby told him.

Justin flashed his torch down the steeply curving passageway. 'Why haven't you shown me this before?' he whispered in an awestruck voice.

'It's a place for the dead – not the living,' explained Sir Willoughby. 'And I didn't want you getting lost. Apart from the main vault there are numerous other interconnecting chambers, and beyond them, miles of catacombs.'

'Excellent!' said Justin. 'No one'll *ever* find your time machine down there, Dad.'

'No – not even *you*,' replied Willoughby, leaning his full weight against the trolley. 'That's why I opened the passage door while you were upstairs. Come on ... give me a hand ... and hold that torch up; I need to see where we're going.'

Justin felt a prickle of irritation at his father's lack of trust in him. 'Can't I at least *see it* first?'

'Well ... I suppose,' Sir Willoughby muttered. Then, with one of his sudden grins, he added: 'Have to admit ... wouldn't mind a proper look m'self. Only caught a quick glimpse of it when the police rescued me.' He tugged the sheet off and stepped back, shooting a sidelong glance at his son. 'The *Prototype Automatic Spatiotemporal Transporter*,' he announced. 'What d'you think?'

Justin was almost lost for words. He hadn't expected anything half so beautifully crafted. The machine was roughly the size of a photobooth – but there the similarity ended. It was made of finest walnut and rosewood with brass fittings, and had the old-fashioned steampunk look of something designed by a Hollywood props department.

'Dad ... it's ... it's *stunning*!' he whispered.

'M'afraid some of the metal's got a bit tarnished,' said Sir Willoughby, frowning at a countersunk grommet housing as he rubbed it with his pocket handkerchief. He opened the time machine's door and unfolded a lattice chrome step. Justin eased himself inside, perched on a small burgundy leather seat and gazed at the dashboard. It was polished malachite – and instead of the touch-sensitive computer screen he was used to, it had a long row of brass dials and gauges surrounded by levers and switches.

'This is beyond cool,' he murmured. 'What a shame it alters the traveller's age. Would you consider letting me make a few minor adap—'

'Don't even *think* about it,' Sir Willoughby interrupted – then, with an impulsive chuckle, he lowered his voice: 'Just between the two of us, I did the adaptations myself at *TOT* thirteen years ago. Top secret, of course; told X it couldn't be fixed. And, sure enough, it *would've* altered his age if *he'd* used it. But ...' He leaned over Justin's shoulder and ran his fingers along the underside of the dashboard. There was a soft click, and a hidden keypad slid out; Willoughby typed IMNNME2X and pushed it back. Then, with a gentle whirring sound, a dash-panel flipped over revealing another row of dials and switches. '... *These* override the fault,' he continued. 'Can you imagine ... the idiot's had a fully operative dual-function time machine all these years without knowing it?'

Justin's mind reeled. In an instant he felt a dozen conflicting emotions: astonishment at this unexpected revelation, relief that Agent X hadn't discovered the truth, delight knowing Robyn could be returned to her youth, anger that his father had once again withheld the truth, and a delicious bubbling excitement at the prospect of more time travel ... as long as the machine wasn't dismantled.

But it can't be, Justin reminded himself – *not if what Beowulf said was true.*

'You're not *really* going to destroy it, are you, Dad?'

'Not tonight,' said Willoughby. 'Too dashed tired. It'll be safe enough in the crypt for a few days; there's not another living person knows how to access this passage.'

'Well, let's get it down there, then,' said Justin, dragging the sheet back over the machine. He kept his face blank, hoping his father wouldn't guess he was frantically formulating a plan to discover how the crypt was opened.

Apart from the occasional grunt and groan, they descended in silence. Fergus, however, refused to follow them, and stayed by the entrance, whining unhappily.

The tunnel down to the crypt wasn't especially long, but it was steep and uneven underfoot; it took all their concentration to keep the time machine from tipping over. At the bottom there was a huge iron-studded door. As Sir Willoughby pushed it open and stepped inside, Justin noticed a dull thrumming noise from somewhere beyond.

'What's that?' he asked.

'Generator,' replied Willoughby, looking suddenly uncomfortable.

'You mean there's electricity down here?'

Sir Willoughby hesitated. He took a box of matches out of his jacket pocket, and lit several candles in a rusty wall-bracket before replying. 'Not in the main chamber.' He walked off before Justin could ask anything else, his footsteps echoing as he strode across the floor.

Justin shivered; it was almost cold enough to see his own breath. In the flickering light he gazed round. The crypt was cavernous – cathedral-like – with a high vaulted ceiling supported by towering columns. The walls were the same stone used throughout the castle, but here each block had been intricately engraved with everything from rudimentary letters and symbols to stylised flora and fauna; some were crumbling with age, while others were covered in a mottled shroud of grey-green moss.

The crypt itself was octagonal in shape, with rows of sarcophagi arranged around the edge. There were simple stone coffins, vast granite slabs bearing medieval knights in carved armour, and grand marble tombs with effigies of sleeping lairds or serene ladies in repose. Justin shone his torch on a tiny white sarcophagus and read its epitaph:

Take your time and Time will take you
Morton Thyme – 1809 ~16

A sudden thought occurred to him: 'Why are Grandma Isabel and Uncle Deighton buried up on Harbinger Hill?'

Sir Willoughby sighed. 'Pops couldn't bear the thought of them trapped down here in this gloomy old place. Can't say I blame him. Hey, look at this peculiar whatnot.' He gestured to a tall basalt obelisk.

Justin could tell he was trying to change the subject. 'Hmm ... yeah,' he said. His attention was fixed on a narrow gothic archway in the opposite wall; as he walked towards it the sound of the generator grew louder. 'What's out here?'

'Oh, nothing,' said his father dismissively. 'Just an old experiment I set up years ago; it's in one of the antechambers ... but you mustn't go wandering through there; it's like a maze. Tradition has it there's even a subterranean lake with an underwater tunnel out to the loch, but no one's ever found it. Come on, son, let's get back up to the library.'

As Justin took a few more steps towards the arch, Sir Willoughby made an impatient huffing noise, then marched back to the main door where he started blowing out the candles. Justin turned reluctantly. He knew that defying his father wouldn't solve the Beowulf problem.

'Have you decided what we're going to do with our spy-baby?' he asked. 'Nanny'll be back with the real Albion tomorrow; we can't have two babies here when Mum gets home.'

Sir Willoughby closed the crypt door, and headed back up to the library. Justin followed, giving him time to think. He could see Fergus waiting in the glowing rectangle of light at the end of the passageway, wagging his tail feebly – and behind him the old Thyme Clock on the mantelpiece.

'I suppose you want me to use my er ... contraption,' said Willoughby. 'Send him back to his own time and age.'

'Can you think of an alternative?' Justin asked reasonably, as they emerged from the tunnel.

Sir Willoughby strode past Fergus and threw himself into his favourite armchair, looking morose and preoccupied. After stroking the little dog's head, Justin sat opposite his father and held his gaze.

'You owe me one, Dad. Not just for telling the police where to find you, but for persuading them to return your time machine.'

Willoughby sank deeper into his armchair and glared at him.

'No? Well, the least you can do is answer me a question,' continued Justin. He took a deep breath: 'Tell me ... are the Thymes part of some ancient cosmic feud you've not told me about?'

Sir Willoughby's head snapped up at the word *cosmic*. 'What's given you that preposterous idea?'

'The joker,' said Justin, pointing to the figure on the clock. '*Cosmic Joker* – arch enemy of Old Father Time. I'm guessing that's you, Dad, being the present Laird of the Clan. And I think Valentine Kiss isn't just some random sneak-thief with a grudge against the Thymes; I suspect the two of you are part of something bigger ... something you won't even admit to yourself ... and this old clock's right at the heart of it.'

'Nonsense!' said Willoughby. There was an icy brusqueness to his reply that convinced Justin he'd struck a nerve. 'That Victorian monstrosity's got nothing to do with Agent X *whatsoever*.'

'You're wrong, Dad. Without that clock I'd never have identified him. When I was looking at it last night I saw the dice in the Joker's hand, and remembered Jock had a similar pair hanging in his mail van.[92] Then I suddenly realised that *Jock McRosie* is an anagram of *Cosmic Joker*.[93] That's never a coincidence.'

Sir Willoughby jumped to his feet, and Justin caught a momentary glimpse of something in his eyes which could've been either anger or fear.

'You're so sharp, one of these days you'll cut yourself,' he muttered.

'What d'you mean?'

---

[92] Pages 136, 241.
[93] Pages 23, 335, 337.

'I ... I mean ... some things are better left alone. X has been caught ... imprisoned ... it's over. Leave it at that!'

'But ...'

'Look, tomorrow – if I send that blasted baby back to his own time, will you promise to stop pestering me with these ridiculous questions?'

'If that's what you want, Dad.'

'It is,' growled Willoughby. 'Now ... off upstairs. I'm going to close the crypt entrance ... and I won't have you watching!'

For the third time the tiny screw slipped out of Justin's tweezers and rolled across his workbench.

'Concentrate!' he told himself sternly. But instead of focussing on the task at hand, his mind kept replaying the conversation with his father.

He was used to Sir Willougby's mercurial mood swings, but that didn't make them any easier to understand. For years he'd assumed they were merely frustration at his memory loss; later, after learning the truth about his dad, he'd put them down to the strain of perpetuating a thirteen year deception; now he wondered if there was more to this whole *Time versus Chance* thing than he'd first thought.

Up to that evening he hadn't taken it seriously – and had only mentioned it to his father guessing he'd rather agree to help Beowulf than face a barrage of awkward questions. It had worked ... but, in a way, Justin almost wished it hadn't. Sir Willoughby's abrupt denial had only fuelled his curiosity. The old library clock with its two mechanical figures *had* to mean something; its connections to all that had happened lately were too uncanny to ignore.

'Well, if Dad won't tell me, maybe there's somebody else who will.'

But deep down he knew there was only one other person he *could* ask, and it wasn't someone the Laird of Thyme would approve of.

Justin gazed at the partly-rebuilt microbot on his workbench; with Miss Garnet's spycam inserted into its head, and a new transmitter aerial sticking out of its abdomen, it reminded him of a one-eyed metal wasp – a wasp that would fly down to the library when Sir Willoughby next opened the crypt. As Justin reattached its titanium exoskeleton, his father's warning echoed in his ears. *Some things are better left alone.*

'I don't have a choice,' he muttered. 'I'm doing this is for my sister.' But even as he spoke the words, he knew he was fooling himself.

He had reasons of his own for wanting to use the time machine ... and *nothing* was going to stop him.

Tuesday morning started badly. As Justin opened his curtains he noticed a piece of notepaper had been pushed under his bedroom door. He unfolded it quickly, recognising Mrs Kof's distinctive handwriting:

Deer Justink,

I is sozzy to incontinent you just a few days beefor adversary party. I beans very haply here, but policy-man is visiting castle too orphan, and I worrits he mite reckon-eyes me. I getting good offal to join circus again, so I goings. I leaf plenty food for party. Praps wheel meat again sum day. Say good-buys to everybodkin.

Big hugs, Missiz Kof.

Justin sank onto the end of his bed, staring at the letter in dismay. Over the years cooks had come and gone, but none like Mrs Kof. In the few weeks she'd worked at Thyme Castle he'd grown to like her enormously, and it saddened him knowing she'd felt compelled to leave in case her past caught up with her.

He thought of Mrs Kof's strange story and, certain of her innocence, heartily wished he'd done something to help her prove it.

Perhaps it was Mrs Kof's unexpected departure, but everyone was distinctly out of sorts that morning. Sir Willoughby complained that his breakfast was cold, and Knightly grumbled to Mrs Gilliechattan about having to make it. The housekeeper, however, was in no mood to sympathise; Burbage had kept her awake all night gloomily reciting Hamlet's soliloquies once he'd realised his master wasn't coming home.

'When the wind is southerly, I know a hawk from a handsaw,' he cackled, as Mrs Gilliechattan mopped the kitchen floor. Tybalt, meanwhile, was prowling round Haggis's basket, licking his lips. Justin decided to take the little doddling up to his lab; it would be safer, he thought, now that Mrs Kof wasn't around to keep an eye on him.

The morning's lessons crawled by, and the professor was unusually snappish when Justin asked for the afternoon off. Even Grandpa Lyall seemed oddly grumpy.

Just before lunchtime, Nanny Verity returned with the real Albion. Both Justin and Willoughby were hugely relieved to see he looked almost identical to Beowulf ... apart from one minor detail: his Thyme streak was just starting to come through.

'D'you think Hen'll notice we've swapped babies?' asked Sir Willoughby.

'Not if we all act like he's still the same,' said Justin. 'The eye sees what the brain expects most of the time. It's called scotoma; a sort of mental blind spot blocking visual input that seems impossible.'

'Yes, yes, I'm familiar with the concept,' Sir Willoughby muttered. He tickled Alby's chin with his forefinger. 'Seems a nice little chap, anyway.'

Albion laughed happily. He'd clearly bonded with Nanny Verity – and if he was missing his foster family, it wasn't obvious. Nanny, however, looked emotionally drained. Her daughter, Hathaway, had been sad to part with "Milo" – even when Nanny explained his real mother wanted him back.

Justin, of course, realised there was a deeper reason for Nanny's troubled countenance. Visiting her children and grandchildren had reminded her of all she stood to lose if she chose to become Robyn again. When Justin asked if she'd come to a decision yet, she shook her head silently, eyes brimming with tears.

At two o'clock sharp Justin sneaked out of the castle and hurried down to the gates where a taxi was waiting for him. He'd purposely kept his plans for the afternoon a secret, knowing his father wouldn't approve.

Half an hour later he walked into Inverness police station; Sergeant Awbrite was waiting for him, looking stern and disapproving.

'I don't like this,' he said, rubbing his moustache uneasily. 'It's been bothering me ever since you phoned.'

Justin concealed a sigh; he'd guessed this wouldn't be easy. 'Prisoners *are* legally entitled to visitors, aren't they?'

'Yes, but technically speaking, he's not in prison ... *yet*. He was only formally charged this morning, and won't be transferred to Shacklebolt until Thursday.' Awbrite put his hand on Justin's shoulder and spoke kindly. 'Criminals don't generally get visits from their victims. Couldn't *I* tell him his dog's okay for you?'

'There's more to it than that,' said Justin. 'I want some answers ... closure, I guess. I know it's an unusual request, but it's important.'

The policeman frowned. 'I'll let you see him – but only because I'm hoping he'll drop his guard and give something away; he hasn't answered *any* of *our* questions.' He paused a moment, then added: 'There's something I *really* don't like about this chap. When you've been in the force as long as I have, you get a nose for these things.'

'What d'you mean, Sergeant?'

'He's too cocky ... too pleased with himself,' Awbrite explained. 'Knox noticed it too. It's like he knows something we don't. I've only seen that kind of arrogance three times before: the first was a foreign ambassador who claimed diplomatic immunity; the second was a fraudster, whose family bribed all the key witnesses; and the third – a murderer – had an accomplice who sprang him out of jail, killing two guards.' Awbrite checked his watch. 'Obviously, I can't leave you alone with him. I'd prefer to supervise things myself, only I've got an appointment with the Chief Inspector in five minutes – but Knox will be on hand the entire time, taking notes. And I've instructed him to remove the prisoner if he becomes threatening or aggressive.'

Justin hid his relief behind a polite smile. 'Thanks, Sergeant.'

'Don't thank me yet,' said Awbrite crisply. 'I can't shake the feeling this is a huge mistake!'

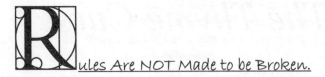

Rules Are NOT Made to be Broken.

Breaking some rules, (duplicating coordinates for example), will result in certain disaster. Other rules may be bent slightly in cases of extreme emergency, but you must be prepared to accept the consequences. If you break a rule there will always be a price to pay. However ...

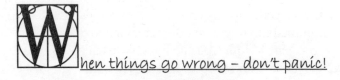

When things go wrong – don't panic!

If something unexpected transpires, maybe it was meant to happen. Perhaps you aren't creating a fork into a parallel universe but completing a loop and fulfilling your destiny. Remember: even if you create an apparently unsolvable paradox, your chances of unravelling it are endless as long as time travel remains in the equation.

CHAPTER TWENTY-TWO

The Thyme Curse

Interview room two was a small bleak cube with a table, a few plastic chairs, and walls the colour of phlegm. Justin sat down and waited. He drummed his fingers on the tabletop, wondering how much he could say to Agent X with Constable Knox listening.

Presently, the door clicked open and the prisoner was ushered in; after seating him opposite Justin, Knox settled on a chair beside the door and took out his notebook.

Valentine Kiss was handcuffed, and instead of his own clothes wore a standard issue orange overall. That much Justin had expected – but what surprised him was how little he resembled Jock McRosie. Yesterday, Justin had watched him straighten up and cast his shy expression aside like an unwanted mask. Today he looked like a different person altogether.

Despite having seen him beside Knox, Justin still struggled to estimate his height; whilst sitting, his posture gave an impression of tallness, yet Jock's stoop had always made him look rather short. If asked to describe the mailman's face, Justin would've used words like: bland, nondescript and unremarkable – yet now he realised that, for his age, Valentine Kiss was still a good-looking man. More than that ... he had an unmistakable inner spark, a vibrant presence that seemed to light up the room. It was curious, Justin thought, how Valentine had the *"X factor"* – whereas Xavier, who resembled him in many ways, didn't.

It was his eyes, Justin decided. Now that he saw them for himself, he realised that both Sir Willoughby's and Nanny's description had failed to do them justice. They were, without doubt, the most vivid electrifying sky-blue imaginable. As Jock, of course, he'd hidden them beneath grey contact lenses. In fact, it was only when Nanny had related how Xavier wore blue lenses to cover his grey eyes that Justin guessed his brother had been doing the exact opposite.[94]

Justin realised that Agent X was staring at him. He was leaning back in his chair, arms folded, wearing a look of faintly amused arrogance. Compared to his venomous rage of yesterday, Justin found it strangely unsettling – and he had to admit Awbrite was correct; there was a slick confidence about X that didn't tally with the prospect of a future behind bars.

'Hello Jock ... I mean Mr Kiss,' Justin began. 'I er ... I suppose you're wondering why I asked to see you.'

'Let me guess: you're planning a career with the Post Office and thought I might give you a reference,' Valentine replied. He had an actor's voice, mellifluous and dripping with sarcasm.

'Actually, I thought you'd be worrying about Fergus,' Justin explained quickly. 'I want you to know I'll take good care of him ... until ... until ...'

'Until I escape?'

Justin forced a polite laugh. 'I left him curled up in front of the library fire, munching a stick of rock ... but I know he's missing you; he keeps whining.'

'Whining and dining – his two favourite occupations.'

Justin hesitated, unsure how to proceed. The unexpected stream of jokes had thrown him off balance, though he guessed that was probably the idea. Before he could reply, Valentine Kiss leaned forward and whispered seriously:

'He likes his ears scratched – that should keep him happy. And tell

---

[94] Pages 326, 344, 97.

Fergus, I miss him, too.' He spoke with such quiet sincerity that, once again, Justin was momentarily taken aback. Valentine sighed. 'Why do I get the feeling there's more to your little visit than a canine news bulletin?'

'Well ... I er ... I do have a question,' Justin admitted.

'Fire away,' said X brightly. He gave Justin a mischievous lopsided grin that reminded him of the Cosmic Joker. 'Don't let PC Big-ears put you off.'

The constable's eyes were fixed on his notebook, but he was listening, Justin was certain.

'Well ... back at Thyme Castle we've got this strange old clock in the library,' he whispered.

Instantly, Valentine's mood changed again, and a look of terrible sadness swept over him. 'Ah yes, the Time and Chance piece ...'

'You *know* about it?' Justin interrupted.

'How could I *not* know about it?' Val replied, his eyes flashing dangerously. 'It's our heritage ... it defines everything that binds us together.'

Justin gasped. He felt oddly disoriented, as if the universe had shuffled its atoms and formed a strange new world around him. Clearly, the bizarre connections he'd noticed hadn't been his imagination. Valentine's use of the words *our* and *us* proved that ... assuming he was telling the truth.

'I don't understand ...' said Justin, trying to quell the knot of panic growing inside him.

'Are you telling me your father hasn't explained *any* of this?' snapped X. His voice was scathing and contemptuous now; his face hard as granite.

'Not ex-exactly,' Justin stammered. 'That's why I wanted to ask *you*.'

'I don't see why I should enlighten you if the Laird of Thyme himself can't be bothered. Tell him to face up to his responsibility.'

Justin slumped back in his chair, suddenly wishing he'd never come. 'Dad says some things are better left alone.'

'I bet he does! Perhaps one day you'll realise your darling daddy has his own agenda, and anything he says should be taken with a huge pinch of salt!'

'Look, I know you two are enemies ... but ...'

'Enemies? Is *that* was he's told you?' X growled. He shook his head, looking bitter and frustrated. '*Of course he has*. That's what *his* father would've told *him*; I'd stake my life on it – and a nastier man never trod this earth.' He paused, as if waiting for an objection, but when Justin remained silent he continued, spitting his words out like poison: 'Down through the centuries, the Lairds of Thyme have become ever more ruthless and arrogant, ever more convinced they're the good guys – but believe me, I've seen what evil some of them are capable of.'

Justin realised Agent X was trying to provoke him; he knew he shouldn't rise to the bait, but he couldn't help it. 'Well, Dad's not like that.'

Valentine Kiss threw his head back and laughed; a long scornful laugh that made Justin feel sick to his stomach. 'Don't play the fool, boy; that's not your role.'

'What d'you mean?'

'I'll tell you what I mean,' snarled Agent X, banging his handcuffed fists on the table. He leaned over, putting his face close to Justin's, his cold cerulean eyes burning with hatred. 'The Thymes are heading for a disaster of epic proportions, and your role will be central to their downfall. Enjoy what little time you have left, boy; your next perform-ance will be PLAYING DEAD – and you *WON'T* BE ACTING!'

'That's it,' said Constable Knox, slamming his notebook down. 'Interview over ... NOW!' He strode over and took hold of the prisoner's arm.

Agent X rose meekly out of his chair, giving the policeman a rueful smile. Justin tried to flash Knox a warning look but he was too late. X turned towards him, holding out his cuffed hands in submissive gesture, then dived across the table, grabbing Knox's notebook. He tore off the top three pages, stuffed them into his mouth and chewed them savagely. After a noisy gulp, he opened his mouth wide.

'Aaaaarrrghhhhhh ... *deee*-licious!' Then with a sly wink at Justin he added: 'I knew I'd have to eat my own words!'

By the time Justin arrived back at the castle, afternoon tea had been cleared away. The smell of hot buttered crumpets still lingered in the air, but the interview with Valentine Kiss had robbed Justin of his appetite.

Oddly enough, it wasn't X's threats that had upset him – he dismissed those as the ranting of a madman; it was his comments about Sir Willoughby that hurt most. After thirteen years of him living a lie, Justin had hoped his father would start being open with him; but he was still hiding something – of that, Justin was certain.

As he reached the end of the portrait gallery, he saw Grandpa Lyall coming out of the great hall, carrying a small blackened book. Not in the mood to talk to his father, Justin tiptoed past the door – but Sir Willoughby spotted him and shouted.

'Ah, *there* you are. Missed your tea, 'm'afraid.'

His voice sounded unusually bobbish. Justin glanced back, half tempted to pretend he hadn't heard, but Sir Willoughby caught his eye and beckoned him in.

'Saved some jam tarts for you and Robyn,' he called, waving towards a plate. 'Nanny said the two of you had gone to Inverness, shopping for the party. Rather relieved, I must say. Haven't seen your sister since I got back; thought she was still angry with me.'

'Well ... you know Bobs,' said Justin, silently praising Nanny's inventiveness. He wondered how long it would be before his dad got suspicious. 'She's er ... just ... errmm. Shall I go and look for her?'

'Never mind now – I've got some good news,' said Willoughby. 'I'm guessing you read the letter I left the night I was kidnapped?'

Justin nodded.

'Then you'll know I thought your grandpa was an impostor. Of course, now you've caught Agent X, I've stopped worrying ... but it turns out the old man has had indisputable proof his identity all along. You see, when Pops went missing he had his latest journal with him, and ...'

'He's still got it?' asked Justin.

'Absolutely,' Willoughby continued. 'Had it in that old bundle he was carrying when he arrived. Binding's been burnt to a crisp, and we can't unlock it yet ... but if he can find the key ... and if its pages are only damaged round the edges ... well, we'll finally discover what happened to him.'

Justin hesitated a moment, then spoke cautiously, not wanting to spoil his father's buoyant mood.

'If it's burnt and you can't open it, how come you're so certain it *is* Grandpa's journal?'

'Because it's written on it,' laughed Sir Willoughby. '*A Journal of Highland Travels by Sir Lyall Austin Thyme*. Charred black in places ... barely visible ... but that's what it says alright. No doubt whatsoever!' He clenched his fists, holding them up in a gesture of triumph. 'The curse is finally broken!'

'Wow, that's *really* excellent, Dad.'

The Laird of Thyme sank back in his chair looking blissfully happy. 'I can't wait to tell Henny.'

'Yeah ... best anniversary present *ever*!' Justin agreed, hoping his mother wouldn't point out that things didn't usually get burned in an avalanche!

That evening, a few minutes after eight, Sir Willoughby knocked on Justin's lab door then strode in, carrying Beowulf.

'All set?' he asked, putting the baby on the floor next to Fergus. 'Your mum just phoned; she'll be back tomorrow ... so we'd better get this done tonight.' He stood with his arms folded and his back to Wulfi.

'Yeah,' said Justin. 'This homework's almo—'

'Now listen,' Willoughby cut in. 'I won't have you sneaking down trying to see how the crypt opens, so I want you to sit over there,' (he pointed to the fireman's pole), 'legs dangling over the edge. Once I'm in the library I'll check I can see you. If I can't ... the crypt stays shut. Got it?'

Justin put on a sulky expression and muttered, 'Okay, Dad,' then trudged over to the hole in the lab floor, hoping he wasn't overplaying it.

Meanwhile, Haggis, who had been peeping over the edge of his basket, squawked feebly and pecked at Sir Willoughby's trouser leg.

'Hmm ... when you come down you'd better bring coordinates for the dodo too,' he said, lifting the basket by its handle. 'I don't want your mum tempted to keep the dratted thing ... you know what she's like.'

'Good idea,' said Justin, pleased he hadn't needed to suggest it himself. The doddling had been looking out-of-sorts for a day or two; being kept indoors and fed human food clearly didn't suit it.

Justin watched his father carry the little bird through the door, then as soon as he heard his footsteps on the stairs, pulled a remote control unit out of his inside pocket. Behind him, a tiny metalic wasp vibrated its wings and swooped off the workbench.

'Hey, what's that?' asked Beowulf, crawling over for a closer look.

'Spy-cam number one,' Justin whispered. '*Spike* for short.'

As the microbot plummeted through the hole, Justin craned his neck to see the computer screen over on his desk; it showed a Spike's eye-view of the south tower, and was a bit like playing a flight-sim game.

Spike zoomed down to the library, then flew over to a shelf behind the door. Seconds later, Willoughby walked in, and as he marched over to the fireman's pole, Justin sent the microbot after him. It landed, feather-light, on his back, then crept up to his shoulder.

Sir Willoughby peered up at his son. 'Good, you're still there,' he shouted. 'Don't budge.'

'Okay!' Justin answered, keeping his eyes pinned on the computer screen. He caught a lightning glimpse of his feet from three floors below before Willoughby turned, strode back to the library door and looked up. Justin swivelled Spike's eye in the same direction, and watched his father's hand reaching towards the keystone high above the door. On it was a stone shield carved with letters and heraldic symbols. After rotating the shield a full turn anticlockwise, Willough-by pressed its lower right quadrant; as it sunk inwards, Justin heard the crypt slide open.

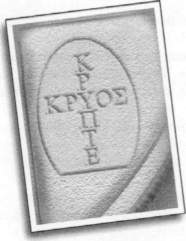

Quickly, he clicked his remote, taking a snapshot of the carving: two lines of intersecting letters inside a sort of arch-shape.

Spike's wings whirred silently. Justin piloted the little microbot to a vase of flowers and sent it crawling inside a tulip, ready to see how the crypt was closed again afterwards. He tucked the remote back in his pocket and peered down through the hole barely a moment before his father reappeared, telling him he could come down.

'Sneaky,' chuckled Beowulf. 'I could've done with one of those myself.'

Justin hurried across to his workbench. He grabbed a backpack and his notebook, then leaned over to scoop the baby off the floor.

'You *are* sure you want to do this?' he said. 'There's a risk you could end up in a parallel future instead of your own.'

'But I *will* be sixteen again, won't I?' asked Wulfi.

'Yeah, you'll get older as you travel forwards in time, but ...'

'Then I want to go.'

Justin shut the lab door behind him and carried Beowulf across the landing. About halfway down the south stairs, Wulfi spoke quietly.

'You've been very fair to me. Like a *real* brother. So there's something I want to tell you.'

'About my future?' asked Justin.

'Yes ... I feel I should war—'

'SHHhhhh! Don't tell me,' said Justin firmly. 'Knowing your own future isn't a good idea; I've seen what it can do to a person.'

'But ...'

'No ... truly! I realise there'll be bad things as well as good – but I'd rather take whatever life throws at me and learn from the experience.'

Beowulf shrugged sadly and turned his head away. Justin walked on in silence – then, at the bottom of the stairs he stopped abruptly.

'Actually, there *is* one thing I *would* like to know,' he whispered. 'It's not about me, though,' he added, seeing Wulfi's surprised expression. 'It's just something that puzzles me. I don't understand why you were sent here in the first place. Your future grandpa must've known you'd be caught and that his past self would end up in prison ... so why bother?'

'Maybe he thought he could change things,' Beowulf suggested.

'Yeah, maybe. That's what happens in stories. It's just ...' Justin stopped and shook his head. 'Did he say anything about his plans? Anything that, looking back, now seems significant?'

Beowulf screwed his face up in a pensive frown. 'Not really. Gramps was pretty old by then; losing his grip. He kept rambling on about chess that day.'

'*Chess*?'

'Yep! Weird, eh? I always thought he preferred cards.'

'Do you remember what he said?'

'Only that it required tremendous patience. And that, sometimes, the best way to win was to fool your opponent into thinking you were losing.'

'A sham sacrifice,' murmured Justin. 'Classic chess strategy. The player allows a major piece to be taken knowing that, ultimately, it'll strengthen his position. It's drastic ... but it often results in victory.'

'So he *knew* I'd fail?' asked Wulfi.

'It looks that way,' said Justin grimly. 'Which means the game isn't over.'

Once they were down in the crypt, Justin helped his father manoeuvre the time machine into the centre of the floor, well away from the surrounding tombs.

While Sir Willoughby set the coordinates for Beowulf's trip, Justin undressed the baby and wrapped him in a tartan blanket. The air in the crypt felt just as damp and cold as it had the previous night, and Haggis, whose basket had been left on a stone coffin, sneezed several times in quick succession.

403

Justin carried Wulfi over to the time machine.

'Dad's sending you back to the exact time you left,' he said. 'We think that'll be safest. But as we don't know your original spatial position, we've chosen a remote spot down by the loch where it's unlikely anyone will see you.'

'You'll have precisely one minute to get out before it returns here,' Sir Willoughby added, wearing an aloof expression. 'And don't think about setting new coordinates because the pre-programmed data will override everything.'

Justin lifted the baby inside, then slid the backpack he'd brought under the seat. 'Clothes for when you arrive,' he explained. 'Mine, I'm afraid; I hope they'll be big enough. There's money too ... and some food, just in case.'

'I'll be fine,' Beowulf assured him. He was shivering now – even more than Haggis – though whether from nerves or cold, Justin couldn't tell.

He shook the baby's hand. 'Bye, Wulfi ... perhaps we'll meet again one day.'

Beowulf stared gravely at Justin, as if there was something he wanted to say – but as he opened his mouth, Sir Willoughby spoke curtly:

'Once you're ready, press *this*.' He indicated a glowing amber button on the instrument panel, then closed the time machine door before Beowulf could reply.

Isolated now, and facing an uncertain future, the spy-baby looked suddenly terrified. Justin peered through the porthole, watching him lean forward and punch the launch button. Seeing Justin's anxious face, he smiled bravely and raised a small chubby hand in farewell ... then he and the time machine vanished.

There was no computerised countdown ... no bursts of plasma, no flashes of light. The machine simply shimmered for a moment and then faded away.

'Coooool!' said Justin admiringly.

Sir Willoughby looked pleased. 'Well, that's *him* dealt with,' he said, rubbing his hands together. 'Now, stand well back. Pretty sure I got the return coordinates right, but best be careful.' He glanced at his wristwatch. 'Look sharp – I only gave us a ten second clearance time.'

They both edged backwards. As Justin stared at the spot where the time machine had stood, he noticed that the floor was engraved with an elaborate eternal knot pattern. He was just thinking it looked rather like a maze, when the air above it seemed to ripple, and the time machine reappeared ... without Beowulf.

'Well, that's a good sign,' remarked Willoughby. 'Now, what about this blasted bird? Got the coordinates?'

'Here, Dad,' said Justin, handing the Laird of Thyme his notebook. 'These are the spatial coordinates for the cave we used in Mauritius. Timewise, hmmm ... not back to his own time of course, or he'll be totally alone; a few years earlier perhaps. The nesting season, so there'll be other doddlings his own age.'

'Righto. Spring 1657.' Sir Willoughby eased himself into the time machine, wedging the dodo's basket between his feet; after adjusting several dials and levers, he shut the door and pressed the amber launch button.

Again, the machine shimmered discreetly and faded from view. Justin gave a long, heartfelt sigh. He was sorry to see Haggis go – but more than a little relieved.

Seconds later the time machine reappeared, materialising as silently as before. Sir Willoughby stepped out, mopping his brow. He looked sunburnt, and his shirt – now open at the collar – was stained with perspiration.

The wicker basket was empty.

It rained on Wednesday; not proper rain, but the kind of drizzle that soaks everything without really trying. After breakfast, Justin wandered into the entrance hall wondering if the Royal Mail had drafted in a replacement postman yet. They had: a grumpy-looking middle-aged hippy, who got very cross when Fergus tried to jump into his van.

Justin flipped through the envelopes as he headed back to the south tower, opening any that looked interesting. The third contained a chilling message:

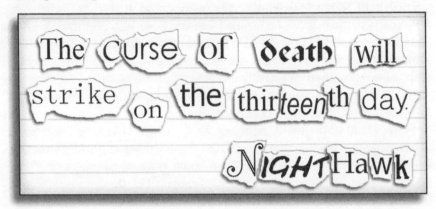

The Curse of death will strike on the thirteenth day. NIGHTHawk

Justin felt sick. His first thought was that it was from Agent X – a follow-up to his menacing diatribe of the previous day.

But no ... that was impossible, he decided; prisoners weren't allowed to pop out and mail death-threats.

Then he wondered about the pseudonym of the sender. Who *was* Nighthawk? Try as he might, Justin couldn't see any connection to Agent X, Valentine Kiss, Random Chance, the Thief of Time or even the Cosmic Joker. Yet something about the name struck a chord, as if he *should* know it ... or had already stumbled across the clues to unravel its mystery.

And the use of the word *curse* unsettled him too. Was it a reference to the Thyme Curse? It claimed that death would strike on the thirteenth day ... and today was the eleventh. Did that mean one of the Thymes would die in just two days' time?

'You're over-analysing it,' Justin told himself sternly. 'It's probably just someone's idea of a joke.' Then Agent X's cold mocking voice echoed in his memory: "*The Thymes are heading for a disaster of epic proportions ... and your next role will be playing dead.*"

'I've decided,' said Nanny Verity. 'Well ... sort of.'

406

It was lunchtime, and Justin had taken a plate of sandwiches up to the nursery so he could get to know his new baby brother.

'I want to be Robyn again,' she continued. 'But only if you can change me back to Verity whenever I want to visit my family.'

Justin shook his head. 'Sorry, Bobs. I can't agree to that. All time travel is risky – but the age-altering kind changes every cell in the body ... a sort of reverse mitosis. The body appears to withstand it once, possibly twice ... but more than that could trigger damage at a molecular level.'

'What if I'm prepared to take that risk?'

'I won't let you. The best I can offer is to try being Robyn for a few days ... *then decide*. But if you choose to become Verity Kiss again, you'll have to stay that way permanently.'

Nanny sighed. Justin had never seen her look so disappointed. He wanted to tell her she wasn't the only one with problems – but he knew if he showed her the Nighthawk note she'd flip into full panic mode and complicate things even more.

'When can we do it?' she asked quietly.

'Tonight – once everyone's asleep. Meet Mum as you are first; tell her you're going away for a few days ... and say Robyn's had an early night.'

'You'll need to arrange for a new nanny, then. But get someone young ... fun; I don't want Alby stuck with some cantankerous old battleaxe.'

'Yeah, I'll phone Napkin's now,' Justin agreed. 'And I'd better see about a replacement cook too – though it'll be short notice with the party tomorrow.'

'Class dismissed,' said Professor Gilbert, frowning at his only pupil.

Justin glanced up at him. It was scarcely three o'clock; afternoon lessons usually ended at four.

'Run along,' Gilbert sighed. 'Your m-mind's been somewhere else all day; your b-body might as well join it ... unless there's something you want to talk about.'

It was tempting, Justin thought – especially now he knew the professor wasn't Agent X – but he shook his head; this was a family matter.

Since the Nighthawk note had arrived that morning, it had awoken in him a disturbing idea: what if the deaths his father had always blamed on the Thyme curse were, in fact, premeditated murders?

Sir Willoughby rarely spoke about his mother, though he'd once told Justin that her drowned body had been found *inside* her boat. Deighton was thrown off his horse, but had it *really* been an accident? And what about old Sir Lyall? Even if by a miracle he'd managed to survive, could the avalanche have been started deliberately?

As Justin headed back to his lab, the endless cycle of questions whirled in his brain like the vanes of a radiometer. He felt sure there was some unseen thread connecting these events – but even if he could travel back in time and actually watch what happened, he knew he wouldn't be able to change anything. For a moment, Justin wondered whether to broach the subject with his father – but he dismissed the idea at once; reawakening Sir Willoughby's paranoia would *not* be a good idea ... especially just before the party.

Thinking of the anniversary reminded Justin of the special surprise he had planned for his mother. It would require the use of his dad's time machine and a considerable amount of preparation – but this time, unlike the dodo project, he had a pretty good idea it would be a success. After all, he'd already seen the Loch Ness monster and guessed time travel was the only rational explanation for her existence. Palaeontologists were divided as to whether plesiosaurs gave birth to live young or were oviparous... but later that night Justin intended to find out for himself.

Most of his equipment was already packed – however, he still needed to construct a simple handheld sonar device he could use to summon Nessie. He hoped that by transmitting a specific NBHF burst-pulse before each feeding session, she'd eventually learn to come when "called". Of course, this was assuming plesiosaurs were biosonar – but from what he had seen of fossilised specimens, their lower jaw structure certainly indicated a rudimentary use of echolocation.

By the end of the afternoon Justin had constructed the perfect miniature sonar-projector, all neatly housed inside a ballpoint pen casing. Pressing the end triggered a powerful electro-acoustic signal capable of travelling the entire length of Loch Ness.

His final job before supper was to prepare an itinerary of his proposed trips through time. As Justin suspected, Sir Willoughby's machine didn't have a memory – so it was vital to keep a written log of all coordinates. He hadn't settled on a specific date for his visit to the late Jurassic period yet – but once Nessie was old enough to leave the incubator and feed herself, he planned to release her in 1925, knowing this would give her enough time to grow into a full-size adult plesiosaur before her first reported sighting.

Justin instructed his computer to select five random dates between 1925 and the present, so he could stop off and check on how she was progressing. He copied them carefully in his notebook:

> May 11th 1938
> July 10th 1951
> March 13th 1964
> May 12th 1977
> March 31st 1990

Now, all that remained was for him to find his way to the underground lake tonight ... and Justin was certain he'd discovered a map of the catacombs down in the crypt.

Henny and her film crew landed about eight o'clock that evening. Fortunately, Mrs Kof had left plenty of food in the pantry, so while Knightly drove to the airport, Nanny Verity laid out a cold meal in the kitchen.

Mrs Gilliechattan had already prepared guestrooms for Hank and Polly, but Lady Henny surprised everyone by inviting the pilot to stay too. While she and her crew chatted, he ate silently at the opposite end of the table, although he rose and bowed deeply to Nanny Verity when she bustled back in with Albion.

Justin hovered behind her, exchanging nervous glances with his father. It was past Albion's bedtime, but Nanny thought it might be best if Henny met him in front of the others.

'Alby wants to say a quick nighty-night,' she announced brightly, hoping he'd remember the two words she'd spent all afternoon teaching him. She gave him an encouraging squeeze. 'Go on, Poppet.'

'Nigh-nigh ... Mommee.'

There was a chorus of *Ahhhhs* from everyone, and Albion chuckled.

Henny reached out for him, then hesitated, looking slightly puzzled. 'He seems ... kinda *different*,' she said.

'Of course he does,' snapped Nanny, plonking the baby on her knee. 'Och, he's growing so fast you can practically see it.'

'And his Thyme streak's starting to come through at last,' added Sir Willoughby.

Albion watched Eliza emerge from the pantry carrying a couple of bananas. He was still unsure of the enormous gorilla, so snuggled close to his mother, clutching her thumb tightly. Lady Henny gazed down at him wearing a radiant smile.

'Well, he looks more adorable than ever,' she said, and leaned forward to kiss the top of his head.

'You'll have to be a more hands-on mum from now on,' said Nanny, fixing Henny with a firm gaze. 'I'm thinking of retiring – moving down to Brighton with my family.'

'But Nanny, Honey – we *need* you,' Lady Henny insisted, waving her objections aside. 'We'll talk about it after the party, darling. Hmm ... a raise, perhaps.' She gave Justin a meaningful look. 'Or a nice vacation ...'

'Nan's already going away for a few days,' Justin told her. 'I've arranged a stand-in nanny; she'll be here tomorrow on a month's trial. Our real problem is replacing Mrs Kof,' he sighed. 'The agency can't

410

supply anyone until next week.'

'But we've *gotta* find someone for the party,' cried Henny.

Hank glanced up from his apple pie. 'Hey, I might be able to help. My old mum was the cook here years ago; I bet she'd come out of retirement for a few days if I asked her. I'll give her a bell if you like.' He pushed his chair back and ambled into the entrance hall. Polly trotted after him saying he ought to phone his daddikins too.

Henny laughed happily. 'Thanks, Hank ... you're an angel,' she called, then glancing round, asked: 'Where's Robyn got to? Not sulking, I hope?'

'She's got a headache,' said Justin hurriedly.

'I made her go to bed,' Nanny added. 'And *no* ... she's *not* sulking; she's grown up a lot since you last saw her. You'll see.'

'Well, I hope she's been looking after that dodo,' Henny whispered. 'It's our last chance of salvaging the Mauritius project.'

'Dad's taken it back,' Justin told her, keeping his voice low. He leaned over, putting his mouth next to her ear so even Sir Willoughby wouldn't hear. 'Don't worry, Mum – *Thyme-Zone* won't be axed. I'm going ahead with the next stage of my plan.'

'You mean ...?'

'Yes. But we can't tell Dad, remember. You'd better keep him well away from the south tower tonight.'

'What are you two whispering about?' asked Willoughby.

'My er ... surprise present,' said Henny, winking at her eldest son.

Justin changed the subject quickly. 'Did you find out why the other dodos died?'

'Avian flu,' Henny replied sadly. 'It was like their immune systems couldn't fight a 21st century virus.'

Suddenly, an image of Haggis sneezing and shivering down in the crypt flashed into Justin's mind. He stole an uneasy glance at Sir Willoughby, and from his horrified expression knew that the same terrible thought had just occurred to him.

It was almost one-thirty in the morning before Hank and Polly potted their last snooker ball and finally went to bed. High above in the laboratory, Justin and Nanny watched them through Spike's micro-cam eye, and breathed a sigh of relief as they closed the library door behind them.

'This is it,' Justin whispered. 'Time for you to become Robyn again.'

Verity smiled nervously, then reached into her apron pocket. She took out a small hand mirror and peered at her face, recalling the thirty years of joy and sorrow that had transformed it, leaving fine threads of silver in her dark hair and laughter-lines around her eyes. Looking back, the time had passed faster than she would have ever believed possible.

'I'm ready,' she said.

The time machine shimmered, vanishing silently into the past – and Justin realised he might have just said goodbye to his dear old nanny forever. On this very spot thirty years in the past, (if the age-reversal had worked), Robyn would be poised for the return half of her pre-programmed trip – standard time travel this time, keeping her age at fourteen and three-quarters.

Justin checked his watch. He'd set the return coordinates fifteen seconds in the future, allowing him just enough time to photograph the crypt floor while the machine was missing. He took out his mobile phone and flipped it to camera-mode, hurriedly snapping pictures of the mazelike engraving beneath his feet. Yesterday, he'd noticed an octagon at the heart of the design; this, he guessed, was the crypt, and the interlocking knot pattern surrounding it, a map of the catacombs.

After taking a final shot of what he hoped might be the subterranean lake, Justin moved back – and moments later the time machine reappeared. He felt a flood of relief as its door burst open and Robyn jumped out, babbling excitedly.

'I feel GREAT!' she shouted, reaching for her hand mirror. One glance at her reflection and she was screaming with delight. 'WOW! Look at my *skin* ... my *hair*!'

'Yeah, and look at your clothes,' said Justin, unable to resist teasing her.

Robyn peered down at her old nanny's uniform and rumpled stockings, and exploded with laughter. 'Crud-crumpets! I should've brought something to change into.'

Justin walked over to where his equipment was stacked against the crypt wall, and picked out a bag. 'One of your rare sensible outfits,' he said, tossing it to his sister. 'I guessed it might be a day or two before you're ready for luminous sequined miniskirts.'

'Don't bet on it,' Robyn sniggered. She slid behind a huge granite sarcophagus and stepped back a minute later looking her usual self. 'Need a hand?' she asked, seeing Justin still hunched over his equipment.

'No. Most of this can stay here, close to the time machine; the incubator goes in the next chamber near the generator – but right now all I really need is *this*,' he said, pulling the little sonar-projector out of a backpack. 'Once we find the underground lake I can summon Nessie and ...'

'*Summon* Nessie? Don't you need to travel back a gazillion years and nick a dinosaur egg first?' asked Robyn, looking confused.

'Sequentially, yes,' said Justin. 'But not chronologically ...'

'Urrghh, stop talking like you've swallowed a dictionary.'

Justin grinned. 'Sorry, Bobs. Look ... I'm planning to release Nessie in 1925. In fact, I'm fairly sure I *must* do that because she already exists ... which *should* mean I survive my trip to the prehistoric past. But I can't rule out the possibility there's another explanation for the Loch Ness Monster – one that has nothing to do with me – and if that's the case then my safety *isn't* guaranteed.'

'But why summon Nessie *now*? How does *that* help?'

'It's like time travel insurance,' Justin continued, thinking of the Nighthawk note and its ominous warning. 'While *my* plesiosaur's still a baby I'm going to train her to answer a unique sonar signal – so if the old Nessie comes when I call her, I'll have proof of the trip's success before I take it.'

'And you won't have to worry about becoming a Jurassic dino-chew,' laughed Robyn.

413

'Exactly!' You see ... I've got a horrible feeling *I* might've caused the dodo's extinction,' Justin admitted gloomily. 'And I don't want *anything* to go wrong this time!'

Sir Willoughby didn't sleep well at the best of times, but when his wife was home he slept even less.

It was dawn, and Lady Henrietta Thyme was doing a remarkable impersonation of a buzz-saw hacking through logs. Willoughby gazed at her, marvelling how lips so beautiful could spew forth such an appalling racket – but even sixteen years of her snoring couldn't spoil his mood tonight. Words couldn't describe the joy finding his long-lost father had brought; better still, he felt a wonderful sense of peace and tranquillity knowing the Thyme Curse was well and truly broken. Finally he could let his mother and brother rest in peace, accepting their deaths were nothing more than two tragic accidents connected by an uncanny coincidence.

He could hardly believe that for the last few weeks he'd been terrified to even glance at the loch in case he saw the dreaded beastie. His fear had made him want to stay in Mauritius; then, after flying home, it'd almost caused a motorbike accident when he'd sped along the road with his head turned away from the water.

No one had ever guessed the true reason he loathed all mention of the monster – and he hadn't told a soul; even Henny assumed it was disbelief ... but Willoughby had never doubted the beast's existence for a moment.

His first memory of her was hazy and incomplete. He'd been just three-and-a-half years old, out sailing with his mother when a dark shadowy shape passed beneath their boat. As he'd leaned over the prow trying to get a better look, something had knocked against the keel and sent him tumbling into the water. His only other memory of that day was waking up back inside the boat ... next to his cold, lifeless mother.

Thirteen years passed before Willoughby's next encounter. He and his brother were riding along the clifftop when a loud splash frightened

414

their horses – and Equinox, who'd always been skittish, reared up, throwing Deighton onto the rocks below.

The third time didn't count now that Sir Lyall had been found – and it was different to the others anyway; but, once again, the Beast of the Loch had crossed his path with disastrous consequences.

For years, Nessie had haunted his dreams; a chilling omen of death ... his personal harbinger of doom. Yet now that he really thought about it, what evidence had there been? A half-glimpsed shadow, a loud splash and a blurred photograph.

But none of that mattered now. The curse was broken.

'It's beautiful!' gasped Robyn. 'The most amazing thing I've ever seen.'

Justin had to agree. After their monotonous trek through the catacombs, the underground lake was indeed breathtaking. It was the size of a football pitch, but tapering at one end like a teardrop. Its surface glowed with a strange bioluminescent algae, which lit the cavern and made the water look like molten gold; there was a narrow beach of soft, dry shingle down one side, and hundreds of long glistening stalactites dangling from the roof like giant icicles.

'There's meant to be an underwater tunnel leading out to the loch,' Justin explained. He crouched on the shingle, lowered his sonar device into the water and transmitted three ten-second signals. 'That should do it. Might take a few minutes for her to get here, though; she'll be in her late seventies by now ... I'm guessing that's pretty old for a plesiosaur.'

Justin straightened up and stood beside his sister. Her cheeks were flushed with excitement, her eyes gleaming like stars. She took hold of his hand and gave it a gentle squeeze.

'I forgot to thank you,' she whispered.

Justin grinned happily. 'And I forgot to say welcome back!'

Sir Willoughby eased himself off the bed and walked towards the window. He drew back the curtains, closed his eyes and took a long, deep breath.

The sun was just starting to rise, and the gentle warmth of it on his skin filled him with a rush of elation ... optimism ... and hope. From now on things would be different: no more regrets ... no more lies ... no more living in fear. With his old enemy in jail, Sir Lyall safely home, and the time machine locked away where no one could ever use it, what *was* there to fear?

Certainly not the Thyme Curse.

'If you mean it, prove it,' he told himself sternly. 'Look at the loch. Make today a new beginning.' He took another deep breath ... then, with a strange feeling of release, opened his eyes.

In the pale dawn sunlight Loch Ness looked magnificent; as calm as a millpond, with clouds of mist drifting languidly across its surface. But as Willoughby laughed at his folly, the mist parted and a monstrous saurian head loomed out of the water.

Time seemed to stand still. The beast turned ... slowly ... until their eyes met. And in that moment, the Laird of Thyme knew with a terrible sickening certainty that a member of his family was going to die.

After filling her lungs, Nessie plunged below the surface, spiralling down through one endless crevasse after another into the darkest murkiest depths of the loch ... heading for the place she always thought of as home.

416

The
Tartan of Thyme
will continue with:

??????? ?????

APPENDIX

This list gives brief definitions to some of the more complex words in this book, however, if you are anything like Justin, you'll know most of them already!

It includes: general vocabulary, Scottish dialect, abbreviations, and greatly simplified explanations of scientific or technical terms.

*Where a word has a number of meanings, only the definition appropriate to the context is given.

A

abattoir - slaughterhouse where animals are butchered.
abdomen - the posterior part of an insect's body, (behind the thorax).
accentuate - highlight or emphasise.
Achilles heel - a fatal weak spot easily overlooked. In *Greek myth*, Achilles was dipped into the river Styx by his mother. This magically protected every part of his body except for the heel she had held him by.
acrostic - a hidden word or phrase spelt out by the initial letters of successive words, or lines of poetry.
Ad infinitum - to infinity (*Latin*).
adamant - determined, unshakeable.
adamantly - determinedly; unshakably.
adherence - sticking to something, or following (rules, perhaps) very closely.
adjacent - near, close or beside.
admonition - a firm but gentle warning.
adversary - enemy; (*used incorrectly by Mrs Kof instead of the word* anniversary).
alluring - temptingly attractive.
alphanumeric - using both numbers and letters of the alphabet.

altercation - a heated argument.
altimeter - an instrument used to show height above sea level.
ambigram - a word written in such a way that it looks the same from more than one angle. From *ambi* (both) + *gram* (word).
ambiguous - difficult to understand. Having more than one possible outcome or meaning.
amicable - friendly. **amicably** - done in a friendly manner.
amnesia - loss of memory.
anagram - arranging the letters of a word or phrase to spell another word or phrase.
Anansi - a trickster of West African and Caribbean folklore who takes the form of a cunning spider.
annihilation - complete destruction. (*used incorrectly by Mrs Kof instead of the word* anniversary).
anomalies - things that are **anomalous** - irregular or abnormal.
anonymously - by someone unknown or withholding their name.
anoraknophobia - an invented word mistakenly used by Mrs Kof instead of arachnophobia - a fear of spiders.
anti-gravity - a repulsive form of gravitation.
apathetic - indifferent.
apparition - *the appearance of something remarkable, unexpected or mysterious.

arachno-feline – something part spider, part cat, combining the words **arachno** - relating to spiders, and **feline** - relating to cats.

archetypal - original, prototype, or typical specimen.

arquebus - *an old-fashioned long-barrelled gun.*

artefacts - *manmade objects.

ASAP - *Abbrev.* **A**s **S**oon **A**s **P**ossible.

assailant - attacker.

audacity - boldness.

automaton - a clockwork or mechanical figure that appears to be self-moving.

aversion - extreme dislike.

avian flu - bird flu.

avid - keen, enthusiastic.

axial rotation - rotation on an axis.

B

BAFTA - British Academy of Film and Television Arts.

bairn - a baby. *(Scottish dialect).*

baklava - a pastry filled with nuts and honey.

balaclava - a woollen helmet covering the head, showing just the eyes.

basalt - a dark rock of volcanic origin.

basilisk - a legendary serpent able to kill by its glance.

baulked - *recoiled or turned away.

Beastie - the Loch Ness Monster, (also known as Nessie).

Bedouin – a member of a nomadic desert-dwelling tribe.

bevy - *a group, usually of girls.

binary - counting using two figures only, (0 & 1) instead of 10 (0, 1, 2, 3, 4, 5, 6, 7, 8 & 9). Using this scale: 1 = 1, 2 = 10, 3 = 11, 4 = 100 etc.

bioluminescent - a luminous light produced certain living organisms.

biosonar - sonar used by certain living organisms (such as bats and dolphins).

blighter - an irritating person or thing. (*British informal*).

blithering - contemptible. (*British informal*).

blotto - *slang.* drunk.

bobbish - cheery. (*British informal*).

bogle - * bogey, a ghost (*Scottish dialect*).

bogus - phony, not genuine.

borborygmus - the sound made by the rumbling of the stomach.

brazen - *bold.

brioche - a soft French bread roll.

brusquely - curtly, in a blunt manner.

brusqueness - bluntness.

bunkum - nonsense.

buoyant - *cheerful.

burgeoning - rapidly growing.

C

cacophonously - discordantly, harshly noisy.

cadaverous - corpselike.

cahoots - in league with, usually for wrongdoing.

cairngorm - yellow or purple gemstones from the Scottish Cairngorm mountains

callous - insensitive, without feeling.

camouflage - the ability (often of animals) to blend with their surroundings to escape the notice of predators.

candelabrum - a branched candleholder.

canny - shrewd, knowing, clever. (*Scottish dialect*).

cantankerous - quarrelsome, bad-tempered.

carnage - mass slaughter.

Casimir effect - negative energy built up

between reflective plates inside a quantum vacuum.

catacombs - a series of maze-like underground tunnels.

cathodical - relating to a cathode (a type of electrode); (*used incorrectly by Mrs Kof instead of the word* cathedral).

CCTV - closed-circuit television.

cerebral - *intelligence, relating the brain.

cerulean - sky-blue.

chaff - 1) the dried husks of seeds/grains. 2) banter or joking.

Chameleon-like - changeable, having the ability to alter ones appearance as rapidly as a chameleon (lizard) can change colour.

château - a French castle or manor.

chintzy - décor using chintz (glazed cotton fabric, often floral.

Chippendale - a style of antique English furniture.

chipper - cheery, lively. (*British informal*).

chivalrously - politely and considerately.

chivvying - nagging.

chloroform - a liquid that gives off a vapour that causes unconsciousness.

chronology - proper sequence of past times, dates or events.

chronologically - in time/date order.

chrononaut - a time traveller.

cinched - *firmly fastened around (like the girth on a horse).

circumstantial evidence - indirect evidence that infers a conclusion rather than directly proving it.

clangour - a loud ringing noise.

clarion - a trumpeting sound calling to action.

clerical - relating to clergy (religious ministers).

cliche - an over-used phrase or idea.

clink - a slang word for prison.

colander - a food-strainer.

compelling - *convincing.

complexion - the appearance of facial skin in colour and general health.

compounded - *added to or intensified.

concierge - a hotel caretaker. (*French*).

concoction - *something made by adding different ingredients.

concurrently - at the same time or location.

concussion - a blow to the head usually causing unconsciousness.

conglomerate - *a big business corporation made up of various companies.

conglomeration - an assorted mass of things.

consequences - *results (often unpleasant) of previous actions.

conspiratorial - in the manner of one sharing a secret.

consummate - *skilfully accomplished.

contemptuous - showing contempt - the feeling of despising something.

continuum - something continuous, with no single part significantly different to any other part. Used in the term *spacetime continuum*, in which the three coordinates of space and one of time can pinpoint the location of any event.

contraption - a device, often mechanical.

contrived - to manage something by means of trickery, manipulation or obvious planning.

conundrum - a riddle or puzzling problem.

conveying - *transporting from one place to another.

copiously - abundantly, in great quantity.

coquettishly - in a flirting manner.
corporate - belonging to, or arranged by a business corporation.
countenance - 1) facial expression. 2) to allow, tolerate or approve.
covert - secret.
cowl - a large, loose hood, often on the habit (robe) of a monk.
credulity – gullibility; a willingness to believe.
crevasse - a deep crack.
crocodilian - *resembling a crocodile.
crone - an ugly old woman.
croquet - an outdoor game in which players use mallets to knock wooden balls through hoops.
crypt - a hidden underground chamber, often where people are entombed or buried.
cryptic - concealing its meaning in a puzzling way.
cursory - hurried and superficial.
cynical - believing the worst of others.

D

daiquiri - a drink containing rum, lime juice and ice.
da Vinci (Leonardo) - Italian painter, inventor and genius, fascinated by the science of art and the art of science. (1452 – 1519).
debilitating – weakening or making feeble.
debonair - charming, sophisticated, well-groomed.
decapitating - beheading.
decryption - *decoding a message.
defecate - to pass waste from the body.
deferential - respectful.
dematerialise - to stop having a material existence; to vanish completely.
deportment - the physical manner in which a person behaves.
déshabillé - carelessly dressed or partly undressed. (*French*).
despicable - someone or something despised, vile or contemptible.
despondent - downcast or dejected.
detachment - *aloofness, lacking emotional connection.
devastating – overwhelming; shocking.
deviated – to have changed course or turned aside.
diabolical - outrageously bad.
diametrically - completely, utterly.
diaphragm - *a vibrating disc that produces sound waves.
diatribe - a bitter verbal attack.
diffident - timid, shy, lacking confidence. *adv* **diffidently** - in this manner.
dilapidated - falling down or in a state of disrepair.
diplomatic immunity - the exemption of diplomats to local law.
discreet - *tactful; not causing social discomfort or embarrassment. *adv* - **discreetly.**
discombobulated - thrown into confusion.
discomfited - made uneasy or embarrassed.
disconcertingly - upsettingly, unsettlingly.
disconsolately - gloomily, beyond comfort.
discordant - a harsh inharmonious noise.
discriminately - showing special favour to a person or thing.
dishevelled - with hair or clothes disarrayed.
displacement behaviour - substituting one behaviour for another.
dissipate - *dissolved.
distraught - agitated, very upset.

Appendix

drivelling - speaking foolishly.
duress - forced to do something by means of threat.
dutiful - having a sense of duty.

E

ebullient - exubrant, bubbling with enthusiasm.
eccentric - *decidedly unusual in behaviour or appearance.
echolocation - a way of determining an object's location by analysing the length and direction of an echo bounced off it.
effigies - *a sculpture of a person.
elated - thrilled, excited.
elementary particles - particles that are less complex than atoms.
embroiled - involved or mixed up in.
encephalophage - brain-eater. a word invented for this story combining
encephalo - indicating the brain, and
phage - something that eats. From *enkephalos* and *phagos*, (*Greek*).
enigma - a puzzle. Something mysterious or difficult to understand.
enigmatic - mysterious.
ephemeral - lasting a short time.
epitaph - an inscription on a tomb.
equilibrium - *a state of balance in which one force cancels out the influence of another.
equinox - the two annual occasions – vernal (spring) and autumnal – when day and night are of equal length.
ETA - *abbrev*: Estimated Time of Arrival.
ethereal - delicate, airy, of very little substance.
etiquette - rules of correct behaviour in society.
Euclid - 3rd century BC Greek mathematician.
Euclidian - relating to Euclid's works

and theories.
evasive - not straightforward; giving an excuse.
evasion - avoidance of responsibility or duty.
exhilarating - exciting, thrilling.
exoskeleton - outer skeleton. the protective out covering or shell of creatures like beetles.
extinction - *the act of making a species extinct by killing off the last living specimens.
extravagance - excessive or wasteful spending.
extricating - removing by disentangling.

F

fabrication - *invention of an untruthful story.
famulus - a sorcerer's servant, (mis*used by Mrs Kof instead of the word* famous).
faze - deter or disconcert.
feckless - irresponsible.
feign – pretend or act.
festooned - *decorated with loops or swags of material.
fey - a state of high excitement once thought to bode imminent death or disaster. (*Scottish*).
fiasco - a humiliating failure.
Fibonacci spirals - spirals based on a sequence of numbers where each is the sum of the previous two. (0,1,1,2,3,5,8, 13, 21 etc.)
filament - *thin wire, or any slender threadlike structures.
filigree - ornately twisted wirework of precious metal.
flailing - to thrash about, moving like a flail (an implement used to thresh grain).

Appendix

flambéed - food served in flaming brandy.

flimflambeau - a "magic" word invented for this story combining **flimflam** - trickery or deception, and **flambeau** - a large ornamental candlestick.

flux - flow. 1) the rate at which fluid, energy or particles flow. 2) a state of continuous change. 3) instability. 4) a medical term for a particularly nasty bout of diarrhoea.

folly - * 1) foolishness, the actions of a fool. 2) a fanciful or eccentric building with no practical purpose other than being decorative.

foraging - searching or rummaging - often for food.

foreboding - an uncanny feeling that trouble lies ahead.

forensic - applied for the purpose of law; usually concerning evidence examined to determine the cause of death.

Fortean - descriptive of anomalous (unusual, puzzling or unexplained) phenomena – after Charles Fort, who spent his life researching mysteries of the universe, like: cryptozoology, teleportation, coincidence, chance and synchronicity.

foundling - an abandoned baby.

fractious - irritable.

frippet - a frivolous young woman.

frugal - meagre and inexpensive.

fuselage - the body of an aircraft.

fusion - thermonuclear reaction - energy created by the fusing of two nuclei into one nucleus.

G

gallant - *brave, honourable and chivalrous.

garbled - muddled.

gaunt - *thin in appearance.

gazillion - an invented word used for any very large number.

gelignite - a type of explosive.

genetically - relating to genes.

goaded - prompted or motivated to do something, (as if with a cattle-prod).

gobsmacked - very surprised. (*British informal*).

gothic - *a style of hair, clothing or makeup designed to give a vampire-like appearance.

GPS - *abbrev*: Global Positioning System.

grotesque - strangely distorted.

guano - dried sea bird droppings.

guttural - harsh sounding.

H

hadron collider - a machine that accelerates hadrons (elementary particles capable of strong nuclear interaction), making them collide with each other. Sometimes called an atom-smasher or particle accelerator.

haggis - a Scottish dish; offal, oatmeal and suet boiled in an animals stomach.

hallucination - seeing something that isn't there.

hangar - a building where aircraft are stored.

hapless - unlucky.

harbinger - a person or thing that heralds an approaching event.

harmonious - *fitting together in a perfectly pleasing and effective manner.

Harpy - *Greek myth*. A bird with the head of a cruel vicious woman.

heraldic - relating to heraldry, (study of family descent).

herbivorous - an animal feeding on plant matter, (*used incorrectly by Mrs*

Kof instead of the word herbal - *made from herbs*).
Hermes - *messenger of the gods. *Greek myth.*
HG (Herbert George) Wells - English author of science fiction novels including "The Time Machine". (1886 – 1946).
hologram/holographic - * three-dimensional images usually produced by lasers.
horologist - watch or clockmaker.
Houdini, Harry - Famous magician and escapologist.
hyperactive - abnormally overactive.
hypnogogic - the state between being awake and fully asleep.
hypothesis - a suggested explanation.
hypothetical - an explanation that is unproved and may not necessarily be true.

I

IATA - International Air Transport Association.
impassive - calm, not showing any emotion.
impenetrably - descriptive of something that cannot be penetrated or understood.
imperative - urgently important.
imperceptibly - too gradually to be noticed.
impertinent - rude, impudent.
impervious - *cannot be influenced.
impetuous - acting rashly, without previous thought.
improv - improvisation, performing (often acting) without preparation or rehearsal.
incarnate - in human form; or the personification of something, such as: *evil incarnate* - a personification of evil.
incentive - a reward that prompts an action.
inclination - *liking or preference.

incoherent - not expressed clearly.
incomprehensible - unable to be understood.
incongruous - unsuitable. Out of place.
inconsolable - cannot be comforted.
incontinent - *having no control over the bowel or bladder.
incriminate - to suggest someone is guilty of a crime; **incriminating** - in this manner.
indisposed - unwell.
indisputable - beyond doubt.
indistinguishable – identical; something that cannot be identified from another.
induction -the bringing on, or causing of something.
indulgent - pampering to someone's every desire; *adv* **indulgently** - in this manner.
ineffectual - having no effect.
inevitable - unavoidable; certain to happen. **inevitability** - inescapable certainty.
inexplicably - unexplainable.
infiltrate - to enter without being noticed - like a spy.
ingratiating - fawning; trying to gain approval.
inkling - suggestion, suspicion.
innate - inborn, natural.
inscrutable - mysterious; hard to make out.
insidious - behaving harmfully without attracting much attention.
instinctively - behaving in away dictated by instinct - the fixed inborn behavioural response of animals.
insubordination - rebelliousness, disobedience.
insubstantial - flimsy; without substance.
integrated - to be included or accepted as part of a whole.

Appendix

interconnectivity - everything connecting to everything else.
intersecting - cutting across.
interspersed - scattered between.
intrinsically - basically; essentially.
invigorating - refreshing, stimulating.
iridescent - showing shimmering rainbow-like colours.
irrefutable - impossible to disprove.
irrevocable - cannot be changed or undone.
itinerary - a written record of a journey, (often planned in advance).

J

jerkin - sleeveless jacket.
jibe - to taunt or jeer.
jiggery-pokery - trickery. (*British informal*).
Jurassic - the period between Triassic and Cretaceous when dinosaurs roamed the earth.

K

ken - understand. *(Scottish dialect).*
keystone - central stone at the top of an arch.
kilt - a knee-length pleated skirt, usually made of tartan material, (worn by both men and women in Scotland).

L

Laird - a Scottish landowner similar to an English Lord. *(Scottish dialect).*
liability - something one is liable (legally responsible) for.
linguistic - relating to language.
lintel - horizontal beam over a door or window.
liveried - wearing livery (the uniform of a servant).
loch – lake. *(Scottish dialect).*
lucid - *clearly understood.
ludicrously - ridiculously; foolishly.
lugubrious - dismal, mournful.
luminescence - light emitted at low temperatures.

M

macabre - gruesome, grim.
malachite - a bright green mineral.
malicious - showing malice, (a desire to harm others).
manipulative - *deviously controlling.
manoeuvre - 1) to manipulate a situation for personal advantage. 2) to move something skilfully.
marinated - (of food) soaked in oil, wine or vinegar.
marionette - a stringed puppet.
martyred - *descriptive of one who is suffering greatly.
masquerading - acting, often in disguise.
massacre - mass killing.
matinee - a daytime theatre performance.
Mauritius - a small island in the Indian ocean, (formerly the habitat of the dodo).
mayhem - violent destruction or chaos.
meagre - an insufficient amount.
mellifluous - (of speech) as smooth and sweet as honey)
memento mori - an object that reminds one of death. (*Latin: remember you must die*).
menagerie - a zoo.
mercurial - changeable; volatile; like

Appendix

mercury.

meridian - *noon. (antemeridian, meaning before noon, abbreviated to a.m.)

mesmerising - hypnotising or fascinating.

methodically - by an orderly logical method; systematically.

meticulous - paying great attention to detail. *adv* **meticulously** - in such a manner.

microbot - microscopic robot.

migraine - a severe headache.

millisecond - one thousandth of a second.

minuscule - *very small.

mirthless - without merriment.

misconception - a mistaken opinion.

mitosis - cell division.

molecular - *relating to molecules, (simple chemical compounds of two or more atoms).

mollified - soothed, pacified.

momentous - of great significance.

monochrome - *in shades of black and white.

monocular - a spyglass.

monologue - a long speech by one person.

monosyllabic - curtly, using words containing only one syllable.

monotonous - repetitive, boring.

monstrosity - *something outrageously ugly.

mornay - (of food) served in a cheese sauce.

morose - gloomy. *adv.* **morosely** - gloomily.

mortified - humiliated.

motivational - inspirational; offering incentive.

motley - 1) a varied collection or mixture of things. 2) the colourful garb of a jester.

multilingual - able to speak more than two languages.

multiverse/multiversal - a theory including multiple parallel universes as oppose to just a single universe.

mundane - ordinary.

N

naive - having poor judgement and showing lack of experience. *adv* **naively**.

naivity - being naïve.

nanosecond - a billionth of a second.

NBHF - Narrow Band High Frequency.

negligence - carelessness; showing neglect.

Nessie - the Loch Ness Monster.

Newtonion - relating to the works and theories of Sir Isaac Newton, English mathematician and physicist, remembered for his law of gravitation and three laws of motion. Author of *Principia Mathematica*. (1643 – 1727).

nonchalant - calm, without showing anxiety or excitement. *adv* **nonchalantly**.

noncommittal - not committing to.

nostalgia - a yearning for the past.

Nyx - *Greek myth.* Goddess of the night, daughter of Chaos. (Roman counterpart: Nox).

O

obelisk - a flat-sided stone pillar tapering towards a pyramid top.

obese - overweight.

oblivion - *a state of unconsciousness or unawareness.

obscenity - an offensive statement or act.

obsequious - in an attentive and servile manner.

och - Scottish interjection like *oh*, often used to preface a remark such as: 'och, no dear.' pronounced *ock. (Scottish dialect).*

okey-dokey - okay.
ominous - ill-omened, threatening evil.
ornithology - the scientific study of birds.
adv **ornithological**.
oscillating - *fluctuating.
ostentatious - showy.
outlandish - strange, bizarre.
oviparous - egg-laying.

P

palaeontologist - someone who studies the fossils of extinct life forms.
pallor - an unnatural paleness.
paltry - insignificant or worthless.
pandemonium - confusion, chaos.
pandora's box - (*Greek myth*) Pandora was given a box but forbidden to open it. Unable to resist, she disobeyed, releasing from it all the ills that trouble mankind, leaving only hope left inside.
paradox - a puzzle or an odd statement or situation that appears to contradict itself.
paradoxical - puzzling.
paranoia - a tendency to mistrust and be wary of others. **paranoid** - behaving this way.
patronising - *treating someone in a superior manner that implies you know better.
peevish - fretful, irritable.
penitent - feeling regret and wanting forgiveness.
peripetia - a sudden and dramatic change of circumstances.
perpetual - everlasting.
perverse - contrary or stubborn.
petersham - strong corded ribbon.
petulant - sullen and irritable.
phenomenal - *extraordinary.
phial - a small bottle.
philosophically - *calmly, in the face of difficulties.
phlegm - *mucus.

phosphenes - the impression of light seen behind tightly closed eyelids.
physiognomical - descriptive of facial features.
physiotherapy - therapeutic exercise or massage.
pictogram - pictures used to represent written words or phrases.
pirouette - spinning on the toes whilst dancing.
pitcher - a large jug.
placate - to pacify, calm or soothe.
plaintively - mournfully.
plasma - *a gas used in modern flat television monitors. Also a hot ionised material consisting of nuclei and electrons present in the sun and fusion reactors.
plausible - believable.
plesiosaur - an aquatic long-necked dinosaur.
plutonium - a highly toxic metallic element often used as reactor fuel. Symbol: Pu. Atomic no: 94.
pneumatic - an area of physics concerned with the mechanical properties of gases.
ponderous - (of movement), slow and heavy; laborious. *adv* **ponderously**.
potpourri - dried petals used to scent the air.
preconceived - an idea formed before all the facts are gathered.
preliminary - *initial; first.
preposterous - ridiculous, unbelievable.
prerogative - a personal right or choice.
pristine - *pure, fresh and clean.
procrastination - delaying an action until a more convenient time.
prodigious - 1) vast in amount. 2) exceptional.
profiterole - small balls of choux pastry, usually filled with cream and covered in chocolate; (*used incorrectly by Mrs Kof instead of the word* professor).

Appendix

propulsion - a propelling force.

prosaic - unimaginative.

prototype - a first example upon which others can be modelled.

protracted - prolonged, drawn-out.

provocation - the act of provoking someone, (making them behave in a certain maner).

pseudonym - false name.

psychedelic - *having vivid colours and intricate patterns.

psychology - scientific study of methods of thought and behaviour.

Puck - a mischievous mythological sprite or hobgoblin of English folklore; also known as Robin Goodfellow.

Pygmalion - (Greek myth), a king who fell in love with a statue he'd made which was then magically brought to life.

Q

quadrant - *a quarter.

quantify - to specify an amount.

quantum entanglement - the corresponding actions of a pair of linked particles which, although separated spatially, remain connected and always behave as one.

quibble - to nitpick, or raise trivial objections.

quid - a pound in money. (*British slang*).

quip - a joke.

quoin - *a wedge used to adjust the elevation of a canon.

R

radical - drastic or far-reaching.

radically - completely.

radioactive - emitting radiation.

radiometer - an instrument for measuring radiant flux, with windmill-like vanes (having dark and light sides) which spin in a vacuum when exposed to light.

Raphus Cucullatus - Latin name for the dodo, an extinct flightless bird of the pigeon family.

rapport - understanding.

redoubtable - formidable, worthy of respect.

regressed - *reverted back to.

repercussion - outcome or consequence.

repertoire - *the complete collection of works/songs etc., that a person can perform.

replete - with one's appetite satisfied.

resounding – loud, ringing, resonant.

retaliate - fight back.

retribution – punishment for wrong-doing.

reverberating – resonant, echoing.

riffled - hurriedly flicked through pages.

rifling - searching through something; rummaging; ransacking or plundering.

rudimentary - incompletely developed.

rue - regret.

rueful - regretful. *adv* **ruefully**.

S

saboteur - a person committing a secret act of damage or disruption.

saccharine - artificially over-sweet.

sarcophagus - a stone coffin or tomb.

sarcophagi (*plural*)

sardonic - scornful, mocking.

saurian - lizard-like.

scarper - to hurry away; flee.

scavenging - *searching for anything edible.

scenario - summary of a plot or sequence of events.

Appendix

sceptical - doubting what others believe.
scimitar - a sword with a curved blade.
scotoma - *a mental blindspot.
scrimshaw - carved decoration of objects by sailors.
scrutinise - examine carefully.
Scullery - area in or near a kitchen where the dishes are washed.
scurrilous - grossly insulting; slanderous.
scythe - a tool for cutting grass having a long handle and a long curved blade.
sedative - sleep-inducing medication.
sequentially - in sequence.
Serengeti - part of north-west Tanzania (in Africa) known for its National Parks and game reserves. From the *Maasai* word meaning *endless plains*.
shabby-chic - worn and threadbare, yet still elegant.
shard - a broken piece.
shinty - a Scottish field game similar to hockey.
simian - a monkey or ape.
simpering - an affected smile or smirk.
simultaneously - at the same time.
sinuously - fluidly, supplely.
skirling - the shrill sound of the bagpipes.
skivvying - working as a menial servant.
sloop - a sailboat with a single mast.
solicitously - considerately.
solidifying - becoming solid.
soliloquies - speeches in a play where an actor speaks to himself.
somnambulation - sleepwalking.
sonar - underwater communication and navigation using echolocation. **so**(*ound*) **na**(*vigation and*) **r**(*anging*).
sonorous - deep and booming.
soporific - sleep-inducing.
spartan - plain, bare or austere.
spatiotemporal - descriptive of the three dimensions of space and one dimension of and time; also referred to as **spacetime**.
spectral - *ghostlike.
sphinx - Egyptian stone statue of a monster with a human's head and a lion's body; in *Greek mythology*, it would ask riddles, killing those who answered incorrectly.
spifflicate - (*British slang*) to destroy.
spontaneous - done without external influence or planning, or arising from impulse.
squab - a baby bird, usually of the pigeon family.
squalid - dirty through neglect.
squiffed - drunk (*British informal*).
stalactite - a long cylindrical mass hanging from a cave roof.
steadfastly - faithfully.
steampunk – a sci-fi sub-genre combining futuristic technology with Victorian style and craftsmanship.
stereotypical - conventional or unoriginal.
steroids - hormones used medically to aid tissue-growth, but often abused by atheletes to overly increase their muscle size and strength.
stickler - a person who makes unreasonable demands.
stygian - dark and hellish; (descriptive of the river Styx – *Greek mythology*).
stimuli - things that stimulate a response.
stollen - sweet German bread.
subatomic - of a process occurring within an atom.
subconscious - acting without awareness – or the part of the mind that is on the fringe of consciousness. *adv* **subconsciously**.
Sub Rosa - in secret. (*Latin for* under the rose - *from a time when a hanging rose was a sign of secrecy*).
substantial - considerable, sizable.
subterranean - situated underground.
suburban - situated in a residential

area.

superfluous - more than is needed.

superimpose - place over something else.

surreptitiously - stealthily.

surveillance - observation; of equipment used to watch people.

swither - to hesitate or dither undecidedly. (*Scottish dialect*).

synchronicity - two or more causally unrelated events that appear almost identical.

synonym - a word that means the same as another word; (*used incorrectly by Mrs Kof instead of the word* cinnamon).

synthesised - produced artificially.

T

tacit - implied but not spoken.

taciturn - silent; not inclined to speak.

tarpaulin - waterproof canvas.

taxidermist - a person who stuffs dead animals.

teleportation - a hypothetical method of transporting a person or object from one place to another instantaneously.

temporal - relating to time.

tempus fugit - *Latin* - time flies.

tenaciously - stubbornly, persistently.

termagant - a bad-tempered mean-spirited woman.

thalamus - two areas of grey matter at the base of the brain.

theodolite - a telescope-like instrument used for measuring horizontal and vertical angles.

theoretical - based on theories (unproven ideas).

theremin - a musical instrument that is played without being touched; volume and pitch determined by the proximity of a player's hands to its two antennas. Invented by Leon Theremin; (*word used incorrectly by Mrs Kof instead of* thermos).

thermos - a vacuum flask used to keep drinks hot.

thespian - 1) an actor or actress. 2) relating to the theatre.

Thymum Sempiternum – *Latin* - Thyme Eternal. (The Thyme Clan motto).

tinnitus - a ringing in the ears.

titanium - a strong lightweight metal.

topiary – the trimming of bushes into artistic shapes.

tosh - nonsense. (*British slang*).

traipse - to plod tiredly.

transcended - surpassed; moved beyond.

translucent - semitransparent.

trigonometry - a branch of mathematics.

trillion - a million million. (1,000,000,000,000).

tyrant - a person who rules unjustly; a bully.

U

Ulam spirals - a numerical pattern discovered by mathematician Stanislaw Ulam, who observed that when ascending numbers are written spiralling out in a rectangular grid, the prime numbers form diagonal lines.

ultimately - *finally.

uncanny - beyond what is expected.

unceremoniously - without ceremony.

unctuous - greasy, or in an oily charming manner.

unmitigated - absolute, complete; not diminished.

unorthodox - unusual; not conventional.

USB – *Universal Serial Bus*; a plug-like interface that allows external devices to

be attached to a computer.
UV - ultraviolet.

V

vagrant - a tramp; a person with no fixed home or job.
varicose veins - a health condition in which veins (especially in the legs) become prominent and swollen.
venison - the edible flesh of a deer.
Vermeer, Jan - a Dutch painter 1632-1675, famed for his paintings of domestic scenes.
vertigo - a feeling of dizziness.
vigilance - the state of being vigilant (on the watch, alert to trouble or danger).
voluminous - of great size or volume.
vortex - a whirling mass of, gas, liquid or flame shaped like a whirlwind.

vulnerable - *open to attack.

W

wee - small. *(Scottish dialect).*
whodunit - a mystery story challenging the reader to deduce who commits a crime by finding clues in the text.
winnow - to separate the grain from the chaff.
wormhole - a tunnel through spacetime connecting two different points in either space, time or both.
wraithlike - ghostlike; lacking in substance.
wry - twisted; mocking.

XYZ

yield - *to give or surrender.

Notes

Clues to what might happen next
can be found within this book!
Use these pages to keep a record
of your suspicions and theories.

Theories

Clues and Suspects

Curious Connections

Codes and Keys

Food for Thought!